OUR TRAGIC UNIVERSE

Books by Scarlett Thomas

Scarlett Thomas

OUR TRAGIC UNIVERSE

HOUGHTON MIFFLIN HARCOURT

Boston   New York

2010

Library of Congress Cataloging-in-Publication Data
Thomas, Scarlett.
Our tragic universe / Scarlett Thomas.
p. cm.
ISBN 978-0-15-101391-3
1. Women authors — Fiction. 2. Self-realization — Fiction.
3. Storytelling — Fiction. 4. End of the world — Fiction.
5. Psychological fiction. I. Title.
PR6120.H66087 2010
823'.92 — dc22   2010005767

Book design by Melissa Lotfy

Printed in the United States of America

DOC 10 9 8 7 6 5 4 3 2 1

For Rod, with love

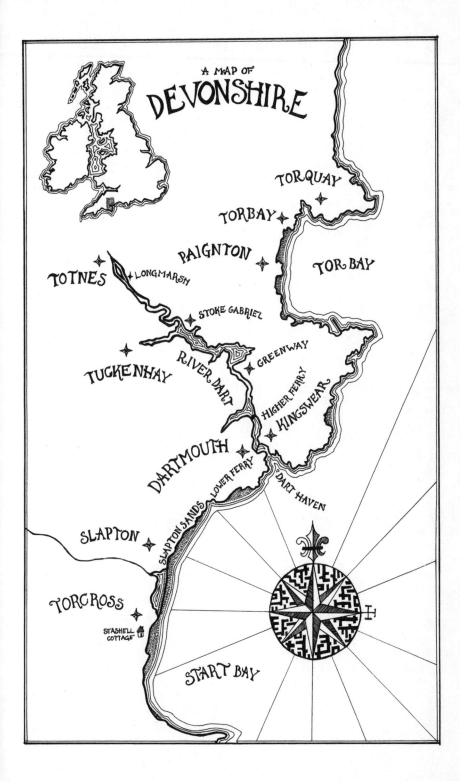

PART ONE

Organise a fake holdup. Verify that your weapons are harmless, and take the most trustworthy hostage, so that no human life will be in danger (or one lapses into the criminal). Demand a ransom, and make it so that the operation creates as much commotion as possible—in short, remain close to the 'truth,' in order to test the reaction of the apparatus to a perfect simulacrum. You won't be able to do it: the network of artificial signs will become inextricably mixed up with real elements (a policeman will really fire on sight; a client of the bank will faint and die of a heart attack; one will actually pay you the phoney ransom), in short, you will immediately find yourself once again, without wishing it, in the real, one of whose functions is precisely to devour any attempt at simulation, to reduce everything to the real . . .

—JEAN BAUDRILLARD, *Simulacra and Simulation*

I WAS READING about how to survive the end of the universe when I got a text message from my friend Libby. Her text said, *Can you be at the Embankment in fifteen minutes? Big disaster.* It was a cold Sunday in early February, and I'd spent most of it curled up in bed in the damp and disintegrating terraced cottage in Dartmouth. Oscar, the literary editor of the newspaper I wrote for, had sent me *The Science of Living Forever* by Kelsey Newman to review, along with a compliments slip with a deadline on it. In those days I'd review anything, because I needed the money. It wasn't so bad: I'd built up some kind of reputation reviewing science books and so Oscar gave me all the best ones. My boyfriend Christopher did unpaid volunteer work on heritage sites, so it was down to me to pay the rent. I never turned down a commission, although I wasn't at all sure what I'd say about Kelsey Newman's book and this idea of surviving beyond the end of time.

In some ways I was already surviving beyond the end of time: beyond deadlines, overdraft limits and ultimatums from my bank manager. I hit deadlines to get money, but not always to give it away. That winter I'd been reduced to cashing all my cheques in a high-commission, no-questions-asked place in Paignton and paying utility bills at the Post Office with cash.

Although what did anyone expect? I was hardly a big-time writer, although I was still planning to be. Every time a white envelope came from the bank Christopher added it to the pile of mail on my desk upstairs. I never opened any of these envelopes. I didn't have much credit on my phone, so I didn't text Libby back; but I put the book down and got off the bed and put on some trainers. I'd vowed never to go out in Dartmouth on a Sunday evening, for complicated reasons. But I couldn't say no to Libby.

The grey afternoon was curling into evening like a frightened woodlouse. I still had fifty pages of *The Science of Living Forever* to read and the deadline for my review was the next day. I'd have to finish the book later and make sure I filed the review on time if I wanted any chance of it being in the paper on Sunday. If it didn't go in until the next week I would miss being paid for a month. Downstairs, Christopher was on the sofa cutting pieces of reclaimed wood to make a toolbox. We didn't have a garden he could work in, just a tiny, completely enclosed and very high-walled concrete yard in which frogs and other small animals sometimes appeared miraculously, as if they had dropped from the sky. As I walked into the sitting room I could see sawdust getting in everything, but I didn't point this out. My guitar was propped up by the fireplace. Every time Christopher moved the saw back or forth the vibration travelled across the room and made the thick E string tremble. The sound was so low and sad and haunting that you could barely hear it. Christopher was sawing hard: his brother Josh had been for lunch yesterday and he still wasn't over it. Josh found it therapeutic talking about their mother's death; Christopher didn't. Josh was happy that their father was dating a 25-year-old waitress; Christopher thought it was disgusting. It had probably been up to me to stop the conversation, but at the time I was worrying that I hadn't even looked to see what book I was supposed to be reviewing, and that the

4

bread was running out and we didn't have any more. Also, I didn't really know how to stop the conversation.

Sometimes when I went downstairs I'd think about saying something, and then I'd imagine how Christopher would be likely to reply and end up saying nothing at all. This time I said, 'Guess what?' and Christopher, still sawing madly, as if into the back of his brother's head, or perhaps Milly's head, said, 'You know I hate it when you start conversations like that, babe.' I apologised, but when he asked me to hold a piece of wood for him I said I had to take the dog out.

'She hasn't been out for ages,' I said. 'And it's getting dark.'

Bess was in the hallway, rolling on a piece of rawhide.

'I thought you walked her this afternoon,' Christopher said.

I put on my anorak and my red wool scarf and left without saying anything else; I didn't even turn back when I heard Christopher's box of nails fall on the floor, although I knew I should have done.

How do you survive the end of time? It's quite simple. By the time the universe is old enough and frail enough to collapse, humans will be able to do whatever they like with it. They'll have had billions of years to learn, and there'll be no matron to stop them, and no liberal broadsheets and no doomy hymns. By then it'll just be a case of wheeling one decrepit planet to one side of the universe while another one pisses itself sadly in another galaxy. And all this while waiting for the final crunch, as everything becomes everything else as the universe begins its beautiful collapse, panting and sweating until all life arcs out of it and all matter in existence is crushed into a single point and then disappears. In the barely audible last gasp of the collapsing universe, its last orgasmic sigh, all its mucus and pus and rancid *jus* will become pure energy, capable of everything imaginable, just for a moment. I didn't know why

I'd contemplated trying to explain this to Christopher. He'd once made me cry because he refused to accept spatial dimensions, and we'd had a massive row because he wouldn't look at my diagram that proved Pythagoras's theorem. According to Christopher the books I reviewed were 'too cerebral, babe'. I didn't know what he'd make of this one, which was a complete head-fuck.

According to Kelsey Newman, the universe, which always was a computer, will, for one moment — not even that — be so dense and have so much energy that it will be able to compute anything at all. So why not simply program it to simulate another universe, a new one that will never end, and in which everyone can live happily ever after? This moment will be called the Omega Point, and, because it has the power to contain everything, will be indistinguishable from God. It will be different from God, though, because it will run on a processing power called *Energia*. As the universe gets ready to collapse, no one will be writing poetry about it or making love for the last time or just bobbing around, stoned and listless, waiting for annihilation, imagining something beautiful and unfathomable on the other side. All hands will be on deck for the ultimate goal: survival. Using only physics and their bare hands, humans will construct the Omega Point, which, with its infinite power, can and for various reasons definitely will, bring everyone back to life — yes, even you — billions of years after you have died, and it will love everyone and create a perfect heaven. At the end of the universe anything could happen, except for one thing.

You can't die, ever again.

It wasn't the kind of book Oscar usually sent me. We reviewed popular science, however wacky, but we drew the line at anything New Age. Was this a New Age book? It was hard to tell. According to the blurb, Newman was a well-respected psychoanalyst from New York who had once advised a president, although it didn't say which one. He had been inspired to write his book by reading the work of the equally well-respected physicist Frank Tipler, who had come up with the idea of the Omega Point and done all the necessary equations to prove that you and I — and everyone who ever lived, and every possible human who never lived — will be resurrected at the end of time, as soon as the power becomes available to do it. Your death will therefore be just a little sleep, and you won't notice any time passing between it and waking up in eternity.

Why bother with anything, in that case? Why bother trying to become a famous novelist? Why bother paying bills, shaving your legs, trying to eat enough vegetables? The sensible thing, if this theory were true, would be to shoot yourself now. But then what? I loved the universe, particularly the juicy bits like relativity, gravity, up and down quarks, evolution, and the wave function, which I almost understood; but I didn't love it so much that I wanted to stay beyond its natural end, stuck with everyone else in some sort of coma, wired up to a cosmic life-support machine. I had been told once — and reminded of it again recently — that I would come to nothing. What on earth would I do with all that heaven? Living for ever would be like marrying yourself, with no possibility of a divorce.

There were thirty-one stone steps down to the street. I walked with B past Reg's place on the corner and across the market square, which was completely deserted except for one seagull pecking at a flapping chip wrapper and making the sound they all make: *ack, ack, ack,* like a lonely machine gun. B hugged the wall under the Butterwalk by Miller's Deli, and stopped to pee as soon as we were in the Royal Avenue Gardens. Everything seemed to be closed, broken, dead or in hibernation. The bandstand was empty and the fountain was dry. The palm trees shivered. There was a smell of salt in the wind, and something seaweedy, which became stronger as we approached the river. No one was around. It was getting darker, and the sky above Kingswear was bruising into a mushy green, brown and purple, like the skin of an apple. The wind was coming in from the sea, and all the little boats danced on their moorings as if they were enchanted, making ghostly sounds.

I put up the hood on my jacket, while B sniffed things. She liked to visit all the benches on the North Embankment, one by one, then go around the Boat Float and home via Coronation Park. She was always slower and sleepier in winter, and at home I kept finding her balled up in the bedclothes as if she was trying to hibernate. But she still followed her routine when we came out. Every day we stopped to look at the mysterious building site in Coronation Park. The previous autumn Libby had heard from Old Mary at her knitting group that it was going to be a small, stone Labyrinth set on a piece of raised and landscaped lawn with a view of the river. But it was still just a hole. The council was funding the project because a study had said it would help calm everybody down. Dartmouth was a sleepy harbour where people came to retire, die, write novels or quietly open a shop. The only people who needed calming down were the cadets at the Royal Naval College, and they would never come to the Labyrinth. My main worry was that the builders might cut down my favourite tree, and almost every day I went and checked it was still there. The wind tore across the park and I hurried B past the building site with its flapping plastic and temporary fencing, looked at my tree and then went back to the Embankment. This February was cold, cruel and spiteful, and I wanted to be at home in bed, even though it wasn't much warmer than outside and the damp in the house made me wheeze. B obviously wanted to go home too, and I imagined her curled under the covers with me, both of us in hibernation.

There was still no one around. Perhaps I'd been worrying over nothing all these months. Perhaps he didn't come any more. Perhaps he'd never come.

Upriver, the Higher Ferry was chugging across the water towards Dartmouth. It had only one car on it, probably Libby's, and its lights danced in the gloom. Things on the river tinkled. I stood there waiting for Libby, looking at all the boats, not looking for *him*. I listened to the *ding-ding-ding* sounds and wondered why they seemed ghostly. I reached into the inside pocket of my anorak. I already knew what was there: a scrap of paper with an email address on it that I knew by heart, and a brown medicine bottle with a pipette. The bottle contained the last dregs of the flower remedy my friend Vi had made me several weeks before. I'd been up to Scotland for Christmas to stay with Vi and her partner Frank in their holiday cottage while Christopher went to Brighton, but it had all gone wrong and now Vi wasn't speaking to me. Because of this, I was objectively lonelier than I had ever been, but it was OK because I had a house and a boyfriend and B, which was more than enough. I also had this remedy, which helped. Her handwriting was still just legible on the label. *Gentian, holly, hornbeam, sweet chestnut, wild oat and wild rose.* I put a few drops of the mixture on my tongue and felt warm, just for a second.

After a couple more minutes the ferry arrived. There was a thump as the flap came down; then the gate opened and the single car drove off and headed down the Embankment. It was Libby's, so I waved. Libby and her husband Bob had closed down their failing comic shop two years before and now ran Miller's Deli, where they sold all sorts of things, including unpasteurised cheeses, goose fat, lemon tart, home-made salads, driftwood sculptures and knitted shawls and blankets made by them or their friends. I made jam and marmalade for Miller's Deli to supplement the income I got from my writing projects. My favourite lunch was a tub of pickled garlic, some home-made fish pâté and a half-baguette, which I often picked up from the shop on winter mornings. Libby was driving slowly, with the window down, her hair going crazy in the wind. When she saw me she stopped the car. She was wearing jeans and a tight T-shirt with a hand-knitted, red shawl tied over the top, as if February was never cruel to her at all, and as if she'd never worn thick glasses, or baggy tops screen-printed with characters from horror films.

'Meg, fuck. Thank God. Christopher isn't here, is he?'

'Of course not,' I said. I looked around. 'No one's here. Why? Are you OK? Aren't you cold?'

'No. Too much adrenaline. I'm in deep shit. Can I say I was at yours?'

'When?'

'Today. All day. Last night as well. Bob came back early. Can you believe they diverted his flight to Exeter because of a slippery runway at Gatwick?'

'Have you spoken to him yet?'

'No, but he's sent messages. He was supposed to text me when his plane landed at Gatwick, which I thought would give me loads of time to get home and change and make the place look lived-in and stuff. When I heard a text come I just thought it was Bob at Gatwick — it was the right sort of time — and I was in bed with Mark, so I didn't look at it immediately. I mean, it's half an hour to get off the plane and out of the airport, and then another half an hour into Victoria, then twenty minutes across to Paddington, and then three hours to Totnes to pick up his car and then another twenty-five minutes to drive back here. So I wasn't exactly panicking. But by the time I looked there was another text saying *See you in half an hour.* Then another one came asking where I was and if I was all right. I almost had a heart attack.'

Libby was having an affair with Mark, a bedraggled guy who had washed up in Churston, a village over the river in Torbay, when he'd inherited a beach hut from his grandfather. He lived in the beach hut, ate fish and picked up any casual work he could get in the boatyards and harbours. He was saving to start his own boat-design company, but Libby said he was about a million miles away from that. Libby worked in the deli with Bob most weekdays, and spent the rest of her time knitting increasingly complicated things and writing

Mark love letters in dark red ink, while Bob played his electric guitars and did the shop accounts. She had invented a book group at Churston library and told Bob that's where she went on a Friday night. She also saw Mark at her knitting group on a Wednesday, although that was more problematic, because there was always the chance that Bob might drop in with left-over cake from the shop, or that one of the old ladies might see Mark touching Libby's knee. This weekend had been different, though, because Bob had gone to see his great-aunt and -uncle in Germany. She'd been with Mark since Friday.

'So you came to mine last night? And . . . ?'

I frowned. We both knew there was no way Libby would ever spend a whole evening at my house. Sometimes, but not so often recently, she'd drop by with a bottle of wine from the shop. Then we'd sit at the kitchen table, while Christopher simmered on the sofa a few feet away, watching American news or documentaries about dictators on our pirated Sky system and mumbling about the corruption of the world, and the rich, and greed. He did this on purpose because Libby had money and he didn't like it. Mostly when I saw Libby it was at the pub, although Christopher often complained about me going out and leaving him on his own. B had been sniffing the ground, but now put her paws up on the side of Libby's car and whimpered through the window. She wanted to get in. She loved going in cars. Libby patted her head, but didn't look at her.

'No . . . I must have lost my keys.' She started brainstorming. 'We, er, me and you went out last night and I lost my keys and had to stay at yours. I was drunk, and I didn't worry about bothering Bob because he was in Germany and I thought I'd go out and look for my keys today, and in fact that's what I was doing when he sent the messages, but I'd left my phone at yours and . . .'

'But you're driving your car. Do you have separate house keys? I thought they were all on the same keyring.'

Libby looked down. 'Maybe I found the keys . . . Holy shit. Oh, Christ. Oh, Meg, what am I going to do? Why would I have driven the car to your house anyway? It's only a five-minute walk. I'm not sure I can fit this together.' She frowned. 'Come on. You're the writer; you know how to plot things.'

I half-laughed. 'Yeah, right. You read. I'm sure you can plot things too.'

'Yeah, but you do it for a living. And teach it.'

'Yeah, but . . .'

'What's the *formula* here?'

Formula, like the stuff you feed to babies. This was my speciality; she was right. After winning a short story competition in 1997 I'd been offered a contract to write a groundbreaking, literary, serious debut novel: the kind of thing that would win more prizes and be displayed in the windows of bookshops. But I'd actually filled most of the last eleven years writing genre fiction, because it was easy money and I always needed to pay rent and bills and buy food. I'd been given a £1,000 advance for my literary novel, and instead of using it to clear my debts I'd bought a laptop, a nice pen and some notebooks. Just as I'd begun to write the plan for it, Claudia from Orb Books rang and offered me two grand if I could knock out a thriller for teenagers in six weeks. The official author of this book, Zeb Ross, needed to publish four novels a year but didn't in fact exist, and Claudia was recruiting new ghostwriters. It was a no-brainer: double my money and then write the real novel. But I was only a couple of chapters into the real novel when I realised I needed to write another Zeb Ross book, and then another one. A couple of years later I branched out and wrote four SF books in a series under my own name, all set in a place called Newtopia. I kept meaning to finish my 'proper' novel but it seemed as if this would never happen, even if I stuck around until the end of time. If Kelsey Newman was right and all possible humans were resurrected by the Omega Point at the end of the universe, then Zeb Ross would have to be one

of them and then he could write his own books. But I'd probably still have rent to pay.

I sighed. 'The thing is, when you plot a book you can go
back and change things that don't work and make everything
add up neatly. You can delete paragraphs, pages, whole manuscripts. I can't go back in time and put you on a bus to Mark's,
which would probably be the best thing.'

'How would that work?'

I shrugged. 'I don't know. Then you could have walked
round to mine and lost your keys and your phone like you
said.'

'But why would I have a weekend bag with me?'

'Yeah. I don't know.'

'There must be a way. Let's go back to basics. How do you
tell a really good story? I mean, in a nutshell.'

I looked at my watch. Christopher would be wondering
where I was.

'Isn't Bob expecting you?' I said.

'I need to get this right, or there'll be no Bob any more.'

'OK. Just keep it simple. Base the story on cause and effect.
Have three acts.'

'Three acts?'

'A beginning, a middle and an end. A problem, a climax
and a solution. You link them. Put someone on the wrong
ship. Then make it sink. Then rescue them. Not literally, obviously. You have to have a problem and make it get worse and
then solve it. Unless it's a tragedy.'

'What if this is a tragedy?'

'Lib . . .'

'All right. So I was out with you and I lost my keys. That's
bad. Then to make it worse I got gang-raped while I was looking for them, and now I've lost my memory and the kidnap-
pers took you away because you were a witness, and only Bess
knows where you are, and she's trying to tell Christopher,
but . . .'

'Too complicated. You need something simpler. You only need to explain the car. The story here is that we went out and you lost your keys, which was a bummer. Then maybe because you lost your keys you lost your car too, which is obviously a bigger bummer. Maybe someone found your keys and stole your car. Who knows? All you know is you lost your keys. The only glitch is you still have your car.'

Yadda, yadda. I seemed to have become a plot-o-matic machine programmed to churn out this kind of thing. But when I was dispensing advice like this to the more junior Orb Books ghostwriters I always said they should believe in their project and not just follow a set of rules. Then again, if they got lost in the wilderness of originality I gently guided them back to the happy path of formula again.

'OK. So how do me and Bob live happily ever after?'

I thought about it for a second.

'Well, obviously you'll have to push your car in the river,' I said, and laughed.

Libby sat there for about ten seconds, her hands becoming paler and paler as she gripped the steering wheel. Then she got out of the car and looked around. The North Embankment still seemed deserted. There were no kids trying to steal boats, no tourists, no other dog-walkers. No men looking for me. Libby made a noise a little like the one B had made before.

'You're right,' she said. 'It's the only thing to do.'

'Lib,' I said. 'I was joking.'

She got back into her car, did a haphazard three-point turn until it was facing the river and, finally, drove it up on the Embankment. For a moment it looked as if she was going to drive her car into the river. I stood there, not knowing if she was messing around, not knowing whether to laugh or try to stop her. Then she got out and walked around to the back of the car. Libby was small but as her biceps tightened I realised how strong her arms were. The car moved; she must have left the handbrake off. She pushed it again, and then the front wheels were over the edge of the Embankment.

'Lib,' I said again.

'I must be mad. What am I doing?' she said.

'Nothing,' I said. 'Come on, don't do this. It's going to be very hard to explain.'

Then she pushed her car into the river and threw the keys in after it.

'I'll say kids must have done it,' she said, over the splashing, sucking sound. 'They must have stolen my keys. Even if it does sound crazy, no one will think I was desperate enough to push my own car in the river, will they? Nothing would motivate me to do something as stupid as that. Holy shit. Thank you, Meg. That was a brilliant idea. I'll call you tomorrow if I'm still alive.'

She looked at her watch and then walked away down the Embankment towards Lemon Cottage, her red shawl moving like a flag in the wind. I remembered a Zen story about a flag in the wind. Does the wind move, or does the flag move? Two monks are arguing about this when a wise man turns up and says, 'The wind is not moving, the flag is not moving. Mind is moving.' I walked on slowly, with B re-sniffing benches as if nothing had happened. Libby didn't look behind her, and I saw her get smaller and smaller until she reached the corner and went off towards Bayard's Cove. Of course, as any scientist would tell you, she didn't really get smaller and smaller; she simply got further away.

The wind breathed heavily down the river, and I half-looked at the little ripples and wakes in the blackish, greenish water as I tried to hurry B home. There was no sign of Libby's car. I was watching the river, not the benches, so when someone said 'Hello,' I jumped. It was a man, half hidden in the gloom. B was already sniffing his ancient walking boots, and he was stroking her between her ears. He was wearing jeans and a duffel coat, and his messy black and grey hair was falling over his face. Had he seen what had happened? He must have done. Did he hear me suggest the whole thing? He looked up. I already knew it was Rowan. So he had come. Had he been coming every Sunday for all this time?

'Hi,' I said. 'You're . . .'

'Hello,' he said. 'Chilly, isn't it?'

'Freezing.'

'You OK?'

'Yeah. I think so. How are you?'

'Cold. Depressed. Needed to get some fresh air. I've been at the Centre all day working on my *Titanic* chapter. Can you believe I'm still at it? I should be grateful I'm still alive, I suppose. Everyone said retiring would kill me.'

Rowan and his partner Lise had relocated to Dartmouth just over a year before to help look after Lise's mother. They lived in a renovated old boathouse near the castle, with spectacular views of the mouth of the harbour. Everything inside it was tasteful and minimal: nothing was old or shabby, although it must have been once. Rowan had not yet retired when I went there for a dinner party. Lise wore too much make-up and spoke to Rowan as if he was a child. She told stories about him getting lost for three hours in a shopping mall, wearing jeans to her company's black-tie Christmas party and breaking the new dishwasher just by touching it. I'd pictured him alone in an airy office at Greenwich University, with an open window and freshly cut grass outside, surrounded by books and drinking a cup of good coffee, secretly dreading these dinner parties. I'd wondered then why he was retiring at all.

'Most people retire and then take up gardening or DIY, don't they?' I said. 'They don't go and get another job as director of a maritime centre. I don't think you really are retired, by most normal definitions of the word.'

He sighed. 'Pottering about with model ships all day. Wind machines. Collections of rocks and barnacles. Interactive tide tables. It's not rocket science. Still, I've had time to take up yoga.'

So he wasn't going to mention Libby and her car. We were going to have a 'normal' conversation, slightly gloomy, slightly flirty, like the ones we used to have when he came to Torquay library every day before the Maritime Centre opened — to do paperwork — and we ended up going for lunch and coffee all the time. Would we kiss at the end of this conversation, as we had done at the end of the last one?

'How's your writing going?' he asked me.

'OK,' I said. 'Well, sort of. I'm back on chapter one of my "proper" novel yet again, re-writing. The other day I worked out that I've deleted something like a million words of this novel in the last ten years. You'd think that would make it really good, but it hasn't. It's a bit of a mess now, but never mind.'

'Are you still using the ghost ships?'

'No. Well, sort of. They might come back.'

'And how was Greece?'

I frowned. 'I didn't go in the end. Had too much other work on here.'

'Oh. That's a shame.'

'Anyway, how about you? How's the chapter?'

'Oh, I keep having to read new things. I just read a hundred-page poem by Hans Magnus Enzensberger about the sinking of the *Titanic*.'

'Was it good?'

'I'll lend it to you. It's about some other stuff as well as the sinking of the *Titanic*. There's a bit where members of a religious cult are waiting on a hill for the end of the world, which is supposed to take place that afternoon. When the world doesn't end, they all have to go out and buy new toothbrushes.'

I laughed, although I was remembering that Rowan had already lent me a book that I hadn't read, even though I'd meant to. It was an Agatha Christie novel called *The Sittaford Mystery*, and I had no idea why Rowan had given it to me. He'd worked on a short local project on Agatha Christie's house on the River Dart, which was how he'd come to read the books. But I couldn't imagine he'd found anything that would interest me. I spent enough time messing around with genre fiction anyway.

'Sounds great,' I said. 'Sounds a bit like a book I'm reviewing, except the book I'm reviewing isn't great.'

'What is it?'

'It's all about how the universe will never end, and how we all get to live for ever. I hate it, and I don't know why.'

'I don't want to live for ever.'

'No. Me neither.'

'What's the point of living for ever? Living now is bad enough.'

'That's what I thought.'

'Are you OK?' he asked me again.

'Yeah. Did you just say you're doing yoga, or did I imagine it?'

'No, you didn't imagine it. I am doing yoga.'

'Why?'

He shrugged. 'Bad knees. Getting old. We're not long back from a yoga holiday in India, actually. Missed Christmas, which was good. Saw some kingfishers too.' Rowan stroked B's head again while I looked away. I knew that his casual 'we' meant he and Lise. Long-term couples often did that, I'd noticed: referred to themselves as 'we' all the time. Whenever I phoned my mother and asked, 'How are you?' she replied, 'We're fine.' I never talked about Christopher and me in that way. Maybe it would come in time. Not that I'd know how to use it, since we hardly ever did anything together. And we were never fine. We were even less fine since I'd kissed Rowan, because I knew that if I could kiss someone else, then I could never kiss Christopher again. In the last five months he hadn't really noticed this.

'How's Lise?' I asked. 'Is she still working on her book?'

I ran retreats twice a year for Orb Books ghostwriters in a clapped-out hotel in Torquay. These were supposed to teach already talented writers the finer points of plotting and structure and the Orb Books 'method'. Orb Books didn't mind if I charged a few local people to come too, so whenever a retreat was scheduled I put up posters in the Harbour Bookshop and usually got three or four takers. Lise had come to one the previous year. She had been planning to use some of her retirement to write a fictionalised account of her parents' experiences in the war, but as far as I knew she hadn't retired yet. She still took the train to London twice a week and worked at home the rest of the time.

Rowan shrugged. 'I don't think so.'

'Oh.'

He reached down and played with one of B's ears, making it stand up and then flop down again.

'Your dog's quite lovely,' he said.

'I know. Thanks. She's being quite patient while you abuse her ears.'

'I think she likes it.'

'Yeah, she probably does.'

'I meant to say . . . I've been looking at some of the cultural premonitions connected with the *Titanic* recently,' Rowan said. 'And I thought of you.' He looked down at the ground, then at one of B's ears and then up at me. 'I mean, I thought you'd be interested. I wondered if I should get in touch with you.'

'Get in touch with me any time.' I blushed. 'Just email me. What's a cultural premonition?'

'Writing about the disaster before it happened, or painting pictures of it. Lots of people did.'

'Seriously?'

'Yeah.'

'So it's paranormal in some way?' I could feel myself wrinkling my nose.

'No. Cultural. The premonitions are cultural rather than supernatural.'

'How?'

'It's like . . . Have you heard of the Cottingley Fairies?'

I shook my head. 'No.'

'Remind me to tell you about them sometime. It's quite an interesting case-study in how people decide to believe in things, and what people want to believe. I'd guess that there are usually cultural explanations for supernatural things if you look hard enough.'

'They weren't on the *Titanic* as well?'

'Huh?'

'These fairies.'

'No. They were in my old home town.'

'I thought your old home town was in the Pacific.'

'After I left San Cristobal I was in Cottingley before I went to Cambridge. My mother came from Cottingley, although she was dead by the time I left San Cristobal. Mind you, the fairies were long before that.' He frowned. 'I'll tell you the whole story sometime, but it's too complicated now. I thought you might have heard of them. Silly, really, bringing them up.'

'Oh. Well, I know a good joke about sheep that's all about how people decide to believe things, if that's of any interest.'

He smiled in the gloom. 'What is it?'

'OK. A biologist, a mathematician, a physicist and a philosopher are on a train in Scotland. They see a black sheep from a train window. The biologist says, "All sheep in Scotland are black!" The physicist says, "You can't generalise like that. But we know at least one sheep in Scotland is black." The mathematician strokes his beard and says, "All we can really say for sure is that one side of one sheep in Scotland is black." The philosopher looks out of the window, thinks about it all for a while and says, "I don't believe in sheep." My father used to tell it as if it said something about the perils of philosophy, although I wondered whether it said something else about the perils of science. My father is a physicist.'

Rowan laughed. 'I like that. I like sheep. I believe in them.'

'Did you know they can remember human faces for ten years, and recognise photographs of individual people?'

'So when they fix you with that stupid look they're actually memorising you?'

'I guess so.'

'Like those machines at Heathrow. But why?'

'Who knows? Maybe sheep will take over the world. Maybe that's their plan. Another plot for Zeb Ross, perhaps. I'll have to tell Orb Books.'

I wasn't really supposed to talk to anyone about Zeb Ross, and everyone who worked on the series signed NDAs. But in reality you can't pretend not to be writing a novel when you are, and pretty much everyone knew that those kinds of books were ghosted — except, perhaps, for their readers, particularly the ones who sent Zeb fan mail asking what colour his eyes were, and whether he was married.

B was now trying to get on Rowan's lap. I pulled her off, wondering what I smelled of as I leaned over him. And I didn't mean to look into his eyes, but when I did I saw that they were shining with tears. 'Hay fever' is what people usually say when they are crying; it's what I say, but not in February. I imagined Christopher walking along the river and finding me looking into Rowan's eyes, and then seeing my eyes suddenly full of tears, because when someone I care about cries I always want to cry too. He never knew about the lunches, or the kiss. Suddenly, joking about sheep didn't seem quite right, even though Rowan was still smiling. I didn't say anything for a moment.

'Why did she do it?' he asked.

'Who?'

'Libby Miller. Why did she push her car in the river?'

'She's the one I told you about ages ago. She's having a tragic love affair. Didn't you hear what we were saying?'

'No. I only got here just as she pushed it in.'

'Oh. Well.'

'I won't say anything.'

'Thanks.'

'Funny how things just go, isn't it?' he said.

'Sorry?'

'The car in the river. It's just *gone*.'

'It's for the best, I'm sure,' I said.

Rowan got up to leave, and I felt like a melting iceberg as I said goodbye and walked away from him. I didn't know what was wrong with me. I could have emailed him any time I'd wanted to. I could have got in touch to tell him I'd read the book he'd lent me, but I hadn't. I could have emailed him to write off the kiss as a mistake and tell him how much I missed our friendship. As I walked away, I imagined going back and asking him if he had come out tonight because of me, and then him looking puzzled and saying it was all just a coincidence.

Was it a coincidence that we'd ended up at the library together? It must have been. I didn't usually tell people that I worked in the library every weekday. It was such a weird thing to do when I had a perfectly good house to work in, and if I ever mentioned my asthma and the damp people didn't understand why I just didn't simply move. I recognised Rowan the first day he came to work at the library. He seemed to recognise me, too. After we'd spent a day or so just nodding and smiling at one another I showed him how to get his emails on his laptop rather than the library computers and then he took me to Lucky's for lunch to say thanks. Over lunch we realised we had friends — Frank and Vi — in common. Frank had been my lecturer almost twenty years before, and he and Vi had been something like a second set of parents for me since then.

Rowan had been at Goldsmiths before he got his chair in history at Greenwich, and had met Frank there. Vi was an anthropologist, and she and Rowan had really hit it off and ended up working together on re-enactment projects. They'd wanted to reconstruct the voyage of the *Beagle,* but could never secure any funding. But they did once spend a successful couple of weeks in Norfolk re-enacting Captain Cook's death on Hawai'i with their postgraduate students.

Cook had been killed by his previously generous hosts when he came back to the island to fix his broken boat. ('It would be like having your parents come to stay,' Vi explained to me once, 'and just after you've settled down to eat with your put-upon partner and vowed never to have them back again, their car breaks down and they return to stay for another week while your local garage sources the part to mend their car.') Was he killed because he demanded too much generosity? Or was it because he'd inadvertently become a character in a ritual, and this character wasn't supposed to return? Vi, Rowan and the students decided to act out a situation as close as possible to the one in which Cook and the islanders had found themselves. They'd hired an old beachfront hotel to function as 'Hawai'i' — a closed community into which Cook came, went and came again. Rowan played Cook, and Vi played the Hawai'ian King and chiefs. The students played islanders, and after the project had to write up how they'd felt about having to bow and scrape to Cook, and wait on him hand and foot. Could this have led one of them to want to kill him, or was there more to it? How much did they believe in the ritual? Rowan wrote about how interesting it was to find yourself allowing and accepting huge amounts of deference and generosity, and, after a while, becoming upset if people don't give you everything you want. An edited version of the experiment was published in *Granta* magazine.

When I'd asked Vi about Rowan, not long after I'd met him, she had told me how fastidious he was about always taking a good map and a pair of walking boots anywhere he went. I couldn't bear to admit to myself that I was interested in him, but I lapped up everything Vi said. I would have found out his shoe size if I could have done. When I discovered that he and Vi shared a birthday I even looked up his astrological chart, despite not believing in astrological charts. From Rowan I heard things about Vi that I mostly knew already. Vi's projects always involved what she provocatively called 'going native'. Over the years she had picked up several colloquial languages, five complicated tattoos, three 'lost' herbarium specimen collections, a drum kit, a dress made from leaves, and malaria. After her long period of Pacific studies, she took more study leave from the university, got a job as a care assistant and embarked on an ethnography of a nursing home in Brighton, which became her bestselling book *I Want to Die, Please*. Now she was working on a project about subculture and style in late-middle-aged people in the UK. Rowan made lots of jokes about that, mainly at his own expense.

Vi never used maps, but relied on a strange kind of 'luck' to find her way around. If she found a tree that had been cut down she apologised to it on behalf of humans. She talked to inanimate objects as if they too were alive, although since working at the nursing home her conversations with these objects often began with 'How the fuck are you, then?' She used tea tree oil as an antiseptic, and ginger to settle a bad stomach. For everything else she used 25+ manuka honey. One time in Scotland I'd gone on a hike with Frank and Vi and she had fixed his sprained ankle with a bottle of vinegar and some daisies. I told Rowan about this in some detail and then felt I'd betrayed Vi by laughing at her. Then again, we laughed at a lot of things.

We found all sorts of excuses to have coffee or lunch at Lucky's and continue the long, rambling conversations we'd started. These included our thoughts on playing guitar, whether it was immoral to use a dictionary when doing cryptic crosswords, why neither of us could sit at a messy table, why we hated shopping and how many ferry disasters there'd ever been on the River Dart. We discovered that we both disliked email: me because I had a psychological problem with replying to them, and Rowan because he got too many of them and preferred pen and paper. We joked about reading each other's minds, and tried to guess each other's lunch order every day. Bizarrely, we'd bumped into each other in a one-off flea market in the hall next to the library, both looking for an antique fountain pen to give to the other as a thank-you present. He was—still—thanking me for helping with his email. I can't remember what I was thanking him for. And we kept parking our cars next to each other in the library car park. Once when there wasn't a space free next to his car I drove round the car park until one did become free, because I didn't want to break the symmetry. A few days later I arrived first, and when I left the library that afternoon and saw his car several rows away from mine I felt like crying.

When Rowan's office in the Maritime Centre was completed we went for our last lunch. On the way there we'd been talking about the *Titanic*, and I'd recited Thomas Hardy's 'The Convergence of the Twain' and told Rowan my theory that it is a tragic love story as well as a disaster poem. After that he looked at me, and his eyes held mine for a second longer than they should have. Over lunch he told me that he was planning to write a completely different book after the one on shipwrecks, something that would involve going back to the Galápagos Islands for at least a year, but not as Darwin or anyone else: just as himself. I could tell he wouldn't hang around in Devon for long. Once Lise's mother was dead and Rowan's book was finished they were bound to sell the converted boathouse and move on. If I was the iceberg and he was the ship, we'd never converge, because he would change course before it was too late. I wouldn't sink him, and he wouldn't destroy me either. There would be no jarring of 'two hemispheres'.

We stayed in Lucky's until gone four, talking about Rowan's plans for exhibitions and conferences, and ways in which I could get involved. We laughed a lot as these collaborations became more and more absurd. We never explicitly said we wanted to see one another again, but we planned thousands of ways it could happen. Our eyes touched again, for longer. I breathed out as he breathed in and the molecules of air between us danced back and forth in a frenzied tango that no one else could see or feel. But we didn't physically touch: we never had. We walked back to our cars together as if we were walking through a force-field. Rowan said quietly, 'I often go for a walk in Dartmouth on a Sunday evening. Maybe we'll bump into one another sometime.' Then, even though I'm sure we meant to just say goodbye by shaking hands or kissing on the cheek, we ended up taking each other's hands and then kissing properly, deeply, gently stroking each other's hair. Afterwards, as I drove home panicking and sweating and moaning his name, I realised that I hadn't kissed anyone like that for almost seven years. We didn't have each other's phone numbers, but we had exchanged email addresses. I felt that an affair was inevitable, even though I didn't want to have one. I'd had plenty of complicated break-ups but never an affair. Who would email the other first, I'd wondered? Who would fashion the iceberg?

Neither of us did.

'Where have you been?'

I looked at the clock on the oven. It was half past seven. It was dark outside, and there was a cold smell in the house. Christopher had turned off the central heating as usual. Nothing was cooking, no washing was drying, my peace lily was slowly dying on the sunless windowsill; if it wasn't for the sawdust and Christopher it would be as if no one had lived here for ages: as if whoever had lived here had died.

'Walking Bess,' I said. 'You knew that.'

'For an hour?' He shook his head. 'And after storming off in such a mood. I don't know why you can't just stay and talk if there's a problem. I'm not a monster. There's nothing for dinner, by the way. I've looked in all the cupboards. And your mother phoned.'

'I really don't know what you're talking about. I didn't storm off.'

'Don't use that tone of voice with me. It's not helpful.'

'What tone of voice?'

'That one.'

'Oh, for God's sake.'

I started going through the cupboards and found some whole-wheat penne and a jar of murky-looking tomato sauce. Our few kitchen cupboards were always full of things that couldn't be thrown away but couldn't be eaten either. I didn't mean to slam all the doors, and thump the jar of sauce down on the table, but I did.

'So you are in a mood. I always know . . .'

'If that's what you want to call being angry, then yes, I am now. I wasn't before. I walked out of the house completely normally, came back after a normal amount of time, and found you shouting at me.' As I said this, I was filling the kettle with my back to Christopher. He didn't say anything until I turned to face him again.

'I'm not shouting,' he said.

'No. But you know what I mean.'

He looked at the floor. 'You always say I'm shouting.'

I looked at the floor too, but a different spot.

'I'm sorry. You're right. I do.'

My mind was like a fishing net with too many thoughts wriggling around in it. My stupid suggestion. Splash. The tears in Rowan's eyes. Splash. Libby's shawl. Splash. Immortality in an artificial heaven. My eyes were filling with tears again, and I was developing a headache. I imagined an eternity with Christopher. I'd been waiting for the last seven years for him to make sense to me, to fall into place; perhaps in an eternity it would happen. Perhaps in an eternity everything would fall into place, but then it wouldn't stay like that, because that's not the point of eternity. Even in a finite universe, a rock doesn't keep being a rock. Things are always disintegrating and becoming other things. In fact, I was quite looking forward to becoming a rock, or perhaps some sand, once I was long dead and decomposed. It would be a lot simpler than being resurrected and having to go through all this again. In an eternity, though, I'd get one night with Rowan, something I'd never get in this life. But like everything else in eternity it would be meaningless.

The kettle had boiled, and I put the penne on.

'I'm sorry,' I said again. 'You're right, I do feel a bit unsettled this evening. I think I'm coming down with a headache.'

The pieces of pasta bobbed about in the pan like little tubes of brown cardboard, the empties from a doll's-house toilet, perhaps, although not even doll's-house people would put little tubes of cardboard in a pan and cook them. I blinked and looked at Christopher. He was looking at the pasta too.

'What's wrong?' he said. 'Has something happened?'

'No. I don't think so. It'll be OK. I'll take some painkillers. What did my mum say?'

'She said she'd ring back tomorrow. Then, as usual, she put the phone down.'

'Oh.'

Without catching his eye I picked up the newspaper from the table and opened it to the cryptic crossword that I did every Sunday. I'd done all of it the previous week except for one answer, which I'd written in the margin but not entered because although I thought it was right I didn't know why. Now I could see the correct answers for last week, and I had been right. I still didn't know why. Rowan and I once finished the crossword together on a rainy Monday morning in the library, after using a big, musty atlas to look up a lake in Australia and the capital of Corsica. That morning had ended oddly, I remembered. We'd planned to go for lunch as usual, but Lise had texted Rowan to say she had a migraine, and he'd gone home instead. His hands had been shaking as he'd packed up his decrepit, cotton knapsack, and he'd rushed off without really saying goodbye. Now I picked up a mechanical pencil from the kitchen work surface and sat down on the sofa. It was hard to concentrate, and I realised Christopher hadn't moved.

'Any news from Josh? Was he OK after yesterday?'

Christopher rolled his eyes. 'Who knows?'

'Any news from your dad? Is Becca any better?'

'No,' Christopher said. 'I don't know. I was going to ring him after dinner.'

We ate in front of the TV, with me still looking at my crossword, and Christopher occasionally looking at my crossword too as if it was my lover and he'd become resigned to discovering us together. But mostly he was watching a programme about haunted houses. I hated programmes about haunted houses and Christopher knew this. I ate so fast I half-choked on a piece of penne. Once I'd finished coughing I put my plate in the sink and headed for the stairs, still carrying my crossword.

'What are you doing now?' Christopher said.

'I'm going to have a bath. Give you some space to talk to your dad.'

'I don't need space,' he said. I went anyway.

'It'll help clear my chest,' I said, coughing again.

I lay there for an hour, until long after Christopher had put the phone back in its cradle and started sawing again. There was always something in the crossword that made me think it could have been written just for me, and I always wanted to tell Rowan about it. Today the clue was 'Cosmos in a single poem (8 letters)'. After a while I put down the crossword on the damp bathroom floor, made myself stop thinking about Rowan and wondered what on earth I could do about my relationship with Christopher. Was there something I could say to him? I still dreamed about Becca sometimes, even after all these years: her freckled, laughing face freezing at the sight of me.

Becca was Christopher's sister. She lived in Brighton with her husband Ant. They'd just had a third daughter and there'd been some complications that meant Becca had temporarily closed the shop where she sold her hand-made jewellery. Ant's brother Drew was an actor, and had been my fiancé in the late nineties when I first met Christopher. For a couple of years we'd all hung around together having silly tea parties and 'happenings' in Becca and Ant's huge house. Just after my first Zeb Ross book had been published Drew had shot his first major drama series, in which he was the young parochial sidekick of a literature-loving detective. A couple of years later there was a Millennium party, where everyone except Christopher and me dressed as bugs. But Brighton soon became very complicated, which was why I had run away to Devon with Christopher, home for him and exotic for me, at least at the beginning. Becca had hardly spoken to either of us since we'd left Brighton, although Christopher had gone there at Christmas to try to patch things up. Drew had blamed Becca somehow, and left the area too. She and Ant 'almost split up' because of it.

I vaguely remembered the first synopsis I'd written for my literary novel, which was at that time called *Sandworld*. It was going to be all about a bunch of youngish, long-haired, thin people living in Brighton. They would take cool drugs and listen to cool music and fuck each other for about 80,000 words and then the novel would end. It fitted with what my agent called the '*Zeitgeist*', but seemed to lack substance, so I'd added a dangerous love-interest for the main character. I also added a philosophy course about hedonism, and made the characters students rather than townies. I wrote lots of pointless sections about nihilism and then deleted them. Then I decided to end the novel with the end of the world, but that didn't work, so I made it so that the end of the world could just be a fireworks display on Sark, or one of the other Channel Islands — but the reader doesn't know for sure. Then I put it aside and wrote another Zeb Ross novel and then another Newtopia novel, because I needed the money.

When I came back to *Sandworld* I deleted most of it, changed the title to *Footprints*, decided to relocate the characters to Devon and started researching some themes about the environment. I made the main character a scientist, and then, perhaps more authentically, a writer who wanted to be a scientist. Recently I'd been trying to make the novel into a great tragedy, but that wasn't working either. I had realised a while ago that I was always trying to make the novel catch up with my life, and then deleting the bits that got too close, wiping them out like videogame aliens in a space-station corridor. I still didn't know what to do about it. I'd invented a writer character from New York who deletes a whole book until it's a haiku and then deletes that, but then I deleted him too. Blammo. Lock and load. In the past few years I'd invented a couple of sisters, called Io and Xanthe, who have lost everything in their lives, a building site with yellow cranes, a run-down B&B owned by a chewed-up old woman called Sylvia, an inconsiderate boyfriend, a married lover, a girl in a coma telling her life story from the beginning in real-time, a life-support machine wired up to the Internet, a charismatic A-level physics teacher called Dylan, a psychic game-show, an extended game of 'Dare' that goes wrong, some people trapped in a sauna, a car accident, a meaningful tattoo, dreams of a post-oil world full of flickering candles, a plane crash, an imposter, a character with OCD who follows any written instructions she sees, some creepy junk mail, a sweet teenage boy on a skateboard and various other things, all of which had now been deleted as well. Ducks in a row, then *bang, bang, bang.*

I heard Christopher come up the stairs, walk across the

small landing to the bathroom door and sigh loudly before walking up the next flight of stairs to the bedroom. Was he going to bed already? He went to bed earlier than me, because on weekdays he took the 6 A.M. bus to Totnes to work as a volunteer on a wall-rebuilding project. But it wasn't even nine o'clock yet. He came down the stairs again and tried the bathroom door, which I'd locked.

'I won't be a minute,' I said.

'Can I come in? I need to piss.'

'I'm just about to get out. Can you hang on?'

'I'm desperate. And I want to get ready for bed. Why have you locked the door anyway? Why have you been in there for so long?'

'I'm going to be like *one minute*. Just hang on.'

He sighed again. 'Don't worry. I'll go and piss in the kitchen sink.'

'Fine,' I said. 'But I will only be a minute if you want to wait.'

I heard him muttering something like 'I don't believe this,' as he went down the stairs again. I wished I knew what to say to him, but I didn't. I didn't know what to say about us, or about his father and Milly, or about Josh and his episodes, or about Becca and her bitterness about everything, or indeed about Christopher's lack of paid work. Could I plot one single thing to say that would make everything better? A Zen koan, maybe fifty words long, could change your whole life; it could, apparently, bring you enlightenment. I knew all about this because the Zeb Ross editorial board had recently rejected a novel where some survivors of a plane crash find a utopian island populated by wise people who tell each other Zen stories all the time. The Zen stories, and indeed the novel itself, had no obviously conventional narrative structure. In one of the stories, a woman gains enlightenment after the reflection of the moon falls out of a bucket of water she is carrying. Another told of a woman Zen master who owns a teashop. People who come to her teashop for tea are well treated, but those who come looking for Zen are beaten with a red-hot poker. In the novel, which I had quite liked but pretended not to, each of the main characters is given a koan, kind of a Zen riddle, to work on, and their lives start to change. But their enlightenment is all about cheering up, doing simple things well, not being too high and mighty, and accepting the unfathomable nature of the universe. Christopher, like most people, didn't like his universe being unfathomable, so I doubted that a Zen koan would help him. Mind you, he did like doing simple things well. He spent every day rebuilding sections of dry-stone wall, after all.

He was broken when I met him, and beautiful. We'd gone to bed together for the first time not long after I'd split up with Drew. Everyone wanted to talk to me about the split, or blame me because Drew had been hospitalised, even though it wasn't my fault. I just wanted to talk to Christopher; although he didn't say much in those days, we seemed to have a special connection. We both recycled everything we could, and both moaned about Becca and Ant leaving all the lights on in their huge house. He said he liked me because I was an 'old-fashioned gal' who used a fountain pen and played an acoustic guitar. That day we'd met in some greasy spoon that no one else liked, and talked half-seriously about running away from Brighton and getting working passages on a ship Christopher had heard of. We wouldn't escape on a plane, of course, because of the environment. Then we drank all day. Christopher had lived in a shared house near the police station. His bedroom walls were painted magnolia and there was a mattress on the floor, and nothing else. I was wearing a new pair of blue knickers with white lace on the edges, and he laughed at them. 'What are you wearing those for?' he'd said. And I thought that meant he wanted me naked, right then, and I threw them in the corner and got under the lumpy duvet and put the spliff he passed me into an ashtray and waited. In some ways I was still waiting. Nothing happened that night except for his long, brown hair spreading out on the pillow, and him stroking my arm until we both fell into a stoned sleep. It didn't seem to matter much. Back then, life felt like something that would happen in the future, not now; and it felt as if you could easily fit the cosmos into a single poem.

After I'd dried off and said goodnight to Christopher I settled down on the sofa with *The Science of Living Forever*. It was dark and quiet outside the cottage, and the only sounds I could hear were the occasional *ack, ack*s of the seagulls, and the odd door slamming up the hill as people got back home from the pub. Sometimes boats would blare their foghorns from way out at sea, but there were no foghorns tonight. I was tired, and glad I had only one chapter and an epilogue to read. In the last chapter of his book, Kelsey Newman discussed the visions of heaven in all the major world religions, and argued that the Omega Point, essentially the God constructed at/by/ in the end of time, was very similar to the Gods we already know. He quoted from the Bible, the Qur'an, the Upanishads, the Torah and the Buddhist scriptures to show that the prophets from history knew all about the Omega Point, and its eternity and power. Was the Omega Point so different from the Hindu God that manifests itself in everything? Was it so different from the Buddhist idea of the interconnectedness of all living things? When the Bible talks about God being the 'alpha and omega', the beginning and end, surely this is what is meant?

As I was reading, I was wondering about basing a Zeb Ross novel on Newman's book. I imagined a girl-hero who decides to rescue humanity from this artificial, shrink-wrapped universe at the end of time. Perhaps she'd have to kill herself in order to get to the Omega Point, and then she'd have to overthrow it, or convince it to let the universe go. This would undoubtedly be rejected by the Zeb Ross editorial board, though, even though I was on it. For one thing, Zeb Ross didn't write about unanswerable mysteries beyond the universe. All the plots, however puzzling, had to have neat resolutions, and anything mysterious had to be ultimately explainable using GCSE-level science or common sense. So, for example, if there was wailing in an attic, and the attic was empty, a Zeb Ross hero would show that there was no ghost, but actually a secret room concealed between the top floor and the attic, where a disturbed teenager was hiding — the long-lost cousin of the hero, perhaps, who would now move into the spare room and would be able to help him fit in better at school. Also, no hero in a Zeb Ross novel could ever commit suicide, even if you could prove, using GCSE-level science, that this would not be the end of her. Along with suicide, Zeb Ross novels were not permitted to contain anorexia, drug use, the words 'fuck' or 'cunt', cannibalism or self-harm. There were a few other things too, all printed on a sheet that we gave to new ghostwriters.

Maybe there was some other way of plotting this end-of-universe novel; I could certainly have used Newman's ideas in one of my Newtopia novels, if I was still writing them. Did I miss them? I wasn't sure. I was tapping my pencil on my leg, and my thoughts were going *tap, tap, tap* too, and I was quite distracted by the time I reached the first lines of Newman's epilogue. I had been wondering whether to skip it altogether. But it was quite arresting.

'So now you won't mind', Newman wrote, 'if I tell you something shocking. You are already dead. You died a long time ago, probably billions of years ago. In fact, you are already immortal, although you may take a few more lives to properly realise it. You are currently living, and re-living, in what I will term the *Second World*, which has been created by the Omega Point as a place where you prepare for the rest of eternity. No one knows much about the First World. It probably looked a lot like the world we are living in now, for reasons I will come to in a moment. It is the world whose scientists originally created the possibility of the Omega Point, and thus ensured the immortality of all its beings. You were certainly one of those beings once. How do we know for sure that we are in the Second World and not the First World? Remember that the Omega Point is infinitely powerful. It can, and therefore will, use its *Energia* to create an infinity of universes that look just like the one you are in right now. There is therefore an infinity-to-one chance that we are *not* living in a universe created by the Omega Point; it is mathematically impossible for us not to be. Compared with the infinity of time in a simulated universe, the physical life of the universe was a mere sneeze. It is far more likely that we are in a post-universe, which is eternal, than in a finite universe, which must be long-gone. So why are we stuck in this Second World? I have just written a whole book telling you that you will go to Heaven when you die, and now I'm telling you that you are already dead, and living in a world that is distinctly unheavenly. But here's where things get exciting. In my next book I will explain in detail how to leave the Second World for the last time and embark on the Road to Perfection, which will take you to the Heaven that I have shown is mathematically not just possible, but inevitable. For now, I will conclude with a few remarks about the nature of the Second World, and the purpose of its creation.

'No one knows', he went on, 'what Heaven will be like. It's unimaginable. But one thing we can say for certain is that all of us, immortal beings though we may be, are not ready for it yet. We were originally wired up for roughly a hundred years of life in a terrestrial environment, and so this is when we begin our immortal lives — just as the Bible says. However, your human brain — and I will show you the science behind this in the next book — has room inside it to store a thousand years' worth of memories. The Omega Point could give it even more. The Road to Perfection is the place you go after you die for the last time in the Second World. It is where you set about collecting these memories, and it can be whatever you want it to be. The Omega Point will find a perfect partner just for you, if that's what you want, and together you can go on great adventures. On the Road to Perfection, you will have a new, improved body, with no aches, pains or defects. You will be consciously immortal and enlightened. But only the properly individuated Self can cope with all this. And to become truly individuated, and to be able to succeed in your great Quest on the Road to Perfection, you need to learn how to become a hero in this world. In short, you get out of the Second World by becoming truly yourself, and overcoming all your personal obstacles. Then you will be ready for enlightenment and transcendence.

'You will receive plenty of Special Invitations in your life: those moments where you are invited to embark on an adventure, where the universe seems to be beckoning you with its finger and saying, *Come here and try this.* Will you sit on your sofa eating pizza and thinking that adventure is not for you? Then you'll take a long time to make it out of the Second World, which, of course, is full of pizza-guzzlers and other no-hopers who have not transcended and therefore not a nice place. Decide what you most desire, and set off on a quest to get it. In my next book, I will describe the nature and possible structures of these quests, and give you some ideas about how to complete one. But in the meantime, you can learn almost everything you need to know about what it means to be a true hero from classic myths, stories and fairy tales.'

My mind was a tangle as I put the book down and picked up my knitting. I had only a small amount of my turquoise wool left, but I stayed up until about midnight making knit-stitch after knit-stitch and purl-stitch after purl-stitch, continuing my K2 P2 rib and wondering why I hated this book so much. No doubt it would give great comfort to people who'd been bereaved, or who were scared of dying. It was certainly very well argued, and the maths made sense, sort of. Perhaps a real scientist would be able to say what was materially wrong with Newman's theory. I just wondered what the Omega Point's motivation was in all this.

My turquoise wool had been a Christmas present from Frank and Vi. Claudia, the publishing director of Orb Books and also Vi's twin sister, had been staying in the holiday cottage in Scotland as well. Things were slightly awkward between us because Orb Books had recently told me they wanted me to focus more on Zeb Ross projects and that they wouldn't be renewing my contract for the Newtopia books. I'd mentioned this to Vi about a week before Christmas, when Claudia was lying down one afternoon and we were in the kitchen of the holiday cottage making beetroot soup. I explained that Orb Books didn't feel my own work was 'commercial' enough any more and that I was taking too many risks with the genre. Vi had clapped me on the back and said, 'Good for you. Fuck them. Finish your own book at last. Screw their bottles of oil.'

This was a reference to Aristophanes' play *The Frogs*, which she was re-reading over the holiday as research for her next project. In the play Dionysus goes to the underworld to stage a competition between the dead poets Aeschylus and Euripides to see who is the better tragedian, and who, therefore, should go back to Earth to save Athens. They take it in turns to criticise one another's work. Euripides says that Aeschylus was too dark, brooding and overwrought, but then Aeschylus proves that any of Euripides' clever but formulaic stories could be about someone losing a bottle of oil. The point seemed to be that every formulaic story starts with a conflict that's later resolved — like losing a bottle of oil and then finding it again.

Vi was grinding pepper for the soup, while I processed oranges into zest, juice and segments. Frank came in for a glass of sherry and then went back to watching the cricket in the sitting room. The dogs were all in front of the fire and Frank's parrot Sebastian was in his cage on the piano. Every so often I could hear him saying half-sense things like 'He really middled it yesterday', 'See you after the break, Grandma' and 'One hundred and eighty!'

'If we go along with Nietzsche's arguments that art and writing should do something much more profound than simply have someone lose a bottle of oil and then find it again, then it is obvious how pointless most stories are,' Vi said, looking up from the pestle and mortar. 'They're just dull repetitions of the same kind of idiot losing the same bottle of oil and then, of course, finding it again and living happily ever after and not being such an idiot any more. But I'm still not sure how, or if, Nietzsche comes into this. I'm not sure what he says about tragedy is quite right. I know you think tragedy is beyond all formula, but I'm not a hundred per cent sure.'

'Why not? In tragedy if someone loses a bottle of oil, it's a really important bottle of oil and they end up dead.'

'It's still a formula.'

'But don't you think it's significant that the end isn't happy?'

'But it is happy for Nietzsche. I think that's my point. He likes it that everyone is cast into primal oblivion.'

I thought for a second. 'That is interesting,' I said.

The kitchen was filling with the sweet smell of roasting beetroot. Vi kept on grinding the peppercorns, breaking them down firmly but gently.

'I can't stop thinking of the stories everyone told at the nursing home,' she said. 'They didn't have beginnings, or they didn't have ends — happy or sad. People often put themselves and their lives into something like a formula, but then they would subvert it. One woman I worked with told me about her kid walking in when she and her husband were having sex on the living-room floor. "I'll only be a minute, love," the father said to this kid. "I'm just slipping your mum a length."'

I laughed. 'How is that subversive?'

'It should be a dramatic moment, but it isn't.'

'I see.'

While Vi carried on talking about nursing-home anecdotes involving blow jobs, false teeth, colostomy bags, thrush
epidemics and ninety-year-olds lap-dancing, I was imagining
using the bottle-of-oil idea as an exercise on an Orb Books
retreat. I imagined telling the new writers about how easy
plotting could be if you just imagined that your character has
lost a bottle of oil and then needs to find it again by the end
of the novel. This wasn't what Vi had in mind, of course. She
was still in the process of working out her theory of the 'storyless story', an idea which had come out of all the anthro-
pological work she'd done. She'd got her professorship relatively late—she was now sixty-four—and was planning to
talk about this storyless story in her inaugural lecture. I didn't
pay too much attention to this stuff any longer, considering
that my entire existence now depended on me being able to
take a good but unhappy character from bad fortune to good
fortune in a credible way, and give them a bottle of oil—if
that was what they wanted—as a prize at the end. I wanted
to make my 'real' novel less formulaic and more literary, of
course, but if I listened to Vi's theories, then my only narrative
strategy would be 'shit happens'.

Being in Scotland with Frank, Vi and Claudia felt like a
proper holiday. During the day we walked on the beach with
the dogs, read, or wrote in our notebooks. Frank had some
marking to do, Claudia was editing a Zeb Ross novel and Vi
was finishing a feature for Oscar, the same literary editor who
commissioned me to review science books. In the evenings
the dogs lay by the fire and Sebastian hopped around in his
huge cage on top of the piano, just as he would at home, inter-
spersing phrases he'd been taught from Shakespeare or picked
up from the cricket with words and phrases he'd taught himself, like 'Banana!' and, regardless of whom he was addressing,
'You're a very hairy man, Frank.' Frank was indeed very hairy.
He was in his early fifties and had a scruffy beard, bushy hair,
ragged fingernails and sharp, green eyes, like some creature

living in the mountains. Vi resembled one of these mountains: tall, jagged and permanent, with the possibility of a dangerous fall if you took the wrong path.

One cold afternoon, while Frank and Claudia were out getting supplies, I asked Vi to teach me how to knit. I'd never knitted before, but I'd bought some wool and knitting needles in Dartmouth on a whim one cold, void-like day earlier that December after a big argument with Christopher. Sometimes arguing with Christopher made me feel as if I were a planet that had been tipped off its axis by some unspeakable cosmic event, so that even rotating normally would now be enough to cause radioactive storms, tectonic shifts and tsunamis. I would stand there in the kitchen scared to do anything, because the tiniest sigh or meaningless glance out of the window could start the whole thing off again. Later, when I reflected on the tiny sigh or the 'meaningless' glance I'd realise that there had been something in it after all, and I'd wonder whether the whole problem with Christopher was actually me.

When I got back from the shops that day the argument hadn't finished.

'Oh, I see,' Christopher had said. 'While I've been sitting here worried sick you've been out *shopping*.'

There had been a breathtakingly icy wind coming off the sea and by the time I got back I couldn't feel my toes or my fingers. It wasn't just that; I could barely feel myself. When we'd first moved to Dartmouth I'd spent afternoons browsing in the shops, imagining myself a millionaire and deciding on this cashmere sweater, that pair of £100 distressed jeans and those dark red, lace-up boots. In Dartmouth you could browse handbags, hardback books, houses, boats, holidays and even swordfish for dinner parties. Most weeks I went to look at a small, yellow, wooden breadbin that cost more than £50. But on this occasion I realised I didn't want any of it, and I suddenly hated the people that did. *We all die,* I wanted to shout at everyone. *Why are we all bothering with these stu-*

pid fucking meaningless things? So I'd hardly had a good time at the shops. After seeing my freaked-out eyes and tired skin in too many boutique mirrors, I'd decided to find somewhere with no mirrors: thus the knitting shop. I'd never been in there before, but I liked the way it didn't sell anything, just the patterns and possibilities and materials for things. There was a bargain bin and I'd found three balls of red wool, and needles to go with them.

'I've bought wool,' I said to Christopher. 'I thought I'd learn to make you socks.' And then I started to cry while he put the kettle on. 'I just wanted to do something nice for you, and I know you could do with some proper socks for the project and . . .'

He chewed on his lip the whole time he was making my tea. 'I'm such a bastard,' he said, when he handed it to me. 'Please forgive me, babe.'

A couple of weeks later he asked how long I thought his socks would take. I'd completely forgotten about them.

'A while, sweets,' I said. 'I haven't even worked out how to knit a scarf yet.'

Being in Scotland meant I actually had time for knitting. Vi and I were curled up in the sitting room, with books, Biros, pencils and notebooks strewn around us, along with Claudia's cross-stitch project and Frank's 'Rainy Day Cricket'. The open fire crackled away and B was lying in front of it with the other dogs, all of them snoring every so often like a very bored chorus. I got the wool out of my battered hemp bag and showed it to Vi. 'Do you know what to do with this?' I asked her.

'How cool!' she said. 'I've never seen you knit. You'll look like an old auntie.'

'Yeah, well, maybe I've reached that age.'

'Ha,' Vi said. 'I knitted when I was a kid. Claudia was better than me, of course. I haven't knitted for years. I once made a lambswool blanket on a ship between Tasmania and England, while Frank read *War and Peace* in Russian. I can teach you how to cast on and get going, I reckon. Claudia will show you the rest. You know she knitted these?' Vi bent down and pulled up the legs of her jeans. I could see the tops of two striped socks emerging from her big, battered DMs. 'When I got back from Tassie that time she actually counted the mistakes in my blanket, the old cow. You can start by making a scarf in garter stitch, which is just knitting, no purling. After that you can make a scarf in a knit-two purl-two rib. I might make one too. I feel the urge, seeing your wool.'

'I want to knit socks,' I said. 'For Christopher.'

Vi looked horrified. 'Why?'

I shrugged. 'I think hand-knitted socks will make him happy.'

'Then get him to knit his own. Frank can knit. It's not that hard.'

I laughed. 'I think the idea of me knitting them for him makes him happy.'

'God.'

'Not in a sinister way. I just think he feels loved when I make an effort.'

'But hand-knitting socks? A pair of socks takes a million billion years. Make some for yourself.'

'Claudia made socks for you.'

'Yeah, but all that old bat does is knit, when she's not line-editing or cross-stitching. She has to make gifts for people. Anyway, she's my sister.'

'Yeah.'

'But socks are a long way off for you. You need to begin with a scarf.'

'OK. Is it hard?'

'If you can write Zeb Ross novels, you can definitely knit a scarf.'

We fiddled around for a while, casting on. Vi showed me how to make a slipknot and then a strange lasso with my fingers. She cast on a few stitches while I watched, and then she

43

just slid them off the needle and pulled the wool into a straight line again. It was like casting a spell and then undoing it. After about an hour of copying this, I'd managed to cast on twenty stitches, so that there was a long row of red on one of the needles, as if it was a sword dripping with blood.

'Now what do I do?' I asked her.

Vi took the needles from me. 'You stab him,' she said, sticking the empty needle through the first cast-on stitch. 'Then you hang him,' she said, bringing the yarn around the needle. 'Then you throw him.' She brought the needle under, over and away, and I could then see that there was a new stitch on it. 'That comes from Claudia, by the way. It was the only way she could remember, when we were learning.'

I sat there doing this for an hour or so, and a very basic fabric began to form. Vi tapped away on her laptop, but stopped every so often to check my progress.

'You're doing very well,' Vi said. 'You're a natural. It's like your healing hands.'

'Ha, ha. I have not got healing hands.'

'You so have.'

'I don't even believe in healing hands.'

'No. But still.'

Years before, when Vi and Frank still lived in Brighton, someone had got Vi a book on Reiki and we'd tried it out one evening. The idea was that you used energy from your hands to heal people without even touching them. When Vi passed her hands over my shoulder — sore from too much writing — it went warm and then felt a bit better. According to Frank, my hands had more energy even than Vi's. Apparently the bunion I passed my hands over just went away about a week later. But after that my shoulder got worse again and I didn't think about Reiki any more.

I knitted a few more rows.

'I might go into business doing this,' I said. 'Like my friend Libby.'

'Just do it to relax,' Vi said. 'Otherwise you'll ruin it.'

'Yeah, maybe. Oh, that reminds me of a joke. Well, it's not exactly a joke, more a story. There's a group of fishermen on a tropical island. Every day they get up when they feel like it, go out on their boats and catch enough fish for themselves and their families, and perhaps for anyone they know who is ill and can't make it out that day. They all have gardens where they grow everything else they need. When they are done fishing, they play with their children, or have a game of cards, or read books in the sunshine. Every night they eat their fish and then go around to one another's houses and tell stories or have parties. One day, an American comes for a holiday on the island — they don't get many tourists there, but the location has just featured in some book of "unspoilt destinations" or something like that. He looks at the way they live, and then says to one of the men, who has taken him out on a fishing trip, "You know, you're missing out on all kinds of opportunities here. If you organised yourselves into a company, you could spend more time fishing, and export the surplus that you don't need to live on, and you could build bigger houses and have your own swimming pools and trust funds for your kids and you could get yourself some proper clothes and travel the world. Soon you wouldn't need to fish for yourselves; you could employ other people to do it. Eventually — imagine this — you could retire with a million in the bank and then . . ." "Then," finished the fisherman, "I suppose I could afford to go on holidays like yours, and find true peace and harmony by simply fishing in the sunshine."'

Vi smiled. 'I like it. It's almost a storyless story. You want a simple life, too, don't you? You said that was why you didn't go to Greece in the autumn. You said having a simple life helped with your writing. Your real writing, I mean. Maybe that's how knitting will be good for you.'

My *real* writing. I thought about how real my Newtopia books were, and my Zeb Ross novels. You could go into any bookshop, almost, and touch at least one of them. My literary novel existed only in my head. It was only as real as the ghosts I'd believed in as a child.

'Christopher wants a *really* simple life,' I said. 'More simple than the life I want, probably. He said recently that he's not going to buy any new clothes ever again, just mend the ones he's already got, which isn't going to help much with the job interviews, I suppose, but it's quite a cool idea.'

'As long as he doesn't expect you to knit his bloody socks.'

We both laughed. Then I knitted a few more rows.

'I haven't admitted this before, but I do sort of wish I'd gone to Greece,' I said.

Vi looked up from her laptop and her face slowly avalanched into a kind version of 'I told you so.'

Back in the summer I'd been accepted to spend October in an artists' colony on a Greek island to work on my 'real' novel. The timing had been pretty good, since I'd just finished a Zeb Ross novel and agreed with Orb Books that I wouldn't do another one for a year. Vi had been to the colony in Greece the year before and said it was an amazing place. Indeed, she'd nominated me for it, written the reference and helped me select some material to submit, most of which had since been deleted. She said that the whole place had a 'campfire' atmosphere, and you got to meet nice people and drink wine and sit on the terrace in the evenings, while being left undisturbed to write, swim, walk or think in the day.

The whole idea of it terrified me. I didn't want to meet people who might be happy and thus illuminate my own unhappiness. I also didn't want to leave Christopher, because I thought I'd never return. It hadn't been very long since Rowan and I had kissed. Although I was determined not to go and meet him on a Sunday evening in Dartmouth, I wanted to go to the opening of the Maritime Centre and at least see his face again. Of course, I didn't think in those terms at the time.

I thought I'd decided not to go because there was no one to look after B, and because I didn't want to add to my carbon footprint by flying. Christopher would be lonely and might starve, because he didn't like going to the supermarket and since vowing to grow all his own fruit and vegetables in window boxes had managed only one tomato and some basil. As usual, I had no spare money at all. The trust that funded the colony paid for flights and accommodation, but residents had to pay for their own food. There was also the problem of buying sandals, sun cream, a bikini, sarongs, insect repellent and sunglasses, none of which I owned.

I hadn't been at all sure that being in Greece would make any difference to anything. People who needed constant new thrills just weren't that good at making the most of what was around them, or even just making things up, I'd decided. I prided myself on being able to get hours — or at least minutes — of excitement from the same beach I went to with B almost every day in Devon. Why should I need anything else? I also felt by then that nothing could surprise me, perhaps apart from really out-there popular science books. Fiction didn't surprise me at all, and once I'd read the blurb on the back of a novel I rarely felt the need to read the whole thing. I sometimes got three-quarters of the way through a novel and then abandoned it, because I knew what the end was going to be. I'd also somehow got into the habit of reading each page of a novel almost-backwards, scanning the last paragraph to confirm I knew what was coming before I started at the top. After I'd played out October in Greece in my head a few different ways, I became certain that there was no need to actually go. I knew what water felt like, and sun, and I had conversations with people all the time. I drank wine. What was the point of doing all this in a slightly different way, in a slightly different time-zone? I loved flying: seeing the world below me like a doodle, and feeling like a friend of the doodler, but

I'd done that before too. I had the results of the experiment already.

I also wasn't sure I would be able to finish my novel under any circumstances, let alone somewhere strange like Greece. It had originally been due for submission in 1999, and every year since then I'd had to email my agent and ask for another extension. The editor who had commissioned the novel had left the publishing house in 2002, and her successor had left in 2004. The publishing house had been bought by another publishing house and had become an imprint. Then the second publishing house was bought by a huge media conglomerate and the imprint changed its name. Every so often I got an email from a new editor asking how the book was coming on, but I hadn't heard anything since about 2006. The contract had probably been left behind in someone's filing cabinet and sent to the dump. I'd almost certainly lost my copy. Even my original agent had long gone — down to Cornwall to work as a schoolteacher — so I didn't have anyone to ask about it.

I sent the email cancelling my trip to Greece about two weeks before I was due to go. I thought this act would make me stop lying awake wheezing for hours every night after Christopher had gone to sleep, but it made it worse. I spent the whole of October Googling the weather in Greece while yawning and almost falling asleep in the library. Since then I'd written about 2,000 words of my novel and deleted about 20,000, which was a net gain of −18,000 words. Was it possible to submit a novel with a negative number of words? I'd changed the title a few more times too, and it was currently called *The Death of the Author.* It was all very frustrating. I had no problem writing formulaic genre books totalling about half a million words to date, and I never deleted things from them or changed their titles. Maybe I was just a formulaic genre writer, and that was why.

'How's it going between you and Christopher now?' Vi asked. 'Really.'

'Oh, it's the same.' I sighed. 'I know I've got to pull myself together. I guess I can learn something from the Greece experience. Next time I get that sort of chance I will take it, I suppose, perhaps. But I guess that's got nothing to do with Christopher.'

'Just don't knit socks for him.'

'No.'

'And I'll make you up a flower remedy. You look exhausted.'

'Thanks.'

The next day Vi went to the village and bought herself some black alpaca and started making a ribbed scarf. It turned out that Claudia had a half-knitted Regency dress tucked away in one of her bags, so she got that out and worked on it beside us. It was like being in a club. My knitting felt real in my hands, and all I had to do was knit stitch after stitch and the fabric got longer. It was much easier than writing my novel. At first I'd stop knitting after every row and look at how long my scarf was, and calculate how long it might be in half an hour, or the following day, but after a while I stopped doing that. It was easier if I kept the yarn wrapped around my fingers in the way Vi had shown me, and each time I finished a row to just turn the needles and begin again on the next one. Whenever I made a mistake, Claudia would take the needles from me and fix it, saying things like 'Yes, this stitch is twisted — look, Vi, at what she's done — and you've dropped this one,' and then she'd give it back to me and I'd tell myself not to make any more mistakes, because they sounded very difficult to undo.

While we knitted, Frank read Russian fairy tales aloud to us. He was writing an introduction to a new edition of Aleksandr Afanas'ev's nineteenth-century collection, and was getting to grips with the translation. On Christmas Eve he finished with a story called 'The Goat Comes Back'. He cleared his throat, and said to Vi, 'You'll like this, my love. Propp has nothing to say about this one.' Then he began.

> Billy goat, billy goat, where have you been?
> *I was grazing horses.*
> And where are the horses?
> *Nikolka led them away.*
> And where is Nikolka?
> *He went to the larder.*
> And where is the larder?
> *It was flooded with water.*
> And where is the water?
> *The oxen drank it.*
> And where are the oxen?
> *They went to the mountain.*
> And where is the mountain?
> *The worms gnawed it away.*
> And where are the worms?
> *The geese ate them all.*
> And where are the geese?
> *They went to the junipers.*
> And where are the junipers?
> *The maids broke them.*
> And where are the maids?
> *They all got married.*
> And where are their husbands?
> *They all died.*

When he'd finished reading it, we were all laughing.

'Sounds like one of my authors explaining why their manuscript is late,' Claudia said, knitting so fast it looked like she had invented a new dance.

Vi smiled and didn't say anything.

'Can you read it again, Frank?' I said. 'And a few more times. It's a great rhythm for my knitting.'

By Christmas Day I'd knitted all my red yarn, and I didn't know what I was going to do next — Claudia suggested starting a new Zeb Ross book. But when I opened my presents from Vi and Frank, I found, as well as a Moleskine notebook and a new translation of Chekhov's letters, several balls of soft, turquoise yarn and some beautiful rosewood needles. We exchanged the rest of our gifts and then ate a late lunch at the big dining-room table. It wasn't until early evening when we found out that a TV satellite had come down in the Pacific and caused a tidal wave that had devastated Lot's Wife, one of the Japanese islands Vi had written about years ago. She'd stayed in a Buddhist monastery there for almost six months. We didn't have a TV in the cottage, but we listened on the radio. Vi was quiet for a long time after this, and knitted next to me for hours, but by Boxing Day evening she had something to say about it.

'So many innocent people killed by bottles of oil,' she said, shaking her head.

Claudia snorted. 'Come on, V. Surely no one had anything to gain from this. It was just an accident. You can't come up with a conspiracy theory for everything. The company themselves said it was a huge loss for them as well.'

'It's an encore to colonialism,' Vi said. 'Yet another encore. Not even the final one. People just keep on clapping.'

'You've even lost me, my love,' Frank said. 'It could have crashed anywhere, surely?'

'Well, maybe. But don't you think there's something horribly poetic about a storyless nation being put to death by other people's "heroic" stories? No one from this island ever did anything to anyone else or went out and conquered anything. But first of all some eighteenth-century explorer turns up and decides to name the island because he thinks it looks like a pillar of salt from a story he's read, and now this. Killed by soap operas and American drama series.'

'How can a nation be "storyless"?' I asked.

Vi sighed. 'OK. I don't think in the end a nation can be storyless. Only a story can be storyless. They did have stories on Lot's Wife. But in recent times mainly Zen stories, which are storyless stories, because they are constructed to help you break away from drama, and hope and desire. Some of them are funny. All of them are unpredictable. They're not tragedies, comedies or epics. They're not even Modernist anti-hero stories, or experimental narratives or metafiction. I lost count of the times someone would say, "I'll tell you a story," and then recite something like an absurdist poem with no conflict and no resolution. One of these "stories" was about a Zen monk who, on the day he was going to die, sent postcards saying, "I am departing from this world. This is my last announcement." Then he died.'

'Isn't this a problem of definition?' Claudia said. 'They obviously weren't telling "stories" as we would understand them. If we say that a story is something with a beginning, a middle and an end, deterministically linked, with at least one main character, then someone else can't come along and say that a story is actually defined as "anything anyone ever says".'

'How about if we define "story" differently again?' Frank said. 'What if a story is simply any representation of agents acting? What if that's all it is, and the shape of the narrative, its determinism, its construction of "good" and "bad" characters and so on are culturally specific?'

'Exactly,' said Vi. 'Thank you, my love. These structuralists who go on and on about the universality of the hero's journey like to talk about the story of the Buddha, because he saw three fucked-up things and then set off on a journey and got enlightened at the end. But they don't pay so much attention to the Chinese story "Monkey", which is another Buddhist story, but with a very silly Trickster hero who doesn't do the right things or ask the right questions, but ends up enlightened as well. They also don't pay any attention at all to the Pacific Trickster Maui, who, according to the stories, fished up at least some of New Zealand with his grandmother's jawbone. Maui eventually dies while attempting to creep inside the goddess of death, Hine-nui-te-po, through her vagina, which is lined with teeth. He's supposedly a hero entering an innermost cave — ha ha! — and hopes to secure immortality for everyone. He has taken some bird companions on his great quest. But one of these, the Piwakawaka, or fantail, laughs at Maui and wakes up the goddess, who crushes him between her legs. These are storyless stories, because they are not Aristotelian, or even *Claudian*.' Vi smiled at her sister as if she was the one now picking out all the mistakes in Claudia's knitted blanket. 'If we go with Frank's definition, then they are stories, but they're not satisfying in the way we expect stories should be in the West. They also make us re-think what we mean by "story" in the first place.'

'Isn't that more or less a normal tragedy?' I said. 'No hero can ever succeed on a quest for immortality. There's too much hubris.'

'Yeah.' Vi nodded. 'I see what you mean. But in its very nature the story takes the piss out of tragedy, because it's funny and absurd, which is not how tragedy is supposed to be. This, for me, is a key feature of storylessness: all structures must contain the possibility of their own non-existence — some zip that undoes them.' She smiled. 'The storyless story is a vagina with teeth.'

There was no sign of Libby's car in the river on Monday morning. I had plenty of time to look, since I got stuck in the ferry queue for half an hour. I was on my way to the library as usual, where I planned to finish my review of *The Science of Living Forever* and then try to work on my novel. I was sleepy but warm, wrapped up in my new turquoise ribbed scarf. I'd woken when Christopher had, at five, and only dozed between then and him leaving. I realised I'd been dreaming Kelsey Newman's words over and over again — *You are already dead* — and of being chased around by the Omega Point, which had become a blueish, cartoonish antagonist that said things like 'Ha, ha, ha,' and twiddled its moustache. I also dreamed some other words, words that I remembered, and which seemed to be connected somehow: *You will never finish what you start. You will not overcome the monster. And in the end, you will come to nothing.* After a quick shower, I'd taken B to the beach. I did this every morning in the winter, and some days it woke me up, but most days it didn't. Today I'd been looking at all the little barnacles clinging to the rocks, and remembering Darwin writing about their evolution, and the female barnacles that at one stage had a 'husband in each pocket' — like Libby, I'd thought with a smile. If we were living in some sort of Second World, what was the point of evolution? I supposed Newman would say that the whole point of evolution in the First World would be the ultimate creation of the right scientists, and then their Omega Point. I wondered what the creationists would make of that idea: that the ultimate purpose of evolution is to create God.

While I'd been looking at barnacles, B had been fishing for a big rock that I kept throwing in the sea for her. She strutted around with it between times as if carrying the rock was her important job. Animals hadn't seemed to figure much in Newman's afterlife. They had in Plato's, I remembered. If you were sick of being a human, you could ask the Spindle of Destiny if you could come back as a dog or a horse or a sparrow and have a less troublesome life. According to Plato, even Odysseus chose to come back as a normal citizen in his next life because he couldn't be bothered to have adventures any more. But it didn't sound as if Newman was a fan of the quiet life. What was wrong with sitting around eating pizza if it made you happy and you didn't hurt anyone? Why was this worse than, say, slaying a dragon or rescuing a maiden? The idea of a thousand years of adventure just made me feel tired.

After a while longer in the ferry queue I thought I was going to drop off, so I started doing the Waterwheel, a breathing exercise I'd learned a long time ago. To breathe like a waterwheel, you breathe through your nose but imagine your breath entering your body at the base of your spine, continuing up your spine, stopping for a second at the bottom of your throat and then tumbling down the front of your body, exiting somewhere around your navel. The Waterwheel eventually creates the sensation that you are breathing in and out at the same time, and that the air is like water constantly flowing around you. It is both relaxing and energising at the same time.

I learned the Waterwheel when I was eight. It was the beginning of October in 1978, and my school was closed because of the strikes. We hadn't had a holiday that year because of my brother Toby being born, but suddenly one day my father said, half to me, and half to my mother, 'Meg would like a holiday, wouldn't you?' and the next day we got in our old car and drove to Suffolk. It wasn't much of a holiday at first. My mother was busy with Toby, and my father was working on an important paper and worrying about his promotion application. We'd rented, or perhaps borrowed, a house on the edge of a forest, and for the first few days I simply sat on my bed and read books about children who go on holiday and find criminals in caves, or enchanted castles or dungeons with treasure in them. My parents occasionally said I should go out and get some fresh air, but I got the impression they didn't much care whether I did or not. Still, when the books ran out I went off to explore the forest. Perhaps I wanted an adventure, like the ones I'd been reading about. Perhaps I did just need some fresh air.

Each morning I would make cheese and pickle sandwiches and a flask of tea and go out for the whole day, wondering what I'd do if I met a fairy, or came across a monster in a lair. I knew I wouldn't tell my father. It was a bright, crisp autumn, and early in the morning cobwebs glowed white with dew between the low branches of trees, and robins and thrushes sang high-pitched songs that echoed through the forest. Cones were beginning to grow on the branches of silvery-green pine trees, like little cosmoses sprouting in the kind of multiverse my father sometimes talked about. On the ground I would sometimes find bright red and white toadstools that had come up suddenly, like the Yorkshire puddings my mother made on a Sunday. There were different sorts of mushrooms everywhere: some were like huge, spongy pancakes lying at the base of tree-trunks; others were tiny, with stalks like spaghetti. Late in the day, the cobwebs would become almost translucent in the low sun, and I would only notice them at all because of the spiders that hung in the middle of them like nuclei. One time I saw a spider catch a wasp. I hated wasps, and I was quite pleased when this one flew drowsily away from me and got stuck in the web. In an instant, the fat spider came and started wrapping up the wasp in its white silk. The wasp struggled at first, and I felt sorry for it. But then it stopped moving. The spider worked away, turning it around, cocooning it, its thin, jagged legs moving this way and that, each one as precise as a needle on a sewing machine. Then it picked up the wasp in its front legs and took it up to the centre of the web the way a human would carry a newborn baby. I watched for ages, but nothing else happened, and when I came back the next day the whole web had gone. Another day I found some string in the damp, creaky holiday house and made a shoulder-strap for my flask. In the forest I made myself a necklace out of wild flowers by piercing each stalk with my thumb-nail and threading the next flower through it, just like a daisy-chain. I ate blackberries from bushes until my hands were dyed purple with the juice. I had stopped brushing my hair. I'd gone wild, and no one seemed to notice.

One bright, chilly afternoon I followed a stream and found a thatched stone cottage that seemed as if it had grown out of the forest. It was covered in a dense, deep-red ivy, with holes for only the windows and the door. It looked like something you might try to draw at school because you'd seen it in a picture book. There was a gate that opened easily, and I walked into a garden and past a small well. Around the side of the cottage there was a wrought-iron gazebo, also covered in climbing plants and half shaded by big, old trees, and inside it there were two wooden rocking chairs and a wooden table on which stood six cups, into which a man was arranging flowers. I'd never seen a man arranging flowers before. In fact, no one I knew arranged flowers.

'Aha! A young adventuress,' he said. 'Well, don't just stand there gawping. Come and help.'

I went and stood closer. He was small, with a big, brown beard the colour of tree bark. He looked as if he had grown out of the forest along with everything else. He was wearing electric-blue suede boots and faded red trousers. He had a blue suede waistcoat too. I liked that colour blue: it was the same as the hairband I was wearing.

'Hold these,' he said, giving me some flowers. 'And if you're lucky I'll show you some magic and maybe even tell your fortune.' He winked. After I'd held several bunches of white flowers while he cut their stalks, he asked me to go and gather some foliage. I didn't know what that was, and I must have looked baffled, because he said, 'Just green stuff. Go on — quickly — or the spell won't work.'

When I'd finished helping him I said, 'Now will you show me some magic?'

He laughed. 'I just did.'

'Oh,' I said, disappointed. Nothing seemed to have changed.

'All right,' he said. 'Watch this.'

He took a matchbox out of his pocket and put it on the little wooden table. He sat down in one of the rocking chairs and looked at it; then it started to rise up in the air. I gasped and it fell down with a little clatter.

'Is it really magic?' I asked.

'Yes,' he said, smiling. 'I suppose so.'

'Will you teach me how to do it?'

'We'll see.'

'And what about my fortune?'

He looked at me seriously. 'I'm not sure it's always good for people to know their fortunes.'

'But you promised,' I said.

He sighed. 'Come back tomorrow if you like. Make sure your parents know where you are, though.' The man said his name was Robert, 'like the herb', and that before I could learn magic, or indeed understand my own fortune, I'd have to learn some other things. He had a friend called Bethany, who would be there tomorrow, but who was very shy and wouldn't want to be disturbed too much. He said she was so shy that I might not even see her at all, but that she would definitely be there.

The next morning I went straight back to the strange little cottage. There was a beautiful young woman there who was wearing a long, wine-coloured dress. She seemed to be Robert's wife, although there were other times when I thought she was his daughter, or even his granddaughter. She would sit and play the flute all morning, and on market-day afternoons she would gather up her things in a drawstring bag and go off into the local town. The first thing that Robert taught me was the Waterwheel. We were sitting in the gazebo, and Bethany was inside the cottage playing a melody that sounded like half-finished birdsong. 'You breathe like this', he said, 'when you want to concentrate, or when you're scared, or', he smiled, 'if you want to do magic.' But he didn't show me any actual magic.

Each day of the rest of the holiday was more or less the same. I'd arrive early at the cottage and Robert would give me some task to do, like organising the woodshed or filling bird feeders, because, he said, Bethany loved seeing the birds, and feeding them 'made the other Faeries happy too'. One day we planted bulbs in the garden: snake's-head fritillaries, irises and grape hyacinths. Another day we made some sort of moonshine in a still at the back of the cottage. Another day we pickled walnuts. One day I gathered blackberries, hawthorn berries and rosehips with Bethany. It was the first time I'd been with her alone. She didn't say much, but at one point she smiled and said, 'Robert's taken a shine to you. He must think you are one of us.' Then she skipped off to the next bush and didn't say another word. Later, we made jam. On the last day of my holiday, I asked Robert if he would please show me just a little bit of magic, because I wouldn't be able to come back again. He sighed and said, 'Are you sure you want to learn?'

'Yes,' I said.

Bethany was still out in the town. I was sitting at the big, pine table in the kitchen, where I had been shelling peas for her. Copper pans, skillets and griddles hung from the ceiling, and there was an axe propped up by the back door. I'd done so many tasks at the table, and I'd got used to gazing over at the strange objects on the dresser, one of which was a ship in a bottle, which particularly fascinated me. I wondered how the ship had come to be in the bottle. It couldn't have fitted through the neck. Perhaps it had come to be there by magic. One time Robert had been out collecting mushrooms and I'd picked up the bottle and looked at the ship inside. It had white muslin sails, and writing on its hull in a white, chalky script. When I looked closely I saw that the writing said 'Cutty Sark'. The ship sat on a waxy blue sea, and the bottle had a cork in its neck. I'd wanted to pull the cork to see if it came out, but hadn't.

'Do you believe you already have the ability to do magic?' Robert asked me.

'Yes,' I said solemnly. 'I think so.'

He smiled. 'I think so too. So does Bethany. Not everybody sees Bethany, you know.' Now he looked down at his hands. 'Some people think you need to be initiated to do magic, and that you need to understand the relationship between the world of the Faeries, this world and the world above before you can even attempt a spell. It's a big commitment, and once you open the doors to the Otherworld, you can't go back. But I happen to think there's a lot of magic you can do on your own. Some people might say that every time you cook something or give someone medicine you're doing magic, because you're changing the states of things by redirecting energy.'

I bit my lip. 'But that's not real magic, is it?'

'That depends on your point of view. You need to understand that good magic is always about bringing harmony to the world, not disorder. And you must also accept that magic has consequences. Do you understand that idea?'

I shook my head. 'Do you mean getting into trouble?'

'When you do magic, you are always involved in the redirecting of energy. You might choose to focus lots of healing energy on someone who is sick, or you might simply sew a good-luck charm into the patchwork quilt you are making for a friend. But you must never do this lightly, because you are always taking energy from somewhere else. Depending on the sort of magic you are doing, you will usually ask for help from the spirits of the underworld — the Faeries; or the spirits from Middle Earth; or the higher spirits that dance among the stars. You might call on the Lord and Lady of Middle Earth to help you with a sick cat, for example, or a Faerie to help you interpret a dream. Some people believe that these magical creatures and deities really exist. Other people believe that they are manifestations of an energy that we can only understand metaphorically, as stories and pictures. In any case, when you ask the Faeries for help with a spell or charm, for example, you always need to do something in return. You might feed the birds in your garden, or plant some new flowers. Faeries like nature. Indeed, they don't come to our world much any more because of what we've done to the natural world. If you don't do what you've promised . . . Well, all I can say is that it's fairly easy to use what you would call "magic" to redirect energy, but it always has consequences.' He frowned and then smiled. 'Oh, dear. You're not following me, are you? Bethany said you were far too young. Maybe she's right.'

I shook my head. 'I'm not too young.' But I was beginning to worry about this. I already had some idea of what 'consequences' were. They were always bad things like burning yourself because you played with matches, or being run over because you didn't use the pelican crossing correctly, or being sent to your room, or being beaten with a slipper, or having to write lines. I didn't like the idea of magic so much any more if it had consequences. I didn't like the idea of offending Faeries who lived in some underworld. What if I forgot to do what I'd promised and they came to get me in the middle of the night?

'Also,' Robert said, 'everything you do returns to you three times. In other words, if you do something magical you get it back multiplied by three. The problem is sometimes not knowing if what you're doing is good or bad. In magic there aren't easy definitions of good and bad, and you can still make mistakes. It's a tricky business. You can create monsters, if you're not very careful. If you use a lot of energy and find you can't redirect it properly, then you can end up with ghosts and ghouls and magical creatures roaming around. It's unpleasant when that happens, because someone with higher powers has to come and put it right.'

An owl hooted somewhere outside, and my stomach suddenly felt as if it was a cold dishcloth being wrung out late on a Sunday evening. I looked out of the window and saw that dusk was falling. It had been coming a little earlier every day. 'I'd better get back,' I said.

He laughed. 'Oh, dear. I've scared you off. Well, you're probably too young anyway. But I can see you have the ability. Maybe when you're older. Will you come back here again on holiday? Bethany would like to see you again.'

'I don't know,' I said.

'Well, call on us if you are ever back in the area.'

Robert started filling his pipe.

'Will you tell my fortune before I go?' I said, feeling suddenly tearful. 'You did promise.' This was the end of my holiday, and the end of coming to the forest, and I had been too much of a coward even to learn any magic. I really wanted to change my mind, but I knew it was too late. And I knew that my family would never come back. Mum had complained of damp in the house, and my father said it was too remote. I realised that I would miss Robert and Bethany and the way they lived their lives.

Robert was still standing by the sink. He put down his pipe, turned and looked out of the window for a minute. When he turned back to face me, his eyes had gone a terrifyingly bright shade of green, and his face was set in an unfamiliar way. Before, he had looked like a wise old tree. Now his face was jagged, like rocks cutting through a choppy sea. He looked as if he was in some sort of trance.

'You will never finish what you start,' he said, in a voice that wasn't quite his own. 'You will not overcome the monster. And in the end, you will come to nothing.'

This day, I knew, was going to be like any other. Because of the ferry queue it had already begun slightly too late. By the time I'd walked B and driven across Torbay it was always gone ten, but today it was already coming up for eleven and I was still driving. This in itself could be read as a good sign: sometimes the radiator overheated and I had to stop and fill it with Radweld, which made me even later. Usually I'd get an hour's work done before lunch, less if I had lots of emails to read, and the afternoon would then be postponed until after two o'clock, and by the time I'd finished whatever I'd started before lunch and done some Orb Books admin, it would be time to go to the supermarket and drive home. How was I supposed to write a novel with no time at all to write it in? It didn't have to be like this. When I had written the second halves of all my completed novels, time had just bloomed everywhere, even in the darkest corners. I'd write at least 500 words at the kitchen table before walking B in the mornings, and make crazy notes over lunch. I even wrote in the supermarket queue sometimes, using the tiny keyboard on my mobile phone. One day I wrote 7,000 words. But I probably wouldn't get much done on my novel today, especially not with a book review to write.

The countryside around me looked too bright in the cold February sunshine as I drove across Torbay with the radio on low, wondering about how to begin my review. Oscar loved it when I really trashed a book, and I was sure he deliberately gave me books he knew I'd hate. I'd therefore decided to really go to town on *The Science of Living Forever,* but I didn't quite know how. It seemed a bit of a soft target. I thought about writing something like *Regular readers will know that I should never be provoked on the subject of infinity.* But that was way too smug. I'd been writing for the paper long enough now that I could get away with first-person reviews, but there were limits. Perhaps I could make the point that when humans fiddle around with anything natural they completely mess it up, and messing around with infinity would therefore be an infinitely bad idea. There was also Tennyson's poem about the Ancient Greek Tithonus, lover of Eos, queen of the day. Tithonus has been given the gift of immortality so that he can love Eos for ever, but whoever has arranged this has not also given him eternal youth. So he is doomed to age and decay for evermore. The poem opens: *The woods decay, the woods decay and fall, / The vapours weep their burthen to the ground, / Man comes and tills the field and lies beneath, / And after many a summer dies the swan. / Me only cruel immortality / Consumes: I wither slowly in thine arms.* Perhaps I'd begin my review with that. But it didn't seem quite right either.

In Newman's never-ending universe there'd be time to write an infinite amount of novels, and even finish reading all the books I'd ever begun, and all the books I'd never begun.

But who'd care about fiction any more? We only need fiction because we die. I turned up the radio when the news came on. A study had revealed that Prozac, taken by forty million people, including my brother Toby, had been working only as a placebo for all this time. As I drove past the Maritime Centre with the sea on my right, I thought again about Rowan. *I wither slowly in thine arms.* Even if we were both single, he was still too old for me. It was a good thing we hadn't started emailing each other. But perhaps there'd be an email from him this morning; I'd said he should email me any time. And then what would I do? I couldn't ever kiss him again, because I wouldn't be able to leave it there. I couldn't face living through the aftermath all over again.

After recycling one of last week's car park tickets, I spent the morning at what had become my usual desk in the library, writing my review. It had once been Rowan's usual desk, but I'd taken it over. Oscar only ever had an 800-word space to spare, which often shrank as advertising came in. His assistant Justine spent most of her time sourcing cheap pictures to go with the reviews. The year before, I'd reviewed a book in which a scientist had used slicing ham as a way of explaining dimensions. The ham is three-dimensional, she'd said; and the slice is two-dimensional. It drove me mad. Two-dimensional 'objects' cannot exist, cannot be; however thin something is, it still has three spatial dimensions. I'd spent half the review explaining why it was impossible to experience a two-dimensional world, especially if one was attempting to travel from a three-dimensional world made of ham. Justine had come up with a nice image of a hock of ham, which she'd placed alongside an image of the scientist and a caption: 'The universe is not ham'. I remembered checking and checking that review, worried that I'd got something wrong, and nervous about criticising a real scientist for not being scientific enough. For weeks afterwards I feared the email I'd get from her, putting me straight. But nothing ever happened. I also imagined my father reading my review and being proud of me, but as far as I knew he never read the literary pages of any newspaper.

The Newman review came far more easily than I'd thought. I ended up just summarising his argument, which, like most long and complicated things, including great tragedies and anyone's life story, sounded far more crazy and improbable in 800 words than it ever could in 80,000. In the end the book trashed itself. I told myself I was glad to be done with it; Newman's simulated post-universe, a ghost ship at the end of time, was really giving me the willies. But in fact, I wasn't really done with Newman at all, since I was wondering if I could further trash his ideas in fiction. The post-universe wouldn't work in a Zeb Ross novel, but it could easily become a sub-plot in my 'real' novel. Having some characters trapped in a frozen moment at the end of time was certainly way better than having them trapped in a sauna.

After I'd filed my review and been across the road to the cheap café for lunch, it was half past two. I logged onto my Orb Books email account and read the two proposals that had come in for Zeb Ross novels. One of the proposals was from someone I remembered from the last Torquay retreat, Tim Small, a faded-looking man in his mid-forties who'd relocated to Dartmouth ten years before with his wife Heidi who worked as an accountant at the Yacht Club and was having a long-term affair. The locals who responded to my poster in the Harbour Bookshop only came for six days. On the seventh day I worked with the ghostwriters individually on their particular project, which could be a Zeb Ross novel, a Pepper Moore novel or the next instalment of the Vampire Island series. The first six days were the same for everyone: an intensive trawl through Plato, Aristotle, Vladimir Propp, Northrop Frye, Joseph Campbell, Jung and Robert McKee. I gave students their own pair of Orb Books scissors, because there was so much cutting up and rearranging of bits of paper: so much fiddling with archetypes, complications, resolutions and helpers. The scissors had been my idea. So had the whole Vampire Island series, although I didn't work on it very much.

Tim was the only local student who'd ever had an idea with the potential to work in the Zeb Ross format. He'd wanted to write about a Beast of Dartmoor, and although he'd had in mind a middle-aged, cuckolded protagonist, I'd taken him aside and told him that if he made it a teenager then it was something we'd probably consider. The whole class had been excited about Tim's Beast. How do you end a story about a Beast? We'd discussed that for hours. Chekhov said if you have a gun in a story it needs to go off. If you have a Beast in a story, does it need to 'go off' too? When? How? I was ashamed because I loved these discussions, with their implied neat and tidy narrative symmetry and clever devices, all endorsed by great writers. My novel, my bloody albatross, *The Death of the Author*, deliberately had no such symmetry, and I was constantly in turmoil because one minute it would have too much narrative: people desperately in love, or waking up from their comas, or lying in ditches contemplating great life changes and so on — just like a formulaic genre novel — then I'd fiddle with it and it would die: a species extinct before it has even begun. In order for a new species to evolve, an already existing species has to split in half, and somehow — genetically, or geographically — members of these halves must stay separate and not go on any dates or have sex for a few hundred or thousand years. If I had my formula fiction and all its dominant genes trapped on one side of a mountain range, and my novel on another, maybe my novel would have a chance to make it. I sighed and unbended a paperclip someone — probably me — had left on the desk. It snapped, and I was left with two useless bits of metal that I was reluctant to drop on the floor. I put them in my pocket. Tim's proposal seemed pretty good, so I sent a note to Claudia recommending that we consider it at the next editorial board in March. The other proposal was about a girl who eats her own parents, which I rejected.

At about three, my phone vibrated. I guessed it was Oscar calling from the paper; but all I ever got on my phone's display was *Withheld number*, regardless of who was calling. As I hurried out of the library I wondered what was wrong with my review. Oscar was only in his early fifties, but acted as if he was a grumpy old man and all his reviewers were his naughty grandchildren, or his wayward pets. He only ever called if there was a problem, and he always smoked on the phone, *suck, suck, pause,* although on the few occasions I'd been to his office there was no evidence of his smoking anywhere.

'I thought you weren't there,' he said in his mild, clipped Caribbean voice. 'I was about to give up on you.'

'I'm at the library. I can't answer the phone inside or the librarians get really upset and shout at me.'

Our conversations usually began in this way, with him telling me off and me saying something amusing about the librarians, who had never, in fact, done anything amusing at all. Most conversations in publishing were vaguely Alzheimic, because everyone suffered from over-thinking and over-reading and no one could remember if this was the first time they'd said something today, or the fifteenth, and whether it was true or made up. You can identify someone who works in publishing because they tell every anecdote as if for the first time, with the same expression as someone giving you a tissue that they have just realised has probably already been used.

'Well, never mind about that.' He sucked and paused. 'This is your strangest trick yet.'

'What is?'

'This review you've sent me. What were you thinking?'

'You didn't like it?'

'I did like it. It's pretty good. Very funny. What a nutter this Kelsey Newman is.'

'So . . . ?'

'Well, you've baffled me this time,' he said. 'You novelists are all the same.'

I couldn't imagine what I'd done.

'This book was published in 2006. Sometimes we're a bit late with a review, but never two years late. Where did you find it?'

'You sent it to me. Didn't you?'

Obviously he hadn't.

'Don't be so silly,' he said. 'You novelists don't know the difference between fiction and reality; I've always said so. But don't worry, I won't write you off as insane this time. It's not the first time someone's reviewed the wrong book, after all. Don't bother to review the book I did send, though. It's too late now, and some extra advertising has come in for the next few weeks.'

'God, I'm so embarrassed,' I said. 'I'm sorry. I don't know how . . . I mean, it's weird. I don't know what happened.' As well as being embarrassed, I'd just lost about £400, as well as all that time on Sunday that I could have spent writing my novel.

'It's a shame, really. It was a good review. Still, it's given me an idea that you might like. We should put these books under the microscope, I think. Enough bloody people read them . . . I've got the proof of the new Kelsey Newman book here somewhere. It's out this month. It's not the kind of thing we'd normally review, but since you've read the other one . . . What's the new one called? What does the blurb say? Hang on.' There was the sound of paper being shuffled around, and then more sucking and pausing. 'Oh, here it is. *Second World.* It's got quotes on it from a couple of wackos — oh, and one from your friend Vi Hayes. She says it "provides a blueprint for living based on what we have learned from the most well-loved fiction". You could just review it — same sort of style as the one you sent today — or, if you felt like it, I could send you all the New Age, self-help, blueprint-for-living-style books I've got in the cupboard and you could do a two-thousand-word feature on this kind of phenomenon and the way these nutcases write about . . .'

Some deep part of my brain now started speaking to me in a calm voice, as if it was talking me — or, I guess, my ego — down from a thin ledge on a tall building. *Say no. Say you'd rather starve. Write your novel. Don't bring yet another species of commercial writing into its fragile ecosystem. Say no. No. No. No.*

'That's such a good idea,' I said. 'The feature, I mean. It would be . . .' I remembered last time I was in Arcturus, a New Age book and crystal shop in Totnes. I'd gone there to buy a birthday present for Josh and decided to browse some of the other crazy books while I was there. At the time, I was writing the third book in my Newtopia series. In these novels, which were set roughly fifty years or so in the future, a corporation has colonised everyone's unconscious, so that people have two lives: one in the 'real' world, and another in a fantasy realm accessed via a chip in their brain. This alternative world has its own currency, fashions, language and conventions, and although many years ago people had to sign up for user accounts and choose to log into them, by the time my novels took place people had no choice about it: everyone was simply microchipped at birth. Also, everyone was by then unaware that they were living two lives. The chip in people's brains was programmed to make the best use of the mind's down-time, and the minute someone's brainwaves slowed down — during sleep, on a coffee break or simply between thoughts — they would be switched over to this alternative world, which I had called Newtopia.

The whole series had been inspired by a news story I'd seen where two fat people were divorcing in real life because their thin online avatars had both married other thin avatars that stood in place of other real-life fat people. I'd wondered what would happen if it became so normal to have this kind of second life that people were unaware they were even having one. In my Newtopia novels, a girl-hero discovers The Truth, which is more or less to do with something called the Corporation, which has colonised everything in sight and beyond, and then she sets about finding other people who Know. Between them they find a way of hiding their unconscious selves on the edges of the cells in the mobile-phone network, although they can't do this for long each time before they are discovered. They have adventures and relationships between the two worlds, with various dramas to do with unconscious betrayal, confused identities, awakenings and the rising arc of the greed and power of the Corporation. In the third book I thought I'd explain exactly how this unconscious world was structured, and I'd had some crazy ideas about the Corporation colonising something like the astral plane. I knew nothing about such things, but Arcturus was full of books about the astral plane.

Two women had come into the shop just after me. They browsed the astral plane books too, before moving on to books about co-dependency and 'not loving too much', photographing your own aura and developing magical powers. 'I'll get you this one, love,' the older woman said to what must have been her daughter, probably in her thirties. The younger woman was holding about three other books and had just opened her purse. 'I've got five pounds left on this credit card,' she said. 'And about seven pounds fifty on this one. So if you get me that one as well, then . . .' 'I'll get you two, love,' the older woman said. 'And then we'll get the bus back. I know you need them.' What were these four life-changing books? I never got to see.

'I've got it!' I said to Oscar. 'I'll do like a first-person thing.'
'How?'
'Send me the books and I'll pick maybe four or five of them. Each one will tell me to do or think something different, and each one will promise that my life will change because of it. I'll

do what each one says and see what happens. Then I'll write about it. It'll be a kind of gonzo project. Almost an ethnography, if I meet some weird people.'

'Excellent. I love it.' He paused. 'Make it funny.'

'Oh, I will.'

'Deliver at the beginning of April,' he said. 'Make it three thousand words if you like. We'll do a double-page spread with a picture. Paul is very into first-person features just now.' Paul was the editor of the paper.

'OK. That's great. Thanks, Oscar. Sorry about the fuck-up.'

'That's all right. I know what you novelists are like.'

Then he was gone. Before I put my phone away I checked my credit. It was down to fifteen pence. Still, my mistake had worked out quite well. I had lost £400 and some weekend time, but gained about £1,500 and whatever I could get from selling the New Age books afterwards. But by the end of the process I would have lost a lot more time. *You should have said no,* said my brain. Perhaps I could recoup the lost time by using the research in my novel somehow. Could my poor, bashed-about protagonist, once metafictionally called Meg, but now nameless, also do a first-person, almost-ethnographic project? The novel could always take new layers, especially as I was always stripping them out. I was a big believer in layers, and taught a whole day on them on the retreats, emphasising to the students that a novel is never one storyline, but many layers of storylines. Something like an ethnography — and I could make it full-blown in the novel — would enable my protagonist to do things she wouldn't normally do, which would be good. Lately I couldn't motivate her to even go out of the house. Perhaps she could be an anthropologist who objects to exoticism and therefore decides to do an ethnography of her home town: that would give her an excuse to be out taking part in life and I wouldn't need to mess around with rainforest locations and tribespeople. But that must already have been done. I had long ago realised that I needed a love-interest too, but my protagonist wouldn't fall in love with anyone normal. Maybe an older man?

I thought about writing a few notes, but when I took the lid off my pen I just sat there with it poised in midair while the fluid of my conversation with Oscar drained out of my mind. Once this had happened I thought I'd be able to work, but instead I found I was left with a great amount of sediment which amounted to this: where the fuck had the Kelsey Newman book come from? How in God's name had I managed to review a book Oscar hadn't even sent? I'd messed up reviews in all sorts of ways in the past, but I'd never reviewed the wrong book. I sighed. Perhaps Vi had sent it. It didn't seem likely; I doubted Vi would send me anything ever again. But if she'd blurbed it, she'd definitely read it. But how could she have blurbed it? It sounded like the kind of project she would hate. Then again, what was it doing with a note from Oscar in it? For the rest of the afternoon my phone kept vibrating and whoever it was left messages, but I didn't have the funds left to pick them up, or call anyone back.

On Boxing Day evening in Scotland we'd all gone to bed early. The discussion about Zen stories had looked as if it might turn nasty, and everyone was still upset about Lot's Wife, especially when Vi talked about some of the people she remembered from the monastery. The next day I went to the beach early with Frank and Vi. While Vi sat on a rock, looking out to sea, Frank did t'ai chi. I sat on my own rock, watching them both. After a while Vi stripped down to an old red-and-white striped bathing costume, screamed, dived into the freezing water and screamed again. For the next few minutes she thrashed around like a fairground goldfish, although a rare one with a voice: 'Ow, ow, it's cold, oh fucking shit, it's cold.' Then she started doing a kind of backwards butterfly stroke that looked both silly and graceful at the same time. I knew that by doing this Vi was, in her own way, becoming one with the universe, and the universe had therefore also become silly and graceful at the same time. For me this kind of connection seemed impossible. I knew that if I tried to become one with the universe it would reject me in the same way the sea rejected the boats whose skeletons framed the shore.

'You OK?' Frank called to me.

'Yeah. Just cold,' I said. 'Especially watching Vi. She's giving me goosebumps.'

'Do you want to do some of this?' he asked.

'What? T'ai chi?'

'Yeah. Come on. It'll warm you up.'

I shrugged and walked over to him. He showed me a few movements, all of which were too subtle for me to really comprehend. I copied him for a while, but I didn't get very warm. I started jumping up and down instead, while watching him.

'I've been struggling with this,' he said, showing me some fluid-looking movements. 'It's called "Carry Tiger to the Mountain".'

I stopped jumping and smiled. 'That's a nice name. It looks good to me.'

'You're also struggling a bit at the moment? Vi said something.'

Vi's splashing was quieter now. She'd stopped complaining and was swimming out towards the lighthouse. But there was an energy in what she was doing that I just didn't seem to have. I wasn't struggling at all. There didn't seem to be any point. What would I struggle against? Christopher? My mother? Orb Books? My novel? Myself? Would I struggle for Rowan, a man who was too old for me and didn't want me anyway?

'I think I'm a bit depressed. I'll be OK.'

'You know we're always there. Come and stay in London if you like.'

'Thanks. I might do,' I said, although I knew I wouldn't be able to afford the train fare or explain to Christopher why I was going.

'Vi told me once that if you ask the sea for help it never fails you. I tried it a few times. It does make you feel better. You can just ask the sea for help and see what happens, or, alternatively, you can give it your problems. It's big enough to take them, after all. You could choose some large stones, make each one represent one of your problems and throw them in the water.' He shrugged. 'Probably sounds a bit hippy for you. I know you're more down to earth than we are — but sometimes you just need something to help you focus and let things go.'

'Thanks, Frank. I'd feel too self-conscious doing it now, but if things get any worse I'll certainly think about it. I'll go to Slapton Sands when I get home. There are lots of big stones there.'

On our last night in Scotland we all got drunk on sloe gin, and Claudia and I started recounting the most ridiculous Zeb Ross proposals we'd ever rejected, including one for a novel narrated by a cat, and another where one character turns out to be a manifestation of the Buddha.

'What was that really weird Zen story from that manuscript?' Claudia asked me.

'There were quite a lot,' I said.

'The one with the psycho old woman who burns down the monk's hut.'

'Oh, yes,' I said. 'That narrows it down. How did it go?'

'There is an old woman who looks after a monk while he meditates for twenty years,' Vi said. 'Is this it? She gives him food and water and makes his clothes and eventually sends a prostitute to throw herself at him because she wants to see what he does with all his wisdom. He's taken a vow of chastity, but will he be tempted? The monk says something poetic to the prostitute about an old tree growing on a cold rock, and tells her there is "no warmth". When the spurned prostitute tells of this, the old woman is angry that she has supported

74

someone who after twenty years has not learned compassion. Then she goes and burns his hut down.'

'Yes. I hated that one,' Claudia said.

'Why?' I said. 'I liked it.'

'It doesn't tell you anything useful,' she said. 'All it says is that this psychotic old bitch has got this poor monk in her clutches and has resorted to violence because he isn't exactly what she thinks he should be. It's a horror story, really, of someone who sets out to ruin someone's life, like an obsessive stalker.'

'Only if it's seen from the monk's perspective,' I said.

We drank a bit more, and then Claudia reminded me of the manuscript about a teenager who takes up gardening and accidentally grows lots of carnivorous plants that speak to her all the time and become her only friends. We both started giggling and trying to remember terrible lines from it, like 'We've been growing since the beginning of time, Melissa!' or 'You too will taste the exquisite blood of the bluebottle and become one of us!'

Then, out of the blue, Vi said to me, 'My God, Meg. When exactly are you going to realise that the world is more complicated than a predictable formula? You're so scared of taking things seriously, it's no wonder you can't get on with your real novel.'

If she hadn't begun by using my name I would have assumed she was talking to Claudia. It was the first time she'd ever said anything to me that wasn't supportive, kind or indulgent. I didn't react to it very well.

'I am so sick of this,' I said back, before I'd really thought about what I should say. 'Don't you realise that anyone can put together a story that has no shape? *Anyone* can make up a few random actions and string them together. Children do it all the time. The real skill is as Claudia says: you need to find original ways of doing everything Aristotle said you should do, which isn't at all as easy as just following his instructions. It takes some real hard work to create a reversal that's not clichéd, to have a recognition that isn't based on a token, or a "sudden realisation", or something the hero knew all along—but on the rising action and tension in the whole plot. You should read Aristotle again, because he tells you not just how to write those bottle-of-oil stories, but proper, meaningful tragedies. And yes, they're predictable too, sort of. But he says that one of the key things the writer has to do is to make the person who hears or reads the story feel astonished, even though the story itself has a formula and is written in accordance with probability and cause and effect. It's a great art to make someone surprised to see the picture, and even more surprised when they realise they had all the pieces all along.'

'But that's the trick,' Vi said. 'Making people feel astonished when they hear the same old story is just the same as making people want a new kitchen every two years, and new clothes, and makeovers. People somehow forget that they've "heard it all before". These narratives don't make them see anything new. They don't defamiliarise anything in their lives.'

'How does throwing together some random events help people to see things anew? Every time I go out I see random events. It's not art. Art needs artfulness.'

'No one said that there's nothing in the vast space between formulaic narrative and completely random events,' Vi said. 'Life at its least artful is life that is trying to follow a formulaic narrative. Don't you think?'

I didn't know quite what she meant, so I said, 'No.' I paused, but she didn't say anything, so I went on. 'You think Chekhov's so great . . .' I did too, of course, as she well knew. 'But even Chekhov couldn't get it together to write a novel. He found it too hard. He kept all his best observations and images for it, and they came to nothing, because actually making a plot hang together over eighty thousand words or more is almost impossible.'

'He was busy making money with his short fiction and his plays,' Frank said. 'He was keeping his family afloat.'

'Aren't we all,' I said.

Chekhov's plan for his novel had been simple. He described it in a letter in 1888: 'The novel will take in several families and a whole district, complete with woods, rivers, ferry boats, railways. At the centre of this landscape are two principal figures, a man and a woman, with other individuals grouped around them like pawns. I do not yet aspire to a coherent political, religious and philosophical world view; my opinions change every month, and therefore I must confine myself to describing how my characters love, get married, have children, die, and how they speak.' To make a novel come together, perhaps you have to have a world view, even if it's wrong. But I hadn't settled on my own world view either, even one that was wrong.

'You're just making excuses,' Vi said, sighing. 'You have to start writing seriously before it's too late. At least Chekhov wrote classic short stories while he wasn't writing his novel. You've so far managed not much more than a few thin novels that preach neo-liberal morality to unsuspecting teenagers. You tell them that the world is OK if you can find a way of owning it, and possessing it and making "your own" sense of it. You tell them, indirectly, that everything fits into some predetermined story-structure where you can do whatever you want, but only if you're the hero. You tell them what a happy ending consists of, which is always individual success. You tell them that nothing irrational exists in this world, which is a lie. You tell them that conflict exists only to be neatly resolved, and that everyone who is poor wants to be rich, and everyone who is ill wants to get better, and everyone who gets involved with crime comes to a bad end, and that love should be pure. You tell them that despite all this they are special, that the world revolves around them . . .'

'For God's sake,' I said. 'It's not that simple, and you know it. I'm not saying that Zeb Ross novels are high art, but some of them have marginalised characters who learn that it's OK to be who they are . . .'

'To accept their lot in life and not make a fuss . . .'

'But they do make a fuss. Stories are all about fuss. You seem to think a three-act narrative comes together like knitting a scarf, but it doesn't. It's bloody hard work. Have you ever tried it? No, of course you haven't. You haven't even tried to write one of the flabby, plotless stories you seem to think are so much better, that any six-year-old could string together in about five minutes. Your writing is easy because you go somewhere and do things and just write them down. But fiction is different. It's fucking hard and at least I try to do it, which is more than can be said for you.'

As I got up to leave the room I saw Frank move towards Vi and put a hand on her shoulder. Before I left the next morning I saw only Claudia, who said, 'Gosh. I've been wanting to say all that for years. Good on you, girl.' Sebastian was still saying 'Good on you, girl' when I went, and Claudia was trying to bribe him, with a piece of banana, to go back to his Shakespeare quotations before Frank and Vi got up. I hadn't spoken to Frank or Vi since.

Almost a week later, on New Year's Day, I'd woken up in the house in Dartmouth, pressed my leg against Christopher's and then watched as he got up without looking at me and left the room. He'd clearly been unsettled by Christmas too, although he hadn't yet said why. The day ahead was gaping like a black hole. I couldn't go to the library, because it wasn't open. I couldn't read a book, because Christopher thought you should spend a day reading a book only if you were ill, or if someone was paying you to do it. He'd hardly said anything since he got back from Brighton, but he had mumbled something the day before about building a new kitchen cupboard.

I imagined holding nails, sanding things and then waiting for the cupboard to fall off the wall.

It wasn't Christopher's fault: things fell off our walls because under the white plaster they were made of nothing more than wattle and daub, a Neolithic concoction still used in the nineteenth century when our house was built. According to a History Channel documentary, wattle and daub consisted of thin wooden strips held together with dung and straw. When things like cupboards fell off walls, Christopher would weep on the sofa and I would make him cups of tea, tell him he wasn't a failure and find a historical programme for us to watch on TV. I would want to escape to the bath with a book, but I'd end up watching something about the Cheddar man, or Boadicea, or glaciers, or Stonehenge, and tell myself it wasn't a waste of time, because these things could easily find a place in a Zeb Ross novel, or even, until I felt the need to delete them, my own. Then I would start coughing, because of the damp in the house, and my lungs would put themselves in a weird kind of Safe Mode until I could go outside again. I'd never directly told Christopher that the damp in the house made my asthma worse, thinking only an idiot wouldn't be able to see that. This was a bit passive aggressive, of course, as was the way I hammed up my coughing when we were arguing. Sometimes I dredged up stuff from my lungs that felt as if it had been there since the beginning of time.

The New Year's Day black hole had been sucking me in, which is what black holes do. While Christopher loudly brushed his teeth and went to the toilet, I took four drops of the flower remedy Vi had made me in Scotland, and looked out of the bedroom window onto the rooftops. I imagined the sea beyond them, and the castle. The castle was just a postcard to me, and the sea didn't go anywhere. I suddenly thought that I could get up every morning for the rest of my life and look at the rooftops and it was possible that nothing would ever change. If nothing changed, I may as well be dead. Perhaps some people began every day with this thought, but it was new to me. I thought I'd already had all the depressing thoughts it was possible to have. Then I felt ungrateful, although towards whom or what I didn't know. It wasn't even as if I could stand at the window yearning for something, apart from money. I'd given up yearning for Rowan. I did want to apologise to Vi, but I didn't know how. She was due to come down and open the Labyrinth in March. Once I'd found out what it was and heard they were looking for a celebrity to open it, I'd suggested Vi. She'd been on TV a couple of times, as well as having a bestselling book, and I thought she might like the Labyrinth. I knew I'd have to find some way of apologising before then.

In the end I'd driven out to Slapton Sands with B and stood on the shingle beach wondering what it would be like to walk into the flat blue sea and never come out again. Of course, I didn't walk into the sea. I looked down, and instead thought about the way you could move shingle around and it would still be shingle. It should have been freezing, but the air was clammy and a light, warm spray settled on my hair. B was hyper-alert at Slapton Sands, even in the winter, her paws touching the shingle lightly as if it was made of jagged pieces of broken glass. I felt almost as bleak as I had done in Dartmouth when I'd bought my wool, and on the long car journey with B back from Scotland. This time I did ask the sea for help. I stood there, looking down at the breaking waves, and I said, 'Help me,' and then added, 'Please.' The act of asking for help made my eyes fill with tears. But the sea said nothing, just splashed more waves at me. So I picked up some large stones and imagined that each of them represented one of my problems. My argument with Vi. My continuing lack of money. Christopher's despair. My despair. The damp house. My novel. Sex. It could have gone on, but I thought I should stop there. Then I threw the stones into the sea, and didn't feel like I had thrown them away at all; I felt like I should go in after them. If I did, would Christopher be embarrassed at my funeral? Would there be an obituary?

Shallow, shallow. And the sea was deep. *In a solitude of the sea / Deep from human vanity / And the Pride of Life that planned her, stilly couches she.* My favourite poem, and the only one I knew by heart, was about the sinking of the *Titanic*. I said the rest of it out loud to the sea, as I had done to Rowan, and for a while I imagined that the sea could hear me. I wondered if it would think much of this poem, in which it functioned not as protagonist or antagonist but merely as the neutral fluid in which the iceberg and the ship are destined to collide, and in which the wreck of the *Titanic* eventually lies, with 'dim moon-eyed fishes' looking on. And then, quite suddenly, on that warm, wet first day of 2008, the sea did spit something out. It was a ship in a bottle, a perfect ship in a slightly chipped and sand-smoothed bottle, and it landed right at my feet. It had been in the sea a long time, but I recognised it. The bottle had a waxy blue sea inside, and the boat on this sea had the same inscription, 'Cutty Sark', on its hull. Then I told myself it was impossible that I'd recognised it, and I closed my eyes, and then opened them again. It was still there. I couldn't believe it. Was this the sea's idea of help? 'What the hell does this mean?' I said to the sea. It said nothing back. Shakily, I picked up the ship in the bottle and took it home. It had sat on a shelf ever since, while I tried to work out what it might mean, and whom I could ask about it now that I wasn't speaking to Vi any more, since I didn't know anyone else who would even believe what had happened.

The tide was up as I drove along Torquay seafront on Monday evening and I half-hoped that waves would splash over the car, but they only did that during storms, and at spring tide. If the car got washed away I'd probably escape and then I could claim the insurance money and get a new car. Maybe I should just push it in the river like Libby had done with hers. One of the billboards at a bus stop on the main street into Paignton was still advertising the opening of the new Maritime Centre last October, although the sign was torn and flapping. I hadn't gone to the opening; I didn't even get an invitation. The rest of Paignton was the same as usual: magical mystery tours on offer in two local travel agents, and Madame Verity's fortune-telling shop doing business next to the pet beautician. The wind had picked up, and clouds moved across the sky thinly, as if being pulled from a dispenser. While I was waiting for the Higher Ferry to take me back across the river to Dartmouth I got a text message from Libby: *Police totally bought car story, so did Bob. Come for dinner on Saturday week? Mark coming too!!! Yikes! You up for a drink this Friday?*

I parked illegally outside Reg's place, although the yellow line was so worn that it wasn't really there any more. I felt a bit breathless going up the steps. Maybe I needed to take iron supplements, or eat more greens? My mother was a big believer in iron. If anyone felt ill, it was always mild anaemia. Maybe I needed a jar of manuka honey. I opened the front door to find B waiting for me, with bits of shredded book-proof everywhere: rare for a Monday. I was far from famous, but I was alive and had published something not that long ago, so I was often sent proofs of new SF novels by young women, along with form letters asking for blurbs. B ate them all. Or, to be more precise, she chewed them and spat them out. She'd once done this to a book I was supposed to review for Oscar, and after that I'd had to arrange for everything important to be sent to a PO box in Totnes, and for Christopher to pick up my post on his way back from the project. Oscar's speech about how a novelist like me should be able to come up with something better than 'the dog ate it' was one of his classics. B loved books, but particularly proofs, with their cheap, shiny paper, even more than she loved the filled bones they sold in the market on a Saturday. Sometimes I imagined I saw pieces of novel coming out in her shit and always saw this as my own novel, which of course she couldn't have eaten because it wasn't finished. I saw a website once about all the weird stuff that comes out in dog shit: Barbie doll heads, toy cars, Lego, spoons. B loved books, and the bubble wrap inside padded envelopes, but never touched letters, perhaps because they were insubstantial, and I could see an intact bank statement on the floor. It would go with the others. Oh—and something that looked like it could be a cheque from the paper. Fantastic. There was also the form letter that had come with the proof. Apparently, what B had eaten this time was 'Futuristic noir for a post-MTV, post-cyberpunk generation'.

To celebrate the money coming for delivery of my last Zeb Ross manuscript, I'd bought a hand-held vacuum cleaner to deal with B's chewed-up paper and Christopher's sawdust. Now I pulled it out of its cradle and started sucking up the pieces of paper slowly. The book had been so mangled that I couldn't even see how thick it had been, but I caught the odd undigested paragraph here and there: something about a woman penetrating herself with a gun encrusted with diamonds, and, further up the hallway, a short scene where presumably the same woman lets a man rub his dick between her breasts while she is flying a car. After the book was cleared up I moved into the sitting room to deal with the debris from Christopher's sawing. As the house filled with a concentrated smell of rancid dog, I wondered again about the Newman book. If Oscar hadn't sent it, then where had it come from? Christopher never got any mail, ever. In some part of his mind he'd never properly moved to Brighton, let alone moved in with me, and I assumed all his post still went to his father's flat in Totnes. If he had been sent a book, here, B would surely have eaten it. Not that Christopher read books. Although he read *The Guardian* from cover to cover every day, all the books people gave him about recycling, heritage sites and globalisation remained barely skimmed. He'd been in the middle of a politics degree when his mother died. He must have read books then, but I couldn't imagine what they would have been.

Before walking B I went up to my study and tried to prepare the space for some proper writing later. I plugged in my laptop and switched on the lamp. Things lit up, dimly, including my poster of the Periodic Table of Elements, which I put up wherever I lived. It comforted me: whenever life got complicated I looked at it and reminded myself that all matter in the universe could be broken down in terms of those boxes. My blue shelves were crammed with uneaten proofs of my own books, finished copies of the same books, manuscripts and copies of the few interviews I'd been asked to do, mainly with small SF magazines. Their journalists, who usually conducted interviews via email at one A.M., or else were bearded and anoraked parodies of themselves, asked me things like 'What is the role of women in science fiction?' and 'Have you seen the film *The Matrix*?' and told me that my author photo did me no favours. I'd never been much good at interviews, and my carefully constructed answers made me feel about as real as Zeb Ross; as if I was making myself up as I went along. Apart from my own novels — at least, while I was writing them — I didn't much like science fiction. I never admitted this; instead, every so often I would read three-quarters of an SF 'classic' so that I'd have something to say in interviews. I did like *The Matrix*, of course, and had read all kinds of essays on it, including Baudrillard saying it didn't represent his ideas at all and was, in fact, a re-working of Plato's *Simile of the Cave*. My interview answer about it now went on for about half an hour, and made even the most geeky journos glaze over.

Zeb Ross didn't have any kind of public profile yet, which Orb Books had decided was a bad thing. He was one of the few people left in the Western world without a Facebook page or a MySpace account, and he didn't even have an email address. He had good reason for this, namely that he didn't really exist; but we didn't want his readers to know that. We'd therefore decided to recruit someone to construct all his social networking pages and hang around non-paedophilic chatrooms being him, and I had promised to recommend Christopher's brother Josh at the next editorial board.

On the top of my blue shelves my ship in a bottle was getting dusty. I still hadn't done anything with it. I'd thought about taking it to the Maritime Centre to show Rowan, but probably wouldn't. Sometimes, late at night, I visualised going there. But I couldn't tell Rowan how I'd come to have it, and I also couldn't tell him why it was important. My fantasy also ended up with us kissing again, which was another reason not to go. I'd thought, of course, about simply putting all this, minus the kiss, in my novel. Perhaps the damn ship had washed up in the first place because it wanted to be in my novel. But what function would it perform? I'd already included, and then deleted, various MacGuffins, including a secret map and a mysterious statue, both of which embarrassed me when I thought of them now. I taught MacGuffins on the retreats, which of course meant I shouldn't use them in my serious novel about the Real World, in which people must want meaningful, if problematic, objects and can't just obligingly want random things that move their plots along. The term 'MacGuffin' was introduced by Alfred Hitchcock, and describes an object that has no meaning in itself, but motivates action in a plot because many of the characters want to obtain it. It could be a document, a key, a diamond, a statue or anything, even a bottle of oil. Aristotle said that using a random object to motivate action or force a recognition was lazy plotting, and I agreed. My plotting was definitely not lazy, just ineffective. I wondered if everything that everyone wanted was a MacGuffin, but the thought was so depressing I abandoned it.

I picked up my ship in a bottle and rubbed some of the dust off with my sleeve. No one wanted this object; not even me. I sighed. The top of my shelves was where I filed unfathomable things, or, at least, things that were unfathomable in a different way from my tax forms and royalty statements. There was a framed photograph of a brown, mushroomy £10 note that I had found lying in some leaves in the rain more than twenty years before, after asking the universe to please give me some money from somewhere, anywhere, because I needed to get the train out to Essex to see my friend Rosa, who'd just broken up with her boyfriend. There was also a scrap of paper with Drew's phone number on it, which I'd found five miles away from where I lost it. There was an embroidered purse that had once contained tobacco, and which I'd found a few years back when I still smoked, in Danbury Woods, miles from anywhere, just after I'd realised I'd left my tobacco at home. I'd once planned a feature for a science magazine where I explained how all these things, which had seemed to happen by 'luck', were really matters of unremarkable chance and probability. There'd been a few cases around then of people finding their wedding rings washed up on beaches three hundred miles away from where they'd lost them, and people answering ringing phones in telephone boxes to find their long-lost relative on the line. I didn't like these things, and so had wanted to plot them away. To this end, I had been planning to write about *apophenia,* the perception of meaningful connections where in fact there are none. But the editor who'd commissioned the piece left the magazine and I'd had to abandon it.

I had two desks. One now had my laptop on it, along with an empty document stand, and various wrist-rests and arm-rests that my mother gave me to prevent RSI. The other was covered in as yet unboxed bank statements, the letters that came with the proofs B ate, book contracts, film options, incomprehensible Russian royalty statements, cheques for amounts like £5.50 and £7.95 that my overdraft would swallow if I ever banked them, increasingly nasty letters from the Inland Revenue, unfiled paperwork from Orb Books, two ring-bound notebooks and the books and proofs sent to my PO box and delivered by Christopher. Many of the items on the desk were there because whenever I wasn't around Christopher trawled the house fishing up anything belonging to me, and then put it all on this desk. So where was the book I should have reviewed? I'd come up and got the Kelsey Newman book just after Christopher left to walk Josh to the bus stop on Saturday afternoon. Of course, I didn't check the publication date because I was only looking for my deadline. This was on the compliments slip in the Newman book, and so I'd read it and reviewed it.

Now I looked properly and found a book on the Golden Section, with a press release inside it with a publication date of 'March o8'. That must have been it. If only I opened my own post things would have been different, but Christopher recycled all the padded envelopes from the PO box before I even saw them. I once told him why I didn't like all this random crap ending up on my desk, and how I wished he wouldn't open my mail. He said if I wanted things to be different I should be tidier and more organised, stay at home all day like normal writers, research using the Internet rather than the library and learn to control my dog. I thought he was probably right about all that, so I didn't push it, or say that I couldn't stay in the house all day because it was hard to breathe. I blamed him for that more than I should have: he'd organised this place on the cheap through a friend called Dougie from the project, who hadn't wanted bank references or a deposit. So how could I ask him about this? I wanted to know precisely how the compliments slip had transmigrated from one book to another without him being completely responsible. And where had the bloody Newman book come from in the first place?

I took B on her usual evening walk: down the steps, across the Market Square, through the Royal Avenue Gardens, down the Embankment, round the Boat Float and then to Coronation Park. I couldn't quite visualise how the Labyrinth was going to look when it was finished. Today there were two yellow diggers, and jagged tracks in the mud around the hole. There were also new piles of grey, stone slabs underneath some plastic. My tree was still there. I wished I knew what kind of tree it was, but despite spending the last few years sitting in the biology section of the library, I hadn't remembered to look it up. It was brown, and had a trunk and branches. I wouldn't even know how to look it up, except that in the winter it grew these little things we used to call 'helicopters' at school. B was sniffing around the stone slabs when my phone rang. It was my mother.

'You're there!' she said, as if she'd used a séance to reach me.

'I'm always here,' I said, laughing. 'I've told you before to ring my mobile, especially if you want to avoid Christopher.'

'I know. I keep forgetting I've got the number written down.'

'How are you?'

'We're fine,' she said. 'Busy. What's that noise?'

'The wind. I'm walking the dog. By the way, what do you call those trees that grow little helicopters?'

'Helicopters?'

'Yeah; like a little seed in a case with a tail. You throw them and the little tail goes around and around like a helicopter.'

'A sycamore tree?'

'Oh, of course. Thank you.'

'Is this for a new novel?'

'Not exactly. *Bess!* Sorry. The dog was trying to get in this big hole.'

'How is she?'

'She's fine.' My mother always asked how I was, and how B was, but not Christopher. I just about managed to afford to take the train to London every couple of months with B to stay with Mum and Taz, my stepfather, for the weekend, but Mum never came to visit me. Often I combined my visits to them with some business in London so I could claim my fare on expenses, although I always stayed with Frank and Vi if there was an editorial board meeting, so that we could laugh about Claudia's latest plans for Zeb Ross. I'd last gone to London before Christmas. I'd had a meeting with a woman called Fred, who was the head of a production company called Harlequin Entertainment. They were thinking of optioning my Newtopia novels for a TV series. The meeting had frightened me. Did I have any ideas for new episodes? Would I mind if they just took the characters and setting and then invented completely different stories to go with them? It felt as if I would be signing up to stop existing in yet another way. But I told my agent's replacement that I'd take the money if they offered it, and I told my mother all about the glitzy place Fred had taken me to for lunch, and how we'd eaten velouté and swordfish. I never heard from Fred again.

'How's your archive going?' I asked my mother now.

My mother was compiling an archive of all our family photos on her new laptop. Some of these were already digital, but others had to be sent by mail order to somewhere where they digitised them, put them on a CD and sent them back. She was also compiling a family tree using census websites and Mormon records of UK ancestry. My brother Toby had once pointed out that we were potentially the final generation of our family, because neither of us planned to have children. Our family was therefore about to become extinct. I had a feeling my mother knew this, and that it was one reason for the photograph archive and the family tree. Every time we talked about her research I remembered that I had never filled in the 2001 census, even when the council chased me for it. I still felt guilty, although I wasn't sure why. I kept imagining descendants of mine filled with despair in some futuristic archive because the records were missing, and then reminding myself that there would be no descendants, and no one in the future would ever care what I was or was not doing in 2001.

'I've almost finished 1982,' she said. 'You must come and look at them.'

'I will. Probably soon. I've got an editorial board coming up.'

'Aren't you staying with your friends, Frank and Whatsit?'

'No. They're going away.'

'Oh, that reminds me. Have you seen the papers recently?'

'No. Not really. Just the *Observer* crossword. Why?'

'There was a big interview with Rosa over the weekend.'

'Gosh,' I said, in a more deadpan tone than I intended. Lately there'd been lots of news from my mother about Rosa. I hadn't seen Rosa for years, but we'd been neighbours in Essex and, even after I moved away to London, best friends. Then we'd started to drift apart when we were about eighteen. I'd wanted to do drama but ended up doing comparative litera-ture; she'd wanted to do drama but had ended up at art col-lege. Our plans to go to RADA together and become famous method actresses came to nothing. When I was in my first year at Sussex, Rosa came to visit. She arrived at the station looking pale and spaced out, wearing a red dress and false eyelashes, and with some bedraggled guy following her down the platform, begging her to marry him, while she smiled, said, 'No, honey, but you're very sweet for asking,' looked over her shoulder and slowed down every so often for him to catch her up. For the rest of the weekend she ate nothing except for some acid another guy on the train had given her and kept go-ing on about travelling to India to sort out her chakras. No one knew about chakras in those days, but Rosa's brother Ca-leb had gone to India, which meant she had become an ex-pert in everything to do with it. She slept with my boyfriend, slept with my housemate's boyfriend, then got upset because she thought that she'd alienated us for ever and was found at

3 A.M. on the Sunday morning trying to drown herself in the duck pond in the local park. Not long after that, she was discovered by a producer while she was walking on Hampstead Heath. She'd started throwing sticks for his dog and he'd asked her to come and audition for a part in a major drama series about the supernatural goings-on in an English village. The legend went that Rosa thought he wasn't serious and didn't bother going for the audition, but he'd tracked her down and offered her the part on the spot. It was to play the female lead: a vicar's psychic daughter, who falls in love with the paranormal investigator. She won a BAFTA for it, and then became one of the most sought-after actresses in Britain. My ex-fiancé, Drew, had once spent a month asking me to introduce him to her to 'help his career'.

'I think you'll find it interesting,' my mother said now.

'I doubt it.'

'Now, you're not going to get silly about this again, are you?'

'What do you mean?'

'You know what I mean. I won't tell you if you don't want to know.'

'Well, you've half-told me now.'

'All right, well, one thing is that she's been cast to play the lead in a big Hollywood re-make of *Anna Karenina*. The rumours are that she's getting millions.'

'Oh. Well, good for Rosa.'

'Meg . . .'

'What?'

'You could sound more happy for her.'

'Why? I'm not happy for her. I don't care. I mean, I'd care if she wasn't doing well; I'd feel sorry for her and hope that things got better. I'm glad she's doing well, up to a point. But I hate celebrity culture; it's just another form of clichéd narrative entertainment but with real people as the protagonists. I saw some of it with Drew, don't forget. And he so wanted to be part of it all and I so didn't. It's completely blah. Also, why cast her to play Anna? She's so not Anna. Anna is dark and mysterious. Rosa's like a little puff of smoke, or a feather, or a bubble someone's just blown. She's far too insubstantial and self-obsessed. She'd make a good Princess Betsy, but not Anna. Mind you, I suppose if it's some lame Hollywood re-make . . .'

My mother laughed.

'What?' I said.

'Are we a little bit jealous?'

'For God's sake. No. I'm more than happy with my own life. If I'd wanted to be an actress I'd have gone to that stage school. I don't want millions of pounds. I wouldn't know what to do with it. I'd have to spend all my time worrying about my hair and whether I was wearing the right dress. It must *cost* millions to keep up that lifestyle. Please, Mum, can we change the subject?'

Mum was still laughing. 'I shouldn't tease you,' she said. 'You know I'm very proud of you. I'd much rather have a daughter who writes books, even if no one buys them, than one who spends all her time on red carpets and in and out of the tabloids . . .'

'You're making it worse,' I said.

'I know. I'm sorry.'

We both collapsed in giggles.

'Oh, Lord,' I said. 'Bloody Rosa. How's Taz? Toby? The dogs?'

For the rest of my walk I listened to my mother tell me about Taz's commission for the new St Pancras station, and Toby's weird boyfriend who insisted on saying Grace before dinner, and how one of the dogs had chased his own tail and actually caught it, which meant the whole place had been covered with blood until Taz came home and cleared it up. After we'd said goodbye I looked across the river. In the beginnings of the twilight the deep pink earth looked like the soft skin on the inside leg of some huge, mythical animal that had fallen asleep by the water, furred with pubic clumps of dark green trees, and scarred and stretch-marked with roads. If the other side of the river was a sleeping creature's open leg, then Kingswear would be the long, thin toe it was dipping lazily in the water. As the hills darkened I walked home the back way, thinking how much more eerie the silence seemed to be now, and how much better my mother's archive would be if I was more like Rosa, and how much more point her family tree would have if I'd had children.

On Friday night it was raining hard. I'd left the library early, gone home, picked up B and walked to the Three Ships before Christopher got back. On Monday night when he'd got in I'd asked him about the mix-up with the books. He hadn't listened properly to what had happened and suggested that I should tidy my spare desk and actually use the two filing cabinets he'd made for me: one for Meg Carpenter and the other for Zeb Ross. Of course, I kept asking questions about the Newman book, for example whether he remembered opening the envelope, and whether it was possible that he could have lost something from the package, like a letter or a card, maybe from Vi, but this led to an argument at the end of which Christopher told me I could pick up my own 'fucking books' from the PO box if I didn't like the way he did it. This argument had thrown a shadow over the whole week and neither of us was quite over it. I had decided I would apologise for my part in it if he apologised first.

B was lying damply under the table in the pub, growling every time someone walked in. She did this just loudly enough so that the person she was growling at could hear, but not the landlord, Tony — who spent most of his time in deep conversation with regulars at the bar — or the pub cat, George, a really mangy old tabby, who would try to scratch out B's eyes if he knew she was here. George's eyesight wasn't great, and B seemed to know that, hiding in the shadows under the table, behind my legs. I was still trying to work out how to recycle the research I would do for my feature and use it in my novel. My nameless protagonist didn't believe in anything, and maybe sending her off on an odyssey into a world of tea-leaf reading, fork-bending and jugglery would reinforce her faith in the material universe. But I wasn't sure I had any faith in the material universe, or even any kind of universe.

I'd brought my notebook with me, and as I was reading through it, looking at rejected idea after rejected idea, all the dodgy brake pads, lockable saunas and other embarrassments, something struck me. Perhaps the *notebook* was the novel. Maybe the whole novel could take place inside its own construction, as our girl-hero tries, and fails, to plan out her novel in her notebook. It would be like a building made out of scaffolding, or one of those skirts with the seams on the outside. I immediately made a note — 'Maybe notebook is novel?' — and then realised that if the notebook was the novel, then the note about the notebook being the novel would also be part of the novel, and then I felt a bit dizzy. I'd already tried once to make the novel metafictional. Still, the notebook idea was better. One of the big problems with the novel had been that everything I really wanted to write about was out of bounds, and so I kept making things up that didn't ring true. I'd have loved to explore my break-up with Drew and my relationship with Christopher. I wanted to write about Libby and her affair. My parents' divorce was a bit clichéd, but still interesting, at least to me. I kind of wanted to write about Rosa too, and her weird attachment to her brother Caleb.

I'd already tried the obvious things, like changing everyone's names and hair colours, but what if these stories and characters — or very similar ones — emerged as faint outlines in the hazy spaces between the notes in the notebook, like little ghost ships? What if my protagonist — the writer of the notebook — was trying to write a crappy genre novel but real life kept breaking in? She would also write down other things, like shopping lists, and these could subtly show her life for what it was. For example, there could be some item on the list that she obviously buys for her boyfriend, something cheap and masculine like baked beans, or massive amounts of economy loo roll, and then this item could disappear from the lists. They'd have broken up, but I wouldn't need to write about it directly. In fact, maybe she'd even use her notebook to reflect on the fact that she couldn't write about what she really wanted to write about. I had a couple of old, rejected Zeb Ross plots — with authentic notes — that I could recycle as a kind of background noise, as her failing ideas. Perhaps she'd try to write about a simulated universe at the end of time too. That's how I could get Newman in, and make sure the time I'd spent reading his book hadn't been wasted. In fact, I could recycle all the work I had ever done that hadn't been published. My girl-hero could be a reluctant science fiction writer who nevertheless can't help but bring science fiction into everything. Maybe there'd also be doodles on the pages: spaceships and equations. And then all this could fade down as she falls in love with an older man and formulates a secret code so that she can express her feelings in her notebook without revealing anything solid at all. The reader would be given clues to this code, but Christopher would never work it out in a million years. The whole novel would be a trace of itself; a mirage; a half-remembered dream. Genius. But this would mean re-writing from the very beginning, again. I sighed. *Notebook*. It would make a good title too. Or maybe *Notebooking*.

Libby came in just after seven, wearing a yellow fisherman's hat, a blue anorak and red waterproof trousers. I was drinking a Bloody Mary, with a big stick of celery in it, thinking that I could easily skip dinner if I was drinking two portions of vegetables. The day before, I'd taken my latest cheque to Easy Cash in Paignton, and come out with £463. Easy Cash would have been interesting had I not been one of its customers. Instead, I was still trying to forget that I was one of the spectral people who drifted in and out apologetically, looking nothing like the pictures of the colourfully clothed, white-teethed members of families in the posters on the walls. I'd decided that the rent could probably wait for a bit as long as Christopher took Dougie for a pint next week, but there were a couple of bills that now had debt collectors attached to them. Once those were paid, I'd have £230. That meant twenty days' money for food, petrol and the ferry, and £30 left over. This £30 was my 'bonus': something I needed to break the monotony of living on £10 a day. I was planning to spend only about £10 tonight, and go out tomorrow and buy shampoo and some new yarn. I wasn't sure what I would knit next, but I was feeling excited about looking at patterns in the shop, and touching all the different balls of wool. B saw Libby, made a happy little sound, came out, waited for her head to be stroked, looked around, saw George on the bar and then went back under the table.

'Good idea,' Libby said to me, once she'd stripped off all her waterproofs. 'Drink that's also food.' She looked a bit pale, and when she ran her fingers through the damp ends of her hair I saw her hands were shaking.

'That's what I thought,' I said. 'Celery for dinner. I'm sure there's a diet book about that. Or we could write one. Not that I'm interested in diets, but you do get bestsellers that way. Are you OK?'

'Sort of. I reckon I can manage some celery. Do you want another one?'

'Yeah, thanks. Only one shot of vodka, though, whatever Tony says.'

Libby stood at the bar looking like something that has been hastily added at the end of a painting that hasn't quite dried yet. I imagined her dissolving down the canvas like Miró drips, or freezing into one of Turner's red splodges that Taz liked so much.

'Are you sure you're OK?' I asked her when she got back.

'No.'

She frowned and looked at her drink. We'd first met about five years before when I'd done a signing in the local bookshop. Libby had read both of the Newtopia novels I'd published then, which seemed miraculous, because I thought no one had done that apart from me, and possibly Josh, whose OCD meant that if he'd read one book by an author he had to read all of them. Libby and I had gone for coffee the day after the signing, and been friends ever since. I'd let her into all Zeb Ross's secrets, of course, and she told me all about how she was leaving her long-term boyfriend, Richard, for Bob, a rich kid from Kingswear who played guitar in a band and wanted to start his own comic shop. She talked about knitting, food and reading; I talked about popular science, food and writing. For Christmas that year I gave her home-made jam; she knitted me 'the fabric of the universe': a black cashmere square with cross-stitched, silver stars. I used it once to demonstrate gravity to Christopher, and he said, 'That's just stupid.' Perhaps he was right. It hadn't helped that the only planet in my makeshift universe was B's well-chewed rubber ball.

'What's wrong?' I asked Libby now.

She looked around the pub. I'd deliberately chosen the red booth by the door because it was furthest from the bar and it was harder for anyone to overhear what we were saying. Joni, the fishmonger, was at the cigarette machine just across from us, saying something to it in Icelandic.

'I'll tell you in a minute,' Libby said. 'How are you?'

'I'm OK,' I said. 'I may have just had a breakthrough with my novel.'

'What, your *novel* novel? Your real one?'

'Yeah. How cool is this: I'm going to structure the whole thing as a writer's notebook, just like one of mine. It's going to be all non-linear and experimental and the reader will have to put together the story for him- or herself. I thought it meant I'd have to start again from the very beginning — again — but I've just realised I can use loads of stuff I've already written, sort of as "draft material" that's been composed in the note-book. In fact, I think I might make the writer dead. Maybe her notebook has washed up like a message in a bottle or some-thing, and then the reader has to work out what's happened to her from fragments of her real and fictional narratives.' I was thinking as I was speaking and as usual my thoughts were tak-ing me somewhere I didn't want to go. 'But no, that's all too plot-driven again. So it probably won't be exactly that. Still, I'm happy with the notebook idea. What do you think?'

Libby frowned. 'So there won't be any story, just notes?'

'Yeah, but the notes will come together to make a story, or maybe two stories. I guess it's hard to describe, but I can see exactly how it will work. I think you can have too much story. I want it to be like real life, so making the whole thing a kind of artefact could really work.'

'But it'll be a fictional artefact?'

'Yeah.'

'Sounds interesting.'

The door tinkled and a man came in wearing a full-length, black raincoat with a large hood. B growled. He raised a hand to greet me and then walked over to the bar. Once he'd taken off his dripping coat I realised it was Tim Small, whom I hadn't seen for ages. I waited for him to look again, and then I waved back. B growled again, then yawned, then fell asleep under the table with her head on my foot.

'Who's that?' Libby asked.

'Tim Small. He's writing a Zeb Ross novel about the Beast of Dartmoor. He's the only local who's ever got anywhere with Zeb. It's not completely final yet, but I'm very excited. Don't tell anyone.'

'I won't.' She bit one of her nails. 'Is there a Beast of Dart-moor?'

'No, I don't think so. It's kind of based on the Beast of Bod-min Moor, but of course we don't want the Beast of Bodmin Moor to sue, so . . . No, seriously, Tim knows Dartmoor much better, so it makes sense. I think it's going to be really good. He came on the retreat last year. There were a few good projects that came out of that one, actually — not all for Zeb Ross either. You know Andrew Glass from the Foghorn? He's writing a fantastic memoir about the D-Day simulation that went wrong at Torcross.'

People said there were ghosts there, at Slapton and Torcross, on the beach and in the sea: American and British servicemen who'd been practising for the D-Day landings. In the 1960s, when he was a boy, Andrew Glass had started hearing the sound of men screaming from the sea. He'd come up with a theory that there'd been a terrible accident at Slapton at some time during the war, but no one believed him. Then he grew up and eventually went away to sea himself, as a medical officer in the Navy. Now everyone knew that the D-Day simulation had taken place, and that more than 700 men died in one day after they were attacked by German torpedo boats that had picked up on all the wireless activity in the area. In 1984 another local man had dredged up a tank, which sat blackly, like a lump of tar, in a corner of the car park at Torcross, with Slapton Ley behind it.

'How can it be a memoir?' Libby said. 'He wasn't there, was he?'

'No, but he's had connections with it all his life. He's doing a first-person investigation, putting himself in the story and seeing where it leads him. I think he's working other stories into it, like some of the experiences he had when he was in the Navy. He was on a ship once where the commanding officer saw a sea monster and wouldn't admit it to anyone apart from Andrew. He went and declared that he was having a nervous breakdown, and demanded that Andrew give him something for it. From what I can remember, Andrew gave him some sort of sugar pill or placebo, because the Navy wouldn't let them have tranquillisers on the boats, and he was fine. The whole thing is about imagination, belief, and the sea of course.' I looked behind me. Joni was still hanging around, taking the Cellophane off a packet of Marlboro. I sipped my drink and carried on talking.

'This other woman, from Kingsbridge, called Clare, I think, was writing about someone who believes she is so ugly that she can't leave the house. The woman decides she wants to die, but can't contemplate suicide, so she does all these dangerous things in the hope that she'll die by accident and not have to take responsibility for it. She starts off doing lots of DIY and trying to have household accidents, but she only manages to cut off one thumb, so then she moves into the outside world and ends up trekking through the jungle and doing extreme sports. She loses body parts as she goes, but somehow gains herself in the process. It's very funny. I hope she finds a publisher for it. It could be quite culty.'

Libby sipped her drink and made a face.

'I thought about throwing myself under a train the other day.'

'What train?'

'The steam train.'

'Why?'

'Because it's closest.'

'You'd have to get a winter timetable. Those tourist things are very haphazard. I thought about walking into the sea recently. The sea's always there.'

'You don't need to walk into the sea. You're a well-known writer.'

'Lots of writers drown themselves. Anyway, I'm not well known.'

'You are around here.'

'This is a small town. Everyone's well known in a small town.'

I looked around the pub. In one corner, Reg was demonstrating the size of something with his arms. Reg hated seagulls and was working on a device that would get rid of them. He was now talking to Joni, who was known for his oysters, and Rob, who was known for always winning the event in the regatta where you build your own raft and cross the river on it. Tim had settled, alone, in another corner with a pint of Guinness and a book. He wasn't known for anything yet. Libby was known for her knitted shawls, socks and blankets, which she sold in the delicatessen along with the jam and marmalade I made, and driftwood sculptures made by Bob's mother. She'd briefly thought of selling jumpers and hats that Mark made too, but decided that would lead to too many questions from Bob. I may have been known for my writing, but nobody let on. People in the town always asked me when I was next going to make rhubarb jam.

'It would be wet and cold in the sea,' Libby said.

'I know. That's what I thought. A train would be noisy and messy. Why were you thinking of throwing yourself under a train? It doesn't sound like much fun.'

'I've really fucked things up,' she said. 'It's over with me and Mark. As of yesterday. Killing myself might be the only option.'

'God. Oh, Libby. Shit. I thought you were joking . . .'

'And he's still coming for dinner next week. But that's a long story. And I'm so in the shit over the car as well.'

'Why?'

'The policeman came back yesterday and said that this woman at the Royal Castle Hotel reported seeing someone push a car in the river on Sunday night. She didn't have her glasses on, so what she saw was a bit blurry. Then he said that most cars don't wash up at all, but when one does the police usually find it was the owner who pushed it in so they could claim on the insurance. Ha, ha! How we all laughed about the idea of that. I pointed out that my car was too nice to push in a river, and that I don't exactly need insurance money, and I gave him some biscuits, but I'm fucked if it does surface.'

'Why? I thought the story was that kids pushed it in?'

'Yeah. But apparently Devon and Cornwall Police are piloting some new way of getting fingerprints from objects that have been underwater. It's been very successful so far. The policeman said it was very exciting because if the car surfaces they'll be able to work out how many people pushed it and probably even who did it. I said it sounded great and very hi-tech, but I was shitting myself.'

'I'm sure it won't surface. Even if it does, I bet their technique won't work. Just stick to your story. Anyway, what happened with Mark?'

'It was because of the car as well. Sort of. And the ring. We had a big argument.'

Mark had saved up and bought Libby a silver and black mother-of-pearl ring for Christmas, which she hardly ever wore. She bought jewellery for herself, but never rings, and she knew that Bob would find it suspicious if he saw her wearing it. So she left it in the beach hut, and planned to wear it only when she was with Mark. He had ended up throwing it in the river one stormy Wednesday night after he'd brought it to Dartmouth thinking she'd forgotten it.

'Do you think I should have left Bob?' Libby said.

'I can't answer that,' I said.

'Mark said I should have. Rather than . . .'

'The car?'

'Yeah.' She frowned. 'What was that story you told me about the horses?'

'Horses? Oh, the one about blessing and disaster.'

'Yeah. Exactly. Tell it to me again. I think it might help, but I can't remember it.'

'OK, so this is the story of a Chinese father and son and their best horse. The horse runs away, for no reason, and lives with some nomads across the border. The son is very upset that the horse has gone, and the father says to him, "What makes you so sure this isn't a blessing?" Then the horse comes back, a few months later, with a beautiful nomad stallion. The son is thrilled, but the father says to him, "What makes you so sure this isn't a disaster?" The son loves riding the new horse, but one day falls and breaks his leg. Everyone is sad for him, and his father says, wait for it, "What makes you so sure this isn't a blessing?" At some point the nomads invade, and every able-bodied young man has to go off to battle. The nomads basically wipe out all the men, but the son is safe because he is lame, and so he and his father live on and look after one another.'

'It would piss you off, having a father as smug as that,' Libby said.

I laughed. 'Yeah, I know.'

'I like it. I'm not sure it's as useful as I thought, though.'

'What, in helping you decide whether to leave Bob?'

'Yeah. The more I think about it, I realise I can't just let things happen by themselves. Not now. That's what Mark said. He was so pissed off about the car. He said he couldn't believe that I'd go to such lengths to avoid facing up to everything. He said it was the ideal opportunity to come clean and just tell Bob everything and go and move in with him.'

'Move into a beach hut?'

'Yeah, exactly.' She sighed. 'I guess we wouldn't stay in the beach hut, though. But if I split up with Bob I'd be poor. Not that it matters. Or it shouldn't matter.'

'It can come to matter.'

I'd never really said much to Libby about my financial problems, but I guessed she knew I had them. Whenever we went out for dinner, she would say, 'It must be my turn this time,' even though she always paid. I'd been out on the yacht a couple of times with her and Bob, and they always brought a hamper from the shop and told me not to bring anything. She happened to have a 'spare' life jacket that I could keep and Bob claimed to have found a dog life jacket somewhere in the boat, 'perhaps from the previous owners', although there hadn't been any previous owners because his father had designed and built it himself.

'How would you be poor, though?' I said. 'It doesn't make sense. You own half the house and the shop, don't you?'

'Yeah, of course, but if I left Bob I wouldn't ask him to sell everything so I could have half of it. I just couldn't. You know when we went to Italy recently? We were at this big market, and Bob was tasting some sun-dried tomatoes. He turned around and looked for me in the crowd, and when he saw me he smiled in such a happy, comfortable way. He looked, well, like Bob, with his baggy jeans and stupid red lumberjack shirt, and his crazy beard, and I thought about how I never, ever, wanted to go to bed with him again — the thought of it made me sick — but that I loved him, intensely, the way you might love a brother. At that moment I realised that I never wanted to do anything to make him cry. I never wanted to be sitting there facing him, with his face all crumpled up and everything in tatters because of me. He just doesn't deserve it. I can't fuck up his whole life and take away everything that means something to him just because I think I've found my soul mate.'

'Yeah, but . . .'

'Yeah, *but*. I know. Having found my soul mate, how cruel is it for me to stay with Bob, pretending I feel more for him than I do and preventing him from going out and finding someone who loves him the way I love Mark?'

'You can't be responsible for other people's feelings,' I said. This was something my mother used to say a lot after leaving my father. I wasn't quite sure what it meant, or whether it was even right.

'If you threw a brick at someone you would be responsible for them feeling pain, presumably,' Libby said.

'But if you do the right thing and it makes someone feel bad, isn't that their problem? Then again, how do you even know what the right thing is? Who decides?'

'It's so confusing. I am sure about Mark, but I was sure about Bob before that, and Richard before that. Maybe Mark isn't for ever, I just think he is now when I can't have him. I have to face up to this about myself. I fall in love like that.' She clicked her fingers. 'I always have. For other people, love is like some rare orchid that can only grow in one place under a certain set of conditions. For me it's like bindweed. It grows with no encouragement at all, under any conditions, and just strangles everything else. Good metaphor, huh?'

'Maybe you should write a novel,' I said, smiling.

'Oh, well, I can teach you to knit socks now,' she said. 'I'll have plenty of time.' I'd been bugging Libby to teach me how to knit socks since I'd got back from Scotland. 'I think Mark's right. I'm not ready, and I'm not committed enough. But when I think of being with Bob, only Bob, for ever, I just want to kill myself now. This is great, isn't it? I'm only thirty-eight. I can't have ruined my whole life already, can I?'

'I think maybe this is one of those things where time will help, whatever happens, whether you end up with Mark or Bob.'

'We'll knit socks,' she said. 'It'll take my mind off everything. It's really hard.'

'Yeah. Maybe I was a bit hasty with that. I'm still not sure I'll be able to cope with four needles,' I said. 'I can't even cope very well with two.' I was wearing my turquoise scarf, and I fiddled with the end of it. I had made a slipknot to cast on, and then, when I'd finished, woven in both ends of the wool just like Vi had shown me. But the knot was still there, sticking out like some sort of fabric scab. 'Mind you, I'm a dab hand with the knit-stitch now, and purling. But I should probably try something else first that has increases and decreases and stuff—and an actual pattern to follow. I'm going to get new wool tomorrow, and a pattern. I'm very excited. After that I will do socks.'

'Why exactly do you want to knit socks?'

'Originally I was going to make them for Christopher, but I'm not so sure now. I know it takes ages, but I still like the idea of it. It just seems like something you can always be doing, and it seems quite compact. I saw someone doing it on a train, and it looked soothing. I like the idea of knitting a whole thing at once. Maybe I'll go into business knitting designer socks and I can compose novels in my head — or even onto a Dictaphone — while I do it. Then again, I flicked through a book in the library and there was lots of stuff about picking up stitches, which I didn't like the look of. I'd like to have sock-knitting in the novel, ideally. Maybe include a pattern or something. I'd probably have to have a man doing it so it doesn't seem too mumsy. I'm just going to practise a little bit more first before you teach me. I'm no good at fixing mistakes, yet. I should probably make some on purpose so I can fix them. At the moment I'm just very careful, because I know if I fuck something up I'll have to abandon the whole thing.'

'I can fix mistakes in knitting,' Libby said. 'Just not in my actual life. I'd like to start again, ideally. Any idea how to do that?'

'In my experience you just pull at the end and watch the whole thing unravel, ping, ping, ping, and then it's very complicated trying to get the crinkly stuff into a ball again.' I laughed. That was how my turquoise scarf had started. 'Sorry. If it's any help I did just read a book that says that we're all immortal, only we don't realise it, and that we have lots of chances to live a perfect life. But I'm not sure that would be better. Who says what a perfect life is?'

Libby asked about the book, so I summarised Newman's argument in the same way I had in my review.

'That sounds a bit improbable,' she said.

'The science is right,' I said. 'Well, as far as I know. It's like having a knitting pattern for something where all the instructions are correct, but the actual thing you make is awful, because it traps you.'

'Like knitting yourself into a big sack.'

'Yeah, exactly.'

'But if I did kill myself I'd get another go, and then when I got it right I'd end up in heaven?' she said. 'Which would seem lovely even if it is a big sack?'

'Well, sort of. It depends whether the theory is true, of course.'

'Christ. This is what I think will happen: I'll leave Bob because of, basically, sex, and lose everything, and he'll be magnanimous but heartbroken, and he will cry, and me and Mark will run away and get bored with one another and we'll have nothing to talk about once the whole situation is resolved and he'll end up watching football all the time with his mates and I won't have any mates and we won't have sex any more and then I'll get PMT and go and throw myself under a train. It's totally *Anna Karenina*. Maybe I'm a tragic heroine. But I bet that doesn't count. So maybe I should just throw myself under a train now and get it over with.'

'By that logic we should all kill ourselves now. Anyway, I don't think Tolstoy implies that Anna has PMT.' I'd given Libby *Anna Karenina* for her birthday a couple of years before, wondering if she'd get into it, considering all the terrible SF, fantasy and horror books she liked reading. But she'd already read it twice and was always coming up with new theories about it.

'Honestly, Meg, that's total PMT. Read it again. She is irritable and "senselessly jealous". She hates the smell of paint. Then there's all that stuff about hating everyone and everything, and desire being like "dirty ice-cream" when she's on her way to the train station. Don't tell me you don't feel like that before your period. Oh, well, I suppose if this Newman guy is right, then if I threw myself under a train now I could start again with a clean slate. New life, new disasters. Maybe I would get it right if I started again.'

'My mother rang me yesterday with more news of Rosa,

by the way. She's going to be playing Anna Karenina in a big Hollywood blockbuster. Maybe I'll email her with the PMT tip.'

'Don't worry,' Libby said. 'It'll probably be a big flop.'

'Oh, I don't want it to be a flop exactly. But why my favourite book, of all things? My mother thinks I'm jealous, and she's probably right, I suppose, although I don't know why I'm jealous of something I don't want. Who's to say that Rosa, with all her success, is getting life any more right than anyone else? Her brother's an accountant at a charity and I bet no one makes a fuss over him, but maybe in his quiet way he's making a better job of life. Who knows? I think getting it right is a total mystery.'

'Anna Karenina certainly didn't get it right.'

'Didn't she?' I raised an eyebrow.

'What do you mean? How could she have got it right?'

'I don't know exactly. But she sees the light,' I said. 'At least she sees the light, just before she dies. Her passion gives her some sort of insight that the other characters don't have. Mind you, then it goes dark for ever.' I sipped my drink. 'God. I wouldn't want to be Rosa trying to act that.' Or me, trying to write something with half as much depth and weight.

I'd first read *Anna Karenina* at university, but had re-read it about three years after we'd moved to Devon while I was having a brief flirtation with Christopher's brother Josh. I'd thought it would warn me off. He had just turned twenty-eight, and couldn't find a girlfriend. He kept saying everything would be great if he could find a woman like me who played the guitar, and was happy to have a kick around with a football in the park, and read books. 'I need a writer,' he'd say, and I'd respond that most writers were weirdos who never did anything physical at all. I told him he probably needed a yoga instructor, or someone on a gap year. He hung around with us a lot in those days, and it was nice having someone to confirm that Christopher had not really spoken for the previous twenty-four hours, or that his reaction to spilling a cup of tea was unusual, or that he would often disagree with an opinion if I expressed it, but not if the same opinion was expressed by someone on television. Where Christopher was mercurial and irrational, Josh was highly rational, or even beyond rational. He carried a tape measure with him, partly because he couldn't buy a book that wasn't the same size as books he already had, but also because sometimes, if no one was looking, he would measure walls and doorways 'just to know' how high or wide they were. He told me once that he had to count to thirty-two every time he washed his hands. If he lost count, or didn't switch the tap off in time, he'd start again. When he made tea he would squeeze the tea-bag in the cup exactly eight times. He would wear only an even number of articles of clothing at once. If he was reading a book, he couldn't stop reading on page 6, or 15, or 23, because these were bad numbers. He wouldn't read page 13 of any book, or page 36, and he said this meant he never missed much, usually. Once, he hadn't been able to read any prime-numbered pages, but this meant always missing the beginning, and he'd got over that.

I was convinced that Josh had had OCD since he was a child, especially after he told me he'd had to go to the Steiner School because Pi made him throw up in normal maths lessons, but the rest of his family believed it started properly after his mother died. I'd once found him exhausted and close to tears, switching the light off and on in his bedroom. He'd done this 1,200 times already, he said, and still had to get to 5,000. I couldn't make him stop. Later, when I asked him why he'd had to do this, he said that if he didn't do it, then someone would die, or become very ill: perhaps his father, perhaps even me. I was flattered that he'd switch a light off and on 5,000 times to save me. Once I'd become convinced that there was a burglar in the house and Christopher had refused to switch the light on even once. Josh didn't quite believe that it was anything like 'God' that was planning to harm me or his father, but rather a complicated network of energies and cosmic checks and balances. He'd picked up on a vibration that something bad would happen, and switching the light on and off was a form of focusing his energy in order to stop the bad thing from happening. Josh had been an excellent footballer as a child, and had been selected to play in the under-13 team of a London club. But his mother hadn't wanted him to live away from home and grow up as a footballer; she'd wanted him to be a writer or a painter. He'd been unemployed for as long as I'd known him, because he still wasn't stable enough to hold down a job. I'd begun to fantasise that I could help him somehow, and we'd spent quite a lot of time together.

By the time I re-read *Anna Karenina* I was becoming interested in tragedy in general. I used the Sophocles play *Oedipus Rex* on the retreats, mainly because our key text, Aristotle's *Poetics,* referred to it all the time. *Oedipus* is an almost perfect example of the deterministic, cause-and-effect-based plot, where Y can only happen because X has happened first, and that was how I used it. But every time I re-read it I marvelled at how a narrative could do so much more than just tell a satisfying story with a beginning, a middle and an end, which was basically what I was always teaching the people on the retreat to do, and what I'd always done myself. Somehow, *Oedipus* seemed to dramatise a fundamental puzzle of human existence. *Anna Karenina* did this as well. So did *Hamlet.* I read Nietzsche's book on tragedy and this made the situation with Josh worse for a while, because I started fancying myself as a tragic heroine with nothing to lose. Tragedy wasn't about people living happily ever after in banal domesticity, but going beyond the rational into a different kind of knowledge on their way to certain death. I managed to resist Josh, mainly because I was so terrified of Christopher's reaction if anything happened between us, and instead tried to make my own novel into a great tragedy. It just ended up being depressing. I could see that most narrative was an equation that balanced, a zero-sum game, and that tragedy was special because you got more out of the equation than you put in, but I had no idea how to write like that. The mechanics of *Oedipus* were simple enough to grasp, but where did one get all that *feeling* from?

I'd once speculated about what would have happened if Zeb Ross had written *Hamlet.* There'd be no ghost, for a start. Or at least, the ghost would be reduced to a troubled teenager's hallucination, and Hamlet, with the help of his plucky love-interest Ophelia, would come to realise that his new stepfather didn't really do something as improbable and stupid as pour poison in his father's ear, and in fact had actually tried to save his life! Hamlet would start seeing a counsellor — perhaps Polonius, who dabbles in the self-help industry himself, would recommend someone — and come to terms with his bereavement and realise that it's OK for his mother to have sex with her new husband (although there'd be no 'rank sweat of an enseamed bed' or anything icky like that) and he'd go back to university happy, having now accepted the change in his family circumstances, with Ophelia in tow. Then I realised that if I'd written *Hamlet* it would probably have been like that too.

'Sometimes I wish I'd never read *Anna Karenina*,' Libby said.

'Why?'

'Because the ending is so perfect, but for Anna so sad. And now, whenever I think about what would happen with Mark, I think it must be something tragic, because I deserve it, and because that's the way the story seems to be going. But what if we'd just be really happy together?'

It hadn't stopped raining by ten o'clock, and droplets of water were still crawling like bugs down the stained glass window as B snored at my feet. Libby kept sighing and checking her phone for text messages from Mark, and we kept drinking Bloody Marys.

'How's Christopher?' Libby asked, putting her phone away.

'Still sulking?'

'What? Oh, probably. When did you last see him?'

'God, it was . . . Must have been at our place for that dinner before Christmas. It feels as if it must have been more recent somehow.'

'Was he sulking then?'

'Oh, yes.' Libby pushed her hair out of her eyes. 'What was it about? Oh, yeah, he thought he was going to be made supervisor on his building project and then he wasn't.'

'Oh, God. That was tough. Mind you, it should have been him.'

'Is he still working on that wall?'

'Just for another couple of months until it's finished.'

'But he's applying for things now? Like, real jobs?'

'Yeah. But it's all so competitive. It'll be OK.'

I knew Libby wondered, but didn't ask, why Christopher didn't just get a job he hated like everyone else. She checked her phone again, rolled her eyes and then shook her head at me.

'Nothing?' I said.

'Nothing. If we had children . . .' Libby began.

'I know,' I said. 'Then we wouldn't have time to worry about everything so much. It would probably be a blessing.'

'It would probably be a disaster. We'd turn into those people who are completely obsessed with our offspring.'

'As opposed to being completely obsessed with ourselves.'

Libby picked up her phone, looked at it briefly and then put it down again.

'By the way, did I tell you that Mark got a big contract?'

'What for? A boat?'

'Yes. It's amazing. Good money that will last a year. But guess who the contract's with?'

I thought about it for a minute. 'Bob's father?' I said.

'Precisely.'

I groaned. 'So that's why Mark's coming to dinner next Saturday?' I said.

'Yep. Me and Bob, my mother- and father-in-law, Bob's aunt and uncle, and my now ex-lover. Bob's parents were supposed to be having it at their house, but their building work's still not finished. Apparently the fireplace won't be put back in for another month. Please say you can come. I'm going to get very drunk and I may need someone to hold my hair while I throw up.'

'How could I miss that?'

'Holy shit, Meg, why doesn't this kind of thing happen to you?'

'It used to. It's not as if I could ever go back to Brighton, for example.'

'But you're settled now.'

'I guess.' She was right. In seven years I hadn't been anywhere near another man; not really, unless you counted the kiss with Rowan. 'I don't know,' I said. 'I'm not exactly happy all the time, but maybe that's normal after seven years. And I can't imagine any man is going to be that different from Christopher. I think I only find men exciting before I actually get to know them. And look at me. I'm hardly breathtakingly gorgeous any more. It's not as if . . .'

'You do sort of look the way Christopher wants you to look.'

That wasn't strictly true. I had rejected fashion for my own reasons. I thought I looked OK in the clothes I had, though: three pairs of faded and fraying jeans, a denim skirt, four organic cotton shirts, a few black T-shirts and a couple of black cardigans. In the winter I wore trainers, and in the summer I wore flip-flops. If I wanted to cheer myself up I put on my silver bird earrings. If I went to a dinner party I wore a long black patchwork skirt with the fabric of the universe — which also functioned as a shawl. Even though my wardrobe was limited I ironed everything, and I carefully planned outfits for the week ahead on a Sunday night. I'd stopped plucking my eyebrows for several years because Christopher saw me doing it one day and said, 'I hope you're not doing that for me.' When I asked what he meant he told me how much more sexy it was to look 'natural', and how women in commercials, and, by implication, me, looked glossy and wrong, and how his ideal woman was someone who wore shapeless things in cotton and denim and didn't bother to change between working on, say, a fruit farm or a heritage site and then going down the pub afterwards. He didn't like perfume either, or make-up. 'I want the real you, Meg. Not some cardboard cut-out.' Did he say that last bit, or did I imagine it? In any case, after I'd met Rowan in the library the first time, I had started plucking my eyebrows again. Not for him, but for some unfathomable reason.

'Hello.' Tim had left his corner of the pub and was now standing by our table holding his book. I could see now that it was the edition of Chekhov's letters that I'd admitted was my favourite book about writing when the people on the retreat last year had kept asking me. B stirred and lazily sniffed his feet and then turned around and went back to sleep. I imagined that since she'd already growled at him a couple of times she thought that job was done.

'Hi,' I said. 'I thought it was you under that impressive rain-coat. This is Libby. Libby, this is Tim Small.'

'Can I get you more drinks?' he said.

'Yeah. Vodka and tonics, I think,' said Libby. 'If you don't mind. I can't drink any more tomato juice. Meg?'

'Yeah. That's really kind. Thanks.'

Tim got our drinks, plus another Guinness for himself, and then sat down next to Libby. He was wearing a faded blue rugby shirt, and jeans that were wearing around the knees. Tim spent a lot of time on his knees. He worked as a handy-man, assembling flat-pack furniture and putting up shelves. He had a rugged, faded face, from years of spending his spare time gardening and walking on the moors. On the retreat last year we'd ended up talking about flat-packs for almost the whole first day. Clare, who already knew what she wanted to write about but had no structure, which was why she had come, started asking him a lot of questions about unusual DIY accidents, and then someone else said that they could never understand flat-packs, and most other people agreed.

'But they're completely logical,' Tim had said. 'Of course, I'm not complaining that most people can't understand them. After all, I get work out of it. But flat-packs are probably the greatest invention of the twentieth century. Everything there in a box, with a picture of an object on the outside, and everything you need to construct it inside. You follow each step and at the end the object is made.' He'd looked at me. 'Please tell me writing a novel is like that,' he'd said, and we all laughed as I shook my head. I didn't say what I was thinking, though, which was that writing Zeb Ross novels was like that once you knew how. My next thought I hardly admitted to myself: *My Newtopia novels, and everything I have ever written, are also flat-packs, and all I've done is screw the parts together in exactly the way anyone would expect.* Almost everyone who came along to spend the week in the hotel in Torquay seemed to have the idea that all novels possessed the same sort of value, and took roughly the same amount of effort from the author, and that Tolstoy was 'a novelist' in the same way that the latest chick-lit author was 'a novelist'. 'How do you even begin to write eighty thousand words?' someone would always ask, admiringly. And I'd always explain that 80,000 words is not that much, really, and that you could do it in eight weekends if you really wanted to, using Aristotle's *Poetics* as an instruction manual. Making the 80,000 words any good is the hard bit: making them actually important. But I didn't really need to talk about importance on the Orb Books retreats, so I would usually talk about unified plots instead, and how hard it can sometimes be to make the 80,000 words hang together the way Aristotle said they should, in a deterministic, three-act plot. On the retreats I ignored what he said about creating fiction as an imitation of life in order that one can examine life more easily.

'Hey,' Tim said to me now. 'Guess what I'm doing at Easter?'

'What?'

'Research trip. Camping on Dartmoor. I've bought a new tent. I got it off the Internet. Can you believe they deliver tents nowadays, to your door? It's fantastic.'

'It's going to be freezing at Easter,' said Libby. 'It's really early this year.'

'Sounds like it'll be fun, though,' I said. 'Who's going with you?'

'No one. Not Heidi. Heidi'll welcome the chance to have her lover over, I'm sure.' He looked at Libby and smiled sadly. 'My wife's having an affair. I like to make it easy for her sometimes. Go away on trips so she can have the house to herself. It's like a kind of compromise, I guess. The kind of thing old people in the local paper say is the secret of their fifty-year marriage.' He shrugged and sipped his drink.

Libby's eyebrows almost hit her hairline. 'Seriously? You have an open relationship? You're fine with it and everything?'

'Between you and me? When I first found out, I wanted to kill him. I've never been violent, but I used to have fantasies about all the different ways I could do it. Machete, chainsaw, toothpick. The toothpick was the best. It sounds improbable, but in the eyes, and the throat . . . And I used to cry in my van between jobs, thinking it was all over, and we'd get divorced, and I'd have to go speed-dating or something else that I wouldn't understand.' He smiled. 'I gave it all a lot of thought. But then I realised that it was probably best not to say anything. I thought that if she wanted to leave me, she would. But she obviously didn't. And I suppose I do still love her. She's very nice to me when we are together, and maybe I am a bit past it in some ways, so — this is going to sound awful — I sort of thought, why not let him do all the work, and provide all the romance? I'm not so good at that kind of thing; I know I'm not. So now I've got time to write my novel, and go camping, which she hates, and do my garden in peace. It's worked out fine. I've realised you just have to consider these things from all angles before making a decision. Every Christmas we go to my parents and she and my mum cook dinner, and everyone gets on well. Every New Year I pretend to have a terrible headache and she goes out with him. He's married too. It's functional. It's modern.' He laughed. 'My marriage is basically a piece of furniture. Probably too bulky to get rid of too. Probably nailed together at the back.'

'And she knows you know?'

'God, no. No, she just feels very guilty all the time. And so she . . .'

'What?'

'I'm a bit pissed. Sorry; I shouldn't say anything else. You'll think I'm . . .'

'No, go on. Just say it. What? She feels so guilty that she gives you blow jobs whenever you want them? Runs you nice baths? Rubs your calloused feet?' Libby looked down at the table. 'God, I think I'm pissed too. Shit. Sorry, Bob.'

'It's Tim,' he said, blushing. 'And you're right. Yeah. I'm a bastard.'

What was worse? Getting home first, or getting home second? If I was first, I'd wait for Christopher's mood; if I was second, I'd walk into it. Christopher was one of those people — there are others, including my brother Toby and my father — who could fill an entire house with emotion. When Christopher was happy, everyone couldn't help being happy too. But when he wasn't, it was terrible. Sometimes there were signs: sawing, or heavy footsteps on the stairs, or sighing, or having the

TV on too loud. But sometimes when all wasn't well there was nothing except an emotional rumble, like the heavy throb of a diesel engine turning over and over right outside the window while you are trying to sleep, or think, or just be. Sometimes the rumbling and the throbbing became so intense that it was more like having a Chinook helicopter hovering over the house.

Once I said this to him, sort of, and he said, 'How do you know it's not you?'

He was right. I was a common factor. Maybe it was my throb, not his. After all, I had once apparently been able to fill houses with my emotions as well. Sometimes I wondered if everything that went wrong with Christopher and me was actually my fault.

The weekly rubbish collection was due the next morning, and as I walked back there were black bags outside most of the houses, and seagulls beginning to break them apart and *ack, ack, ack*ing at one another in the rain. Seagulls in Dartmouth are fat. They have yellow beaks, red webbed feet, white heads and necks, black and white wing-tips and mean eyes. When they are not *ack, ack*ing they screech from the million-greyed sky, *you, you,* like the chorus in a tragedy. I had to keep pulling B away; she was fascinated with these big ugly creatures that weren't at all interested in her. When I got to the bottom of Brown's Hill steps I saw Reg, back from the pub and now out in full waterproofs, putting his rubbish in the wooden box he had built to stop the seagulls getting to it. The steps were strewn with rubbish from other people's bags that had already been split open. In Dartmouth there are three options with rubbish. You put it out five minutes before the bin men come, you put it in a wooden box with a locked lid, or you make sure you don't throw away anything that you wouldn't want your neighbours to see laid out in front of their houses. But there were new people in one of the cottages on Brown's Hill, and in front of me I saw tampons, plastic cartons from ready meals, takeaway pizza boxes, empty dog food tins and a pair of old trainers with holes in both soles.

When I saw the dog food tins, which would have been re-cycled had they not been so dangerous to wash out, and the trainers, I realised that at least some of this rubbish was ours, and that Christopher, who wasn't at all bothered about the em-barrassment the seagulls could cause, had put the rubbish out too early again. I hoped he hadn't seen the trainers. They were his, and they were revolting. I'd finally thrown them out be-cause I couldn't cope with the smell coming from the bedroom cupboard. He wouldn't have thrown them out by himself. He never threw anything away. It struck me then that he would say the same about me, and I wondered whether we needed one another, even just to sub-edit each other's existence.

'Disgusting,' Reg said, nodding at all the debris in the rain.

'I know,' I said. 'Bloody seagulls.'

'I'm going to exterminate them all,' he said. 'They're the plague of this town. Rats with wings, that's what they are.'

We'd had this conversation many times.

'I suppose they're just trying to live, like the rest of us,' I said. 'It can't be easy being a seagull in winter. I mean, they annoy me too, but I understand why they're doing it. They probably think we put the rubbish out specially for them as a treat.'

'Pah! You young people. You're too bloody understanding. You wait. You'll see. These monsters need to be vanquished. They're vermin. They're pests. Everyone will thank me when they're gone. Of course, the council should do it but they've spent all their money on that stupid maze in the park. Mrs Morgan up the hill says she'll throw a big party to celebrate once I've got rid of them. You know one of them made off with her cat? Picked it up and carried it out to sea, just like that.'

I did know this. I wasn't sure whether I believed it, though.

'Well, good luck,' I said, stepping over one of the trainers. I already knew I wouldn't say anything to Christopher about the rubbish. As I climbed the remaining wet steps to the house I decided that once I got in I'd check my email. Maybe I would find that something amazing had happened to me. This wasn't very likely; nothing amazing happened to me. Even if it had I wouldn't know. Well, if it had anything to do with Orb Books I'd know. I couldn't access my personal email account because I hadn't paid the ISP for so long that, even though they were friends of Christopher's from school, they'd cut me off months ago. Still, if I went straight up to my study, I could avoid a conversation about the rubbish, and if I distracted myself with new proposals and admin, then I wouldn't think about Libby crying all the way back to her place, and I wouldn't think about all these broken relationships, and everything would be OK. Maybe Vi would have sent a message to my Orb Books account about the Newman book. Perhaps Claudia would have sent an email telling me how Vi had been trying to contact me for ages, and wanted me to know she'd forgiven me. Maybe there was some cocoa in the cupboard. I'd check my email, wait for Christopher to go to bed, and then I'd make cocoa and read the paper, and there'd be a world outside this one and everything would be OK. Perhaps I'd even finish the crossword and think about what knitting pattern I would get the next day.

As soon as I opened the door, it was clear that everything wasn't OK. I could smell burning, and there was a plopping noise in the corridor. *Plop, plop, plop.* What was that?

'Christopher?'

I put my umbrella to dry by the door, then hung my coat and bag over the banister. I took off B's lead and she ran upstairs and sat by the bathroom, waiting to be dried with her towel. If I didn't come she would knock her towel to the ground and roll around in it until she was dry. She hated being wet.

'Sweets?' Something watery fell on my neck. I looked down and realised I was standing in a puddle. The plopping sound was rainwater falling onto the floor in the corridor, soaking into the carpet. I went to the kitchen and found the pan we used least: an egg poacher that I'd bought after the only holiday we'd ever had. Now I was aware that Christopher was lying in a ball on the sofa, and that the air was throbbing with despair. I thought it would be most sensible to deal with the leak first.

'What are you doing?' he said, in a dead voice.

'Just putting a pan down. This ceiling's leaking again. It's OK.'

'How's the adulteress of Dartmouth?'

'Don't call her that.'

'Why not? It's true. If you acted like her I'd kill you.'

As I put the pan on the floor I slipped and put my knee in the water. It was like kneeling on a cold sponge. 'Fuck,' I said.

'What's got you in a mood tonight?' he said.

I stood up. I was wearing thick woolly tights under my jeans and so now I had two layers of wet material sticking to my skin. I'd have to get changed, but if I went upstairs now I'd probably be accused of storming off, which meant I was stuck with a wet leg.

'Honestly, Christopher, I'm not going to have the "Who's in a mood?" argument tonight. It's obvious there's something wrong with you, but I'm not prepared to spend an hour convincing you there's nothing wrong with me before you'll discuss it. I think I'm just going to get a glass of water and go upstairs and work for a while.'

He said nothing. As I walked into the kitchen again the burning smell got worse. The grill pan was out and two sausages, burned almost to charcoal, lay on it like the remains of a peat-bog person's fingers. I took out a clean tea-towel and started dabbing my knee with it. If Christopher saw me doing this would he think I was making a big deal about the leak, and how he hadn't put a pan down? Would it be seen as a hostile action? Suddenly I wanted to scream. This was all in my head. I had to stop thinking and just do what a normal person would do, without second-guessing everything all the time. I filled the kettle and put it on.

'What's happened here?' I said, looking at the grill pan. 'Christopher? Sorry I snapped. I'm a bit tired. Is everything all right?'

There was an open letter on the counter, which had obviously been screwed up and then flattened out again. A corner of it had sunk into a pool of water from where Christopher must have made coffee earlier. It was as if I'd been left clues: the kind of thing you'd get on a children's game-show or activity holiday. So he'd made sausages at some point that evening, and then abandoned them. He hadn't bothered to clean up after himself, which wasn't like him. He'd ignored the leaking ceiling and curled up in a ball on the sofa. I picked up the letter and read it. It was another rejection, this time from Moor Trees. He'd had the interview two weeks ago, and hadn't even been sure he wanted the job. He preferred walls and old buildings to trees, but most of the heritage places didn't even offer him an interview.

'Oh, sweets, I'm sorry,' I said.

I walked over to the sofa and sat on the edge of it, and then put my hand on his back. Now I realised that he was quietly sobbing, his body bobbing up and down like a storm-shattered boat in a calming sea. He shrugged my hand off him, and I sighed again.

'I'm a fucking failure,' he said. 'I might as well admit it. I can't even cook sausages. I can't even put a pan down under a leak. My father's going to move in with a twenty-five-year-old waitress, my brother's going nuts and my sister told me at Christmas that she "just doesn't like me any more". Everything's shit. I can't do anything without making a mess of it.'

'No, that's not true,' I said. 'Becca doesn't mean it; she's just trying to hurt you. She always used to get stressed and ratty at Christmas. Come on. Why don't you sit up?'

'I can't. You don't understand. Everything has stopped.'

'OK, well, stay there then. Hey, maybe there's something on TV.'

'I don't want to watch TV.'

'I can go if you want to be on your own.'

'Don't go.' He reached for my hand and clasped it. 'Why do you put up with me?'

'Sweets . . .'

'I didn't mean what I said before. I wouldn't kill you. I wouldn't even blame you. And I don't hate Libby. Not really. Christ, my head hurts. I don't think I can move.'

'Do you want some painkillers?'

'Yeah.'

'And a cup of tea?'

'Yeah.' But he didn't let go of my hand. 'What's happened, babe?'

'Hmm?'

'What's happened to us? I don't know if I'm even good for you any more. I fuck everything up. It's even my fault that you reviewed the wrong book.'

'I'll make that tea.'

'Meg?'

'What?'

'Nothing. I'm sorry. I'm sorry about the book.'

'It's all right. It wasn't your fault. I'm sorry too. Look, I'll be back in a moment. I'm just going to get changed, and then I'll get you some tea.'

In the next day's jeans I stood in the kitchen re-boiling the kettle while eating a tangerine. If Christopher had been in a normal state of mind he would probably have said something about boiling the water twice for the same cups of tea. He often said that he wanted to minimise the footprint he was making on the environment, but I sometimes wondered whether really he didn't want the environment to make a footprint on him as it trudged on into an unknown future. I wondered what it would be like if he decided to split up with me. I looked at his thin back, and his dark hair falling on his shoulders. We used to say that we'd be together for ever. We wouldn't be like other couples. No clichés, we'd promised each other. Whatever happened, we wouldn't turn into a cliché like Becca and Ant and the other couples we'd known. Now what?

The rain was still coming down hard outside, and every so often there was a metallic sound as another drip fell into the pan in the corridor. B padded down the stairs and curled up on the armchair, not looking at either of us.

'What if I don't ever get a job?' Christopher said.

He'd sat up on the sofa and was drinking his tea.

'You will,' I said.

'But . . .'

'You could look in other areas. We could move. I wouldn't mind.'

He frowned. 'You've never said that before. I thought you liked being here.'

'I do. It's just . . .' I started coughing, and reached for my inhaler.

'What?' Christopher said, once I'd put the inhaler back down.

'Nothing. Look, like I said, it'll all be all right.'

'I mean, seriously, we're never really going to be able to afford to leave here, are we? Not until I get a really good job, or one of your books takes off. And even then, neither of us will ever be able to get a mortgage, and renting's impossible now with all the checks they do. I've still got a criminal record, babe, don't forget. Neither of us can get a bank reference, and we still haven't got a deposit, or any furniture. But I could look for a shit job around here. Maybe that's what I should do. Nine to five in some beige office with a boss and a photocopier.'

'No, sweets. It's OK. We agreed that we wouldn't do that.'

The plan when we'd moved to Devon had been simple. After everything that had happened in Brighton, we'd just be ourselves here. No bosses. No nine-to-fives. I'd always had some shit job or other in the years before we met, and I'd have one again if I had to, but Christopher was still prone to crying and punching walls if people tried to tell him what to do. When I met Christopher he owned one pair of jeans and two T-shirts and spent all his dole money on skunk. But when he bought me a plant after the first night we'd spent together, he was able to tell me all about how to take care of it, and I ended up feeling that if I killed it, I would have destroyed us. This plant, my peace lily, was now finally dying in this house, but I refused to read anything into this. It was just because of the damp and lack of light, that was all, and the fact that it liked being watered more often than I remembered. It had always been a bit half dead.

He was right. Here was quirky. Here was real. Here was also cheap, and near his family. Still, I could barely afford the price of the ferry every day now, and I wasn't sure I'd ever be able to do anything more liberating than just cross the river and then come back at the end of the day. But watching the sun go down was free, and my morning walks on the beach were free, and you could get a cup of tea in the kiosk for 35p, although Christopher didn't like the polystyrene cups. Once I'd wanted to be a university lecturer, like my father, and I'd imagined having my own office, and a little terraced house in a cathedral city with tree-lined streets, long shadows in late summer and people cycling home from work looking in through my window and seeing lots of books and flourishing plants. That wasn't going to happen now. But I did teach, sort of, and the river and the sea were beautiful, and I didn't have a boss watching me all the time. Surely it didn't matter where you were, as long as you were happy?

'It's not a failure to not get everything you apply for,' I said. 'I fail all the time, but it's just not so obvious. No one really buys my books, for example. But life isn't all about success. We don't all have to be Rosa Cooper. It's OK to just be. That's what we're doing, isn't it?'

'I just want to make an honest living, babe. That's all I want. Save up, maybe buy some cheap land. We could build our farm and live off the land. Then none of it would matter. You still want that, don't you?'

'Of course. But . . .'

'What?'

'You've been completely shutting me out recently. Please — we have to try to talk more, and perhaps not judge each other so much. Can we at least try for a bit and see how we get on? If we are going to go and live on a farm together then we have to stop having these stupid arguments, and we have to be able to not get frosty with each other the whole time.'

I didn't say it, but I suddenly thought about the process of writing a second draft of a novel. That was what we needed: a second draft of our relationship, where all the conflict was pushed into act one, and everything that was wrong with us became an obstacle that we'd already overcome. We would live happily ever after because of all that stuff, not despite it. If we stopped arguing, could I live on a farm with him? What if he started reading books? Maybe his character just needed a little tweaking. Or maybe mine did. Christopher had never much wanted to have sex, but I'd initiated it every so often. But since kissing Rowan I hadn't been able to do it either. What would we do about that?

Christopher started crying again. 'I am a monster. Fuck. I said I wasn't, but I am. Babe, can you forgive me? I'm a real shit sometimes, but I do love you.'

'Shh,' I said. 'It's OK.'

'I don't deserve you.'

'Don't be silly.'

I yawned. Then I felt anxious because I'd yawned. But nothing happened. He didn't accuse me of not taking him seriously, or being tired for no good reason. Instead, he leaned over and kissed me on the cheek.

'You're tired,' he said. 'Let's go to bed.'

In my entire life I'd never used any version of the phrase 'making love'. I'd noticed it about myself, and I had never been sure why. I'd had some boyfriends who'd used it, but I always talked about 'having sex' or 'fucking'. Was it because making love sounded like a drippy, hippy thing from my parents' era? In darker moments I asked myself whether it was simply because I'd never been in love. Sometimes Libby talked about what she felt for Mark, and I just couldn't understand it. She seemed to want *him*, not what he could give her. Sex, when it worked, was just a physical pleasure for me, like eating and exercise, or even sneezing. That night we went through three condoms before we could even get started. Christopher hated condoms because he could never put them on properly, and I didn't like them much either. But as we hardly ever had sex it seemed pointless to use any other form of contraception. Eventually I managed to get a condom to stay on, and then Christopher pulled me on top of him and started poking around, looking for a way in. 'You're too dry, babe,' he said, so I did something I'd never done before: I thought of Rowan until my body did what it was supposed to do. Then we had sex.

I got up afterwards and went to the kitchen and found some cocoa. Then I realised that I felt quite nauseous, as if Christopher was a stranger I'd just fucked in the toilet during a party while my real partner slept at home. I couldn't face cocoa, so I just drank a glass of water instead. Then I fed the burned sausages to B and washed up the grill pan. I sat and did the crossword for a while, wishing I could have a shower without Christopher knowing. Before I went back to bed I went upstairs to my study and looked at my ship, and tried to fathom how it had washed up at my feet. For a second, it was just me and the ship there, in our bottle, and nothing outside existed. There were no bank statements, no dust and neglect, and no man sleeping downstairs who I knew needed me, but did not really love me.

I'd just turned nine when the Coopers moved into the house next door. We were the end terrace in a street near the cathedral, and the house next to us had been empty for a long time. Mr Cooper had a big beard and taught at the same university as my father, but in humanities, not science. He went off every morning on his bicycle with a large brown satchel and a flask full of oxtail soup. Mrs Cooper wore jeans all the time and had her red hair cut short. She was a mature student at the university, studying psychology. They had one son and one daughter. Caleb was a teenager with long hair who didn't wear shoes, except when he was at school. Rosa was a year younger than me and pale all over: her skin was bright white, her hair was light red and her freckles were the colour of very weak tea. The Coopers had several cats, and not long after they moved in I saw Mrs Cooper on her hands and knees by their back door installing a cat-flap. There was lots of banging and drilling for the first couple of weeks. My father said we had to be understanding about this, but my mother complained all the time that the banging woke Toby. Still, our two families quickly became friends. For some reason we rarely went to their house, but there was usually a Cooper in our house, even if it was just one of the cats. Every Tuesday afternoon I walked home with Rosa and she had her tea at our place, because Mrs Cooper had a late seminar. My father and Mr Cooper played chess together in our dining room every Friday evening, and were always talking about the university: the relative merits of the different deans, the underlying motivation of the Vice Chancellor and which common room had the best cheese rolls. Even Caleb came sometimes to talk about the true nature of the universe with my father, who lent him books full of equations.

After the Coopers had been in the house for about a month, strange things began happening. Every night, at about nine o'clock, just after I went to bed, there'd be a big crashing sound, followed by a series of dense thuds, like books falling on the floor. After this there would be the sound of footsteps, and sometimes someone crying: I knew it was Rosa, although I never said anything. The cats would make echoey mewling sounds and clatter out of the cat-flap as if they were being chased by a pack of dogs. This would go on until about one in the morning, and then I'd finally get to sleep for an hour or so before Toby woke up. Then I'd lie there awake again, listening to my mother as she padded down to his room and then up and down the corridor trying to soothe him. Sometimes my father would come out and remind her that the best thing to do with a crying baby is leave it to cry. It was almost impossible to get any sleep.

My mother and father had long conversations about the noises next door. Should they say something to the Coopers or not? If they did, would it embarrass them? Would they be seen as interfering? My mother thought that maybe mild Mr Cooper was beating his wife. My father suggested that what we were hearing was probably just the radio, or Caleb doing something crazy, or even our imaginations. It was a cold November, and the air smelled of smoke, apples and fireworks. I was back at school after the strike finished, and was still haunted by my experiences in the forest with Robert and Bethany. Every night when I went to bed I imagined the monster coming, and not being able to overcome it. At one point I decided that this monster couldn't see you unless you could see it, and I could almost fall asleep with my blankets over my head even though it was hot, and a bit difficult to breathe. Of course, the noises next door made all this worse, and soon I was falling asleep at school, and crying whenever we had a spelling test.

My teacher was called Miss Scott, and everyone loved her. She was young and beautiful and wore long dresses in soft colours. Other classrooms had gerbils and guinea pigs, but we had a bright white rat called Herman. Other classes did science experiments with litmus paper and lemon juice, but Miss Scott brought in a camping stove one day and boiled eggs and told us that the whole process was science, but made it sound magical. One day she asked me to stay in the classroom when the other children went out for playtime.

'Meg,' she said. 'You seem very unhappy.'

I couldn't help it. I started to cry again. 'I am,' I said.

'Do you want to tell me about it?' she said.

I shook my head.

'You need to tell someone. What about your parents?'

'They'll get cross.'

'I won't get cross. I promise.'

Something in her eyes made me think I could trust her, so I told her everything about going to the forest and meeting Robert and Bethany and how I'd been too scared to learn any magic and how Robert had told my fortune.

'And now I'm scared of the monster,' I said. 'I don't know when it's going to come and get me. If I'd learned magic properly maybe I would be able to overcome it, but now I can't. I can't sleep, and everything's scary. And there are noises next door all the time, and I'm sure it's the monster coming to get me.'

'Gosh,' she said. 'Well, that does sound a bit frightening.'

'Are you cross?' I asked.

'Why would I be cross?' She picked up a piece of red chalk and then put it down again. 'Now, Meg. Do you know the difference between a lie and a story?'

'I'm not lying! And it's not a story.'

'It's all right. I'm not saying you're lying. But you are good at stories — you won a special prize for telling stories, didn't you? It's not a bad thing to be good at telling stories, and in some ways everything we tell is a story, but sometimes it's good to remember which parts of the stories we tell are true, and which parts are made up.'

'You don't believe me,' I said. 'It is true. It did happen. I know it did.'

'I do believe you. I just . . .' Miss Scott frowned. 'Oh, dear.'

I started crying again. 'I wanted to tell my mum,' I said. 'But my dad . . .'

'What about your dad?'

'Nothing. He gets cross about things like this. He's a materialist.'

A couple of years before, I'd sat on my father's lap and asked him what he did all day at the university. He told me that he spent most days looking at numbers and doing calculations in order to try to find out how old the universe was. He said his whole job was like being a detective where you look at clues and find out what things are made of or how old they are. I asked why he wanted to know how old the universe was, and he said that was a good question, but a difficult one. I remembered something from school assembly and suggested that perhaps he wanted to know more about God, and his smile died and he put me down on the floor and told me it was time for bed.

Miss Scott smiled. 'Look,' she said. 'Let's assume that it happened just as you said. Robert was right when he said that not everybody should know their fortune. For one thing, your fortune isn't set in stone. It tells you more about your character than what's actually going to happen to you in the future. I think that what Robert was telling you was that you're not the kind of person to overcome monsters. That's a good thing, isn't it? Remember the story of Beauty and the Beast? The Beast looked like a monster, but all he needed was love, and then when Beauty really loved him he turned into a prince. In that story, Beauty didn't overcome the monster either; she loved him, and they lived happily ever after. Look at Herman.' I looked over to the corner of the room, where Herman was meandering through one of his cardboard tubes. 'Lots of people would think Herman was a monster. They'd say,

"Urrgh! A rat!", and maybe they'd want to try to "overcome" him with rat poison. That wouldn't be very nice, would it?'

I shook my head. 'No.'

'Have you heard about something called the Vietnam War?' Miss Scott asked me.

'I don't know,' I said. I had heard the words, but I didn't know what they meant.

'America, which is a very big country, decided that it would overcome the monster of communism,' she said. Then she laughed. 'Oh, dear, I think this example is going to become too complicated. But do you understand what I've been saying so far?'

I nodded.

'Basically, I don't think there are any such things as monsters,' Miss Scott said.

'All grown-ups say that.'

'Ah — yes, I see what you mean. But what I'm saying is that if a monster, or something you call a monster, comes to see you and you become its friend, it stops being a monster, at least to you. In that sense, there don't have to be any such things as monsters. You have to decide something is a monster before it becomes one.'

'What if the monster doesn't want to be your friend?'

'Well, then I suppose in an ideal world you would go your separate ways and leave each other alone. The main thing is that you don't have to be violent towards something just because you don't like it. I think that's what your friend Robert meant. I think he was saying that you are naturally a kind person. That's a good thing.'

'But he also said I'd come to nothing.'

'Well, that is more tricky,' said Miss Scott, 'I agree. How did he say it?'

'He had a scary face, and scary eyes.'

'What was his voice like?'

I tried to remember. 'It wasn't quite as scary as everything else.'

'Do you think he was also saying that this might be a good thing?'

'How can it be a good thing?'

Miss Scott smiled. 'Some religions think nothing is the best thing of all.'

'How can they say that?'

'It sounds a bit odd, I know. But I think that the "nothing" they talk about is more of a mystery than a nothingness. It's about leaving the physical world behind and embracing something more spiritual. Have you heard of Taoism?'

'Dow-ism?' I repeated.

'It's more of a "way" than a religion. In Taoism, it's only nothingness that gives anything meaning. A cup is only useful because it has an empty space inside for your tea, for example. The best part of a house isn't the walls and the roof, but the space inside, where you live. There's a lovely passage from the *Tao Te Ching* — "The Book of the Way" — about the world being formed from a void. All the physical things you see are cut out of a big sheet of material, and this material is nothingness, or the void. The Tao says you should use the things, but remember the essence of the void. I don't know if this is what your friend meant, but again, "coming to nothing" could be coming to a place of peace or simplicity, a place where you understand the fabric of the universe, not just the patterns you can cut from it. Or perhaps it means you won't be successful in a conventional sense . . .'

'You're using lots of complicated words,' I said.

'Sorry.' She smiled. 'You're right. Look, I have a very dear friend whom I can't help but think of. Someone once told him he would come to nothing too. He was at a very strict school where they had the cane, and freezing cold showers, and the headmaster told him one day that he was a very lazy boy and would "never make anything of himself". Have you heard that expression?'

I nodded. 'I think so.'

'When grown-ups say that, they mean you won't become famous or successful. You won't become a prime minister, or even get a good job in a bank. You'll, in a sense, come to nothing. In a way, the headmaster was right. My friend lives in a caravan and reads books all afternoon. At night he goes to work in a factory, and then he sleeps all morning. He once went around India in a bus! In a sense you could say he hasn't made anything of himself, because he hasn't become rich and famous, and he doesn't have a family and a house, but he's very happy with his simple life. He knows lots of things from the books he's read. He learned how to make his own wine, and how to fix the engine on his car, just from books.'

I couldn't quite visualise all the things Miss Scott was talking about, but somehow I felt better from talking to her. Just before the bell rang for the end of playtime, she went to her desk and took out a little bottle of liquid with a tiny pipette in it. She told me to open my mouth, and then she put two drops of the liquid on my tongue.

'This will make you feel a lot better,' she said.

The strange noises continued next door, but I wasn't so bothered by them. I was sleeping more soundly, but my parents weren't. Some nights I would wake up and overhear things. One night my mother was crying and saying, 'I can't take it any more. What are we going to do about the children?' Another night she was saying, 'You're so cold,' over and over again, in a high, breathless voice. I tried not to think about all of this. Every evening after tea I would be sent to my room to read on my own for an hour. This was in preparation for homework, which I would be getting for the first time the following year. I'd decided that this hour would be my magical training time. If Miss Scott was right, and Robert had meant to tell me kind things, then surely there was nothing wrong with trying just a little bit of magic. If I could do magic, I thought, I could make everything all right, and stop my parents from arguing and do things to make their lives easier, like make Toby sleep better and cure my father's headaches. I had a matchbox that I'd taken from downstairs, and I would put it in my desk and concentrate on it. But I'd be half-thinking all sorts of things as I willed it to rise, and of course it didn't work.

One Saturday my mother took Rosa and me to a jumble sale in the church down the road. I'd always worn jumble-sale clothes, and I needed new jeans. Toby was in his pushchair sucking on a rusk, and Mum gave Rosa and me 20p each, supposedly to buy whatever we wanted, although we knew to check with her first before we handed the money over for something. In the past, kids we knew had bought all kinds of unsuitable things at jumble sales, including cap guns, sparklers, scented erasers, snuff and, apparently, from a half-blind old woman, *The Joy of Sex*. We went straight to the book stall and started looking for things that we weren't allowed to buy, because we knew from experience that we could read quite a lot of dirty bits before it was time to go home. Then, while Rosa was lost in something called *Teach Yourself Tantric Sex*, I saw it: a thin, red paperback called *ESP: The Sixth Sense*. It was a Macdonald Guidelines book, with a terrifying cover depicting a huge eye with a ghostly woman inside it. I picked it up and started flicking through it. There was a picture of Uri Geller bending a spoon and various images of séances, people walking through fire, dream symbols, dowsing and faith healing. Although the picture on the front was too horrible to look at for very long, I felt something stirring in me as I looked through the rest of the book. The last section showed you how to develop your own extra-sensory skills. I had to have it. It was 15p. I picked up an Enid Blyton book I didn't already have and wandered over to my mother, who was deep in conversation with one of the neighbours.

'Mum, can I get these?' I said.

She hardly looked at the book underneath the Enid Blyton.

'Yes, love,' she said.

Later, in my bedroom, as I lay on my bed completely absorbed in my book, Rosa, who had finished her Secret Seven novel, got up from the beanbag she'd been curled up on and wandered over, yawning. She got on the bed with me and bounced a bit.

'Stop it,' I said. 'I'm reading.'

'What's it about?'

'ESP,' I said. 'But it's a secret, so don't tell anyone.'

'What's that?' she said, looking over my shoulder and pointing at a picture.

'This bit's about poltergeists,' I said, stumbling slightly over the word.

'Oh,' she said coolly. 'We've got one of those.'

'I told you we often have ferry disasters,' I said to Rowan.

It was Tuesday morning, and the Higher Ferry, also known as the Floating Bridge, had broken down. All the locals had got out of their cars and were making phone calls, lighting cigarettes or inspecting whatever piece of the ferry they thought wasn't working. The few tourists and out-of-towners were sitting in their cars watching the ferry men. Rowan, who never usually got the ferry at this time, had been leaning over the safety rail looking at one of the waterwheels, but was now looking at me. I was looking back at him, and suddenly something happened with our eyes: they touched. Somewhere in the air between us, we touched without touching. I didn't want to let go, and perhaps he didn't either, because we held each other's gaze like this for almost ten seconds. It was as if we were about to kiss again.

'You also told me never to go on the Lower Ferry,' he said, dropping his eyes.

'It feels worse,' I said, dropping mine and looking briefly

down the river and out to sea. How would you describe a moment like that? How could you know anything had happened at all?

Rowan took off his glasses and rubbed his eyes. Thin folds of skin puffed around his eyes like rows of underfed basking sharks, and his face was the pale grey of a moonlit sea. He looked as if he hadn't slept for a week. He was wearing his duffel coat and jeans as usual and his hair stuck out at crazy angles.

'But this is the one that always seems to be breaking down,' he said, leaning over the safety rail again, dangling his glasses.

'This is a magnificent piece of Victorian engineering,' I said.

'You're right,' Rowan said. 'Year of construction?'

'Pass,' I said. 'Some local engineer stole the idea from a Scottish student, though.'

'1831,' Rowan said. 'At least that's when it was opened. The engineer was James Rendel, and the Scottish student was James Nasmyth. He didn't exactly "steal" the idea. Or maybe he did. Nasmyth was an engineer when Rendel met him, but he told him about this mad idea he'd had when he was a student, about boats being attached to cables, and Rendel decided to give it a try.'

'Aha,' I said. 'This is why you're a historian and I'm a novelist. I sort of knew most of that, but I'd forgotten it. How do you know so much about the Higher Ferry?'

'The Greenway project,' Rowan said. 'Before Agatha Christie and her husband lived there it was owned by James Marwood Elton, the High Sheriff of Devon. He didn't want a bridge, which was why people were interested in finding some other way of crossing the river. The Floating Bridge was originally powered by a couple of horses. Agatha Christie would have travelled on the ferry.'

'When she disappeared?'

I already knew from Rowan that Agatha Christie had become so pissed off with her husband's affair that she'd staged a disappearance. She'd left her car in a ditch and gone to a spa in Harrogate, where she checked in under a false name, perhaps even, I remembered, the name of her husband's mistress. When the newspapers found out, they went so wild that Agatha Christie had to pretend to have had a nervous breakdown. A year or so later she filed for divorce, went on an archaeological dig and met the man who would become her second husband. He was fourteen years younger than her and was apparently pushing her in her wheelchair when she died of natural causes at the age of eighty-five. I remembered the way Rowan had told me that detail, with a pessimistic smile.

'No,' he said. 'She only moved to Greenway after she had married Max Mallowan, the archaeologist.' He put his glasses back on and leaned against the safety rail, facing me. 'Apparently on sat-nav the Higher Ferry shows up as a B-road.'

'I heard that some sat-navs really freak out when you cross the river. I don't know if it's an urban myth or not. One of Libby's out-of-town friends claims that when she drove onto the Lower Ferry the sat-nav started saying, "Turn back now! You are in danger! You have driven into a river." Or something like that.' I looked at his car. 'You've got sat-nav in there, presumably?'

'Yeah, Lise had it installed,' he said. 'But I keep it switched off. I think I know where I'm going, most of the time.' He looked over the side of the ferry again. 'Where are these cables, do you think?'

I went and stood next to him, and we both hung over the rail. Our arms were separated by at least four layers of clothing and about two inches of air.

'Underneath, I guess. They must run across the river bed.'

'Apparently one time when it sank a herd of cows were on board, and they had to swim to safety.' He paused. 'Didn't you tell me that?'

'Yeah. And there was that time in the eighties when the cables snapped and the ferry was swept downriver. It was like what happened last year, but worse. It mowed down something like twelve yachts. It also had an ambulance on it, carrying a woman to hospital, and she died. Some people say that on stormy nights you can see the faint outline of an ambulance on the ferry, and hear her weakening cries.'

Rowan went pale. 'God,' he said. 'That's awful.'

'Yeah. Well, I'm sure most of it isn't true.'

He turned and faced upriver, but I wasn't sure what he was looking at.

'How's the chapter going?' I asked.

'Oh. Probably too much research, not enough writing.'

'You mentioned cultural premonitions before,' I said. 'I meant to look up some examples, because I was intrigued. But I forgot.'

'Well, the most famous one is from 1898, fourteen years before the *Titanic* sank, when a writer called Morgan Robertson wrote a novel called *The Wreck of the Titan,* all about a supposedly unsinkable ship that is sunk by an iceberg on its maiden voyage. The two and a half thousand passengers drown because there aren't enough lifeboats, just like on the actual *Titanic.* They don't bother to have them because the ship is apparently indestructible.'

'But you don't think this was a real premonition?'

'No, of course not. In the chapter, I'm arguing that if you were a novelist writing about an unsinkable ship, and you wanted to name it, you'd presumably be in the same mindset as someone naming a real ship. *Titan, Titanic:* it's plausible that both the novelist and the person naming the real ship would think along the same lines. It's not as if the word "Titanic" wasn't used frequently before the boat came along, and it's always used to describe some great thing that is eventually overthrown. Byron used it to describe Rome before it fell. "In the same dust and blackness, and we pass / The skeleton of her Titanic form, / Wrecks of another world, whose ashes still are warm." And when it comes down to it, if a boat like that sinks, people will usually drown because the authorities, believing the ship is unsinkable, don't take sufficient precautions, and don't install enough lifeboats. None of it's that far-fetched. So it's not so much a supernatural premonition of the future, but a different kind of premonition, or prediction, based on cultural factors and things people would reasonably know, or guess.'

I started peeling a tangerine from my anorak pocket. 'It's interesting that whoever named the real *Titanic* called it that. I'd never thought about it before. It's almost as if they wanted it to sink, or they knew it would. I mean, the Titans were defeated by the Olympians, weren't they, and the word "Titanic" has a sense of tragedy and doom before you even start. It goes with the vaingloriousness that Hardy writes about: "Dim moon-eyed fishes near / Gaze at the gilded gear / And query: 'What does this vaingloriousness down here?'"'

'This is what I wanted to talk to you about,' he said. 'I wanted to run my tragedy theory past you. Do you mind if I do it now? It looks like we're stuck here for a while, and there's no one else to really talk to about this.'

Not even Lise? I thought. But this wasn't really a surprise, since no one seemed to talk to their long-term partners about the things they were really interested in. Bob knew nothing about Libby's knitting; she barely knew how many strings a guitar had. Whenever Taz finished a painting, my mother would say it was very beautiful but far too complicated for her to properly understand. It seemed to be one of the small sadnesses of contemporary life that there was always someone in the office, or down the road, or across the river who understood your inner soul better than your partner did, not that I had any such person. Christopher had seemed to understand my inner soul once, I remembered, but he was well out of date on that score now. I wasn't even sure he knew how many books I'd published. But who was I kidding? Lise might not know about the *Titanic*, but she would know everything else that was important about Rowan: his favourite colour, his middle name, how he liked his tea, whether or not he snored, why they'd never had children. The list could go on for ever. And Rowan couldn't have been that desperate to talk to me. He still hadn't emailed me after all.

'I don't mind,' I said. 'I'm thinking of putting something about the *Titanic* in my novel. I thought I might start with the Hardy poem, or include it somehow. So talking to you is research for me too. It's also an interesting conversation to have while we wait to drown.'

Rowan pulled himself up on the safety rail and leaned over the edge of the ferry. For a moment I thought he might fall in the river. His feet were no longer on the deck. He turned himself around and hoisted himself up further so that he was now sitting on the safety rail, with nothing behind him but air, and below that, water.

'OK, so the whole book—my book—is about disaster. Obviously it's around shipwrecks and disasters at sea, but I wanted to theorise it partly through ideas of *affect*, but also around the structuring of disaster. I wanted to look at whether disasters "just happen" and then people become unhappy, or whether there's more to it than that. Perhaps the narrative runs the other way: people become unhappy, and then there is disaster. When I started the *Titanic* chapter I thought I was arguing that there's no way to tell the difference between a fictionalised disaster and a real one, using the philosopher Baudrillard. My plan at first with this chapter was to suggest that the cultural premonitions were the simulations, a bit like shipwreck-themed Disneylands, that existed to cover up the fact that these disasters are real and inevitable.'

'I've come across Baudrillard,' I said. '*The Matrix* was supposedly a dramatisation of his ideas, but he said it didn't work because he was more or less saying that when everything becomes signs referring to other signs, then there's no way out, and in *The Matrix* there is a way out. I think that's it.'

'That's right. He talks about things like the map that becomes so detailed that it turns into the thing it was supposed to represent. It's about how you represent the real, and whether this affects the real in some way. If you fictionalise everything, does everything become fictional, for example? If you organise a fake holdup, how do you keep it "fake" when the people who are frightened by it and believe it to be real are feeling actual fear? For me this was an unfamiliar way of thinking about familiar things, but very useful. Then I started reading Paul Virilio on disaster, and found that he suggests disaster is built into every man-made system, so then I started thinking that we can expect not just disasters, but premonitions of disasters, around every piece of technology, and that's *why* they're inevitable. Something similar to, but a bit more complicated than, a self-fulfilling prophecy.'

I ate a piece of my tangerine. 'Sounds very interesting. Are you throwing yourself overboard?'

Rowan looked as if he'd forgotten he was sitting on the rail. He looked over his shoulder and then back at me. His hands gripped the rail more tightly and the wooden bracelet he always wore — made from pieces of the shipwreck that left his grandfather stranded on the Galápagos Islands — shifted and then settled on his wrist. He smiled. 'Wouldn't be a bad idea.'

'But that really would be a disaster,' I said, quietly.

He shrugged. 'Maybe it's true that disaster is built into everything. Anyway, it's OK. I'm holding on.'

'So how does tragedy come into all this?' I asked.

'Virilio makes a distinction between artificial accidents and natural ones. He says whenever you build something like an unsinkable ship you have to invent, along with the ship, the possibility of it sinking. I'm arguing that premonition then becomes entirely reasonable and rational because people are simply reading technology as tragic. People somehow know that technology is always doomed. All that hubris. Anything "unsinkable" is destined to sink eventually.'

'That's probably true,' I said. 'So in act one you have something big and shiny and vainglorious. You're right. By act three it has to be sunk, or whatever, otherwise the narrative wouldn't work.'

'But why exactly is that?' Rowan said.

I shrugged. 'Because narrative is about change. All stories of success begin with failure, and the reverse. Love stories begin with loneliness; loneliness stories begin with love.'

'But is life the same as narrative?'

If it was, then was I in a love story, a loneliness story or both?

I laughed. 'Well, by definition, no. But also by definition, yes.'

'Because . . . ?'

'Well, all narrative is simulation, as you say. Narrative is representation, or imitation, or mimesis — it stands in for something that it is not. Your *Titanic* premonitions are narratives that seem to chime with a "real" narrative. But even a "true story" isn't life, by definition. Life is life. But on the other hand all we know about it is what exists as narrative. As Plato says, there are true stories and there are false stories. The only difference, presumably, between a premonition story about the *Titanic* and a real account of it is the timing and perhaps some detail, for us, since I'm guessing that neither of us has ever seen the *Titanic* or met anyone who was on board. For us, the *Titanic* is also a story, because everything we know about it comes through narrative and not through experience. Sorry; I'm brainstorming out loud. I think what I'm saying is that narrative has to have patterns, otherwise it wouldn't be narrative, and while life doesn't have to have patterns, the minute we express it as narrative it does have to have patterns; it has to make sense. Therefore we impose patterns on life in order that we can express it as narrative. Whenever something good happens, for example, we start anticipating its end.'

'What about poems, or sculptures? They're not narratives, but they still tell us about life. Life doesn't only have to be made sense of by narrative, does it?'

'I still think there's a narrative implied in poems and sculptures. You get a "fragment" or a "moment" and you then try to put it into some sort of whole. It's like trying to solve a puzzle. Warhol's Brillo Pad boxes, for example, only work when you reconstruct a narrative to go with them from the clues that you have. When you look at them close up, you see that although they seem to represent or imitate mass-produced items, they are clearly not mass-produced, because each one's different and obviously hand-painted. So you ask yourself, "Why has someone bothered to do this? Why has someone obviously taken time over this crap?" And this poses a dramatic question, where you're part of the story, because it's only in realising that you are examining these boxes that you also realise that you wouldn't bother if they were mass-produced, and that you think about the labour of an artist differently than you think about the labour of a factory worker. You also realise how many things you don't bother to examine closely. The packaging of every object tells a story, but we take those stories for granted and forget to defamiliarise them. The setting of a problem is always the beginning of a narrative. It's a knot that exists to be untied . . . God, sorry. I never get to talk about this stuff either, unless I'm teaching, and even then I can't say what I really want. I'm wittering on.'

'No; it's interesting. So you're saying that in narrative, and therefore in life, every moment can be read as part of a bigger narrative in which anything successful is doomed to failure, and anything big and shiny is doomed to crash and burn, and all rags will eventually turn to riches, which must therefore turn back to rags again, and so on?'

'Yes. More or less. But not necessarily all in the same story.'

'So in that case it's probably true, then: premonitions are people predicting narrative, rather than events. Telling tragic stories about things where tragedy appears to be inevitable. And then when the stories are compared — the "fictional" story and the "true" story — they are similar because they are stories.'

'I bet almost all stories with ships in them have some kind of disaster at sea, just like all stories with animals in them put the animals in peril. In narrative any equilibrium must become a disequilibrium. All narrative involves change from one state to another: happy to sad, or sad to happy usually. But it can be alive to dead, broken to fixed, confused to comprehensible, separate to together — anything.'

'Every ship is a shipwreck waiting to happen.'

'Yeah. After all, every ship is destroyed in the end, even if it's on purpose, at the end of its useful life. But the reason tragedy is so mysterious is because it isn't exactly predictable. There's always a moment in tragedy where disaster can be avoided, and what's interesting is looking at why the hero or heroine doesn't take this course of action. It's not a simple formula. Also, people probably get a feeling that an unsinkable ship will sink, because that seems like a good narrative formula, but plenty of people go on unsinkable ships. People don't only believe in formula and nothing else.'

He looked as if he might cry again, although maybe that was the effect of the cloud that had just obscured the weak sun.

'So the premonitions exist and don't exist at the same time?'

'Maybe. Mind you, and I don't know if it's relevant, but I did once read about a study of train crashes. Some researcher found that trains that crashed had fewer people on them than other trains. He thought this was because people "sensed" the impending accident. Also, the most badly damaged carriages had fewer people in them, suggesting, apparently, the same thing. But who knows how that study was done. It's a narrative itself.'

'Sounds worth following up, though,' Rowan said. 'Where did you read it?'

'Just some silly book on ESP from the seventies,' I said. 'Probably not a good source.'

'Oh. That's a shame. Can you give me the title anyway?'

'I think I've forgotten it. I can look it up, though.' I finished eating my tangerine and then threw the peel in the river. 'I'll email you.'

'No, don't go to any trouble,' he said quickly. 'Just tell me next time I see you. Next time we're in a shipwreck together.'

I shrugged. 'OK.'

'Did I tell you about the spiritualist on board the *Titanic*?' Rowan said. I shook my head, and he continued. 'W. T. Stead. He'd apparently drawn pictures of ocean liners, and his own death by drowning, years before. He'd also written about shipwrecks. Apparently he helped women and children into lifeboats, then went into the first-class smoking lounge, started reading a book and waited to drown. Although I don't know how anyone actually knows that. I wonder what book he was reading.'

The ferry lurched slightly, and someone said, 'Oh, God.' Rowan got down off the safety rail, half pushed off by the movement of the boat. If it had lurched in the other direction he probably would have fallen in the river. I wanted to take his arm, or his hand, but I didn't.

'Do you think the other people left on the *Titanic* were having conversations about great shipwrecks and disaster theory as it went down?' I said.

Rowan laughed. 'We're very brave.'

Then there was a shudder, and the sound of the engines

starting, and one of the ferry men came around saying, 'Crisis over, folks.' Then everyone got back in their cars. Rowan and I were the last to go. I almost said something about my ship in a bottle, and I suddenly wanted to arrange to take it to show Rowan one day soon, but I wasn't sure I could explain it properly in the few seconds it took to get to our cars. Instead, just before Rowan got in his car, and before I'd stopped to think about what I was doing, I slightly breathlessly asked him if he wanted to have lunch again one day soon. He turned and looked up from reading something on his mobile phone.

'I don't think that would be such a good idea at the moment,' he said, his eyes not meeting mine. 'Sorry.'

I had a long list of things to do that day, including beginning my new draft of my novel, but I could barely concentrate on anything for hours. I had my notebook out, and, perhaps fittingly for someone planning to re-fictionalise herself, I was scribbling in it as if I'd gone crazy; as if I'd been given one of those terrible 'automatic writing' exercises. There were pages of this stuff in the end. *Protagonist feels rejected by Love Interest. Need to get a sense of this as an actual, tangible, PAINFUL feeling. Show with action? What action? She can hardly sit in the library and cry all day. Also — there is a kind of hope in his rejection, because he obviously feels something for her. Otherwise, of course, there'd be no harm in lunch. So what would she do in response to this? Maybe just write in her notebook. (Ha, ha! Is this project in danger of becoming too meta-metafictional?) Protagonist writes a long list of reasons as to why he is unsuitable as a Love Interest for her, including his age, his gloominess, the fact that he is in a relationship. She can't believe that he has rejected her. Can he afford to reject her like this? Will he get any other chances? Maybe women throw themselves at him all the time. Maybe he'll never split up with his actual partner, even though he obviously doesn't love her. Or maybe he will leave her and end up going on country walks*

147

*with grey-haired, arty widows from singles ads because the
protagonist is TOO YOUNG. But also need some sense of this
connection between them, despite the age difference, and what
he does to her with his eyes and all the possibilities of his body
and . . .* At this point I stopped writing. I just couldn't imagine
him with anything other than black hair and strong forearms,
standing there in his knackered old jeans. Maybe I wouldn't
include a physical description of him in the novel. It probably
wasn't the kind of thing someone would write in a notebook,
especially if they had a partner who might read it at any time.

Before lunch, I checked my Orb Books email account, and
found nothing from Vi, as usual. Perhaps she'd written to my
other address; or maybe not. Anyway, there was plenty to read
from Orb Books. At our last editorial board meeting we'd
ended up brainstorming a rough character outline for Zeb
Ross, so that we could better think about how to present him
online. Claudia had finally typed up the profile and I was reminded that we'd decided that Zeb should be a mysterious recluse, who can go on the Internet, but never appear in magazines or in person. His vague profile on his various web pages
would say that he has dark hair and blue eyes, a medium build,
and dresses mainly in jeans and T-shirts. He had gone to a
boys' grammar school in Nottingham, where he was a loner
who enjoyed science and English. His parents were suburban
drones, who wanted him to go into finance or insurance, but
Zeb had other ideas. While working in a bookshop, he decided that he could easily write a novel himself, and so he did.
At the end of this Claudia had asked people for further ideas.
*Why is Zeb a recluse? Is he disfigured in some way and, if so,
how? Could we invent an accident for him? Let's make Zeb less
bland! Ideas, please, people!*

Over a salad, sandwich, some soup and another tangerine, I
spent almost all of lunchtime disfiguring Zeb. I imagined him
falling in a vat of acid, crashing his sports car, being attacked
by men with knives, cutting the wrong wire when trying to

defuse a bomb, running through a pane of glass or, indeed, being one of the few people who chooses to sit in a train carriage that is destined to derail and tumble over and over down an embankment until it eventually catches fire and the only way out is by smashing a window with a little hammer. I imagined him lost at sea, drowning. But drowning is total. You can't half-drown, and come back with the scars to prove it; not really. I imagined Zeb shipwrecked, and then I wondered why the word 'shipwrecked', applied to a person, implies a survivor: someone marooned and alone but alive.

After lunch I opened up the remains of the last draft of my novel to see what could be saved. There it all was: just over 30,000 words that were as familiar and boring to me as my own pallid face on winter mornings. I must have read my opening paragraph more than a thousand times; I could certainly repeat it by heart. It hadn't changed in two years, but now it was time for it to go. I created a new file with all the same styling as the old one, and typed *NOTEBOOK* at the top of the first page. The idea was that I would copy-and-paste anything usable into this file, and then construct notebook entries around it, perhaps even including the one I'd written this morning. After an hour I hadn't found anything I wanted to keep. This worried me, so I started a list instead in a new file: *Problems with this novel (again).* The items on it were: *It is boring; it has no focus; it is self-indulgent; I hate the central character; it's too depressing; no one wants anything; no one does anything; there are no questions to be resolved; there is too much narration.* Then I thought this would make a nice opening to *Notebook,* so I pasted the whole list onto the first page. I smiled at my own audacity. Surely no one, not even the most metafictional and post-modern of writers, had ever begun a novel with a list of its own faults?

My word-count for the novel was now 43, and it felt like I'd just had an enema. I spent the next hour or so reading over my real notebook, wondering how it would look in print.

Then I realised that what I'd written this morning had some narrative drive, so I typed it up under the list of *Problems with this novel (again)*. I looked at what I had. So far my new draft was a cheesy romance with some confusing metafiction. I deleted the bit about the love-interest and copied it into a new file called *Further Bits*. I checked the word-count again; it was back to a manageable 43. Then I didn't know what to do next, so I decided I may as well ditch the library and go to pick up my post from the PO box in Totnes, since this had turned out to be the new arrangement with Christopher. Forty-three words must be a record low for a day's writing, unmatched by even the most ponderous modernists. I wondered whether Zeb's disfigurement could have been the result of some early writer's block, before he found himself miraculously able to write four novels a year. Perhaps he poked out both his eyes with the same pencil.

Oscar had sent the books he'd promised. There they were in Totnes post office, in a huge mail sack, along with what looked like an unearned-royalty statement from my literary agency, which I wasn't in a hurry to open. They contrasted oddly, the thin envelope and the big grey sack, and on the way down the hill I felt like a burglar on my way to return some stolen goods, and carrying an apology note. I remembered another Zen story. A Zen master is in his hut when a robber turns up. The Zen master has nothing to steal: all he owns are the clothes on his back. Feeling sorry for the robber, who has come such a long way and made such an effort, the Zen master offers him these clothes. The robber takes them and runs off into the night, and the Zen master looks up at the sky and thinks, 'Poor fellow. I wish I could also give him this beautiful moon.'

It was just before four when I put the books in the car, and I realised that if I hung around for another forty-five minutes or so I could surprise Christopher by picking him up from the bus stop. I walked back up the hill and browsed for a while in the bookshop, looking for books on the *Titanic,* and trying to work out what Byron poem Rowan had been talking about. I tried randomly flipping open the pages of *Don Juan,* and then *Childe Harold's Pilgrimage.* On about the fourth flip I found the reference in *Childe Harold's Pilgrimage.* I considered buying the book, but it was almost £10 and seemed to tell a long, tragic story in verse. It was the kind of thing I would always mean to read, but never actually would. After all, I'd failed even to read an Agatha Christie novel that meant something to Rowan.

I was planning to get something for dinner from the Happy Apple, and I couldn't really afford to spend any more money, but I went to the Barrel House for a large soya latte anyway, thinking that there was probably a can of beans in the cupboard at home. There was a big pile of newspapers on a table in the corner, including the most recent *Sunday Times.* And there, on the front cover, was a picture of Rosa. She was perched on a wooden table with her legs crossed, looking as deeply into the camera as she could with her pale, faraway eyes.

Her interview was printed in one of the supplements over a double-page spread, and there was a pull-out quote of her saying, 'Of course I believe in ghosts.' It had never occurred to me that she would ever go public with the story of her family's poltergeist, but here she was talking about how terrified they'd all been to see books flying around the house every night, and how she still couldn't bring herself to buy a breakable ornament, just in case. She talked about the research she'd done for her part in *Bump in the Night,* and how it had further convinced her that there were unexplainable things out there. 'At some point in history, starting a fire would have looked like magic,' she said. 'Or listening to the radio, or speaking on the telephone, or using remote central locking on a car. Things seem like magic only when we don't understand the underlying forces that make them happen.' The structure of the piece followed the intertwined paths of Rosa's career and life to date, using the supernatural aspects of both as a focus. There was just one paragraph at the end about *Anna Karenina*, which she was due to start shooting in May. I half-read, half-scanned the article until I saw the detail that my mother had clearly felt she couldn't tell me: the actor due to play Vronsky was Andrew Grey. Drew. So they did get together in the end. Or they would now. I knew why my mother hadn't mentioned this, of course, but I wondered why she hadn't mentioned the detail about the poltergeist. Then I realised that we had never spoken about that episode since about 1980, when it had bizarrely become one of the 'irreconcilable differences' in my parents' divorce case.

Christopher wasn't at the bus stop, and when I went round to the project he wasn't there either. As darkness fell I drove home to Dartmouth on the back roads, known as the Lanes. These were ancient tracks on which people had probably travelled when compiling the Domesday Book. They had hedgerows on both sides and witchy cottages with smoke curling out of chimneys. On the Lanes I often got a strange feeling, as if I was back in that mysterious forest that I still wasn't sure I hadn't imagined in 1978. It was almost like becoming a fictional character in a world containing something more than the Standard Model and evolutionary theory, and in this world anything was possible, and things made a different, mysterious kind of sense. I wondered about Christopher, and where he was. He was probably at home, wondering where I was. If I told him I'd tried to pick him up he'd be happy, but then when he realised I'd failed he'd be sad. Perhaps he'd been killed in an accident on the project, and that was why he hadn't been at the bus stop. If he had been killed, I found myself thinking, then I'd be free. I erased the thought from my mind, but I couldn't undo the fact that I'd had the thought in the first place.

• • •

Christopher usually returned home at around half past five, but there was no sign of him by six. I barely noticed his continued absence until then, so busy was I with the contents of Oscar's sack. Anyone walking into the sitting room would probably think that I had lost my mind. There, laid out in front of me, were three gigantic piles of New Age, esoteric and self-help books, roughly separated into three categories: 'Stupid', 'Offensively stupid' and 'Absurd but well-meaning'. Where was something sensible like *New Scientist* when I needed it? Here, in front of me, were so many different kinds of madness that I could hardly breathe. Even B looked baffled, and had already knocked over the 'Stupid' pile once by wagging her tail at it. This particular way B had of wagging her tail was, to my mind, her way of asking, 'What on earth are you doing?' It was a half-wag, a low wag, that stopped and started like a misfiring propeller. I re-stacked the 'Stupid' pile and wondered if there really were that many people who felt so victimised by contemporary life, with its electromagnetic fields, meetings, childcare worries, pollution, radiation, mobile-phone masts, caffeine, sugar, monosodium glutamate, logical husbands and emotional wives, that they needed a book, or several books, to get over it and learn things like downshifting, going organic, positive thinking, saying no to people, overcoming anxiety, loving without conditions, establishing boundaries, asserting themselves and breathing correctly.

My 'Absurd but well-meaning' pile was the smallest, and B knocked this over next on her way to curl up on the armchair. As well as *Second World* by Kelsey Newman, this pile included a book on dog psychology called *The Dog Whisperer*, with which I vaguely threatened B as she went past. There was also an academic-looking book called *Radical Healing*; a book called *The Fool and His Journey* that came with a pack of Tarot cards; a book called *Mapping the Astral Plane*; and one I'd set aside partly for myself, but also for Tim, called *Taming the Beast.* These might create the beginnings of a good feature, I thought.

In contrast, my 'Offensively stupid' pile, which had remained erect, contained books that were big and brash and that each featured a TV psychic or a white-teethed guru with a list of at least twenty other publications to his or her name. Many of these books had garish covers, large type, pictures of beaches, palm trees, angels or the moon, and blurbs full of exclamation marks. They were obviously aimed at people who recognised the TV psychics as old friends, and who would use anything the cosmos had to offer in order to try to win the Lottery and go to bed with more people. There were DIY kits that enabled you to connect with your guardian angel or spirit guide; collections of love spells; teach-yourself books on harnessing the power of runes, the I-Ching and astrology; primers on connecting with your past lives and finding out whether you were indeed Cleopatra, Shakespeare or Elizabeth I; achieving success; and — heavens above — cosmic ordering. The cosmic-ordering book had a quote on it from a washed-up game-show host from the eighties. The esoteric had gone horribly mainstream. I rang Libby.

'I can't cope,' I said.

'What with?'

I giggled. 'I've got a book here that says all I need to do if I want something is ask the universe for it. You can, apparently, even "super fast track" your order. I've got about fifty similar books. I said I'd write a feature on them for the paper. I must have lost my mind.'

'Maybe you could ask the universe to write the feature for you.'

'Good idea. This book, which, by the way, is all of fifty pages long, was featured on afternoon TV. "You too can have everything you desire!" That's what it says on the back. Apparently the author went from "zero to hero" using this method and earned lots of pound-signs.'

'Presumably nobody ever desires anything like world peace.'

'No.'

'Or hand-knitted socks.'

'That would be useful, actually. By the way, how are you?'

'Oh, awful. The same.'

'Can you talk?'

'Not really.'

'Bob's there?'

'Yeah. Bob's got a new book of guitar riffs. He's about to crank up his amp and start rocking out, aren't you, dear?'

'Oh, well, say hi to him for me.'

'Meg says "Hi",' Libby said. I could hear Bob say something cheerful back.

'You'll never guess what,' I said.

'What?'

'Drew's playing Vronsky in *Anna Karenina*. With Rosa.'

'What, Drew-your-ex?'

'Yeah. How sick is that? He always fancied her.'

'God.' She sighed. 'Why is life so complicated?'

'Don't ask me. So what am I going to do with all these books?'

'I don't know. All that stuff would give me a headache,' Libby said.

'It's giving me one,' I said. 'I find it all so depressing, but I don't know why. Actually, I do know why. In the past I've always got a bit pissed off with those broadsheet sceptics who make their living being passionately angry about homoeopathy, God, synchronicity or whatever, because it's as if they can't get beyond their emotions, and in their rage they become as faith-driven as the beliefs they criticise. I always said they give scientists a bad name. After all, science has to be about asking unthinkable questions, not closing down debate. But I can honestly see where they're coming from now. I mean, so much of this New Age stuff is obviously just a total rip-off.

Half the books try to get you to pay to join a premium website at the end if you want to read more, just like those tabloid horoscopes where you get a couple of sentences on your career and then have to phone in to find out if it's your week for love. How can people do this to other people? How can they exploit vulnerable people's hopes and dreams like this?'

'Maybe people enjoy imagining this stuff. Maybe they don't think it's real.'

'Half the books claim to be able to improve people's love lives and career prospects, though, so they kind of are being encouraged to think of it as real.'

'It sucks.'

'It really does.'

'Do you think you're pissed off about Drew and Rosa and projecting it onto these books?'

'I don't know. Probably. And Christopher's disappeared as well. But honestly, these books are really terrible. If you could see them . . .'

'Well, never mind. Let's cosmically order something,' Libby said.

I laughed. 'We don't know how.'

'It can't be that hard if you said the book's so short. What does it say you have to do?'

I skimmed it. 'Um. OK, well, this'll work for my feature, at least. Did I mention that it's a gonzo feature?'

'What's that?'

'Where you do the thing you're writing about. So if you were writing about wrestling, you'd have a go at doing it. Or instead of going and writing about a village fête, you'd try to grow a prize marrow yourself. It's a bit like travel writing, because the writer is always in the story. I don't know if I want to be in this story at all. I'll have to become a complete idiot.'

'What's the point of being in the story, though, ideally?'

'It's so you can see what something's actually like, rather than make assumptions about it. I've got a friend who says that the human being is a big computer that can compute everything that machines can't — feeling, emotion and so on. For the human, no sum is too big. It's true, really. You can't learn about love from reading books. You have to experience it, especially if you want to write about it.'

'If you can only experience things through experience and not books, what's the point in writing books of your experiences?'

'I guess because you can only experience some things in one lifetime, so everyone experiences and writes different things. Or maybe having experienced love, or hate or whatever in one context, people are interested in reading about it in another context. You always ask such difficult questions.'

'Sorry. So . . . Cosmic ordering?'

I skimmed some more of the book.

'Right. You have to believe everyone's connected, which isn't that hard considering we must have a common ancestor, and then, blah, blah, just kind of ask the universe for stuff. There's lots of waffle. You have to activate your cosmic eye.'

'Your what?'

'It's in the middle of your forehead.'

'OK. Is that it? I've done it. So what do you want?'

I thought I didn't know what I wanted, but now I said, 'Money.' I breathed in deeply and felt an asthmatic crackle in my lungs. 'You know what?' I said, and coughed. 'I also want to move out of this damp, crappy house, and I want Christopher to start taking an interest in me, and I want some passion in my life. I want to know how to write my novel. Oh, and I'd quite like the ability to knit socks.'

Libby laughed. 'Easy. OK. So what do I want?'

'I don't know. What do you want?'

She sighed. 'God. This is hard.'

'You want Mark?'

'I don't know. I think so.' She dropped her voice to a whisper as the sound of an electric guitar started up in the background, with lots of reverb. Then there was the sound of a door closing, and the guitar noise dulled. Libby's voice became normal again. 'I'm in the kitchen.' She sighed. 'Yes, I do want Mark. But I also want Bob not to hate me. And I want Saturday night not to be a disaster and I really want my yarn to come so that I can start knitting the labyrinth . . .'

'I thought big men were building the Labyrinth.'

'Ha, ha. Didn't I tell you about the crazy book I got? It's called *Knit Your Own Fantasy Story.* Old Mary saw me with it at knitting club and started flicking through it for ideas for raffle prizes. You know they're having a raffle for the opening of the Labyrinth? She worked out that we could easily knit a labyrinth based on the maze pattern, and then sew it onto a landscape. She also wants to knit an enchanted forest and some mythical animals. So I'm doing the labyrinth and a couple of trees. Old Mary's knitting the landscape and the rest of the forest. I don't know why we're doing the forest, but Old Mary said she wanted the challenge. Did you get your wool, by the way?'

'Yeah. It's kind of silvery blue, with mohair in it. And I got a pattern for slippers. But I don't know when I'm going to have time to make them, what with this feature to do and my novel to write. You have to "block" them at the end. I was supposed to block my scarf. Is it worth it?'

'Yes.'

'Oh. It sounded a bit lame. Do you really have to pin things to a board?'

'Sometimes. Mostly I just shape things on a towel and leave them to dry on a clear table or something.'

'I don't have a clear table. Hang on a minute.'

I put the phone on the arm of the sofa and took off my cardigan. This house never warmed up, not even in the summer, but it had been getting more and more humid as I spoke to Libby, as if a storm was approaching. I picked up the phone again just as lightning flashed outside. 'God,' I said to Libby. 'Lightning.'

'Where?'

'Didn't you see it?'

'No.'

'You must have done.'

'You're probably imagining it. So what am I going to ask the universe for?'

'I don't know. True love?'

'Holy shit. You want money first; I want love, although I wouldn't say no to some money of my own either, and I'd like to be better at gardening. What else is there to want apart from money, love and creative talent?'

'World peace?'

'If everyone had money and love and creative talent there'd be no need for world peace. OK. Yes, I want love. I want Mark. Hey — what would happen if Bob found this book and cosmically ordered me to love him more than I love Mark?'

'The world would probably end,' I said.

By eight there hadn't been any more lightning, and Christopher still wasn't home. He didn't have a mobile phone, and I thought about ringing his father but didn't. Instead I sat looking at my knitting pattern for a while. Then I cast on the three stitches I needed to start the side of one slipper at the toe, and knitted one row. This took about one minute. The next row had an M1 increase, and so I had to go upstairs and get my *How to Knit* book so that I could study the diagram and find out how to do it. Then I made a cup of coffee and tried to do it, failed, and unravelled all my stitches and cast on again. The beautiful silvery blue wool was becoming worn and grubby already. I cut off the end and started again.

This was like my bloody novel. Everything I'd ever thought about it had seemed like a good idea once, and then I had another 'good idea' and had to delete the one before. Now I wondered how on earth I was going to use all these New Age books. OK, the feature provided a structure and focus for my protagonist, and would get her out and about a bit, but how would I use the notebook format to convey that she was embarking on this feature and not just randomly reading crap? And how would the books change my protagonist? Would she find that science triumphs over irrationality, or the reverse? Was there any other option? I sighed and unravelled my knitting again. Still no Christopher, and I was hungry.

I raided my coin jar, thinking there might be a couple of pounds in there, which would mean fish and chips for dinner, not beans on stale toast. But there was nothing more than 1p and 2p pieces, and I couldn't face taking a pile of them to the chip shop. If Christopher came home and asked, as he was likely to, what was for dinner, I thought that I might explode. Could he not decide what was for dinner just once? In the end I had beans on toast, washed down by very strong coffee, with *Second World* held open in front of me on the kitchen table. I couldn't help but be intrigued by Newman's new book, especially with that quote from Vi on it. Had she sent me his previous book? I would have to get in touch with her if I wanted to find out, but I still didn't know how.

While I ate my dinner, B did the same. Every night I would fill her bowl with mixer and one small tin of dog food. She would wolf down the tinned food, but then she would pick up a single piece of mixer — a biscuit the size of a small pebble — in her front teeth, carry it to the hallway, throw it up in the air, roll on it, and then eat it, *crunch, crunch,* like a radio sound effect for someone walking across gravel. Then she would come back and take another one. It took for ever. Sometimes she would 'bury' a piece of mixer or a rawhide chew. She never actually buried anything, of course, because the house wasn't full of earth, but merely went through a primal-looking set of movements that implied 'burying'. The final one of these movements made B look as if she was pushing imaginary earth over the biscuit with her nose. She did this very carefully, with a faraway look in her eyes, as if imagining herself the heroine in some dog-story.

While B and I ate, seagulls *ack, ack*ed outside, and the lonely wind waltzed slowly down the Brown's Hill steps and all around the town until it finally reached the river, where it found boats to dance with and swoon over, and everything tinkled.

Second World was in two parts. The first part, called 'The Science of the Second World', recapped the idea that we are being reincarnated again and again at the end of time into a world created by, and contained within, the Omega Point, which is made of *Energia*. The second part was called 'The Hero's Journey', and seemed to owe a lot to Joseph Campbell and Carl Jung. Newman referenced them both. At one point he said, 'What Jung termed the "Collective Unconscious" I am calling the Omega Point, although of course I have been able to use Frank Tipler's science to further hypothesise a conscious, infinite entity from which the archetypes emerge. Inside the Omega Point, we are all plagiarists: we all recognise the fundamental archetypes and use them in our dramas and dreams, fictional or otherwise. Could it be possible that the Omega Point invented the first stories to show us the ways we should and should not live? When we meet a Wise Old Man on one of our many Roads of Adventure, are we really meeting a manifestation of the Omega Point?'

Newman's argument was familiar. Life is a great quest, he said, and you are its hero. The purpose of life is the completion of the quest. To complete the quest you must work out what you most want to find in some faraway cave, then take some weapons, go out and find the cave and get this thing. Anything that stands in your way is a monster. How simple it all was, and how unlikely that the cave would turn out to be a vagina lined with teeth and that you would fail because of some laughing birds. But in any case, Newman didn't solve, or even acknowledge, his own central paradox. He didn't explain how you find out whether you are a hero or a monster. Some beings have to be monsters, because otherwise how do you define other beings as heroes? Instead of solving this problem, Newman spent a lot of time rejecting Greek tragedy as 'depraved', and Modernism as 'pathetic'. His reading of *Oedipus Rex* was particularly perplexing. Oedipus was no longer a profound symbol of the curse of knowledge and desire, and became instead, in Newman's world, a failed project, a Game Over, an aborted quest. In order to have a properly happy ending, Oedipus would need to die, be born again and start from scratch. It just wasn't any good to find out that you are a monster and overcome yourself: the monster has to be outside you, and you have to kill it and move on until you get your treasure and your princess and become enlightened and then ascend to the Road to Perfection. This was such a profound misunderstanding of tragedy that I wanted to email someone and rant about it. But who was there? Only Rowan. I sighed.

Reading Newman's book made me want to hand in my resignation as a writer. Most of what he said about conventional narrative structure in the quest, the comedy and the romance was right: even the Zen novel I read for Orb Books was fuelled by desire for change and for characters to lead better lives. At first the protagonists want to get off the island, and then they realise that if they stay they may achieve enlightenment and cast off all desire — so, paradoxically, they start to want that. All narrative is about people wanting their lives to be better, and then this being fucked up, either permanently by the protagonist him- or herself, or temporarily by his or her parents — or some equivalent. All you have to do, I would tell the writers who came on my retreats, is get one of these strands, knot it, put it in the centre of your narrative, and then add as many other strands as you like and weave them together so the resulting fabric looks like a whole. When I said this I had in mind the Fair Isle garments that Libby used to knit, and I even showed the ghostwriters pictures of Fair Isle knitting so they would get the point. They always laughed at the jumpers and cardigans with giant snowflakes and reindeer, and this made everyone bond.

After closing the book I made more coffee and then ate another tangerine. It had a little mini-tangerine inside it, at the top, as if it had given birth to a miniature version of itself while it was hanging on its tree. Where was Christopher? I probably should have rung his dad's place by now. There was that stupid royalty statement lying by the kettle. I hated those things: they were unintelligible, and came with no money. Sometimes they told me that I'd sold three copies of my book in South Africa, and another eleven in Canada. Whoopee. As if life wasn't disappointing enough already. But I opened it anyway, as I usually did in the end, thinking that maybe it would at least tell me I hadn't long to break even on a particular title, even though it was probably out of print. When I took out the single sheet of paper, I saw immediately that it wasn't an unearned-royalty statement at all. It was remittance advice from my literary agency. *Harlequin Entertainment,* it said. *£28,000, less Agency Commission of £2,800. Transfer to bank: £25,200.*

'What the fuck?' I whispered to myself. If it was true — and it couldn't be — then this meant I could go down the hill for fish and chips, and I could buy as many tangerines as I wanted, and I could take Libby a bunch of flowers and a bottle of wine on Saturday night, and I could buy some clothes and fix the car and God knows what else. I wouldn't have to worry about my train fare to London for the March editorial board. I could buy a new pen. I could get some credit for my mobile phone. I could get my email account back up and running. I could pay a few months' rent in advance and perhaps then get a good night's sleep once in a while. Maybe I could take my mother and Taz on holiday. They kept having to remortgage their house to help Toby, and although Taz sometimes made a lot of money from his art, some months he made nothing at all. I could go to Greece after all, on my own, and I'd even be able to buy a bikini first. I would finally be able to write my novel without any distractions. Maybe I could rent some office space to work in during the day, and go there instead of the library. But it probably wasn't true. There was probably no money. Then again, I had met Fred, and she had made all these promises; I just hadn't believed them.

The year the National Lottery first started I was in Brighton doing my degree, and I went home to London most weekends because I'd get free food at my mother's place and it was warmer there in the winter. Taz said he thought the Lottery was a waste of time and a tax on optimism, but my mother and I both bought tickets for the first draw. For almost the whole afternoon before it happened we planned what we'd do with the millions one of us was bound to win. We imagined big houses with swimming pools, and travel, and all the usual stuff. But it was more interesting thinking how we'd give some of it away. My mother said she'd start a women's refuge, with designer furniture and luxury toiletries. I said I'd find a student, someone in exactly the same situation I was in—heading for a First, but with no real career prospects, no financial stability and no house—and give them £100,000. By the time I lived in Dartmouth, I hadn't bought a Lottery ticket for years, but I still wondered why more people bought them on rollover weeks. Unless you were already a millionaire, surely five million wouldn't change your life much more than a million would. Surely a million was still worth winning. But if that was true, why didn't I ever buy a ticket?

I went upstairs to my study and logged onto my Internet banking service, not daring to believe this might be real. But there it was: a new balance in my business account of £22,340. So that was the business overdraft cleared, then. I transferred some money to my personal account to clear the overdraft there, and gave myself some spending money. When I'd finished, I was roughly £5,000 in credit on my personal account, and £15,000 in credit on my business account. I'd never had that much money in my life. I sent a PayPal payment to my email service provider, and once I'd put some credit on my phone I was able to retrieve my agent's replacement's messages that told me that the money was in, and they were doing a transfer. He said he was concerned because I'd never responded to the emails he'd sent about the offer, and he hoped it was OK that he'd signed the contract on my behalf. He also wondered whether we should meet to talk about current and future projects.

Just as I was about to reply I heard a scratching sound coming from downstairs: wild and insistent. B often shut herself in the bathroom and scratched on the door to tell me to let her out, but when I looked the door was open and she wasn't there. I went downstairs and found B asleep on the sofa, and the scratching noise was gone.

PART
TWO

When a piece of brown biscuit is offered to a terrier of mine and she is not hungry (and I have heard of similar instances) she first tosses it about and worries it, as if it were a rat or other prey; she then repeatedly rolls on it precisely as if it were a piece of carrion, and at last eats it. It would appear that an imaginary relish has to be given to the distasteful morsel; and to effect this the dog acts in his habitual manner, as if the biscuit was a live animal or smelt like carrion, although he knows better than we do that this is not the case.

—CHARLES DARWIN, *The Expression of the Emotions in Man and Animals*

AT ABOUT TEN the phone rang. It was Josh.

'Can you come to Dad's?' he said. 'Christopher's here and he's kicking off.'

So that's where he was.

'What's happened?' I said. 'Why's he kicking off?'

'It's about Milly moving in. But can you come?'

'Yeah, sure. I'll see you in a bit.'

I filled my car with petrol, bought two new bottles of Radweld and, after putting one of them into the car radiator, drove to Totnes down the Lanes. My hands, which did not look like the big, masculine hands on the diagram on the Radweld bottle, smelled of engine. At night you could go down the Lanes pretty fast, because it was so dark that any car lights ahead were visible for miles. You had to watch out for nocturnal animals, of course, and walkers without torches. But I didn't drive fast. I drove as slowly as I would in the day. It was a beautiful night, with thousands of stars scattered across the clear black sky. All the stars I could see were long dead, of course, unless we were living in the Second World, in which case they were what? Alive again? Fictional? The backdrop to long-dead people's heroic journeys? But I didn't think too much about the stars that night. Sometimes badgers scuttled out of hedgerows at night on the Lanes. I wondered what it would be like in a badgers' set. If I broke down and crawled into one, would the badgers accept me? Perhaps Christopher and his family would eventually forget that they'd been waiting for me. Of course, I'd get there and make it OK somehow. Christopher would be happy that I'd come to rescue him, would see it as a dramatic act of love, and then I'd tell him about the money, and how we'd be able to move to a farm, and he'd be so happy. Suddenly I felt so breathless that I had to pull over. I switched off the headlamps and sat for a few seconds in almost total blackness. Then I realised: I wasn't going to tell him about the money. I'd tell him there was some, a little bit. But I would keep the rest of the contents of my bank account a secret. There'd be no farm.

Christopher's father Peter lived in a big, sprawling flat above his vegetarian café in Totnes. Josh still lived in the attic, a perfectly square room with shelves and shelves of books arranged by height, a drum kit and a completely clean desk with only a white laptop on it. The rest of the flat was over two floors, both of which had polished floorboards covered with large rugs, as well as lots of wall-hangings, plants, sculptures and, I discovered when I got there, now a harp, Milly's harp, right in the middle of the cavernous, deep-red sitting room.

Only Peter was around. He'd let me in through the café, and was now standing by the harp running his fingers through his curly white hair. He'd already thanked me for coming. Now he asked if Josh had told me what had happened.

'Not in a lot of detail,' I said. 'Where's Christopher?'

'The boys have already gone to the hospital. Josh took Christopher in my car.'

'The hospital?'

'Christopher has hurt his hand. Quite badly, I think.'

'He did this . . . ?'

'Punching the wall.' Peter looked away from me and touched the harp. 'Milly's gone too.'

This didn't make sense. 'Not to the hospital?'

'No. I mean she's gone. I don't know where.'

'She'll be back, though?'

'I don't know.' He shrugged, and his whole body seemed to slump like a sack replaced on the floor after its contents have been shaken. After a couple of moments he said, 'You'll follow the boys on to the hospital, won't you?'

'Yes, I guess so. Are you OK?'

'I expect it'll take a long time in casualty. Last time I went with Josh for his foot it was something like three hours. I forgot to make sure they had change for the machine. Josh gets very thirsty when he's worried.'

Peter talked a little more about how long it might take to wait for an X-ray, and how long he and Josh last waited for an X-ray, and whether or not it would take longer at night, and how Christopher wouldn't be able to work with a broken hand. The whole time he spoke he had his hand on the harp, and at one point stroked one of the strings so gently that it didn't make a sound.

'What actually happened?' I asked, when he finished talking.

'I expect the boys will tell you. Christopher will tell you. It's not really a mystery to me, but I'm too tired of it all to try to understand.'

'He's been quite down lately,' I said.

'He's always been down. Even before his mother died. She used to call him Eeyore. I bet he never told you that. Maybe every family has an Eeyore. Once, when . . .' But Peter didn't finish that sentence; he sighed instead, and then touched the harp again. 'I'll get you some change from the till,' he said. 'You can take it with you.'

We went back down the stairs into the café, which smelled of good coffee and wholemeal pastry. There was a notice-board near the till, advertising the usual Totnes things and a few house-shares and flats for rent. Next to that was a poster for a talk in a few weeks' time. The title was 'Succeeding in the Second World'. The speaker was Kelsey Newman. What? Kelsey Newman coming to Totnes? This was like being haunted. I blinked, but when I opened my eyes the poster was still there. I stopped looking at it and instead watched while Peter opened the till and took out five £1 coins and a few 50p pieces, which he pressed into my hand. This would have been a small fortune to me just a few hours before. Now it was just change for a machine.

'Please, Meg,' he said, 'could you pass on a message to Christopher for me?'

'Of course,' I said.

'It's . . .' There was a long pause while Peter looked out of the window. A woman walked past, dressed in a long black skirt and a grey wool shawl. Once she was gone he looked at me again. 'On second thoughts, there isn't a message.'

'I can tell him whatever it is,' I said.

'No. I was going to say I was sorry and I hoped his hand felt better, but actually I'm not sorry and I hope it drops off. Oh, look, I didn't say any of that. Please forget it.'

Peter was so mild, so concerned about his sons all the time. He'd never said anything like this to me before.

'I understand,' I said. 'I wouldn't be sorry either, if I was you.'

He frowned. 'Really?'

'Yes. Sorry is the last thing I'd be. I hope Milly comes back soon.'

We exchanged a look, and I think he understood that I meant it.

'Why is age such a crime?' Peter said. 'People think that when a younger woman and an older man get together, then it's always about sex for him and money for her. Age buys beauty. But I'm not rich and Milly's not beautiful.' He half-blushed. 'She is to me, of course, but you wouldn't find a woman like her in a glossy magazine.' He sighed. 'Perhaps you could get

Christopher to stop calling her a "twenty-five-year-old wait-ress", especially as she's twenty-eight and has a PhD in music. She only works in the café to help me out, for goodness' sake. And while you're at it, tell him not to come back here. I've had enough of him this time.' He paused and sighed again heavily. 'Of course, you can't tell him that. I'll speak to him at some point. I'm so sorry, Meg. I've ranted at you. It's unforgivable.'

'I really don't mind,' I said. 'I don't find Christopher the easiest person in the world either. I thought it was all my fault.'

'It's not your fault. He's always been like this.'

I found Josh sitting on a bench out the front of Torbay Hospital casualty. He was wearing pale blue flares, a black T-shirt and a zip-up grey cardigan, and looked as if he'd been cast to play a student in a hospital drama about the perils of drugs, skateboarding or cults. His hair was the same length as mine, but was tied back in a ponytail. I sat down next to him and peeled a tangerine from my bag. I offered Josh half, but he shook his head.

'So?' I said.

'He's in there. He's still in a right strop.'

'Oh.'

'I said I'd come out and wait for you in case you didn't know where to go. We can wait for you for a lot longer if you like. Did Dad tell you what happened?'

'Not really. Just that he punched the wall.'

'He's such a complete knob sometimes.' Josh looked at the ground in front of us. 'I don't understand it.'

'What was the stuff about Milly moving in?'

'Dad wants to clear out Christopher's old room and redecorate the house. Christopher has hardly been in his room for years, except that time when you stayed with us. As you'll remember, there are still Euro '96 posters in there, and Oasis tapes. Milly's going to use it as a study for writing her music book, which was Dad's great idea. He must have known

Christopher would freak out because of the mural. When Christopher turned up today out of the blue, Milly was cooking dinner and Dad asked if he wanted to stay. After dinner, the subject of his room came up and he hit the roof. I guess I do sort of know why. It was a bit insensitive of Dad to pick that room.'

Christopher's mother had painted the mural for him before he was born. It was a forest scene, with an enchanted castle on the top of a faraway hill and a brown, earthy path leading to it. In the foreground, a big white unicorn bowed its head, as if waiting to be stroked. A few years before, when we were waiting to move into our current house, Christopher and I had stayed with Peter and Josh for a few weeks. We'd slept together in Christopher's old, lumpy single bed, even though Peter offered the spare room. Every night I undressed in front of the mural and imagined what it would be like to be pregnant, to give birth, to hope and dream for a child as well as yourself. I had never felt the urge to have children, and I kept looking at the mural and trying to have it and failing. It wouldn't have been any use if I had conjured it up. Christopher didn't want children either; and we hardly ever had sex, even then.

'I asked him about the mural once,' I said to Josh. 'He didn't say much. It was obviously one of those things I was supposed to know never to mention.'

'There's been all sorts of trouble over that mural,' Josh said. 'When Christopher was a teenager he thought it was childish and covered it over with posters. I remember I wanted to move into that room so I could have it, and he was like, "It's mine," and then covered it up. Then he took all the posters down when he came back after she died. Just those: he didn't change anything else in the room. I guess I like the mural too, but things have to move on. I think Dad just wants to get on with his life. You can't keep something like that for ever. If we sold the flat, or if it burned down, it would be gone anyway. Maybe memories are better on their own. Dad has offered to have a high-resolution digital photograph taken of it, and to frame a big copy for Christopher.'

'Yeah. I can see why he freaked out, though.'

'He went up quite calmly, and then the next thing we heard was a load of tearing and smashing, and we rushed upstairs and found that he'd started breaking things in the room, and ripping his posters down and kicking things about. He ended up by punching the wall, right by the unicorn, which I thought was kind of significant, not that anyone really cares what I think. Then he looked at Milly and said, "And you're not my fucking mother," as if that even had anything to do with it. Then he walked out. That was when I phoned you. I found him in the pub with his hand all bleeding, and some guy trying to throw him out because of HIV. It was horrible. I hate blood, as you know. Once he was properly bandaged up I got Dad's car and brought him here for an X-ray. It's like a nightmare in there. Too many clocks and too much mess.'

'I didn't even know he was coming round to your place tonight,' I said.

'No. But he just turns up. Does it all the time. Usually lunchtimes.'

'Are you OK?'

'Yeah. Dad's not, though.'

'I know. He said Milly had gone.'

'She'll come back. But they should ban Christopher from coming round at all until he can get over whatever it is. Milly's so nice. She doesn't deserve all this.'

'He's having a pretty bad week. He got knocked back from another job.'

'There's always something.'

Peter had more or less said this too. But was it really true? I was sure that Christopher went for long periods without there being anything bothering him at all. I tried to remember when one of these periods had been. Perhaps in the run-up to last Christmas. We'd decided to home-make all our presents, and there was a nice weekend when I was sewing little rectangles and Christopher was filling them with lavender through a funnel he'd made, but which kept breaking. He'd had a problem with his eyes, I suddenly remembered. That was why the funnel had broken. He'd never needed glasses, but said everything had gone blurry. We couldn't easily afford an optician's appointment, but I worked out that if we took a bit more money out of the Christmas fund and lived on nine, instead of ten, pounds a day for a bit, then it would be OK. I bathed his eyes and didn't say anything when he threw the remote control across the room later that evening because he couldn't see the buttons. I thought that once his eyes were better, then we'd go back to normal; if only his eyes hadn't been bothering him, it would have been a perfect weekend. Maybe Josh was right. Maybe there was always something. But there was also always the sense that if the something could be fixed, then all would be perfect.

I looked into the sky. There were no stars now, just the orange haze of Torbay.

'By the way,' Josh said, 'did you get the book I left for you?'

'What book?'

'The Kelsey Newman book. *The Science of Living Forever.* I gave it to Christopher to give to you.'

'Ah.' I rolled my eyes and smiled. 'That explains everything.'

'What do you mean?'

'Oh, I reviewed it by accident. It got mixed up with another book.'

'Mixed up with another book?' Josh raised both eyebrows.

I laughed. 'Yeah. I thought my editor at the paper had sent it, and so I just reviewed it like some sort of robot.'

'You knob.'

'Of course, Christopher didn't actually tell me you'd given it to me; he just left it on my desk, with a note from my editor in it. So that didn't help.'

'He's such a twat. I bet he did it on purpose.'

'Who knows. Probably they both fell on the floor and he just stuck the note in the wrong book when he put them back. I'll never know, because I can never ask him about it again. You know how you can only ever talk about a problem once with Christopher and then if you bring it up again he goes totally crackers? We've already had one big row about the mix-up.'

'What did you think of the book?' Josh asked.

'I'm not sure. What about you?'

The entrance to casualty was through two sets of automatic doors. These now opened, and Christopher walked out. His hand was neatly bandaged, but apart from that he looked a mess. His hair was all over the place, and he was still wearing the clothes he used on the project: shapeless tracksuit bottoms and a paint-spattered T-shirt.

'What's going on?' he said, looking first at Josh and then at me.

'Nothing,' Josh said, standing up. 'Meg just got here.'

'Well, why are you sitting out here?'

'I was just finishing my tangerine,' I said, standing up as well. 'How are you?'

'Couldn't you have done that before you got here? I've got to go through to radiology now. I've already seen a nurse.'

Josh said, 'I had to tell Meg what happened.'

'And you couldn't have done that inside? Whatever. Come on. We've got to go.'

As I got up I remembered the change Peter had given me.

'I brought this from your dad,' I said, giving it to Christopher. 'For the machine.'

'That's a lot of use now.'

The radiology waiting room was at the end of a long red line painted on the floor. There were only three other people there. There was a shrivelled man in a wheelchair, who looked dead already, and a mother with a boy of about eleven. The mother and boy were called through almost immediately, and we were left with the shrivelled man.

Christopher was holding his paperwork in his good hand, which was shaking.

'How are you feeling?' Josh asked him. His voice echoed in the big empty space. Everything was different shades of blue, and one of the lights flickered.

'Shit,' he said.

Josh shrugged, and leaned across him to pick up a magazine that had been lying at a strange angle on the wood-veneer table.

'For fuck's sake,' Christopher said loudly, dropping his paperwork. The shrivelled man stirred in his wheelchair.

'What?' Josh said.

'My hand. God. Be more careful.'

I bent down and picked up the papers Christopher had dropped.

'I think we should try to keep the noise down,' I said.

Josh got up and took the magazine over to the other side of the room, where there was a disorderly pile of magazines on an identical table. He added the magazine he'd picked up to this pile, counted the items in it and then straightened it. Then he looked at it again and made the magazines into two piles. I watched him concentrate as he did this, oblivious to Christopher sighing and rolling his eyes. When the magazines looked neat and symmetrical he came back. We all sat in silence until Christopher was called in for his X-ray.

'You OK?' I said to Josh, when Christopher had gone.

'Yeah. I've been trying to think of hospital jokes to lighten the mood,' he said. 'All I could remember is one my analyst told me, which is kind of sick. Thought I'd better not tell Christopher, but . . .'

'Go on,' I said.

'OK. Mary and John are patients in a mental hospital. One day they're walking by the swimming pool, and John, who can't swim, throws himself in the deep end and waits to drown. Mary jumps in and rescues him. The doctor sees what Mary has done, and decides she is safe to be released, since her heroic act shows she's mentally stable. He calls her into his office and says, "Well, there's some good news and some bad news. The good news is that you're being released. You saved a man's life and it's quite clear you're ready to enter society again. But I'm afraid there's bad news too. The man you saved, John, hanged himself shortly after the incident in the swimming pool and is now dead. I'm so sorry." "Oh," Mary said, "he didn't hang himself. I hung him up to dry." See? I told you it was sick.'

When I'd finished laughing, I said, 'Why did your analyst tell you that?'

'She tells a lot of jokes and stories,' Josh said. 'I'm supposed to reflect on them.'

'So what did you learn from this story?'

'I think I learned that there's more than one way of seeing your actions.'

'Or, I guess, other people's actions.'

'Yeah. So what did you think of all the science in the Kelsey Newman book? I was pretty impressed by it. I've got the original Frank Tipler book too. It's all there. The science, I mean. It makes a lot of sense, although in the Tipler book there's a slightly disconcerting description of exactly how humans would have to colonise the whole universe before the Omega Point could be of any use. On page forty-eight he talks about test-tube babies being born from artificial wombs and being brought up by robot nannies in other galaxies. This surely would be a universe full of maladjusted psychos. Or already is, if he's right. They'll be the ones running things, of course.'

I smiled. Josh always remembered what page something was on. I'd learned a lot about Josh's relationship with numbers when I'd snuck him onto a Zeb Ross retreat for free a few years ago, just before our flirtation had begun. I used to do an afternoon session on the mathematics of narrative, where we looked first at unity, then pairing, then incidences of the number three in fairy tales and myths, then Jung's theory of quaternity and so on. Josh had an encyclopaedic knowledge of instances of any number in almost anything, and had added much to the discussions, including an incredible list of threes that began with the Three Little Pigs, and ended, after about fifty other items, with the Three Wise Men. He'd even talked about the meanings of the threes in Tarot cards: the Threes of Wands, Cups, Swords and Pentacles. It was only much later that I discovered that he was using his knowledge of threes as a stalling device: a way of avoiding getting to the discussion of sixes.

After 9/11, Uri Geller put forward a theory that the attack had been cosmically connected with the number 11 because, for example, the Twin Towers looked like the number 11, New York was the 11th state added to the union, and flight number 11 had 92 people on board and 9 + 2 = 11. He even put a list on the relevant page of his website of significant people whose names had eleven letters, which included Tutankhamen, Harry Potter, Nostradamus and Josef Stalin. Josh had written a long blog about how you could choose any number and do this kind of idiotic thing with it, just as you could predict or confirm just about anything you wanted, with any text, if you followed the principles of the Bible Code. Josh could be a real sceptic when he wanted to be, which made his belief in aliens and sea monsters all the more interesting.

'What do you think about Newman's ideas, though?' I said now.

'I think that apart from the robot nannies it's very exciting. It makes a lot of sense. And I guess it is comforting too.'

'Because of your mum?'

'Yeah, but also because it means I'm not as mad as I thought I was. Lots of things that I've always believed in are possible in Newman's system, even probable, and completely consistent with the laws of physics. It proves the universe *was* designed — by human beings. How cool is that?'

I kind of shrugged. Before Newman came along Josh had thought, with the astronomer Fred Hoyle, that human DNA came not from evolution but from outer space.

'The Omega Point makes sense of everything,' Josh said. 'Every supposedly irrational thing I've ever come across: ghosts, telepathy, magic, astrology, reincarnation, Tarot, morphic resonance; they are all totally rational in Newman's universe. If we're already beyond the end of time, and living in this Second World in a never-ending afterlife, then everything makes sense. If every possible scenario exists in the mind of the Omega Point, then of course you'd see ghosts and monsters from time to time. It would mean that the universe, run on the physics of *Energia,* rather than matter, would be capable of a lot more than we ever thought. If the future has already happened, or, at least, if it's possible to compute, then of course you can predict it. If we are all conscious within the same system, and we all in some way share consciousness with the Omega Point, and therefore each other, then why wouldn't you be able to know what someone else is thinking sometimes? *Energia* is something you can do magic with. Why not? Doing magic in this system would be just like putting a shortcut on a desktop.'

Josh was always collecting evidence for magic and telepathy. He was very fond of B, and when we'd stayed in the flat he'd become interested in the way she seemed to know when someone was coming home. It was catching: Peter and I — and even Christopher, for a while — all became interested as well. At first we hypothesised that B heard the cars coming and believed her hearing to be extraordinary, especially as we all had to park down a side-street about a hundred yards from the flat. But she even picked up on people walking home. One time Peter was returning from London on the train and although he was supposed to let us know what time his train was due in so that someone could collect him, he decided to walk back from the station instead. About three minutes before he arrived, B started running around the flat, looking out of windows and wagging her tail, before ending up at the front door with her favourite ball in her mouth just as Peter turned his key in the lock. Each time something like this happened, the people who were in the flat would try to convince the person who'd just arrived that B had known they were coming. It was hard to believe when you were the person arriving, but hard not to when you saw her deliberately go through her preparations for greeting someone minutes before it would be possible to hear their footsteps, or their cough, or even smell them. Josh knew all about Rupert Sheldrake's experiments to find out if dogs really do know when people are coming home. Sheldrake argued that the universe has morphic fields, and morphic resonance, which involve memories being stored not in an individual, but outside, along with everyone else's. This, if true, would enable telepathy, among other things, since if a person's thoughts are not kept in their head, but outside in a collective space, then anyone can access them. I never admitted it, and I was sure there was a more conventionally scientific explanation for it, but B was so telepathic — or something — that on a walk if I even thought the word 'squirrel' she'd be off after it. If I thought to myself, 'Perhaps we'll go past the pet shop and get beef sticks later,' then B would seem to start anticipating it, and would pull in that direction. Sheldrake's theories also, Josh said, accounted for why I found it easier to do my crossword on a Thursday than I did on the Sunday it was published. By the Thursday, he said, so many people would have got the answers that they'd be the morphic resonance equivalent of neon, glowing from some nearby dimension. By Thursday I'd be simply plucking the answers out of the air. Josh ended up keeping a detailed record of B's telepathy and sent the results to Sheldrake, although I never found out what he made of them, if anything.

'So why isn't everyone doing magic and predicting the future if it's all possible?' I said.

'I think because we're encouraged to believe it's not possible. Maybe the Omega Point stops people. That bit I'm not quite sure about.'

'And why are there so many frauds out there pretending to bend spoons? Why is it that every stage magician you see is so obviously not doing real magic? If it was out there, I'm sure people would be doing it. You'd see people doing it. People would really bend spoons.'

'Maybe the people who really do it, do it quietly. Also, I think the wrong type of person senses that there's more power out there than they've been given access to, and so they pretend they've got it. Again, I'm not sure. But I'm very intrigued by this Second World, and I think it has the potential to answer a lot of these questions. Kelsey Newman is coming to Totnes to speak, by the way, so I'm going to ask about all of this. I thought you might want to come. Even to tell me what's wrong with what he says back. You could be my devil's advocate or something.'

'I saw the poster in the café,' I said. 'Why's he coming to Totnes?'

'He's been before. He's connected to Dartington in some way. I saw him last time he came; that was how I found out about his theories.'

I sighed. 'Oh, well, at least Kelsey Newman doesn't tell you that you have to pay money into his foundation or sign up for his website. He doesn't have a range of clothing, or jewellery that "might bring you luck".'

'You're really down on these people today,' Josh said. 'More than usual.'

'Oh — I'm doing this feature for the paper on New Age self-help books. My editor thought it was a good idea after he saw my review of Newman. I had no real idea about just how much crap there is out there. You know what I don't understand? Say there was a mysterious life force, or energy, or Qi, or *Energia*, or whatever in the universe that meant you could heal people or tell the future. Say you found out how to use it. Surely you'd be a very enlightened person, in tune with everything, and you wouldn't need to flog books to the public about it? If you did write a book about harmony with the universe, surely you'd give it away for free? Or you'd at least write it and be done with it — not churn out another ten books on the same subject because your publisher's putting pressure on you because there's such a market for your bullshit. In fact, if you were in harmony with the universe you'd probably write brilliant novels or something, or paint great pictures — not write self-help books. I read this book on cosmic ordering that has clearly earned the author more money than he's got from cosmic ordering, which just goes to show. And none of these people can write a sentence.'

'Ouch,' Josh said. 'You're right, of course. But I do think all of that is just there to distract you from the real stuff.'

'What, as in a conspiracy?'

'Not necessarily. Just that you're always going to see fraudsters and tricksters out there on the street, peddling what they've got, because there's no other way for them to live. If you could do real magic you wouldn't need to have a stage show, I assume. Or write a book about it. You'd live quietly in a cottage somewhere and no one would know. Just because you can't see something doesn't mean it isn't there: think of genes, for example, or sound waves. And for every hundred terrible books on Tarot or poltergeists, there's one good one that does expand your understanding of the world somehow. You just have to know where to find it.'

'But what's the point of it all?' I said. 'This universe that's just data. I mean, let's say you're right, and magic is as easy as putting a shortcut on a desktop if only we knew it, and that Newman's right and you have to live a heroic life and prove yourself before you can properly access all this. What's it for?

Even if there are magic and dragons and adventures on flying carpets in eternity with your perfect soul mate — what would make anyone bothered about it? Why would anyone do anything at all? If nothing *is* matter, how can anything matter? If nothing's material, then everything's immaterial, if you see what I mean. Death has to be what defines life, since living things are those things that will die but are not yet dead.'

As I spoke I saw Dartmouth in my mind: the same winter scene in which I'd bought my first balls of wool, just before Christmas. I saw people trudging to the shops in the gloom to buy items to magic the gloom away. As I had at the time, I saw the people themselves, already bad copies of pictures in magazines, ageing, breaking, dying, for no reason at all, just like everything they ever bought. Not long after that I'd drafted something like a science fiction story about a society of people who have been cursed to think that everything is more exciting than it is. So each time two of them kiss in a disco, they imagine they are embarking on a perfect romance. Their daily lives are spent trading what they believe to be very complex items. The people will lie, kill or steal for these items, which they believe to be love potions, beauty creams, elixirs of success or even flat-pack fairy castles. But in fact all they are trading are empty cardboard boxes, which they stack up in their houses until there are too many and then they throw some away.

Josh tilted his head. 'What do you mean? Why would you choose to die if there was an alternative?'

'I don't know. But there must be more to life than ending up in a cave fighting a monster and then coming back and doing it all again in some other way.'

The shrivelled man in the wheelchair suddenly gasped and threw back his head as if he was dying: a real-life death, if that was possible, not just something from my imagination or a hypothetical discussion. I got up, took a step towards him and then didn't know what to do. His head was frozen at a strange angle, and his mouth was open. I looked at Josh, but he had turned the other way. I tiptoed towards the man, but as I did his head fell forwards again and he let out the second half of his snore. I sat back down and Josh giggled.

'That's amazing,' he said. 'I thought he was dead.'

'Me too. My God.'

'That's the best snore I've ever heard.'

'You should hear Christopher.'

'I have,' he said. 'On those hideous camping holidays when we were kids. I'm sure they contributed to my psychological problems.' He yawned. 'Anyway, I think you're completely wrong about everything, and I think Newman will resolve all these issues in his new book.'

'He doesn't. I've read it. It's yet more blah about how your life is a big quest narrative. There's lots about being a hero and not sitting around eating pizza. Remember all that narrative theory I teach about admirable protagonists and character arcs? It's basically that, but at the end of time.'

'How have you read it? It's not out for another month.'

'I've got an uncorrected proof,' I said. 'From the newspaper. I'll lend it to you if you like.'

Josh smiled. 'Thanks,' he said. 'I've been waiting for that book for ages. I bet there's more to it than you say there is.' He looked at the door Christopher had gone through, and then back at me. 'So, even though you clearly have some reservations, will you come?'

'What, to hear Kelsey Newman?'

'Yeah. I think it'll be really interesting. It was last time. He explains things really well.'

'I don't know. Maybe. What date is it again?'

'The twentieth of March.'

That was the day before the opening of the Labyrinth. I'd had plans to take Frank and Vi out that night, but of course those plans were all shot to pieces now.

'I'll need to check my diary.'

'Well, let me know when you decide. We can go together. Maybe eat first, like have a pizza at Rumour or something?'

'Yeah. I'll let you know.'

'Oh — on a different note, any news on the Zeb Ross job?'

'I'll know in mid March,' I said. 'But keep your fingers crossed. You — or whoever does it — will be a recluse with some sort of disfigurement. That's all I know.'

'What sort of disfigurement?'

'We're just trying to work that out.'

'Like, a real one? Am I going to have to have surgery?'

I laughed. 'You knob,' I said. 'Of course not.'

Josh laughed too. Indeed, we were both still laughing when Christopher came out with the X-ray results, which showed he had broken his hand in three places and would not be able to do any manual work for at least six weeks.

The ferries would have stopped for the night, so I drove back to Totnes and then down the Lanes to Dartmouth. Every time we went over any sort of bump, Christopher whimpered and clutched his hand, but apart from that he said nothing. I half-wanted to say sorry, but I didn't, because I also half-wanted to scream at him that it was his own fault, that everything he was upset about was his own fault. I knew he probably wanted to say something to me about Josh. Had I been flirting with him again? Why had we been laughing together? And what would I say back to that? *No, I'm not in love with your brother; I'm strangely attracted to a man twenty-five years older than me whom I can never have. But in any case I'm not sure I love you any more, and I didn't want to be anywhere near you this evening because you're a fucking lunatic.* My thoughts were storming through my head like a mob with pitchforks. What the hell had he been thinking, punching walls and ruining everyone's evening? How dare he be silent now? If he wanted to say something stupid about Josh why didn't he just do it? But after a while I let the angry mob go their own way. I was tired, and the hedgerows on the Lanes made me feel protected, although from what I wasn't sure. I imagined, again, crawling into a badgers' set, although this time Rowan was with me. We became Mr and Mrs Badger and lived happily ever after, cosy and snug underground.

I couldn't believe I'd mentioned that ESP book to Rowan. It had activities in the back that I had done as a child, and although I had vague recollections of Rosa being impressed that I was able to move a pendulum in a glass just by concentrating on it I imagined that Rowan would think I was a complete idiot if he knew. Rosa and I once spent a rainy Saturday afternoon making up cards with symbols on them, and we took it in turns to guess which one the other was looking at. We also practised remote viewing, and we used to go to the park and take it in turns to be blindfolded and follow the other's telepathic instructions to arrive at a marker on the ground. I remembered that we'd had some spectacular results, or at least we thought we had at the time.

Between times, as we drank fizzy drinks and ate biscuits in my bedroom, we had delicious, half-whispered conversations about Rosa's poltergeist. It didn't hurt anyone, apparently, just threw things around every night. Her parents had booked an exorcist, but she made me promise not to tell my parents this. Apparently her father had said my father would not approve. Of course, my father did find out, probably from Caleb. He didn't disapprove at all; not exactly. He said the poltergeist was a figment of the Coopers' imaginations, and that if they needed to believe that an exorcist had got rid of the poltergeist in order to remove it from their imaginations, then it was probably a good idea to get one. My mother asked him how imagination made books fall off shelves and fly around the room, and he simply said that this was not happening. My mother said, 'But we hear it every night,' and then he said, 'We don't know what we are hearing.' My thoughts continued to drift as I drove down the Lanes. There were no cars, no people, no animals. I remembered one time when we were on holiday we'd been driving down roads like this and my father suddenly stopped the car, switched off the headlamps and urged us all to look into the darkness. 'I bet you've never seen darkness like this before,' he said. And then we all got out and looked up at the stars, and my father put his hands in his pockets, leaned backwards and said, 'This is what it's like to live on a planet!'

I hadn't spoken to my father for more than ten years, but I heard he'd become a professor at the university. When he discovered my ESP book and my experiments he didn't get quite as cross as I'd feared. Instead, he sat and lectured me, for hours, long past my bedtime, on every reason why it was stupid to believe in the paranormal. I argued back. I told him that the Chinese used animal precognition to help tell them when earthquakes were likely to happen, and that the Queen had a homoeopath. He asked me why nothing paranormal had ever been conclusively proven in the history of the whole entire world, and I told him, in a small voice, something else I'd read in my ESP book: that paranormal events don't work so well when they are being observed and tested. Then, feeling overwhelmed and tired, I burst into tears. Instead of comforting me, as I thought he would, he said, in a cold voice, 'You are just like your mother,' and left the room. I knew then that I'd lost him for ever.

Not long after that, Caleb declared that he had converted to Hinduism after reading a book that said something about us all being the 'dance of God.' Mrs Cooper and my mother did not approve at all, and said dark things over cups of tea about the oppression of women, and caste systems, and having to marry a man with more qualifications than you, even if you had a PhD, but my father was always ready for a cheerful discussion about the meaning of the universe — as long as it was with Caleb. One day I saw Caleb and my father lying on the Coopers' patio, staring through the cat-flap. Rosa later told me they'd been doing an experiment. Caleb had said that our current understanding of the universe was like watching a cat walk past in front of a small hole. You see the head, and then the body and then the tail, but not the whole cat at once. So you believe the head causes the body to appear, and the body causes the tail to appear, but it's actually a whole cat with no cause and effect at all beyond its simple 'catness'. My father had patiently argued that from this perspective the head does cause the body to appear and so on, and that if you were watching a cat walk past in front of a small hole you would never see the body of the cat first, and then the head and then the tail, not because of a mysterious 'catness' but because cats, walking in a straight line, tend to go head first, and in that sense the movement of the cat, its physiognomy, the structure of its legs and so on do cause the head to appear first, and this does in some way cause the rest to 'happen'. It was this discussion that had caused Caleb and my father to end up lying there watching through the cat-flap, both hoping for a real-life illustration of their particular argument. The cats, however, were all asleep in the laundry basket upstairs and so my father and Caleb just watched an empty kitchen for a while before the football started.

The Lanes were still silent. I drove down the bumpy road past the Sharpham Estate and down the hill towards Bow Creek. Christopher clutched his hand as we went over the hump-back bridge by the Waterman's Arms. We passed the Maltster's Arms and Tuckenhay Mill, and then went over another bumpy section of road. Christopher whimpered again.

'Can you *please* try to be more careful?' he said.

'I can hardly get a steamroller and flatten all the bumps.'

'You could have gone on the main road.'

I sighed. Indeed I could. I could also have cheered him up by telling him the half-truth I'd constructed, that about £3,000 had suddenly come into my account. We could clear our debts, and he could get some new clothes, and perhaps he could do a short course in heritage studies, or conservation, or something that would help him get the kind of job he wanted. I knew if he could do something he loved every day, then he'd feel a lot better. Perhaps then we'd be OK. But for some reason I didn't say anything. I was still thinking about what Rosa had said in her interview. Of course, they did get an exorcist in the end, but he wasn't able to do anything. He explained why this was. Apparently, in virtually all cases, the reason for a poltergeist like theirs was the effects of the disturbed energy of a pre-teenage child in the immediate vicinity. Real ghosts could be sent back to the Otherworld, or wherever it was that ghosts were supposed to be, but not poltergeists. Poltergeists were a manifestation of misery, angst and childhood uncertainty, and would stop bothering everyone only when the child either grew up or became happier. Poor Rosa was immediately interrogated about all the disturbing things that had happened to her in her life, but the poltergeist went only when Toby and I left with our mother, about six months later.

The next morning it was raining again. Christopher was out of it in bed on the strong painkillers they'd given him at the hospital, but had begged me not to leave him alone. I'd been planning to see Libby that evening, but it looked as if that was going to be impossible. The rain made things trickle and gurgle outside, and while Christopher slept I sat on the sofa with my laptop, re-establishing my personal email account. There was nothing at all from Vi. There was lots of stuff about the TV deal, though. My new agent had also asked more questions about my novel, and wanted to know whether I might finish it this year. I wrote him a long email about the notebook idea but it looked wrong, so I deleted it all. Then I wrote another long email about how I hoped my career would now be able to progress more in the way I'd originally intended. I hinted that I was embarrassed about my Newtopia books, and asked whether my name would have to appear on the credits if the TV series was actually made. I explained that I wanted to leave genre fiction behind and become known as a serious writer. I tried again to summarise the notebook idea. I looked at what I'd written and realised that I was trying to say something I could not yet say, as if I was designing my own afterlife. I deleted it all and wrote a couple of lines confirming that I would try to finish the novel this year. I'd finish the novel and let that speak for itself.

Just after I'd gone on the Internet to look at Greek islands, there was a little bleep that told me I had a new email. Had the agent responded already? I flipped from the browser to my inbox and there was a message from Rowan. The subject header was 'Lunch?' The email itself was brief, but it was as if there was a Catherine wheel inside me as I read it. He was sorry he'd been 'odd' on the ferry the other day, and was I free to have lunch any day next week after all? I didn't know what to say back. *Yes?* Or *No?* Should I insert an Aristotelian reversal and tell him I didn't think it was a good idea, or just accept and take the ship in a bottle along as an excuse?

In my Orb Books account there were various messages from board members and regular ghostwriters on the subject of Zeb's disfigurement. These had become rather silly, and Claudia had sent a new message telling everyone off for being childish, and reminding us that Zeb needed a proper character arc, based on cause and effect, and could not have been simply 'abducted by aliens that look like taps'. Could he have learned something from his disability? How has his disability helped him to write? What everyday activities does he struggle with, and how does this help build his character? Someone had almost immediately written back: *OK, so back in the '90s Zeb is this moronic rich kid with a Porsche. One day he's on his way from seeing a beautiful girl for lunch, and he's heading to the gym to tone his glistening abs when he gets a flat tyre. He pulls over by the side of the road to fix it and then hears a little yapping noise coming from the electricity generator nearby. Oh no! It's a puppy! Zeb jumps in to rescue the puppy, takes a few thousand volts/amps/whatever it is you get in electricity generators and is then paralysed for ever.* In hospital he listens to audiobooks, and because they help him through he decides to help others by writing books, which he must now do with his EYELASHES or at least by dictation, although maybe he has lost all speech . . . Someone else had responded: *Good—but flat tyre is too much of a random act of God. Maybe a bit episodic? Why does Z feel compelled to save the puppy? Did he have a puppy as a child, before all the rich-kid stuff made him hollow and shallow? Is he trying to get back to this state?* Then Claudia had reminded everyone that the disability would probably be better as a simple disfigurement, as originally suggested, and must be attractive. *We're thinking more Harry Potter's scar than the Hunchback of Notre-Dame, people!* she said. *The kind of thing you'd put on a visa application as a distinguishing feature. Under NO CIRCUMSTANCES does Zeb write novels with his eyelashes.*

After lunch I felt a bit sleepy, and I was sick of looking at my laptop screen. I hadn't yet replied to Rowan. My novel still stood at 43 words. I closed the lid of my laptop and put it on the table. I hardly ever played my guitar when Christopher was around, but since he was still out cold I picked it up, brushed off some of the dust, checked it was tuned and started playing a few of my favourite chords: B7, E7, A minor, D7. My fingers hurt a bit, but I carried on. Last time I'd played had been before Christmas. But Bob would probably get his guitar out at some point on Saturday night, and I didn't want to be too rusty in case he suggested playing something. He was into carefully structured blues licks, and practised his scales every day. I didn't know any scales, and liked chords more than notes. I loved the almost-dissonance of changing from E7 to B7, and that move from C minor up to G# always made me sigh. Somehow I played well with Josh and not so well with Bob. Josh and I were both counters, him consciously, of course, and me less so. Me on rhythm guitar and him on drums; we never lost time, and he didn't care that I occasionally made some odd chord changes. As long as we kept time, he was OK. But Christopher didn't like us playing together, so we'd stopped.

Towards the end of the day I put on my raincoat and walked B round the Royal Avenue Gardens and down the Embankment. I went to the cashpoint as well, and withdrew £100. After that, I went to Libby's shop. I opened the door a bit and stuck my head in.

'Can we come in?' I said. 'The dog's wet.'

'Yeah, sure. The health-and-safety guy was here yesterday. I doubt he'll come again today. He told me some terrifying stories. A wet dog near food is nothing in his world. Come out the back. I'll find a towel.'

The back room of the deli smelled of strong coffee, cheese, salami and raw silk. There were two really old chintz armchairs, a Turkish rug and a sink with an electric kettle in it. Libby had gone through a phase of cross-stitching her favourite quotes from books, and several of these hung on the wall. The longest one was from *Anna Karenina*. It read: *Understanding clearly then for the first time that for every man and for himself nothing lay ahead but suffering, death and eternal oblivion, he decided that it was impossible to live that way, that he had either to explain his life so that it did not look like the wicked mockery of some devil, or shoot himself.*

There were two old towels hanging on a radiator. Libby took one of these and held it up as if she was a matador and B was a bull.

'Can I do her?' she said, flapping the towel around. 'Come on, Bess! Who's a good girl? Come to Auntie Libby.'

I took off B's lead and she ran over to Libby, wagging not just her tail but her whole back half, which made her look as if she was scuttling sideways, like a crab. Libby started rubbing

B's face, which she knew B liked best. Then she told B to roll over and did her stomach and her paws.

'Busy day?' I said.

'No. It's been dead. Bloody rain. Do you want a coffee?'

'Yes, please. Do you want me to do it? What did the health-and-safety guy say about the kettle in the sink, by the way?'

She smiled. 'Oh, I moved it before he came.'

'So you do agree it's dangerous?'

'I'm still alive.'

After filling the kettle with water from the tap, I put it back in the sink, which really was the only place it could go, because its power lead was so short. I switched it off at the wall, then pressed its 'on' switch, then turned the power back on at the wall. It started to boil slowly. I went and sat in one of the chairs.

'How are you?' I asked. 'Beyond being alive, I mean.'

'Pretty shit. I keep having to go and cry in the toilet. You?'

'Yeah. Also shit. Christopher broke his hand punching a wall. I spent half of last night with him in casualty. I did a bit of crying in the bathroom when we got home too.'

Libby groaned. 'Fucking hell.'

'I know. I can't stay long. He's knocked out on painkillers and he'll want to know where I am when he wakes up. I don't think I can come out tonight, unfortunately, which is such a bummer because I so don't want to be at home. The damp's terrible with all this rain.'

'Don't worry; I'd have been lame company anyway. But you'll still come on Saturday?'

'Of course.'

'I can't cope without you. I'm cooking nine fish. In my kitchen. I can't tell you how much I'm dreading the whole thing.'

'I'll come really early and help.' I looked at the wall and read Libby's cross-stitch again. 'Lib?' I said.

She was spooning coffee in a cafetière. 'What?' She looked at me. 'Are you OK?'

'I'm not sure.'

'What is it?'

'I don't know. Oh, just ignore me. It's stupid.'

'Come on. You can tell me.'

'Well, the cosmic ordering worked. After I finished speaking to you the other night I opened this envelope that I thought was an unearned-royalty statement, but instead I found out that this TV company has bought the rights to all my science fiction books. I earned some pound-signs.'

'That's very cool!' She came over and hugged me. 'But that's not cosmic ordering, you idiot. What did Christopher say?'

'I haven't told him.'

'Ah. Interesting.'

'Yeah. I know. So you don't . . . You don't think I've somehow unbalanced the universe with this cosmic ordering stuff?'

'Don't be so stupid. It's not real. I didn't get what I asked for. I haven't heard anything from Mark. I really do think it's over.'

'Oh, Lib. I'm so sorry.'

'It's all right. I'm OK, apart from crying in the toilet. In fact, I think it might be for the best. Bob was so nice over the weekend. I had terrible period pains and he went out and got me DVDs, magazines, painkillers and a new hot water bottle without me even saying anything.' She looked out of the small window, smeared with rain, and then looked back at me. 'Hey — do you want to hear a really gross story?'

'Go on.'

'So this health inspector was in a pub on Dartmoor the day before yesterday. He was looking at the kitchens, and there were feathers under the cooker, so he asked the landlord whether he let his pet cockerels or ducks come into the kitchen. He said, No, of course not. Then the next thing that happened was that a cockerel ran in, followed by a fox with one of the ducks in its mouth, and one of the other cockerels on its back, and the cockerels pecked out the fox's eyes while the fox killed the duck and then, blindly I suppose, killed the cockerels too. There was blood everywhere. The inspector closed the kitchen down.'

'Oh, yuck,' I said. 'Poor cockerels. Poor fox. Poor duck.'

'Bess would do the same given half a chance.'

'She would not. She caught up with a squirrel she was chasing once on the moors and then she didn't know what to do. They both sort of looked at each other, and then they ran in opposite directions. Since then she doesn't bother to chase them.'

Libby stroked B's head. 'You're very domesticated, aren't you?' she said. 'Oh, thinking of crazy things on Dartmoor, didn't you say that guy Tim was writing about a Beast or something?'

'Yeah.'

'Well, have you heard the news about the real one? You should tell him.'

'What news about a real one?'

'The health inspector told me about it. It was the "fun" story on the local news this morning as well. There's been howling, weird footprints, ginormous piles of foul-smelling shit and all sorts of things. People have seen "something" much larger than a cat or a dog prowling around, and some local had a photograph of a black blob that looked a bit like the Loch Ness Monster, except it was in a field. They reckon that it's probably a puma or a wolf that someone got as a pet and can't look after any more. One woman said that all the dog food she kept in her garden shed disappeared late one night, and when she got up there were just empty bags all over her garden. She said it had cost her about a hundred quid. Imagine spending that on dog food.'

When I left the deli the evening had shrugged itself onto the town, and the whole place was slicked with the reflections of car headlamps and dim, flickering streetlamps. It was turning into the kind of night where you walked the streets alone, heard other people's TVs and wished you were indoors yourself. I walked slowly across the market square, not much wishing I was indoors at all. When I got to Brown's Hill I remembered that if each time I took a step I covered half the distance to the front door, then I'd never get home. Was it worth a try? Was it possible to act out a paradox the way that Rowan and Vi acted out historical events? Or was it that people acted out paradoxes and historical events all the time anyway?

On Thursday morning, the phone rang. It was Tim Small.

'I'm sorry to ring you at home,' he said. 'Are you busy?'

Was I busy? Christopher would need to be given his pain-killers soon, because he couldn't get them out of the packet with his left hand. He was up and about today, but that meant he needed my undivided attention. He would need something for lunch, and a new, hypo-allergenic bandage, which I would have to buy and then put on. He also required constant soothing because the pain was so great, and also because the pain-killers, made by a heartless corporation with a patent stolen from tribespeople somewhere, gave him unbearable side-effects, including dizziness and mild hallucinations. I'd promised to look in my *Radical Healing* book for a solution to all this, and then go into Totnes later that afternoon to buy whatever alternative remedies it suggested, as well as the bandage. So I was still working on my feature as well as looking after Christopher. I had no idea how much longer this was going to go on. The doctor had said six weeks, but surely Christopher would get better before that.

It all reminded me of a hospital joke I should have told Josh on Tuesday night. A wife is summoned to the consultant's room. He says to her: 'Your husband has a very rare and serious illness. Unless you are able to do everything for him — cooking, cleaning, wiping his arse, washing him and so on — he will die. If you can do these things, then in about a year or so he'll recover. But you'll literally have to do everything for him before then.' The wife goes out to the husband. 'What did the doctor say?' he asks. 'I'm sorry, honey,' she says back. 'It's terminal.' Of course, people did look after others in this way, sometimes for years. What was so wrong with me that I could barely manage it for a day? I couldn't stop thinking about Rowan, and his suggestion of lunch, but I still hadn't replied to him. It wasn't clear when I'd next get out of the house for long enough to have lunch anyway.

'No, not very,' I said to Tim. 'I'm assuming you've seen the news.'

'Yeah,' he said. 'I'm really worried.'

I wasn't expecting that. 'Why?'

'Well, I got an email saying that my proposal's going to some sort of editorial board, and apparently that's really good because only one per cent of proposals go through. I've been really quite excited. But now I'm worried that this editorial board is going to think I copied the idea from real life. I mean, can I even write about this Beast, now there is one?'

'It's OK,' I said. 'Don't worry. I'm on the editorial board. And don't worry about the Beast being real. There's no copyright on Beasts. I mean, there's already *The Hound of the Baskervilles*, but that certainly doesn't mean no one can ever write another novel about a supernatural creature on Dartmoor. I guess you'd need to do something different with the idea, though, and show you were aware of what's gone before, but we discussed that already.'

'So I'm worrying about nothing?'

'Yes.' I laughed. 'But I do understand. I'm sure I've worried about similar things in the past. In fact, one time I found out that my book had the same title as another book and I thought it would have to be pulled off the shelves or something, but there's no copyright on titles either, it turns out.'

'That's weird.'

'I know.'

'Well, thanks,' he said. 'I feel better.'

'Good.'

'And I've been doing some research into other fictional and historical Beasts,' Tim said. 'I'm guessing you think that's the right approach?'

'Definitely. But don't overdo it. Remember that your audience is made up of teenagers with short attention spans.'

'There's a great Beast in Robert Louis Stevenson's *Travels with a Donkey*', he said. I could hear Oscar-like sounds of paper being moved and pages being turned in the background. 'Do you know the book?'

'No.'

'It's very funny. Stevenson is travelling around the Cévennes region of France with a donkey called Modestine, who is a real character. At one point they go to a region with a famous Beast. Can I read you a bit?'

Christopher whimpered on the sofa. He seemed to have dropped the remote control, but I couldn't work out why he didn't just pick it up with his good hand. I turned away so I could pretend I'd been looking out of the kitchen window the whole time.

'Yes, go on.'

'"Wolves, alas! like bandits, seem to flee the traveller's advance; and you may trudge through all our comfortable Europe, and not meet with an adventure worth the name. But here, if anywhere, a man was on the frontiers of hope. For this was the land of the ever-memorable BEAST, the Napoleon Bonaparte of wolves. What a career was his! He lived ten months at free quarters in Gévaudan and Vivarais; he ate women and children and 'shepherdesses celebrated for their beauty'; he pursued armed horsemen; he has been seen at broad noonday chasing a post-chaise and outrider along the king's high road . . ." There's a bit more after that,' Tim said. 'Sometime later Stevenson is lost, and meets two young girls who won't give him directions. One pokes her tongue out at him, and the other just tells him to follow the cows. He says then, "The Beast of Gévaudan ate about a hundred children of this district; I began to think of him with sympathy."'

I laughed. 'I don't think the Beast of Dartmoor has eaten anyone yet, although I can think of some people he could start with.'

'Well,' he said, 'I hope I'm not the first. I'm going to look for it myself. See what it is. In fact, I'd decided to do that even if it had turned out that the whole novel was screwed up. I've brought my camping trip forward.'

'Really? That's brave. When are you going?'

'As soon as possible. Need to clear it with Heidi, and shift a few jobs around first. But I've got my tent. I'll build a campfire and wait for it to come to me. I'll take a good camera too.'

I couldn't say what I was thinking, which was that Tim should forget about writing this novel for Orb Books, make the protagonist middle-aged and cuckolded again and write it up as a proper novel. The idea that he was going to all this trouble for a Zeb Ross book made me feel guilty for ever suggesting he write one.

I heard a heavy thud and turned around. Christopher had fallen off the sofa.

'Thanks,' Tim said. 'You've been a great help.'

'Well, good luck,' I said. 'Let me know when you're going.'

'You can pray for me.'

'Indeed.'

I put the phone down and went over to the sofa. Christopher was lying on the floor where he'd fallen. For a second I thought he was dead.

'Christopher?'

'Who was that?' he asked.

'An Orb Books author,' I said. 'Why are you down there? What happened?'

'What were you talking about? I heard something about Beasts. I thought I might be hallucinating again.'

'It was just work. Don't worry about it.'

'You were laughing.'

'Well, sometimes work is funny.' I sighed.

'Babe, I'm so dizzy,' he said. 'Where am I?'

'You seem to be on the floor. Did you fall off the sofa?'

'I can't remember. Everything's such a blur.'

'Come on, I think you should get up. Would you like a blanket?'

'Yes, please.'

'And a cup of tea?'

'Yes. Meg?'

'What?'

'Please don't leave me alone. The world's sort of vibrating.'

I managed to find a blanket for Christopher that was only partially covered in dog hair and settled him back on the sofa with the remote control and a cup of tea. I willed the phone to ring again. It didn't. For the next couple of hours I sat there at the kitchen table reading *Radical Healing*, while Christopher loudly watched a programme about Aztec civilisation, and then one on Stonehenge, both of which I was sure he'd seen before. Weak early-spring sunlight stroked the table-top, and B started to amuse herself by going to the top of the stairs, dropping a tennis ball down to the bottom and then fetching it herself and taking it back to the top again. I put this together from what I could see and hear: first an almost-regular *thud, thud, thud* sound of the ball on the stairs, followed by the ball itself, bald now, its green fabric long gone, bouncing and rolling into the hallway. Then I would hear the miniature galloping sound of B coming down the stairs, and then I'd see her black body gathering the ball and turning. Then I would hear the *pad, pad, pad* of her going back up the stairs, more slowly now she had the ball. She would lie at the top of the stairs chewing it for an unspecific amount of time, and then the whole thing would begin again. Christopher tried glaring first at her, and then at me, and then he simply turned up the volume on the TV. The next time he glared at me I had a coughing fit and had to drink three glasses of water before I could go upstairs to get my inhaler.

Radical Healing wasn't quite what I expected, and I couldn't work out why it had been lumped in with the New Age self-help books in Oscar's cupboard. It certainly didn't seem to be something that would help Christopher. It was an anthology of writings about the placebo effect and the way that the mind can be seen to control the body, and would have been more properly filed with popular science, or the history of medicine. One of the first pieces was an excerpt from the *Malleus Maleficarum,* a medieval text on the evils of witchcraft. The excerpt included a discussion on the ways in which witches removed the 'virile member' of men. The medieval authors argued that the witches did not remove it exactly, but rather made the man believe it wasn't there. There was also a discussion on impotence, which included the following: 'When the member is in no way stirred, and can never perform the act of coition, this is a sign of frigidity of nature; but when it is stirred and becomes erect, but yet cannot perform, it is a sign of witchcraft.' There was also a piece by a late-nineteenth-century homoeopath about the power of *Sac Lac,* the homoeopathic version of a sugar pill, and how he thought it was advisable to give this to homoeopathic patients who did not believe they were being cured by very few doses of the 'real' stuff. There were essays from medical historians and anthropologists about the history of the placebo effect, and how it had affected different groups of people over time. One study suggested that cultures whose members believed they were receiving the best care available thrived, whereas those in which the rich and powerful had access to medicines denied to the rest, didn't.

Part Two looked at contemporary responses to the placebo effect. One essay referenced a study that showed that blue pills made people relax and pink pills woke them up, even when the pills were inert; another study had apparently proved that animals and plants also respond to placebos. The penultimate chapter asked whether, if animals and plants responded to placebos, the placebo effect was happening in the mind of the healer, not the patient, and what that might mean. The last chapter had been written by a fairly well-known scientist, Claude Dubois, who was still in disgrace for leading a study that proved that homoeopathic remedies had perceivable effects. There had seemed to be nothing wrong with his experiment at the time, and *Nature* magazine had published the results. Then a bunch of famous sceptics turned up at his lab to investigate. They tried to repeat his experiment, with no success, and found all sorts of errors in the original study. They ended up concluding that Dubois had consciously or unconsciously tampered with his results and that his study was flawed. In his essay in *Radical Healing*, Dubois looked at the effects of the mind not just on one's own illnesses, but also on scientific experiments. Can you 'will' a study to come out with the results you want, in the same way you can will yourself better? If that was true, he argued, then surely the opposite is possible. Did his positive result and the sceptics' negative result prove not something definite about nature, but simply about their own beliefs?

After I'd finished reading the book, made lunch for Christopher, washed up and checked he had everything he needed, I put my coat on and got my stuff together. This included the proof of *Second World*, which I was planning to drop off with

Josh and had therefore hidden in a carrier bag. Christopher was by then watching a programme about Atlantis, the lost continent. It seemed mainly to involve a CGI reconstruction of the beginning and end of the civilisation, according to what Plato and others had said about it. Currently, they were in about 8000 BC, and the vast, artificial-looking land mass had split into two parts. On screen there was a montage of jewelled palaces, long stone roads, a vast moat, temples with sacred eyes painted in them and olive-skinned people with very high cheekbones. Suddenly, the ground started to shake. It was a huge earthquake, followed by tidal waves and explosions. The voiceover on screen said, 'Is this the end of Atlantis?' And then they cut to commercials.

'Good job they had camcorders back then, isn't it?' I said.

'It's a reconstruction,' Christopher said.

'I know that. I was joking.'

'I know.' He turned around. 'Where are you going?'

'To look for remedies for you. I'll walk the dog as well. She could do with some exercise. I need some air too.'

B had been lying on the armchair, asleep, with her tennis ball by her head, for most of the last hour. But she'd jumped up as soon as I'd finished the washing up, and had been shadowing me ever since. Now she was standing by the door with the ball in her mouth, glancing from me to Christopher and then back again. I coughed a couple of times.

'Did you find something in that book?'

'Yeah, I think so. Might be a bit complicated to find, but I'll try.'

'Don't be too long, babe. I can't manage on my own.'

'I'll be as quick as I can.'

He smiled weakly. 'Thanks for helping me out. Sorry I'm such a mess.'

'Don't worry,' I said. 'How's it feeling now?'

'It's better when I don't think about it.'

'OK, well, I'll leave you to find out whether the Atlantans really did build Stonehenge, and whether lemmings really are trying to get back there when they jump off cliffs.'

'Don't take the piss. I'm enjoying this. It's making me feel better.'

What a killjoy I was. And I hadn't even told him about the money yet.

I put the local radio on in the car. The Beast of Dartmoor was still a news item, and the presenter was in the middle of interviewing a historian from Exeter University about previous Beasts in Devon. I hoped Tim was listening. The professor was talking about the once-famous case of the Devil's Footprints, when on the night of 8th February 1855 an unidentifiable set of animal's footprints had been found in the snow. The footprints, which were said to be similar to those of a donkey, but cloven, seemed to belong to a single creature, and covered a distance of more than twenty miles from Exmouth to Lympstone, Powderham, Starcross, Dawlish, Teignmouth and Totnes. They scaled rooftops, and appeared to pass through walls and haystacks. The event had been the subject of much speculation in the newspapers of the time, particularly *The Illustrated London News*. People suggested that the prints belonged to a badger, a bird, or even a kangaroo, two of which had escaped in the region not long before. The professor said that the matter had never been satisfactorily settled.

'So no one knows what actually happened?' asked the presenter.

'That's right. The most compelling case so far is that the prints were made by pranksters.'

'What, people having a laugh?'

'Exactly. But there weren't any human footprints found. Perhaps the jokers had special shoes made. Who knows? But it is interesting to note that on the night of the seventh of February the Teignmouth Useful Knowledge Society had listened to a lecture given by a Mr Plumtre of Dawlish. The subject of the lecture was "The Influence of Superstition on Natural History". This was described by G. A. Household—one of the only authorities on this subject—as a "remarkable coincidence". It seems likely to me that there is a connection between the lecture and the footprints, but I have yet to find evidence of what it might be.'

'And the Beast that allegedly roams Dartmoor now—you think this could be a practical joke as well? Just a fabrication?'

'Anything's possible.'

Slapton Sands was deserted apart from a few fishermen in dark raincoats and a man scrubbing down a small, yellow fishing boat. Out on the misty horizon I could see the blackish shapes of huge ships. I parked at the Torcross end and then walked along with B under the pale grey sky with sea on my right. All the endless hours of dog-walking I did enabled me to contemplate many objects from nature as B peed on them, sniffed them for traces of other dogs' pee, walked on them, jumped on them, chewed them, ran away from them or brought them for me to throw. I also ended up gazing at other animals, birds and trees in the distance and thinking things my father would find repulsive: *Birds must be happy when they fly,* or *That weird plant must really like growing in sand.*

I once tried to explain evolution and natural selection to Christopher, and I used the usual example of the giraffe. I didn't want to get into an argument about the elements of speciation that I imagined he would find hard to believe, so I told him a simplified version. In the days before giraffes had long necks, and were therefore just horse-things or donkey-things, I told him, one of them is suddenly born with a ginormously long neck, all the better to reach the leaves at the top of the tree. He's the king of the forest because of this, and his mutated genes are easily passed on because all the girl-giraffes want to be fucked by him, and his sons and daughters also get the evolutionary advantage of being able to reach the highest leaves, and eventually the other giraffes die out, perhaps from sadness, because they can't get to the leaves at the top of the tree, and this happened so long ago that you never see the in-between giraffes, only the 'finished' ones. 'That's cool, babe,' Christopher had said. Since this was the first time he'd ever understood anything scientific, I didn't point out that this all meant that even now giraffes aren't completely finished, because evolution keeps on trucking until the end of time, which is never tomorrow, even though we all think it might be. And I'd wondered to myself what else these giraffes want, beyond treetops. Do they want the moon? Or do they not want anything at all?

I couldn't believe that Christopher just accepted evolution as 'cool' and didn't find it at all astonishing. After all, there's a big difference between all the pieces of the giraffe — and me, and you — lying around in the universe, and us all actually being here and assembled and functioning. Surely anything that existed and could think would find itself astonishing. But we'd had a big argument about the speed of light the week before, and perhaps Christopher had just been humouring me. As I approached the kiosk, I thought again about Kelsey New-man's post-universe, where nothing would evolve ever again. Everyone would be a hero struggling for sex and victory, for no reason whatsoever. Everything would be predictable, but nothing would be astonishing.

When I reached the kiosk I bought fish and chips for me, and a sausage for B. Then I sat on a bench looking at the sea, wondering what remedies to get for Christopher. If the book I'd read was right, then anything would do, so long as he — and possibly I — believed in it. It was cold, and I thought I might nip into the Foghorn for a quick half and warm up by the fire. When I took my rubbish back to the kiosk I noticed that a sign had just been put up. *Fisherman's Cottage. Winter Let. £300 per month.* That was very cheap; it was around what I'd been thinking of paying for an office.

'Excuse me,' I said to the girl in the kiosk. 'Who would I ask about this?'

'Andrew Glass,' she said. 'In the Foghorn.'

'Oh, I'm just on my way there. Thanks.'

I walked further along the esplanade until I came to a weathered red door with old crab pots, ropes and fishing nets dangled around it. You could easily miss the Foghorn if you didn't know it was there. There was a wooden sign, but it was overgrown even in the winter. I thought Andrew liked it that way: it meant he got only locals and regulars and didn't have to deal with tourists. There were enough people around who knew that the Foghorn was the place to go for real ale, half a pint of local shrimp, a dozen local oysters or fish straight out of the sea. The red wooden door opened with a tinkle. Inside there was always some interesting music playing: often it was an album I knew well, or was suddenly pleased to be hearing again after a long time. Last time I'd been in — with Libby, for oysters, her treat — it had been a compilation of contemporary sea-shanties, and we'd sat by the fire and sang along to the Tom Waits ones, and afterwards Libby told me she'd met a man called Mark who had the most amazing eyes, and she'd wanted to kiss him as soon as she saw him. He'd come to her knitting group; he was the only man who had ever come to the knitting group. Even though Libby had been knitting for years, she hadn't known that it's much easier to draw yarn out of the middle of the ball, rather than the edge. Mark had shown her this, and a few other things. In return, she'd shown him Kitchener stitch. Mark knitted with one needle tucked under his arm, like a bagpipe. He said his male ancestors in Northumberland had all knitted like that.

Today the Carpenters song 'Superstar' was playing. Andrew Glass was about fifty and driftwood-thin, with a storm-battered face, blond hair and deep navy blue eyes that shone out from behind his round, wire-framed glasses. He was leaning on the bar reading *The Guardian*. There was a pile of magazines next to his elbow: *The Economist, New Scientist, The Spectator, Private Eye;* not what you'd usually find in a Devon pub. There was only a handful of customers, each settled in a nook or cranny with a pint of something. One man was reading a paperback thriller by the fire and B went over and sniffed his legs. He didn't even look up. He was about two-thirds of the way through his book, and it seemed as if the world could end and that wouldn't stop him reading. I called B back and leaned on the bar.

'Andrew,' I said. 'Hello. Any chance of half a pint of Beast?'

Beast was an Exmoor ale, and it seemed even more appropriate than usual. Andrew looked up from the paper.

'Meg,' he said, smiling, coming over and clasping one of my hands across the bar. 'Long time.'

'I know. How's the book going?'

He groaned. 'Been completely rushed off my feet here. So much for retiring from the Navy to have time to write. Haven't done anything for over a month now. But I've got a new barman starting next week, so it should get a bit easier. How are you? How's your writing?'

'I think I've just deleted a whole novel, but otherwise it's fine. I guess I can't seem to get started properly. I'm jealous of you. You're, what, over twenty thousand words in now?'

'Something like that. I did what you said, by the way.'

'What did I say? I hope it was good.'

'To put my own experience into it more and use a conventional narrative structure. Tell the story not just of the disaster but my experiences finding out about it, and include more of my life at sea. I'd just started in on revising the first bit when Danny got called up — you know he's gone to Iraq with the TA?' He gave me my drink. 'On the house. Anyway, once the new barman's in it'll be full steam ahead.'

'Thanks. Oh, I'm drinking Beast partly in celebration, by the way.'

'You always drink it.'

'Yeah, OK. But you remember Tim Small? He's done pretty well with his proposal and Orb Books are considering commissioning it. Not just that, but there's a real Beast and Tim's off on the trail of it.'

'Well, here's to Tim.' Andrew raised his cup of tea.

I raised my glass. 'Absolutely. Oh, also, what's this about a winter let? That sign in the kiosk.'

'Oh, Seashell Cottage. That's right. You interested?'

'I don't know. Where is it? What's it like? Is it damp?'

'It's next door. Bit basic but lovely views. No damp. You want to have a look?'

'Yeah, I think so. I'm sort of looking for an office to work in during the day.'

'You know it's a whole cottage?'

'Yeah. Can I look anyway?'

'Sure. I'll just lock up the till.' He looked around the pub. 'No one'll want me for a few minutes, I'm sure. Come on, we'll go now while it's quiet. Have your drink when we get back.'

Seashell Cottage was certainly basic. It had a sitting room and kitchen on the ground floor and one bedroom and a bathroom upstairs. The floors were simple wooden boards throughout, except in the kitchen, where the floor was grey stone. All the walls were whitewashed. However, the sitting room had a large open fireplace and, as Andrew had said, a wonderful view straight out to sea. It had a big sofa in the middle of the room, facing the fireplace, and a little desk and chair facing the window. I breathed in deeply. The air was dry, cold and clean, if a little dusty.

'House-clearance people take everything,' Andrew said, 'even the doorknobs if you don't stop them. I got them to leave the sofa and the desk, though. Thought they might be useful. I can take them out if you don't want them.'

'Who does the cottage belong to? You?'

'Yeah. It was my uncle's place when he had the pub. After he died my aunt stayed on, really made it her own. It was very different then. But she's dead now as well, of course.' I remembered something of the aunt from Andrew's book. She'd been the only person who'd believed that he'd heard the ghosts of the men in the sea.

'I'm sorry,' I said.

'She was in a home for years in the end. She really hated it; I felt so guilty. She'll be happier now. And I've finally inherited the cottage, which means I have to do something with it.'

'You don't want to live in it?' I said.

'No. Too big for me. I'm happy upstairs in the pub. I got used to confined spaces in the Navy.'

I walked around a bit more, wondering what had been there before the house-clearance people came. They had done a good job; it was perfectly bleak and bare.

'Does the fireplace work?' I asked.

'Yep. Chimney's just been cleaned. And I can throw in logs if you like for twenty quid a month extra,' he said. 'You'd help yourself from the shed around the back of the pub. And you could use the pub's Wi-Fi if you wanted as well.'

B was sniffing around the fireplace and wagging her tail.

'Dog likes it,' Andrew said.

I did too. I imagined sitting at the desk in the window, writing with the fountain pen Rowan had given me and watching the boats in the distance. B would be able to come to work with me. I wouldn't have asthma attacks all the time. We'd come here in the morning and light a fire and we'd walk on the beach and eat fish and chips for lunch, or even have oysters in the pub. I'd need some shelves and a couple of rugs as well as the desk. It felt like mine already. Already, I didn't want to go home.

'I love it,' I said. 'Can I think about it?'

'Sure, but I've got someone else coming to look at it at four this afternoon. I suppose I could tell them I've given you first refusal, but you'd have to let me know by tomorrow morning. Sorry to rush you, but these things seem to happen quite fast.'

'Actually, I don't really need to think about it,' I said. 'Are you happy for me to take it?'

'Delighted.' He grinned.

'Do you need references and stuff like that?'

'No. I know you. Can you pay a month up front?'

'Yeah, of course. I'll want the logs too. I'll write you a cheque now, shall I?'

We went back into the pub. I wrote a cheque, and Andrew gave me the keys.

'I put "winter let" on the sign, but I really don't know what I'm going to do with the place,' he said. 'It's definitely yours until June or so, but probably longer if you want it. In a couple of years I might sell, or convert it into a holiday let. But for now we could just take it month by month.'

'That's great. That's really great. Thanks.'

I put the keys in the pocket of my anorak. My drink was still on the bar where I'd left it. I took a sip. It was musky and earthy.

'Oh, Andrew,' I said. 'While I'm here I wanted to ask you something, if you've got a minute.'

'What is it?'

'It's about the placebo effect. I remember you talking about it once . . .'

He nodded. 'Yeah. Go on.'

'Well, I've just read this book that basically says pretty much all medicine works better if you believe in it. I'm just wondering how valid the whole thing is.'

'You've heard about Prozac, presumably?' he said. 'Big news story.'

'Yeah. I thought that was pretty weird. My brother's on it. Says it completely changed his life. How can that be just in his mind?'

Andrew shrugged. 'I suppose a lot of disease is in the mind in the first place. Especially depression. There's an article in the latest *New Scientist* about how Valium only works if people know they're taking it,' he said. 'Evidence for the placebo effect builds up all the time. I saw it quite often in the Navy. One time, one of the sergeants got a chest infection and my commanding officer told me that we had these new antibiotics that we were trying out. Supposed to be stronger and better—we often did have weird new things like that. I gave the sergeant these pills and they cleared up the infection no problem. It was only much later that my commanding officer told me that in fact someone had forgotten to put the box of antibiotics on board, and I'd given this guy out-of-date vitamin tablets. God knows why we had those. Boxes and boxes of them, it turned out. That was the first time I encountered the placebo effect, and it really stuck with me. Of course, you can't tell most people you've done that kind of thing, because they think you're a nut-job. Then there's the nocebo effect. You heard of that?'

'No. What is it? Like the reverse of the placebo effect?'

'Yeah, sort of. It's when people think they're ill when they're not. It's how people say voodoo curses work. If someone believes they're really cursed and they're going to die, they just do. Again, there's been loads of studies.'

'How does anyone make sense of this stuff?' I said, sipping my beer.

'Ha,' Andrew said. 'Maybe that's the point.'

'What, to leave it not making sense?'

'Well, maybe. But then you've got the problem of how you even do medicine. If there's no point giving people chemicals when it's their minds doing all the work . . . Or maybe it's just some of the work. I heard of an experiment once where they gave people with headaches one of what looked like a choice of two tablets, but were actually four: branded aspirin, normal aspirin, branded placebo—branded the same as the branded

214

aspirin, of course — and unbranded placebo. The normal aspirin worked better than the placebo, of course, but there was only a tiny difference between the normal aspirin and the branded placebo. The brand therefore actually had a tangible effect on the healing process. Just goes to show how much of the process is all in the mind. But you can't send people off to pray or dance to bongo music when they think they need an anti-depressant, not in this day and age. So you're going to write about this book?'

'I don't know,' I said. 'I'm supposed to. Along with a book on cosmic ordering, one on dog psychology, and something about Tarot. But I want to do a sort of experiment of my own; I just don't know how.'

'What kind of experiment?'

'I want to try to cure someone with the placebo effect.'

He laughed. 'Well, good luck. You'll need it.'

'I thought you said it had worked for you?'

'Not most of the time. You tell stories about the extraordinary events, not the ordinary ones, don't you? Half the time, even real medicine doesn't do anything at all. No placebo effect, no nothing. It can go both ways. And I don't think it helps if you know you're giving something that's not likely to work. That's why my commanding officer got me to give the vitamin tablets to that sergeant all those years ago. I think he knew it would work better if I believed in it too.'

'There was another essay in this book about that,' I said, 'although it's one of the ones I skimmed. You convey it to the patient or something — your knowledge that they're not really being treated at all, or your belief in the medicine you are giving them. It's all in subtle body language, apparently.'

'Yeah. Unless it's your mind that's doing it.'

'Huh?'

'The placebo effect might not be the results of the patient's mind, but your mind.'

'What, me believing something has worked when it hasn't?'

'No — you using your mind to heal.'

'Like some sort of witch doctor?'

'Or just a witch. Yeah.'

I frowned. I wanted to ask Andrew how it was possible to go from being a medical officer in the Navy, surrounded by hard men and war, to being somebody who seriously suggests that there might be something in witchcraft. But I knew the answer to that really; it was all in his book. When you've heard dead men screaming in the sea, you're going to end up believing things other people don't believe.

Someone came to the bar and ordered a pint of Old Moggie.

'Well, I'd better get going,' I said. 'Thanks so much for the cottage.'

'I hope you enjoy the views and everything and get some good writing done,' Andrew said, putting his glasses back on. 'And good luck with your experiment.'

'Well, like you said, I'll need it.' I sighed. 'I suppose I won't be able to use the placebo effect just like that to heal someone, will I?'

'Not if you call it the placebo effect,' Andrew said. 'Not if you don't believe in it.'

'No.'

Andrew gave the customer his beer and took the money. 'Cheers, mate,' he said. Then he said to me, 'What's the problem? What is it you want to cure?'

'Oh, my boyfriend broke his hand. He isn't getting on well with the painkillers and says he wants something more natural. I don't know where to start and all this placebo-effect stuff sounded quite easy, really. Give someone anything at all and they get better. But I can see it isn't that easy. I suppose if it was, then everyone would be doing it.'

'If you want a natural painkiller,' Andrew said, 'get white willow bark. It's what aspirin is based on. Works a treat. You can get it in tablets from health food shops. I take it because aspirin gives me indigestion.'

'White willow bark?'

'Yeah.'

Before I drove to Totnes I texted Josh: *Have book. Are you at home?* Totnes was sleepy and quiet and I parked easily on Fore Street, right outside Greenlife. B was asleep on the back seat of the car, but woke up when we stopped, and sat up, yawned and looked out of the window. I'd been looking at the clock on the dashboard of the car all the way there and trying to work out, minute by minute, how I could explain what I'd been doing when I got home. I'd left the house at about two. Now it was gone four and the sky was darkening and breaking into pieces of pre-blackout grey. I could still taste Beast in my mouth. Christopher would know from my breath that I'd been to the pub. I'd have to get some mints. But much worse than that: how would I explain the set of house keys in my pocket? I wouldn't be able to, ever. Compared with having a set of house keys in my pocket, explaining why I'd been out so long should be easy.

While B yawned and stretched I calculated that I could spend about five minutes buying white willow bark for Christopher and mints for me, drive up the hill, illegally park, quickly give the book to Josh, and then be home about half an hour after that. That meant it would be gone five by the time I got in. It would be OK, though. I could say I'd been in the bank dealing with the money for most of the afternoon. I could suggest courses and new clothes and maybe even some kind of eco-holiday, and then perhaps life would sparkle again. But really I didn't want to go home at all. I wanted to go back to Seashell Cottage, eat dinner in the Foghorn and sleep alone.

It was easy to find white willow bark in Greenlife, but one bottle of pills really wasn't much for three hours out of the house, so I browsed a little and also picked up some arnica bath, which was, it said on the box, good for bruising, sprains and broken bones. Also, on a whim, I bought a whole set of Bach flower remedies, and a book to go with them. I saw myself standing in the kitchen like Vi, mixing up some combination for Christopher. I flicked through the book and saw a couple of names that I recognised from the remedy Vi had made for me. Each had an entry of two or three pages. Crab apple, which I hadn't had, was apparently for stressed, anally retentive people who had to tidy everything up and were terrified of dirt. I wondered what 'my' remedies would say about me. Just as I was paying at the counter my phone vibrated. It was a text message from Josh. *Crisis. Am in card shop. Bad numbers. Help?* I had a fair idea what this meant, and I got back in the car to drive up the hill. B gave me a look that I anthropomorphised into 'What on earth are we doing *now?*', so I explained to her that we were going to go and rescue Josh and then drive home to Dartmouth, and we might see some squirrels on the Lanes and when we got back it would definitely be time for her dinner. She cocked her head sharply each time she recognised a word: *Josh, home, squirrels, dinner.* I wondered if I could communicate with B more efficiently by using only nouns and then stringing them in the rough order that they were going to happen. Was that what the world was to B? Was it all just nouns on a timeline? There had to be a bit more to it than that: she was visibly thrilled at the idea of squirrels, even though, as I'd said to Libby, she didn't chase them any more. She did look a bit baffled, however, that the squirrels could come between home and dinner, so I changed the order to *Josh, squirrels, home, dinner.* This time she whimpered slightly as I said each word. I reckoned I could probably write a book on dog psychology myself after all these years of study.

Josh was the only customer in the card shop. It was a small, slightly poky place that also sold paper, fountain pens, mechanical pencils, artists' equipment and notebooks. He had his back to the door and appeared to be examining 2008 diaries, which were on special offer. I could see he was shaking, and I wanted to put my hand on his back but thought that might make him jump. He looked fragile standing there in his carefully ironed jeans and his red Mensa hoody.

'Hey,' I said gently.

'I can't turn around,' he said. 'But I think otherwise I'm acting quite normally. No one has tried to throw me out yet. How are you?'

'I'm all right. What's happened?'

'Look by the door.'

I looked. There was a revolving metal stand with children's birthday cards on it. I immediately saw what the problem was. It was as if whoever had arranged the cards had done so in a way designed to cause Josh maximum discomfort. The vertical row of cards you'd have to walk past to get out of the shop had age-badges with big, colourful numbers on them. From the top down, the numbers were 6, 6, 6, 1, 3 and 7 — 666 was just about the worst-possible number for Josh, closely followed by 13.

'At least there's a seven,' I said to him.

'It won't do any good. Oh, God. Why is this happening? I only wanted a birthday card for Dad. They don't usually do children's cards in here. That's why I came, but now I can't get out. I might have to stay here for ever. I thought of just turning the rack around, but I'd still know they were there. Plus I can't go near them. Why did I not see them when I came in? I'm such a knob.'

'It's OK,' I said. 'I'll move them somehow.'

'You'd touch them?'

'Yeah, it's OK.'

'They'll curse you.'

'They won't.' I thought about the nocebo effect. 'I think if you don't believe in them, they can't hurt you.'

'I can't stop believing in them.'

'I know. But you will one day.'

Josh sighed. 'Thank you for coming to help me. I'm very grateful.'

'It's all right.'

'I left a message for Milly, but maybe she won't come. She always used to help.'

I sighed. 'Yeah. It's all a bit complicated, I guess, now she's moved out.'

'Yeah.'

'So does this happen a lot?' I said.

He shrugged. 'It's been better recently, but usually about once a week.'

'And you always call Milly?'

'Yeah. She's very sympathetic. She understands. I don't know what I'm going to do when she goes.'

'Goes? But I thought she'd already . . .'

'I mean when she goes to London.'

'I didn't know she was going to London.'

'She is. She's going back to her parents. Christopher will be thrilled.'

'God.'

We stood there for a few moments looking at the diaries. One of them showed all the Pagan festivals, and the phases of the moon; another had pictures of mushrooms and details of when you could pick the different types; another included tide tables for the Devon coastline. I picked up the mushroom diary and opened it randomly. An entry for October told me about the death cap, which looks similar to the field mushroom except for its white gills. The field mushroom is good on toast; the death cap will kill you if you eat it. I knew this already because I sometimes went foraging with Libby and Bob. Bob had a rule never to pick anything with white gills, because of the death cap, but Libby claimed to know which white-gilled mushrooms were poisonous and which weren't, and so picked whatever she liked. One of their friends had ended up on kidney dialysis after eating what looked like chanterelles but were actually deadly webcaps. Hearing about this hadn't bothered Libby at all. I couldn't imagine being killed by a mushroom. I put the diary back.

'OK,' I said. 'So I think I'm going to go and . . .'

Josh shuddered. 'Do you mind if we just stand here for another minute or so before you touch them? I have to prepare myself. I think we can just look at diaries for a bit longer.'

'OK. Just tell me when you're ready.'

'Did I ever tell you the joke about the flood?'

'No. I don't think so. What is it?'

'A very religious man hears that there's a flood coming. Everyone in his village is evacuated, but when people ask him why he's not going, he says, "God will save me." So the flood comes and the waters get higher and higher. The man ends up on his roof. A boat comes to rescue him, but the man refuses to get on it. "God will save me," he says, and the boat goes away. Then the water gets even higher until there's only a tiny patch of his roof left. A helicopter comes and they let down a rope-ladder, but the man waves them away. "It's all right," he says. "God will save me." Anyway, he drowns and goes to heaven. When he gets there he's pretty pissed off, so he goes straight to God and asks him why he let him die. "I believed you would save me!" he says. "Well," says God, "I did try. I sent you a warning, and then a boat and then a helicopter. What more did you want?"'

I laughed. 'That's a good one. Oh — thinking of heaven, I've brought *Second World* for you.'

'Thanks.'

'It's in the car with Bess. I hope she hasn't eaten it.'

'I hope so too.'

The door tinkled and I turned around. It was Milly.

'Hi,' she said to me.

'Hi,' I said. 'He can't turn around.'

'Milly,' Josh said, with his back to her. 'Sorry to call you again. Thanks so much . . . How are you?'

While he was talking, Milly frowned a question-mark at me, and I tilted my head at the cards. She nodded. She could see what the problem was too. She was younger than me, younger even than my brother Toby, but she seemed ageless. Her hair was red and shiny and her eyes were light grey. She had no wrinkles, but didn't look childlike. We'd met about a year before, at Peter's sixty-fifth birthday party. Christopher had been too ill to go, so I'd gone on my own and helped Josh and Peter with the food. Milly had been playing the harp. After the other guests left, the four of us sat and drank espressos from the machine and we laughed at Josh's jokes and talked about our plans for the following year. Peter was going to do his Grade 5 music theory test and start opening the café in the evenings. Josh was going to write down his theory of everything and try to make peace with one more number. Milly said she was going to learn how to sew and make her own clothes. It felt more like New Year's Eve than someone's birthday. I said I was going to finish my novel, and I couldn't think of anything else. I'd wondered for ages after that about ringing Milly and suggesting coffee or lunch, but I never did because I didn't want to have to lie to Christopher about where I was going. Also, I never had any money for coffee or lunch.

'I've been better,' she said. Then, to me: 'How's Christopher's hand?'

'Broken. But it was all his fault.'

'Yes,' she said. Her eyes filled with tears.

'Are you OK?' I asked.

'I don't know. Oh, ignore me. We need to move these stupid cards somehow.'

'Josh doesn't want us to touch them,' I said.

Milly rolled her eyes and went over to the counter, where the shop assistant was reading a book. After a whispered conversation that I couldn't quite hear, Milly sighed, marched over to the metal rack by the door and started taking out all the cards with numbers on them. Then she walked back over to the desk, dumped them all down and got her purse out of her bag. Josh had his eyes shut through all of this, and when he heard Milly sigh again he reached for my hand.

'You know that's going to be thirty-eight pounds forty?' said the shop assistant.

'Fine,' said Milly. 'You take Visa, presumably?'

A minute or two later Milly walked past with a big paper bag. Josh still had his eyes shut. The door tinkled as she walked out.

'What's happening?' Josh said.

'It's OK. The numbers have gone,' I said.

He opened his eyes. 'Thank God. Where's Milly?'

'I imagine she's disposing of them somehow.'

'It's cost her loads. I'll have to pay her back. And she must be so upset about her and Dad as well and . . . Oh — I'm such a knob.'

'It's OK,' I said again. 'Don't worry.'

Josh was still shaking as we walked out of the shop. 'Will you thank Milly for me when she gets back?' he said. 'I'm too embarrassed to see anyone right now, especially her. I think I'm going to go home and have a lie down. I'm so fucking pathetic I can't believe it.'

'You're not,' I said. 'Come on. Everyone's got things they find hard to do. Wait a moment while I get that book out of the car for you. Will you text me at some point and let me know you're all right?'

'Yeah. Thanks, Meg. I really owe you one. I'm so sorry.'

B had just woken up, and was now up at the window making a squealing sound at Josh, who didn't seem to notice. The book was still in its carrier bag on the dashboard, unchewed. I gave it to Josh, and he walked away up the road with the bag under his arm as if it held a map he'd already consulted.

Shortly after he'd gone, Milly came back.

'What did you do with them?' I asked.

'Charity shop,' she said. 'Poor Josh.' She dropped her head and looked at her hands.

'Hey — are you all right?'

She frowned. 'I could really do with a coffee if you're free.'

'Of course.' I didn't look at my watch, but I decided that it would be easy for the car to have broken down as well. The car was always breaking down.

'I'm not going back to Peter,' Milly said. 'I'm moving to London.'

We were drinking lattes outside the Barrel House, despite the cold, because B had refused to stay in the car. She was now sniffing around under the table, perhaps looking for squirrels. Milly was wearing turquoise fingerless gloves, and had her hands wrapped around her coffee as if it was the only source of warmth in her life.

'But . . .'

'I do love him,' she said. 'But it's impossible.'

She started crying and I gave her my napkin.

'God, I can't even talk. How are you? I wanted to meet you again after that party, but I never did, and now I probably never will again, and it's a shame, because I thought we could have been friends. Oh, I'm rambling. I'm sorry.'

I smiled at her. 'My life's pretty complicated. But fine, really. I felt the same way after the party. But hey, maybe it won't come to this. Maybe you won't leave.'

She carried on crying, and I gave her B's lead to hold while I went inside to get her some more napkins. When I came back, B had got onto Milly's lap and was licking her face. She hated it when people cried, and always wanted to lick their tears away.

'Get down,' I said to B. 'Come on, you silly dog.'

'It's all right,' Milly said. 'She's making me feel better.'

'Oh, well, push her off when you've had enough.'

'It's nice not being judged for once,' she said, once she'd blown her nose and composed herself. 'Animals never judge you. You know, it's not just Christopher. It's Becca too. It's become unbearable.'

'Oh, I've been on the receiving end of Becca,' I said. 'She hasn't spoken to me for the last seven years. You do get over it.'

'I'm not sure Peter will. He's so kind, and so thoughtful, but how can you be kind and thoughtful both with your children and with the woman they disapprove of? Josh has been great, but the other two . . . Well. It's over now. I'm going back to London to stay with my parents. I reckon it'll take me about a year or so to get over Peter, and then maybe I can find an ambitious young conductor, or someone else my mother will approve of. But I won't love anyone the way I love Peter. It's absurd. He's sixty-five and I'm twenty-eight. If only he was ten years younger and I was ten years older. That might be just about OK. Or if he was the woman and I was the man. There aren't so many clichés then.'

'I guess that's true,' I said. 'I've got a couple of friends in a relationship like that, sort of. She's in her sixties and he's just turned fifty-three. She jokes about him being her toyboy and everyone just laughs. It's really unfair that it should work one way and not the other. But you know, not everyone is judging you. Everyone's got something that other people would think was awful if they knew. People like to attack the people who can't or won't hide, because that's all part of their own camouflage.'

Milly sipped her coffee. 'When Becca comes down for the weekend it's understood that I keep out of the way. You know that I was in the process of moving into the flat? Peter wondered if we could just "not tell Becca" for a year or so, and wanted to know whether I'd feel uncomfortable going to London or something and hiding all my stuff on the weekends that she comes. He can't say no to any of his kids, as you'll have seen, so basically all she has to do is ring up and say she's coming, and that's it — I have to change my plans. He wasn't sure about me moving my harp into the flat, because it wouldn't be that easy to hide if Becca did come down. I'm just so sick of feeling like I'm something to be ashamed of. You know, last time Becca came it was my birthday. Peter had booked for us to go to this restaurant on Dartmoor, but he cancelled it, told me he was sorry and asked if we could celebrate my birthday another day. The worst thing is that I don't have children and grandchildren of my own — never will if I stay with Peter — so my whole life's about him, and only a fraction of his is about me. And it won't ever change. I won't ever come first for him, even though I'm the one who is there all the time, and I'm actually interested in him and his life and how the café's doing, and how he's getting on with his sax lessons, and what book he's just read. I'm the one who makes him do his scales and runs him a bath when he doesn't feel very well. Becca only rings when she wants something, or if she's had an argument with her husband and wants to escape for a few days. She's not that interested in Peter at all. But something about them makes him panic. He doesn't mean to hurt my feelings, but he does, all the time, because he's been put in this impossible position. He can't ever suggest to Becca that she comes at a different time because it's my birthday, for example, since he knows Becca will say something back like "How old is she going to be this year? Seventeen?"'

'I just don't understand why they've got such a problem with your relationship,' I said. 'It's not as if their mother died last week. Surely they've got to let him move on.'

A gust of wind blew up the High Street and I did up my jacket. B was still curled up on Milly's lap. Milly now held her coffee with one hand and stroked B with the other. If B had been a cat, she would have purred.

'They don't like it because it's embarrassing,' she said. 'They don't want to have their birthdays and Christmases and holidays spoiled by having to think of me in bed with their father. That's what it comes down to. We live in a very conservative world, really. Becca's an authority because she conforms, and she has a nice big house, I imagine, and a cleaner, and nice furniture, and a husband and three lovely children, and that gives her the right to judge me, and decide how I should live. You know, what's really sad is that she and Christopher don't understand that the spirit doesn't age. You're the same person at sixty-five as you are at twenty-eight, really, with more or less experiences, and more or less wisdom. Peter can be very childish sometimes, and, even though he's got more general knowledge than me, when we talk about really important things we're completely equal. Of course, when we talk about music it's as if I'm the wise old woman and he's just a child. He can't even work out a minor scale yet. So it's not all cut and dried. When Becca and Ant are sixty-five, they'll be the same people as when they were twenty-eight, more or less. So if one of them was twenty-eight now and the other sixty-five, that wouldn't make any difference. It's the same with Christopher. Would he reject you if you were sixty, or twenty?'

I imagined being with Christopher until we were both in our sixties and realised I'd probably rather shoot myself. I didn't say so to Milly, but if either Christopher or I was much older or younger than the other it wouldn't have worked at all. One of the few things we had left in common was both being in our late thirties; another was the fact that we were already together and inertia was winning out over entropy. I remembered seeing Rowan's tanned, ageless forearms resting on the table in Lucky's the first time we'd been there, and realising that I wanted to touch them. This had surprised me, because I'd never found older men particularly attractive. It was when I'd noticed the agelessness of his arms that I'd first realised he was a man, like any other man, and that he would also have feelings and memories and hopes and a heart and a naked body, just there under his clothes.

'You know, Peter told me he was going to tell Christopher not to come round any more,' I said.

'Seriously?'

'Yeah.'

Milly looked up at the blackening sky, and then back at me. 'And has he actually told him that?'

I thought of the get-well card with a £20 note in it that had come that morning. Christopher had torn up the card, but not the £20 note. He'd given it to me to buy the remedies, and I'd taken it, because I hadn't known what else to do.

'I'm not sure,' I said.

By the time I got home it was six o'clock. I'd tried to ring before I left Totnes, but there had been no answer. Surely Christopher could answer the phone with his left hand? I imagined him passed out on the floor after taking too many painkillers; in bed, overcome with pain, all on his own; or just not hearing the phone because his throbbing despair had become so loud. As I drove down the Lanes I developed a kind of acid indigestion that felt like a monster inside me trying to eat its way out. But when I opened the front door the only throb came from some hip-hop bassline that I half-remembered from the early nineties.

'Sweets?' I said. 'You won't believe . . .'

Christopher was on the sofa grinning and half-dancing. My copy of *The Science of Living Forever* was on the sitting-room table in front of him. I didn't remember leaving it there.

'Hey, babe,' he said. 'I've found a new channel. Old-school hip-hop. Come and watch it with me. It'll bring back memories.'

'OK, I'll just put the kettle on. You won't believe the afternoon I've had.'

'Maybe I can manage to put the kettle on for you? You look knackered.'

'No, it's all right. I can do it. Do you want a cup of tea? Have you had your painkillers? If not, don't take them, because I've got some white willow bark for you. It took ages to find, but it looks really good, and . . .'

'Thanks, babe. I will have a cup of tea, if that's OK, and some new tablets. You do look after me. Sorry I've been a dick recently.'

'You haven't exactly . . .'

'No. I have. I've been thinking about it all afternoon. I'm sorry. And I read that book Josh gave you. It's amazing. We're all going to live for ever! I can't believe you didn't tell me, although you probably thought I wouldn't understand it. I haven't been that good at science things in the past. But it's like life has opened up again. I think I'm going to read a lot more science books now.'

On TV, a guy in a shellsuit was pointing at a clock around his neck.

'Really?' I said, filling the kettle. 'Wow.'

'Yeah. It's like, it's so easy to start thinking that life is totally meaningless. I don't think I ever told you this, but after Mum died I used to get terrible night sweats, and I'd wake up cold and shivering and think about all the black nothingness out there. When I was a kid I thought death would happen to other people, but not to me. Then when I grew up and realised it was inevitable for everyone, and then saw it happening to Mum, it was just such a fucking downer, you know? This book has made me feel like a child again. I think I might write to Kelsey Newman and thank him. He made the science so easy to understand as well. I totally get how the collapsing universe would provide all that energy and create the Omega Point. It makes total sense. The only thing I can't work out is this Second World stuff. Have you got the new book somewhere? Oscar sent it to you, didn't he? I'd love to read it.'

'Sorry, sweets, I lent it to someone else. But when they've finished with it you can have it. I didn't know you'd be interested, otherwise I'd have kept it for you, obviously.'

There was a pause, and then he said, 'Who?'

The kettle had boiled and I poured water into our cups. Now I had some money I'd gone back to using one tea-bag each instead of sharing one between us. It always drove me mad that Christopher didn't notice things like this. If he always made nicer tea when he had money, I would always know when he had money. But he never really noticed the kind of tea I made, or even how many tea-bags there were in the bin. Would Rowan notice that kind of thing? While the tea brewed I started unpacking my shopping: the white willow bark tablets, the arnica bath and everything else I'd bought. Christopher switched off the TV, and an empty sound echoed around the kitchen.

'Who did you lend it to?' he said.

'Huh? Oh, just Josh.'

'You saw Josh? When?'

'Well, I was in Totnes buying your remedies, so I just dropped the book off with him on my way home.'

'So you saw him today.'

'That's OK, isn't it?'

Another pause. Christopher looked away.

'Why wouldn't it be?' he said.

'I don't know. You're the one making a fuss about it.'

'I'm not making a fuss. How is he?'

'He seemed fine.'

'Did you see my dad too?'

'No.'

B had been on the armchair scratching behind her ear and waiting for her dinner. Now she got off and slunk upstairs. Perhaps it was because she'd detected something in my voice that she'd heard before and knew led to an argument. But it didn't lead to an argument, exactly. Christopher got off the sofa and came and kissed me on the cheek.

'Don't stress, babe. What's this?' He picked up the white willow bark.

'Oh, it's a natural painkiller. From trees.'

'Brilliant. How many do I have to take?'

I took the bottle from him and read the label.

'Two. Up to four times a day.'

I gave the bottle back to him.

Christopher got a glass and filled it with tap water. He gulped down two of the tablets.

'I feel better already,' he said. 'What's this other stuff?'

'It's also to help your hand heal. The arnica bath, well, I suppose that's self-explanatory. Arnica is for bruising and stuff. Sports people use it a lot. These flower remedies deal with the more, I guess, psychological aspects. I'll need to do some research to make up a remedy specifically for you, but you can have some rescue remedy to start with. I'll just put some drops in some water for you.'

At Christmas I'd asked Vi what I was taking, and that was when she'd written the label for my little brown bottle: *Gentian, holly, hornbeam, sweet chestnut, wild oat and wild rose*. She'd learned about Bach flower remedies relatively recently, in the nursing home. They'd had an experimental programme during which the residents were given holistic therapies of different sorts. Each of them had their own Bach flower combination in a brown bottle, and one of Vi's jobs was to mix up new bottles when the old ones ran out. I knew from what she told me that these remedies contained nothing more than the 'vibrations of plants'. I remembered asking her how 'nothing' could heal. She hadn't said anything about the placebo effect. She'd talked about male and female systems of rationality, and said that the irrational, female world, far from being non-existent, was actually the world of the void, the black hole, the spiritual cave and the 'cosmic vagina' in which you sense the unfathomable dark energies that are as important to the existence of the universe as the male world of matter that you can see and touch and count. Counting numbers — all the positive and negative integers — were male, but imaginary numbers — the square roots of negative numbers — all the way to imaginary infinity, were female. *Doxa* was male, paradox was female.

'Thanks, babe,' Christopher said.

'What were you thinking about exactly?' I asked him, once I'd carefully used the pipette to put four drops of rescue remedy in the water. 'Here. Sip this slowly.' I gave him the glass.

'Huh?'

'You said you'd been thinking this afternoon as well as reading the book.'

He gulped down the water. 'Oh, just stuff.'

'What stuff?'

'Just about, well, about how good things could still be. With us, and the future and everything.'

'Why were you thinking that?'

He must have picked up on something in my voice, just as B had, because he frowned.

'I just was. Is something wrong?'

I sighed heavily. 'Why does something always have to be wrong?'

'Come on, babe. Chill out. You've had a busy afternoon out in the cold. Let me finish the tea.'

'No, it's all right. It's done now.'

I finished making the tea and peeled and ate a tangerine while Christopher talked about how he knew everything was going to be all right because of a new job he'd seen advertised in the free paper, and how Mick from the project had rung him to say he was a definite for it if he applied. Devon Heritage were looking for people to work on restoring an old castle along the coast from there. Christopher had all the right experience, and Mick was going to be heading up the team.

'Which castle is it?' I said.

He told me. I could faintly visualise it. It wasn't far from Torcross. It was little more than a ruin, and, if I remembered rightly, it always had been a ruin, because it had been built that way.

'Isn't that one actually a folly?' I said.

There were lots of follies around South Devon, especially at the mouth of Dartmouth Harbour. The real castles were hundreds of years old, but the follies had gone up mainly in the eighteenth and nineteenth centuries. I wasn't really interested in old buildings and walls, but I loved follies. They were more or less completely useless buildings, but resembled something useful or real, like a watchtower or a lighthouse. Some people even built fake ruins in the grounds of their country houses to give them a 'historical feeling', and this was what I'd thought this structure was. I couldn't remember quite how I knew that, but Libby had found out a lot about Devon castles when she decided she wanted to get married in one. She'd even considered ruins, since, as she put it, she was already ruined herself, and follies, which she said would also strike the right tone.

'No, babe,' Christopher said. 'It's the ruins of a real castle.'

'Oh.'

'Well, I'm not going to go and work on a folly, am I?'

I shrugged. 'I don't know. They have historical importance as well, don't they?'

He laughed. 'Don't be stupid.'

'Why is that stupid? Don't you think it's interesting that people spent loads of time and money building structures for no reason other than to amuse themselves, or have something better than the neighbours, or so they could pretend to be living in the past, or in a fairy tale or something? I mean, surely history is interesting because it tells us about people? I think people who built follies were probably much more interesting than people who built castles.'

'You've lost me, babe. Anyway, Mick reckons that the timing's going to work out perfectly with the wall. We can all finish that and then move straight on to the castle, and we'll actually start getting paid. I mean, it's only going to be a temporary contract if I get it, but fantastic for the CV.'

Christopher carried on talking and I let my thoughts drift elsewhere. As far as I could tell he still didn't say anything about being sorry for punching the wall, or making me drive around Devon in the middle of the night, or being so rude at the hospital, or going silent on me for most of the drive back. I ate another tangerine and thought about the money, and how I should really tell Christopher about it now. But in the end I just said 'Mmm' in the right places, and 'That's brilliant' every so often, and fantasised about the days I would spend alone with B in Seashell Cottage playing my guitar, knitting my slippers and writing my novel. What was wrong with me? All those years I'd wished Christopher would read an interesting book and want to talk to me about it; all those times I wished he would apologise for, as he put it, being 'a dick'. But now I couldn't give a damn about any of it.

After Christopher had gone to bed I sat on the sofa and browsed through the book about flower remedies. What should I choose for him? Chestnut bud was for people who repeated the same mistakes over and over again. Chicory was for people who were egotistical, domineering and judgemental. Honeysuckle was for people who lived in the past, and couldn't get over some traumatic event. Rock water was for people who liked to take the moral high ground. Willow was for moody, sensitive people who spoiled things for people around them. Was all that Christopher, or was it just my idea of him? The book said that you should not prescribe for someone else unless you could be objective about them. Fat chance of that. As I took the brown stock bottles out of the box I felt my eyes fill with tears. I missed Vi, and I was so sick of Christopher I didn't want to heal him at all; I wanted to go upstairs and smother him. I still hadn't emailed Rowan back because I didn't know what to say. Every day I composed responses to him, and every day I constructed neat apologies for Vi, but I didn't actually do anything. I labelled Christopher's remedy and left it on the kitchen table for him, with instructions. I tried to will some placebo effect into the bottle, but my heart wasn't in it.

I made a cup of tea, wiped my eyes and sat back down on the sofa with the flower remedy book to see what it said about the combination that Vi had chosen for me. Gentian was for sceptics who had no faith. Holly was for those who were hardhearted and joyless. Hornbeam was for people who were exhausted and couldn't see the point of life any more. Sweet chestnut was for people who had lost hope. Wild oat was for people without specific ambition who couldn't settle or make up their minds about anything. And wild rose was for people who had become unable to pick up the right 'cosmic life energies'. I flicked back to the entry for Gentian. 'This is a person who wants to believe but cannot,' it began. 'He or she feels the need for faith — in something — but will need this remedy in order to begin to embrace it.'

I switched on the radio and started to mix a new batch of my remedy. The Beast of Dartmoor was now the main story on the local news. A woman from Postbridge claimed that she had seen it prowling around her garden. She described it as a black wolf, twice the size of an Alsatian, with yellow, 'glowing' eyes. 'I just didn't want to go out there,' she said. 'I've never seen an animal that big outside of a zoo. I'm staying inside from now on until it's caught.' I looked at B, lying on the chair in the sitting room. It sounded like an enormous version of her, although her eyes were brown. There were a couple of interviews with the local police and Paignton Zoo. B came and curled up on the sofa next to me, and I carried on knitting until the scratching sound started up again, this time at the front door. B wasn't bothered by it, which meant it was nothing. But I still went to bed and put my head under the duvet and tried to think about work, and daylight. I knew it was probably a seagull, a rat or even a badger, but I didn't want to think about why it would be scratching at my door rather than someone else's.

On Saturday when I woke up there was an unfamiliar bird singing loudly outside. I lay there for a while just listening, but then I got up to look for it. All I could see out of the window were the usual rooftops, with the sun dribbling a thin, brothy light onto them. I couldn't see the bird, but I wished I could; it sounded like an imitation of an arcade game. *Bing, bing, bing, brrr, brrr, dip, dip, dip, woo, woo, bing, bing, bing, dip, dip, ping, ping, ping, brrr.* And then the same, or roughly the same, again. I'd read somewhere, or maybe someone once told me, that the older birds are, the more complex and beautiful are their songs. This song was complex, but not exactly beautiful. Was it a young bird trying out all the possibilities of its voice, or an old bird having a mid-life crisis? I was still standing by the window wondering about this when Christopher came and stood behind me and pressed his body against mine. His right hand dangled uselessly by his side, but he stroked the top of my thigh with his left hand. He smelled of unwashed hair.

'Come back to bed, babe,' he said, his voice thickened by morning.

I suddenly felt as if someone was offering me sand to eat, or sea to drink.

'Oh, sweets, what about your hand?'

'You've got two hands.'

'I know, but . . .'

He dropped his left hand from my thigh. 'Fine. Forget about it.'

Minutes passed. The bird had stopped singing. Christopher

was back in bed. He was under the covers, not moving. The air felt dense. This was probably the first time I'd ever rejected him sexually, but he was an adult, wasn't he? He rejected me all the time. He'd spent the last seven years rejecting me.

'You know we're due at Libby and Bob's tonight?' I said.

There was a muffled reply from under the duvet. 'What?'

'Libby and Bob's? Tonight. I didn't know if you'd remembered.'

'Oh, fuck.' He sat up. 'Fucking hell.'

'Why are you swearing? Is it your hand?'

'No, it's not my hand. I just don't want to go and play happy families with Libby and fucking Bob, of all people, especially when she's shagging someone else. We can't afford it anyway, buying wine and stuff like that. I haven't got anything to wear. Can't you just make an excuse?'

'No,' I said, an edge appearing in my voice. 'I'm going. I just wondered what you were doing. I can afford it, as it happens. And I'm not into morally policing my friends. Or my family, for that matter.'

'What . . .' He ran a shaking left hand through the top of his tangled hair. 'What the *fuck* did that all mean?'

'Nothing.' I folded my arms and looked out of the window. The bird still wasn't singing and the soupy sun had been all soaked up by doughy clouds. 'I'm sorry. Look, there's some money. It came in yesterday. I wanted it to be a surprise, but I've messed it up a bit. I wondered whether . . .'

'No, what was that about friends and family?'

I sighed. 'I saw Milly yesterday.'

'Oh. That fat cow. I'm not surprised she's behind all this somehow.'

'For God's sake, Christopher. You can't call her that. And no one's behind anything.'

'She's messing up my family.'

'No. You and Becca are messing up your family. Josh is fine with it. Why can't you just let your dad be happy?'

'Oh, I see. Now it's even clearer. This is about how wonderful Josh is.'

'Don't be ridiculous.'

'Anyway, me and Becca are half the family. The other half's mad. It's down to us to keep an eye on Dad and make sure he's not screwing up his life. He's been vulnerable ever since Mum died.'

'So while you and Becca live your lives, you expect your father to be doing what, exactly? Just waiting for you to phone, or for Becca to come for a few weekends a year, usually not even to see him, but because she's found out Ant's fucking another London barmaid or he's found out she's been sending more naked pictures of herself over the Internet to another guy in Florida? Apart from that you'd have him just working in the café and watching TV on his own in the evenings and waiting for his boring life to be punctuated by another one of Josh's psychotic episodes?'

'My father has nothing to do with you. Neither has my sister. I wish I'd never told you any of that stuff now. I knew you'd find some way of using it against them. Why can't you keep out of it?'

'If you want me to keep out of it, then don't expect me to come to the bloody hospital with you in the middle of the night, and don't have a go at me because I don't do it perfectly. And don't ask me to change any more of your bandages. I wish I wasn't involved in your family, but I am, especially when you go around punching walls because you can't cope with the simple fact that your father loves someone who isn't you, and isn't your dead mother.'

Christopher put the duvet over his head.

'That's very grown up,' I said, half-thinking he might laugh at this, but not knowing quite what I'd do if he did.

'Fuck off,' he said.

'OK. Fine. I'm going out. I'll probably be back after the dinner party.'

Nothing.

'Christopher?'

'Do what you like,' he said.

The day was in ruins, should have been in ruins. But in a sense it had been ruined all along. I felt quite calm as I drove out of Dartmouth the Warfleet way, past the road to the castle and Rowan's house, and out towards Little Dartmouth. The sky was the colour of cobblestones as I drove through Stoke Fleming and past the entrance to Blackpool Sands, where I walked B most mornings. She made her usual little whimpering sound as we approached, and then breathed all over the back window as we passed it. She would probably realise that we were going to Slapton Sands, but not how long we might be staying. The road ribboned along the cliffs through Strete, lined with a haphazard stone wall beyond which there were mimosa trees, wild primroses and pink sheep grazing in fields. The road jagged round, and down, and soon I was on the straight road between Slapton Sands on the left and Slapton Ley on the right. Torcross village was at the end of this, like the head of a tadpole. I parked by the Second World War tank and then walked along the esplanade to Seashell Cottage. Turning the key in the lock felt like breathing in after spending a long time underwater. Christopher could simmer and stew all day. I wasn't going back until midnight at the earliest. Or maybe I was never going back, or only going back to pick up my stuff. I wasn't sure.

The desk in the bay window looked inviting as a place to sit and contemplate the rest of my life. There was nothing on the desk, of course, and all I could see beyond it were the yellow and blue stripes of shingle, sea and sky, dotted here and there with sea-birds busy with their fishing. But I couldn't settle. If I sat there now, with so much life to contemplate, I felt that I might just watch the sea for ever, and freeze with no fire and starve with no food.

I let B sniff around the house while I nipped out to the local shop. Even though it was off season, there was a limited range of buckets and spades, as well as laxative powder, shoelaces, doorstoppers, paperclips, postcards, local pamphlets on nature and ghosts, string, firelighters, logs, milk, cheese, sandwiches and about a thousand other things. The shelves were a bit dusty and it was pretty gloomy, but I still managed to buy a campfire kettle, some firelighters, bread, a tub of fresh prawns, a dusty packet of penne, a lemon, black peppercorns, coffee, an assortment of herbal tea-bags and some local honey. I put a can of dog food and some dog biscuits in my basket as well, walked around the shop for a bit and then went back and added two more cans, a big rawhide chew and a tin bowl. Then I went to the cleaning section and picked up some dusters, bleach, cream cleanser, J-Cloths, furniture polish and a bucket. After I'd put everything on the counter the woman behind the till raised her eyebrows.

'Anything else?' she said.

I glanced behind her to yet another rack of local publications. There were tide-tables, birdwatching manuals and nature diaries about Slapton Ley. There was also a slim paperback called *Household Tips*, by Iris Glass. That must be Andrew's aunt, whose cottage I had taken over. 'Can I take that book as well, please?' I said. She sighed and reached it down for me. 'You on holiday, love?' she said.

'Sort of.'

When I got back to the cottage B's eyes seemed full of questions, which I half-answered with the rawhide chew. I put all my cleaning stuff in the bucket and left it in the kitchen. Then I went round the side of the pub and got some logs. I came back and started building a fire while my new kettle boiled and my grill heated up.

I'd learned to build fires back at Becca and Ant's place in Brighton. After Drew's drama series had gone into post-production he'd returned to London, the idea being that eventually I'd move there to be with him, or he'd move to Brighton to be with me. In the meantime we spent every weekend at Becca and Ant's place, because we both knew my little flat was cold and depressing. One Sunday morning we were in the four-poster bed together in 'our' room, overlooking the pond in the back garden, when Drew looked at me seriously and said he loved me, and wanted to marry me. I remember looking around at the perfect bedroom and thinking how the wallpaper — which showed scenes from contemporary Brighton — was more tasteful and eccentric than anything I'd ever manage to buy. There was an Aga downstairs, and I knew that Ant would probably be cooking us breakfast on it already. Becca would be lighting the large open fire in the sitting room, as she always did on cold weekend mornings. After breakfast we'd all read the papers together in front of the fire, and talk about things we'd found in the review and style sections. Becca dominated these discussions, and would often go up to London on a Wednesday afternoon when her shop was shut to buy something she'd seen in the paper the week before. While this was going on I'd glance at the crossword, but I wouldn't start doing it until that evening when I got home. Before lunch we'd all have a swim in the indoor pool, then a sauna, and after lunch Drew and I would go upstairs for more by-numbers sex. It felt a little as if my external life had gone from being something the size and colour of a white handkerchief to becoming several yards of beautiful fabric, printed with complicated colours and patterns. The only problem was that Drew was the dull background on this fabric, not the pattern. And I wasn't sure what you could really make out of this fabric, and whether whatever it was would really suit me. But on that Sunday morning I blushed and said I loved Drew too, and even though I didn't really believe in marriage it would probably be a good idea for us to make our relationship official and permanent.

That had also been the day I'd first met Christopher. When Drew and I eventually emerged, newly engaged, from our room, wearing tracksuit bottoms and old hoodies and big smiles, there was no breakfast downstairs and no fire in the sitting room. The kitchen smelled of cigarette smoke, presumably from Becca, who still hadn't managed to give up, because she wasn't yet over her mother's death. But instead of Becca, there was this thin, jaggedly beautiful, blue-eyed guy in ripped jeans sitting at the kitchen table with a £20 note in front of him. When we walked in he picked up the money, stood up, pocketed it, clapped Drew on the shoulder and said something like, 'All right, mate?' Drew introduced him as Christopher, Becca's younger brother, then Ant came in and told us that Becca had gone 'somewhere' to calm down and asked us if we would light the fire while he made breakfast. So the three of us went into the sitting room and pooled our knowledge, which didn't amount to much. Christopher and I started joking around immediately, but Drew took it all very seriously, arranging three logs in the shape of a wigwam and then looking for firelighters and matches.

'You don't want to use firelighters, mate,' Christopher had said to Drew. 'Bad for the environment.'

'Yeah,' I said, not knowing what I was talking about. 'Aren't you supposed to use kindling or something? Or twisted-up bits of newspaper?'

'Firelighters are more efficient,' Drew said.

Christopher went out of the room, and when he came back he had a bottle of vodka, a box of matches and the review section of that day's *Observer* newspaper. Drew still hadn't found the firelighters, and sighed while Christopher screwed up individual pages of the newspaper into little balls and threw them into the fireplace around the logs. Then he poured half the bottle of vodka over the whole lot and set it alight. For a few moments the contents of the fireplace burned like a Christmas pudding, and then, just as suddenly, it went out. We looked into the fireplace and saw a mass of newspaper pulp and wet logs. The whole house smelled of vodka. Drew rolled his eyes at me and I followed him upstairs. As we went I looked back at Christopher. He was pushing the wet logs around with his foot, coating his trainer in vodka and ash and mumbling something about how stupid everything was. I remembered quite clearly thinking at that moment that I was lucky to be with someone like Drew, who did things sensibly and carefully and never lost his temper, and that someone like Christopher, sexy though he was, would be too complicated and high-maintenance and you'd never know what he was going to do next. When we went upstairs, Drew sat on the bed, put his hands in his lap and said, 'You don't think he's attractive, do you?'

'Who?'

'Christopher.'

'Of course not,' I said. 'Why?'

'Most women think he is.'

'Well, I don't. Well, perhaps objectively. But he's not my type. You are.'

In Torcross, in what I was already thinking of as my new home, I used firelighters on my fire: two at the bottom, underneath several of the smaller, drier logs. I left some space for air to circulate, and then put a bigger log on the top. The fire, when it got going, smelled earthy and wintry. The kettle whistled, and I went to the kitchen and made myself some tea and toast with prawns, pepper and lemon. B lay in front of the fire concentrating on her chew. It was only one o'clock, but through the bay window I could see the sky hemmed at the bottom with pale light and then the thin band of the horizon, almost black against it. Then the grey-blue sea creasing a little and then breaking in lacy ruffles onto the shingle. I watched the sea like this, dressing and undressing, for a long time. *What if?* I thought, in time with the waves. *What if?*

About an hour before I went to Libby's I opened up my laptop. The sound from the fan immediately replaced the gentle sound of the waves outside. I logged into my bank account and selected *Transfers*. Christopher's name was there at the top of my list, and I transferred £1,000 to his account. Then I spent a while browsing beds on the Greenfibres website and once I'd decided which one I wanted to buy, I set about composing my reply to Rowan.

'You've done what?' Libby said.

We were in her kitchen, with nine fish lying in front of us, intact, on the worktop. Their eyes bulged, and they each looked as if they'd been just about to say something important when they were caught. Inside their open mouths were perfect sets of miniature teeth. They were freaking me out a bit; reminding me of why I'd once become a vegan. I turned away. B wasn't at all interested in the fish. She'd insisted on bringing her chew from Torcross and was lying in the middle of the kitchen floor with it, looking as if she couldn't wait to get to the end. I turned back to the fish. Libby was still looking at them as well, holding a knife but not doing anything with it.

'I've rented a cottage,' I said. 'At Torcross. I've spent most of the day sitting there by the fire watching the sea come in and then go out again. It was amazing. You know those rocks at the end of the beach? When the tide goes really far out they look like a dragon's bony foot splayed in the water, and you can actually walk around them to the next cove. I never realised that. I usually only walk the dog from the car park to the monument and then back.'

'You've left Christopher?'

'I'm not entirely sure. The plan was that I was going to just use the cottage to work in, but I almost ordered a bed today. I rented the place on a whim yesterday because, well, it was there, and not damp, and it has an open fire, and I could suddenly afford it. Christopher doesn't know about any of it.'

Libby giggled. 'We'd better have a drink,' she said. 'Why

did I not get them to fillet these?' She waved her knife over the fish.

'Because you were planning to bake them?' I said. 'You won't need nine any more, by the way, because Christopher's not coming. What are they?'

'Sea bass.'

'Bake them.'

'You think?'

'Yeah, definitely.'

She got a bottle of white wine out of the fridge. 'This'll be nice,' she said. 'It's a very expensive Sauvignon Bob doesn't know I took from the shop. God. I don't know what's wrong with me at the moment. Of course I should bake these. That's such a sensible thing to do. So why do I want to fillet them all?'

'Because that's the way you are. But we're baking them.'

'Are we?'

'Yes. I've had a massive row with Christopher, and I may have left him. I'm not sure about that bit, but anyway, at the same time, I'm thinking about having an affair — which by the way will remain an affair even if I do leave Christopher, because the, um, third party has got a partner as well. So I'm going to be very distracted, and if I have to fillet a fish I'll probably leave bones in it and kill Bob's aunt. Also, you look like you're waiting for an executioner to turn up or something. Where's Bob?'

'At the shop still.' She poured the wine. 'So tell me everything.'

While she covered the fish in oil, a different white wine and orange zest, and I chopped herbs, I told her about my row with Christopher, and my meeting with Milly and the day I'd kissed Rowan, although I didn't name him. I said that I couldn't get him out of my head even now, a year later.

'Be careful,' she said. 'You probably won't end up leaving Christopher.'

'I don't know about that. But yes, I am planning to be.'

'Just make sure you don't turn into me. Remember you said that you find people more exciting before you actually get to know them.'

'Oh.' I sighed. 'You're right. Well, it's only lunch.'

'You were the one who used the word *affair*,' Libby said.

'What's wrong with this as a hypothetical model: I do find this man exciting, even though he's too old for me, and so let's say he kisses me again — not that he will, and I don't even want him to —'

'You so do.'

'Well, say it happened and then after some modest amount of time we slept together and fell passionately and tragically in love ...'

'Yes?'

'Well, no one would have to know.'

'I'm just not sure it really works like that. You can't really be in love with one person and officially living with another; it has to be both at once. Well, if you're a woman. Do you want some more wine?'

'Yeah. Thanks. God, you're probably right.'

'You'll keep fancying other people all your life. But if you're going to work things out with Christopher you can't go off with someone else at the same time. You have to do one or the other.' She laughed. 'I know the theory. I just can't put it into practice myself. It's like playing pool. I could always tell someone exactly how to pocket the ball, but not always do it myself. Did I ever tell you about the time I really fell in love with this guy who was, like, the king of pool at my local pub when I lived in Bristol? What was his name? Oh — Ollie. Right, so I loved Ollie, and he slept with me and then broke it off. He had the most amazing dick — suntanned, can you believe it? — and a lovely smile, and he wanted to be a writer. God, I loved him. He had four friends, one dark, one blond, one redhead and one bald guy. They were like a boy-band. I went through them all one by one after Ollie rejected me. With the first three I convinced myself I was in love each time. One of them liked Hawkwind, though, and was obsessed with curry. The next one had a really tiny dick and horrible carpet and used to tell his own mother to fuck off. The one after that I can't much remember. But seriously, each time it was like, "He's got nice hair, and reads books; he'll do," or "He's got really good taste in music and likes Buffy," and I'd convince myself he was the one for me. I didn't fancy the bald one at all, but one night he was the only person left to walk me home from the pub, and when we got there he came in, dropped his trousers and tried to put his dick in my mouth. There was no conversation, but I understood, and he understood, that I'd had all his friends and now it was his turn. I sucked him off and then never went back to that pub again. They must have thought I was a right slag. Which just goes to show.'

I laughed. 'That's like some kind of weird Zen story, almost.'

She laughed too.

'So what's happening with Mark?' I asked.

'Well . . .' There was the sound of a key turning in the lock. 'That's Bob. I'll tell you later.'

The three of us spent the next hour preparing food and setting the table. Bob had brought oysters from Joni for a starter, and a lemon tart from the shop for pudding. He put on some Britpop album from the nineties, and we all sang along and danced around the kitchen. They cracked me up: every time a song had two singing parts they'd automatically take one each and harmonise. We moved on to the soundtrack of some big film from the eighties with lots of harmonisation possibilities, finished the bottle of Sauvignon and started another. B had finally got to the end of her chew and went to sleep it off upstairs. By the time Bob's parents turned up everything was ready and we were all knackered and a bit pissed, sprawled on the sofa, listening to a new jazz band that Bob was really into. He and Libby had started a long conversation about this band. Did she know they'd been nominated for the Mercury Prize? Yes, she did, but she hadn't known he had the album and had wanted to get it herself. I was wondering just what was so wrong with their relationship. It wasn't just the harmonies and the easy conversation. I noticed the way they refilled each other's wine glasses, and how Libby, when moving a book of Bob's from the coffee table, carefully inserted a bookmark so he wouldn't lose his place. Did Christopher and I seem like that to the outside world? Probably not. He'd never refilled my wine glass in his entire life.

Bob's father, Conrad, was German and still spoke with a slight accent that I felt I knew from someone else but couldn't remember who it would be. His wife, Sacha, had been a model years ago, but now worked on local art projects and made sculptures from driftwood. I sometimes bumped into her at Blackpool Sands when I was there walking B in the mornings. She had wild, dyed red hair, and a low, confident voice that reminded me of Vi's. Conrad and Sacha were both in their sixties, but looked a lot younger. Bob told some anecdotes about his recent trip to Germany, and brought his parents up to date with news of his great-aunt and -uncle. Just as Bob was talking about his journey back, and his plane being diverted to Exeter, the doorbell went and Libby jumped up to answer it. It was Mark, wearing unironed jeans, a new-looking shirt and black shoes that had mud around their edges. Once he was settled on the edge of a sofa on the opposite side of the room from Libby he asked Sacha some polite questions about what she did, and where she grew up, and then told us all about how his parents still lived on an island in Scotland as part of a hippy community they'd both joined when their marriage hit the rocks when they were in their fifties and Mark was finishing his GCSEs in Newcastle. Mark had ended up having to sleep on a friend's floor through his A-levels. Sacha kept asking things about the island, like 'Isn't it cold?' and 'Is it true there are no trees?' Conrad laughed every so often and at one point said to Bob, 'See, I've always told you that having crazy parents is a good thing.'

'What did you do at university?' Sacha asked Mark now.

'I didn't go at first. Couldn't afford it, and I didn't really have anywhere to go home to in the holidays. In the end I worked on a lighthouse for a couple of years until it got decommissioned and then I started doing peace studies part-time, but I could immediately see there was no future in peace studies.' He laughed.

'Why?' said Sacha.

'Well . . . You know, the Gulf War had just started, and everything seemed so screwed up. Eventually I transferred to engineering. I was an engineer for a while after I graduated, and then, of course, I dropped out and . . .'

'You didn't really drop out,' Libby said. 'You started designing boats.'

'Yeah, I guess.'

Just as I was wondering how Libby could explain knowing this, the doorbell rang and she went to open it. And suddenly there was Rowan, standing in the entrance to the sitting room wearing jeans and a pale blue shirt and not meeting my eyes. He was carrying a bottle of wine, which he gave to Libby.

'Lise can't make it, I'm afraid,' he said, after kissing Sacha on both cheeks and shaking hands with Conrad. 'She's got a really terrible headache. She's taken pills and gone to bed. I'm going to try to be both of us if that's all right.'

'Oh, the poor thing,' said Sacha.

'She always did have headaches,' said Conrad.

Conrad was Lise's brother. Of course. Had I known that and forgotten it? I didn't think so. So Rowan was Bob's uncle. I'd kissed Bob's uncle and then had a million sexual fantasies about him. I was glad I hadn't told Libby whom I was planning to have an affair with, even though, looking at him now, I realised how impossible that would be. But I had told him about her affair, I realised. I downed the rest of my wine and didn't catch his eye.

Over dinner we all ended up talking about paradoxes. Libby had said something about my TV deal, and all the maths I used in my SF novels and the weird stuff I wrote about mobile-phone networks and cellular structures. She was worried about how they were going to translate this onto the screen. I said not to worry, because from what I knew TV options just sat on a shelf gathering dust until they expired, so it was unlikely the books would ever be adapted. Rowan asked whether or not I understood all of the maths and science in my novels, which was a good question, because I didn't always. Or, at least, I did at the time I was writing and then not a year or so later, usually when I had to give a few interviews about it. I tried to explain all this as honestly as I could.

'But you review science books?' Sacha said.

'Yes. It's a bit the same,' I said. 'I understand them at the time I read them, especially if they're well written and have lots of good examples, but whenever someone asks me to explain relativity I can't do it. Or at least I can, sort of. Which is the speed-of-light one?' Everyone looked blank except Conrad.

'Special relativity,' he said.

'General relativity is gravity?'

He laughed and sipped his wine. 'I think so. You're right; one does forget.'

'In my mind I have a jumble of images: a man on a train that's going along at the same speed as a car, and so it seems to him as if the train and the car are standing still, relative to one another, and when he starts walking down the carriage he feels as if he's going at about one mile an hour, but really he's going at the speed of the train plus that. And I can see space-time laid out like a blanket . . .'

'Like the fabric of the universe!' Libby said.

'Exactly like that,' I said, smiling at her.

'You've confused everyone now,' Bob said to Libby.

'Oh. I knitted the fabric of the universe for Meg ages ago. That's all.'

Mark rolled his eyes when Libby wasn't looking.

'"That's all,"' Rowan said, laughing. He caught my eye and then looked away again. 'As if you're a kind of God of knitting.'

'Or God's assistant,' Libby said. 'I had to ask Conrad what the fabric of the universe would look like so that I could knit it.'

'Do you think God made the universe, or just designed it and got someone else to make it?' Sacha said.

'Oh, Mum, don't. You're hurting my brain,' Bob said.

'This is why we didn't bring him up to be religious,' Conrad said to Mark. 'We knew he wouldn't be able to cope with the paradoxes. Robert has a very focused mind.'

'I feel about three years old now,' Bob said. 'So thanks.'

'I can't understand paradoxes either,' Rowan said. He looked at me. 'Do you know Frank and Vi's friend — that philosopher who solves paradoxes?'

I laughed. 'No. My God. That sounds a bit crazy.'

'I thought you couldn't solve a paradox,' Libby said. 'Isn't that the point?'

'Your wife is cleverer than you,' Conrad said to Bob. 'I've always said so.'

'Dad, please shut up.'

'One of the artists I know collects paradoxes,' Sacha said. 'He pins them in a glass case like butterflies whenever he finds one.'

'Finds one?' I said. 'What, just lying around?'

'It may have been a metaphor. Perhaps there were no glass cases really either. We were drunk when we were talking about it, I think.'

Conrad frowned, and finished his glass of wine. He poured another glass, and then topped up everyone else's.

Rowan laughed. 'I've never found a paradox,' he said.

'You will,' said Libby with a dark smile.

Damn it. She knew.

'This is good,' Sacha said. 'It's good that we're discussing this because I've always been too embarrassed to ask him what they actually are. Now one of you can tell me exactly: what is a paradox?'

'It's a self-negating statement,' Mark said.

'Like what?'

'All Cretans are liars,' I said. 'If a Cretan says that to you.'

'A cretin?'

'No. A Cretan, Mum,' Bob said. 'Someone from Crete.'

'Why?'

'Because it's an Ancient Greek thing, I assume.'

Conrad looked up and laughed. 'She's clever,' he said, pointing to Libby, 'but my son isn't stupid either. They are well matched. In any case, there's something more to it than a self-negating statement.'

'It's where you end up using something to prove that it, itself, is ridiculous,' I said, struggling to explain. 'Like the Heap Paradox, where you have a heap of stones, take one away and ask someone if it is still a heap. They'll say yes, of course. You take another one away and ask again. Still a heap. At what point does it stop being a heap? At some point it will be just one stone, and since there is no definition of "heap" you could end up concluding that the single stone is a heap of stones.'

'But that's just a case of proving that a word doesn't have a precise definition, surely?' Rowan said. 'It just shows the difference between an abstract noun and a concrete noun.'

'OK, yes, that's not a great one. But the whole of twentieth-century science is based on paradoxes. Gödel's Incompleteness Theorem, Heisenberg's Uncertainty Principle . . . There's also the Fiction Paradox, or the paradox of fiction. Why is it that we get scared reading a ghost story, for example, when we know it's just a story? Why does fiction have any emotional effect on us at all, considering that we know it's not real? Why, when re-reading a book, or watching a film for the second time, do we still have the same emotional reactions as we did the first time around?'

'That's not a paradox,' Rowan said. 'That's just life.'

'My favourite paradox is the Horse and the Bales of Hay,' Conrad said. 'This is where a horse, given the choice between two identical bales of hay, each the same distance from it, cannot make a rational choice between them and so starves. This demonstrates the paradox of rationality.'

I thought about the woman who couldn't leave her house because she'd seen the Beast in her garden. Would she starve? If so would it be because she was too rational, or too irrational?

'Oh, that reminds me of an even better one,' I said, struggling to remember where I'd read it. 'It's from Thomas Aquinas originally. Aquinas wondered what would happen if God wanted to achieve universal resurrection. In other words, bringing everybody who had ever lived back to life at the same time. What would happen to cannibals, and the people they ate? You couldn't bring them all back at the same time, because the cannibals are made of the people they have eaten. You could have one but not the other. Ha.' I looked at Rowan. 'That's a good example of a paradox.'

'Rowan's got stories about real-life cannibals,' Bob said, but Conrad was pointedly stroking his beard in response to what I'd said about Aquinas, and so Rowan, like everyone else around the table, waited for him to speak.

'This is an interesting conundrum,' Conrad said eventually. 'Aquinas focuses this problem on the cannibal, but in reality everything is made of everything else. Every boat I build used to be a tree, several trees in fact, and perhaps meteorites, iron ore, plants and so on. You can't eat your cake and have it too. I think this is where the paradox comes from.'

Libby laughed. 'Meg's always talking about cannibalism,' she said. 'Ignore her. Who wants some lemon tart before we all sit around like hippies playing guitar, singing and clapping our hands?'

She was right. I used to talk about cannibalism all the time when I was a vegan. When I was a vegan people would ask me if I thought animals felt pain and plants didn't, and what I'd do if I swallowed a fly, or was in a plane crash and had to survive in the jungle by eating corpses and insects. I'd respond by asking people why it was OK to eat pigs, say, which have the intelligence of three-year-old children, but not OK to eat three-year-old children. I'd been a vegetarian ever since B had been a puppy and I'd been idly stroking one of her legs. Suddenly, horribly, I realised that it felt like uncooked meat. It was just like a chicken thigh you'd buy in a supermarket. B already knew her own name, as well as about twenty other words, and had a favourite ball. She rolled on the floor when I played Tom Waits, but left the room if Bob Dylan was on. She was not food; she was my companion. I realised then that I wouldn't be able to eat a mammal's flesh again, although I carried on eating fish for a while and then gave that up too. Not long after that I reviewed a book that argued that vegetarianism, in the way I was practising it, made no sense. Why eat the by-products from the meat industry, like milk and cheese, but not the products themselves, the actual flesh of the animals? How can anyone drink milk knowing that it's really made for those cute calves you see lying in the sun in fields in the spring, who are taken away to be turned into veal, or gassed, or incinerated, so that you can have their milk? I was convinced enough to start existing on a diet of plants: mainly hummus, plain chocolate and salt-and-vinegar crisps. I kept it up for two years before the cracks started to show. It turned out that the fiction of consensus reality, where farm animals are happy drawings on packets and nothing else, was easier to believe than the truth. I never ate mammals, and I still avoided dairy products most of the time, but I no longer thought much about the reasons why.

Libby put the lemon tart on the table and cut it into slices.

'I remember where I read about Aquinas,' I said. 'It was in this crazy book about how you survive the end of time.'

Conrad laughed. 'How do you survive the end of time?'

'You wait for the universe to collapse, and then you get a computer simulation going just at the moment when all the matter in the universe is infinitely dense. You use the infinite power to simulate a new infinite universe: a never-ending afterlife. It's quite neat, but very creepy.'

'I had a horrible dream after you told me about that the other week,' Libby said.

'It is a horrible dream,' I said.

'Isn't it a good thing?' Sacha said. 'I'd like to live for ever.'

'I wouldn't,' said Rowan.

'It's weird when you start thinking about the possibilities of "for ever",' I said. 'The book I read, or books — there are two of them so far — try to imagine this post-universe, and how it might be controlled by the Omega Point, which is the "moment" of infinite energy that becomes a sort-of God. How would "heaven" be arranged? The writer ends up arguing that we all get to live as heroes for a thousand years before we can even go to heaven. It's kind of complicated and disturbing all at once.'

'I think you can't imagine heaven,' Libby said. 'Or what would be the point of it?'

'Hear, hear,' said Conrad.

'But if you know that you're going to exist, with one consciousness, through all infinity,' I said, 'then there is stuff to imagine, and it quickly gets unpleasant. I think that's why this writer suggests a limit of one thousand years before you sort of merge with the God figure, the Omega Point. If you were conscious in an infinity, you'd become a god yourself in the end, because you'd experience everything, and everyone . . .'

'You'd become omniscient,' Rowan said. 'You'd be able to know everything. Nothing would be impossible.'

'You could go back and live through anyone you wanted,'

I said, holding Rowan's gaze for a second. 'You could find out what people around you had really been thinking while you were alive, even if they'd never said anything. You'd know the truth about everything. You'd . . .'

'It would be hell,' Mark said, pushing his plate away. 'Well, for some people. Because you'd realise that you had spent your entire life lying and cheating and betraying people you loved, and that at some point in eternity—which may as well be at the beginning, whenever it happens, since eternity is for ever—everyone you've lied to, and everyone you've cheated, and everyone you've hurt and double-crossed will find out about it. You'll have no secrets. Everything you've ever thought and everything you've ever done will be there for everyone to see. You'll spend the rest of eternity alone, shunned by everyone you've ever messed around.'

Libby got up and left the room.

'That doesn't make any sense, though,' I said, wondering if I should follow her.

'No,' said Rowan. 'Surely in order to know someone else's thoughts, you'd have to become them. You'd have to live through their life from the beginning: you couldn't just "drop into" someone's consciousness. Even if you did drop into someone's consciousness, you'd have all their memories and desires and hang-ups right there in front of you. And as you say, in an eternity you'd get the chance to know everything once enough time had passed. You'd become unable to judge anyone.'

'You'd end up being completely compassionate,' I said. 'You wouldn't be able to judge someone once you understood them and their motivations. You'd *become* them, like Rowan said, and so it would be like judging yourself.'

'And then you would have merged with God,' Conrad said.

The only song that Bob, Rowan and I all knew was 'Hey Joe', so Rowan and I played the chords on Bob's 'spare' acoustic guitars while Bob did the bassline. Libby was going to sing but didn't know the words, so I somehow managed to do it, even with Rowan watching me the whole time. Mark had left shortly after dinner with a 'bad stomach'. After Conrad and Sacha went we all drank a bottle of Lebanese wine Bob had brought from the shop and insisted on decanting, slowly, through a muslin cloth. Libby's eyes grew redder, and her face paler, until she eventually fell asleep on the sofa. Bob didn't seem to notice; he wanted to show us this riff and then that riff, and I sat there with my heart beating fast as I looked at Rowan. Our eyes met again. And again. His eyes seemed to be asking me a question, but I wasn't sure what it was. It wasn't quite 'Can I kiss you again?'; it was more complicated than that, but I didn't know how.

At about half past midnight I called B down from where she'd been sleeping in the spare room. I couldn't drive in my drunken state, so I put her lead on and arranged to pick up my car in the morning. Rowan, who was still fiddling around on one of Bob's acoustic guitars, glanced at me and then said, 'I should make a move as well.' We said our goodbyes and left together.

'Which way are you going?' I said, although I knew.

'Towards the castle,' he said. 'But I'll walk you home. It's late.'

'You don't need to.'

'I want to.'

We set off down the Embankment with B wagging her tail. She stopped and sniffed the first bench. I stopped too, but Rowan carried on. He realised we'd stopped and came back.

'I'm afraid my dog goes a bit slowly,' I said. 'She has to sniff everything.'

'It must be very interesting for her along here. Lots of smells.' He leaned down and rubbed her head. He did it for slightly too long, and I suddenly wondered if he was thinking about touching me as much as I was thinking about touching him.

'Yeah. I think it is,' I said.

The night was foggy and starless and gulls wailed some-where out at sea.

'Meg . . .' Rowan stopped rubbing B's head, stood up and touched my arm. Then he quickly took his hand away.

We both turned towards the river. Then I looked at him. If we kissed again, what would happen next? We couldn't sleep together. Despite my fantasy, he was too old: too old for there to be any future in it. And I was attached, and he was attached, and the world didn't work like that. Still, I was drunk and I knew if he kissed me I would kiss him back.

He dropped his eyes and cleared his throat. 'Lise left me,' he said.

'Oh, God,' I said. 'When?'

'Well, she's back now.' He shivered. 'It was a couple of days ago.'

'She's back? She left you and then came back?'

'She had a change of heart. She wants us to go to couples counselling.'

'And you?'

He did up the zip on his jacket. 'I want a quiet life.'

'Do you? Most people don't.'

I thought of Libby, and how she never wanted her quiet life with Bob. And me. Perhaps I had always wanted a quiet life, which was why, after making a lot of noise and running away with Christopher, I hadn't immediately run away again to London, where Vi had offered me a room for as long as I wanted. The first few days we'd spent in Devon Christopher had been entirely silent. But I'd thought he'd get over it, get over the trauma of falling out with Becca and betraying Drew. But he never did, not really. How could I become happy with Christopher? This had been the defining question of the last seven years. There had to be a way. We were both young, and he was still attractive, objectively, even though he'd started having the same effect on me as the sofa, or the frying pan, or the remote control. Why had I been thinking about this man, the man in front of me, who suddenly looked as thin and vulnerable as a small tree in a hurricane? Why was I still thinking about kissing him again, when there was no point to it, no sense in it?

'Don't they?' Rowan said. 'I thought they did. When you get to my age . . .'

'Does that matter? Does age matter?'

'I turned sixty last week. I think it matters. I'll never be young again. And I don't want to be on my own knocking around in some bachelor flat, probably drinking too much and never seeing anyone.'

B was pulling, not wanting to stay still. There was no traffic around, so I unclipped her lead. After looking at me once to check it was OK, she trotted over and sniffed each leg of a bench one by one. Then she looked over again to see what I would do next. I walked on slowly, and Rowan followed. She walked behind us, sniffing and glancing, and sniffing and glancing.

'Rowan,' I said, as he fell into step beside me, 'why are you telling me this?'

'I thought you'd understand. I thought — maybe hoped — you'd understand that I need a friend. I don't know many people around here who aren't Lise's friends, or Lise's family. She doesn't want anyone to know. I thought maybe I could trust you. I know you're half my age, and . . .'

'I'm almost forty,' I said. 'Well, in a couple of years. I'm not half your age.'

'I'm old enough to be your father.'

'Yes, but you're not my father.'

He sighed. 'Well, that's why I invited you for lunch. I wished I hadn't sent that email, but you can't get emails back. I didn't want you to think I was some sleazy old man making another clumsy pass at you. I just desperately wanted to talk to someone who might understand. But it was probably selfish of me.

I wasn't surprised that you didn't reply, especially after what happened between us, and all I can say is that I'm so sorry.'

The wind whipped down the river, and B wagged her tail and moved on to the next bench.

'I did reply,' I said.

'You did?'

'Yes, earlier today.'

'Oh. I only check my email at work. What did you say?'

'I said I'd love to have lunch with you. So now maybe you think I'm sleazy.' I laughed, although I wasn't finding any of this very funny. 'God — so when I asked you for lunch on the ferry you must have thought I was some sleazy young woman making an even more clumsy pass at you?' I said. 'No. Don't answer that. Why would I think you were a sleazy old man? I can't imagine anyone less like a sleazy old man. That's so stupid.'

He shrugged sadly. 'Sorry you think I'm stupid.'

'Hey — I think it in a nice way,' I said. 'And just for the record, I wasn't asking you on a date on the ferry. I've got this thing I want to show you. A ship in a bottle that I found. I've been meaning to ask you for ages if you'd have a look at it for me and tell me where it might have come from. Maybe if I bring it you could have a look? I sort of want to use it in my novel, but I don't know anything about it.'

'Of course. You know we've got the William H. Dawe collection of ships in bottles on loan at the Maritime Centre at the moment? You can come and look at those if you'd like to, unless you've already seen them in the Dartmouth Museum.'

'I'd love to see them. Promise me you won't tell me how they get in there, though?'

'What — how the ships get into the bottles?'

I nodded. 'I've never known, and I've never wanted to know either.'

'OK.' He looked over at the Higher Ferry crossing the river. 'Where's your partner? I meant to ask.'

'Christopher? Oh, we had a big row this morning.'

'Serious?'

'Oh, probably not in the end.' I sighed. 'I don't know.'

'Well, you can talk to me about that as well if you want to. I'd like to do something in return.'

'As well as showing me ships in bottles.'

He smiled. 'That won't take long. There's one in a light bulb that you might like.'

I bit my lip. 'I'm not sure I'll be able to help you that much. I'm not exactly very wise.'

'Yes you are.'

'Not about relationships.'

'You can't be as bad as me. According to Lise I haven't got the first clue.'

'Well,' I said, 'I'll try.' My eyes were filling with tears. We walked along in silence for a while. We walked past the Boat Float, which looked like a dirty sink with its plug pulled out and its edges all scummy. Then we walked past the Royal Avenue Gardens and the public toilets.

'Would Wednesday be all right?' Rowan said.

'Sorry?'

'For lunch. Wednesday at one o'clock at Lucky's?'

'That's fine,' I said. 'Great. Look, I'll be all right from here. You go home.'

'Are you sure?' He looked at his watch.

'Yes,' I said, shrugging.

And he went.

The house felt empty as soon as I walked in. Where was Christopher? It was too late to call anywhere he might be, not that I would. I ran over our row this morning. He'd told me to fuck off, which was new. I'd refused to have sex with him, which had never happened before. But I had money now, and a future, and I was going to write my novel while Christopher worked on restoring that castle and maybe did a part-time course. Perhaps we could eventually move away from Dartmouth. I'd probably need to finish my novel first, though. There the plan faltered. Even if I could ever finish my novel, Christopher would refuse to read it. He wouldn't even want to come to the launch party. If he did he'd just moan about pretentious people all the way there and all the way back and complain about trees being cut down for books. He'd deliberately wear something unflattering and combine this with his turquoise espadrilles. His Brighton drug-dealer voice would come back and he'd spend the whole night saying 'Yes, mate' and 'No, mate', with a wide-eyed look, taking the piss out of everyone I liked and sniggering into the beard he would inevitably grow for the occasion. He'd tell people he'd been to the University of Life, and if the publisher put us up in a hotel Christopher would make loud jokes about the other guests and insist on scoring a gram of cocaine because for him that was 'living the high life'.

It was almost two in the morning, but I wasn't at all tired. B didn't seem to be either. Whenever we got home after more than a few hours away, she liked to do all her favourite activities as if on fast-forward: she'd already rolled on her old chew and dropped her tennis ball down the stairs. I'd given her a handful of biscuits and she'd eaten a few of those. She'd been in her bed upstairs, in her bed downstairs, on the armchair and around the room chasing her tail. I needed something to read, so I went upstairs and got the book on dog psychology from my pile, then I checked the front door was properly locked and sat down on the sofa. I listened for scratching, but there wasn't any.

The book's introduction summarised various experiments that showed dogs were as intelligent as children. Most recently, a group of scientists had replicated the classic 'forehead' experiment, normally used to assess the analytical capabilities of children. In the original experiment, a child is shown how to switch a light on. The demonstrator does it two different ways. The first way is to use her forehead, but with her hands clearly visible. The second way is also to use her forehead, but this time with her hands under a shawl, and obviously not free. When the demonstrator uses her forehead even though her hands are available, the child does the same. But when the demonstrator's hands are constrained, the child, clearly working out that the demonstrator would have used her hands if she could, uses its hands. In the dog version, a demonstrator dog pulled a lever sometimes with his paw, and sometimes with his paw but with a ball in his mouth. The study found that dogs reason in the same way as the children in the previous test. A dog would rather use its mouth than a paw to pull a lever, and when the demonstrator dog used his paw 'because' he had a ball in his mouth, the dog subject would use its mouth. But when there was no ball, no obvious reason to use a paw rather than a mouth, the dog subject assumed the demonstrator knew better and copied his actions exactly. There were some sweet pictures of dogs pulling levers.

B was now on the sofa next to me.

'Look,' I said to her. 'A dog experiment.'

She whimpered slightly in response.

The main part of the book, which I half-skimmed, suggested that dogs are all born with various instincts that need to be taken into account by their human companions. According to the book, dogs are pack animals who need to know who is pack leader. If you have a domestic dog, the book said, you have to be pack leader, and do the kinds of things pack leaders do, otherwise your dog will become confused and perhaps even depressed. This means never letting your dog sleep in your bed, sit beside you on the sofa, walk out of a door before you or eat before you do. As long as the dog knows you are in control, you can train it to do whatever you want and it will feel secure.

I kept wondering why a dog would want to pull a lever in the first place. The summary of the experiment hadn't mentioned what 'reward' they got. I guessed the dogs would have got treats every time they performed an action 'correctly'. I made a mental list of things I thought B might pull a lever for. Food, of course, and, once, sex. Before she was spayed, she used to come into season and hump everything that moved and howl every night. But she'd also pull a lever on a machine that gave you tennis balls, pussycats, bound proofs and sunlight. There was an electric fan heater hidden in a cupboard upstairs. B couldn't quite switch it on with her paw, but she would try; at least, that's what it looked like. I was never sure whether she was trying to switch it on herself, or miming the movement to tell me to switch it on. In any case, it was impossible to have it anywhere in sight without her demanding that it was switched on. If I put it on low, she'd do the movement again until I put it on high. Once it was on, and up high, she'd turn around in front of it twice and then lie down and stay there quite happily until the room was like a sauna. Then she would start to pant, get up, find a cool section of the room and lie there. With some relief, I'd switch off the heater. Then, after about ten minutes, she would get up from her corner and start the whole process again. This was why the heater ended up in the cupboard. I wondered what a self-help manual for dogs would contain. Presumably it would tell dogs that they, not people, were the real pack leaders, and humans really enjoyed being rounded up, kept to a strict routine and having their faces licked. Perhaps it would also explain what happened to our instincts when we became domesticated, and how silly we look when we mime the movements of our ancestors and try to make our lives more interesting by imagining we are doing things that we are not really doing at all.

When I woke up it was almost ten. The heating hadn't come on and there was a cold, mouldy smell in the house. I coughed a lot, drank a cup of coffee, changed into some tracksuit bottoms and a hoody, cleaned my teeth, put my hair in a ponytail and went to collect my car from Libby's. I hurried B down the Embankment and past the Boat Float, now full of brown water again. I let B off the lead when we got to Bayard's Cove, and she pottered around on the cobbles while I rang Libby's doorbell.

'God, Meg, what's wrong?' she said as soon as she saw me.

'I am leaving him. I'm leaving that bloody poky, damp house. Definitely,' I said. 'I've just come to get the car and then I'm going to pack it up with all my stuff and go to the cottage. I wanted to say it to someone.'

'Shit. Come in and have a cup of tea. Bob's at the shop and I've got the day off because of my hangover. Check out the bags under my eyes. Come on, Bess!'

B stopped sniffing the benches and hurried into Libby's house. I followed.

'I can't stay long, though,' I said. 'I want to get my stuff out before Christopher gets back. I can't deal with another scene today. Oh — your house smells nice.'

'It's lavender. Sacha brought it to say thanks for last night. Where's Christopher?'

'I don't know. He wasn't there when I got back last night.'

'Maybe he's left you.'

I hadn't thought of that. 'Yeah. How are you?'

'Oh, you know. What sort of tea do you want?'

'Whatever.'

Libby's kitchen was bright in the early spring sunshine and I noticed green shoots in her window boxes where bulbs were starting to come up. Libby and Bob did things like that: autumn would come and one day they'd go to a market and buy bulbs and then they would plant them and in the spring they would come up. I had never planted a bulb in my life. For me there was always some crisis or deadline and I had to ring my mother or soothe Christopher or walk B or finish reading something for Oscar. With all that out of the way there was always my novel to work on, always something there to delete. I remembered that there were only 43 words left to delete, and then it would be all gone. Perhaps then I would be able to start again. Libby handed me a cup of redbush tea with honey.

'Well,' she said. 'This is it. This is going to be my life for the foreseeable future.'

'Huh?'

She laughed. 'You're leaving Christopher. Well, my news is that I'm staying with Bob. I decided last night, and I feel really good about it: kind of warm and comfortable inside. Mark wanted me back, but I said no. Didn't think I would, but I did.' She shrugged. 'I had a long talk with Bob in bed afterwards, and I suggested we go travelling together in the summer. We both need to get out of here. We're going stir-crazy.'

'But I thought you said . . .'

'What? That I can't sleep with him any more? Yeah. It is a problem. But everything else between us works so well, and I must admit that I've found that if I drink a bottle of wine and look at some porn on the Internet, and if he has a bath first so he totally smells of soap all over — then it's OK. Oh, God. That sounds awful. But it's no worse than lots of long-term couples. Is it?'

'Me and Christopher never had sex at all, really.'

'Well, there you go.'

'But I am leaving him.'

'Yeah, but for other reasons.'

'You know,' I said, 'I can't believe he didn't want to just have sex all the time. I mean, what, otherwise, is the point of Christopher? Oh, God, I can't believe I just said that. But it's sort of true.'

There was a pause. 'Holy shit,' she said. 'You're really doing it. You're really setting yourself free.'

'Yeah.'

'It's totally the right decision.'

'Yeah. I know. I think.'

'But don't rush into something else. Don't shag Bob's uncle, for example.'

I rolled my eyes. 'Fat chance of that.'

'What? So you're not denying it? He's the one you were talking about having an affair with, isn't he? I knew it. You're so evil.' She grinned.

'Don't get carried away. I think I sort of overreacted to the whole thing. In reality he doesn't fancy me and I don't really fancy him either. We're just friends. I'm meeting him for lunch this week, but there's nothing in it. He's with someone . . .'

'Like Bob's *aunt*.'

'Yes, quite. Although they're not actually married. Anyway, it doesn't matter, because I'm really not into rebound things. Nothing's going to happen.'

'He is kind of sexy. But he's very old.'

'I get the point, Lib.' I put down my empty tea cup. 'That was lovely. OK. I'm off to move house.'

'Good luck.'

Before I left for Torcross I watered the peace lily, but of course I left it behind. In the end I also left most of my books to be collected at some later date, and so the entire contents of the rest of my life ended up fitting into three cardboard boxes and one big suitcase. B had a little box of her own, containing her blanket, three tennis balls in various states of existence, her rubber ball, two half-chewed pieces of rawhide, her bag of dog biscuits and the two tins of food that were left in the cupboard. I put all my unfiled paperwork and bank statements into several recycling sacks and looked for the first time in years at a clear desk. It was as if I had died and become the person lumbered with clearing the house of my useless old things. I barely looked at most of the pieces of paper before throwing them out. I could have done this months ago, and then maybe I'd have been happier there. I took my laptop, my cables, the books I needed for my feature, my notebooks, my best pen, my knitting bag, my jam-making pan and my ship in a bottle and packed them particularly carefully in the suitcase, as if they were the only things I was taking with me into the afterlife. I put everything into the car, including B, and then I went back up the steps to pick up my guitar and the sack of self-help books and check that I hadn't left anything behind. On my way down the steps I bumped into Reg, who was spraying weed-killer into the cracks between the paving stones outside his house.

'A bit brighter today,' he said.

For the first time ever, I didn't simply agree with him. 'You can't just kill everything because you don't like it,' I said. 'Why can't you let everything be?'

I drove out of Dartmouth and after a while Start Bay emerged out of the brightening gloom like the end of a set of parentheses in a book about the natural world. Inside the parentheses was a story about the sea. Outside them, the land: green, red and brown fields, and hills curling over the landscape. I saw small, delicate clumps of snowdrops, big rough patches of gorse, and along the thin road, houses with yellow roses and mimosa growing in their gardens. The mimosa buds were yellow balls that looked like little models of molecules. It was too early for them to flower.

If I apologised, would Christopher have me back? I imagined him going home with a bunch of flowers and finding me gone, and then going straight round to Libby's to force her to tell him where I was. Somehow, in my fantasy, he turned up in Torcross at the same time as Rowan, who had established my whereabouts in roughly the same manner, and I sent Christopher away. But what if Christopher came, with his flowers, and Rowan didn't come? What sort of flowers would he bring? Knowing Christopher, he'd pick some daffodils from the Royal Avenue Gardens. 'Nature's for everyone, babe' is what he'd say when I told him off. And then I'd say that's why the council plants them in the first place, and then we'd have a big row. I hated the smell of daffodils anyway. Pages and pages of speculation clattered through my mind like something being composed on an old typewriter, and each time a page was completed — *ding!* — I imagined ripping it out of the machine and putting it straight in the bin. So now I was deleting writing that didn't even exist.

My cottage in Torcross was like a sheet of paper with nothing typed on it. I couldn't unpack very much because I didn't have any furniture, so I sat at the window for hours just watching. People walked past every so often, and at one point a woman ran down the beach with her daughter, and they both splashed in the freezing cold sea. A man with a beard set up a tripod by the cliffs and started taking pictures of the rocks. An hour or so later, two people walked by my window: a woman who looked like a mountain and a man who looked like a hermit. I rushed to the door and went outside, thinking that of all people it was Vi and Frank who had come to find me here, and I was so happy and grateful. But in the daylight it wasn't them. They had Welsh accents and a West Highland terrier. I went back inside.

Just after six everything outside turned the colour of twilight. The sea and the sky became the same inky blue, separated by a darkening horizon: a blue-black line on a washable blue background. I wanted to take a picture. If I had, it would have been all blue, with only subtle differences in the stripes of sand, sea, sky. When it became too dark to see outside I settled down in front of the fire on the big old sofa with my blankets and a bottle of wine Libby had given me, and drank myself to sleep as some cosmic force ink-jetted the last bits of sky. I thought I heard my mobile ringing a few times in the night, but when I woke up I had no missed calls.

On Monday morning my mother rang.

'You never answer the phone at home,' she complained.

'I'm going to give up trying it altogether and just ring you on your mobile from now on.'

I put down Iris Glass's book, which I'd been reading since I woke up. It had household tips, of course, including instructions on cleaning a drain with baking soda and vinegar, and making your own furniture polish out of olive oil and lavender. But it also had sewing patterns, knitting patterns, music for folk songs to play in the evenings and prayers for sailors. At the end of every chapter were various 'Proverbs of Iris'. Among these were: *There is no such thing as change, although everything is always changing;* and: *Hope blooms uncertainly, like the flowers on a potted plant.* I'd already turned down the page at the beginning of a chapter about knitting and mending socks. There was a shop in Totnes that did sock wool and I was planning to go there at some point and get some. Maybe I could teach myself to knit socks from Iris's instructions.

'Did you get Christopher?'

'No. It just rang and rang. What's wrong? Meg?'

I hadn't thought that I felt sad, but suddenly I heard myself crying.

'Meg? Are you OK?'

'Yes, I am,' I said. 'I'm really OK. I've left Christopher. I've moved out.'

'Oh, thank God. But where are you? Why aren't you here? Come home; we'll look after you.'

'Thanks, Mum, but I'm OK here. I got some money from that TV deal. Remember I met that woman in London last year? The swordfish woman? Well, in the end they decided to option the books. I suddenly found I had some choices and so on a bit of a whim I came here.'

'Where is "here"?'

'Just a little cottage by the sea. Short-term let until I work out what to do.'

'So you're still in Devon.'

'Yeah.' Something in her tone made me add, 'It's my home. And I've got friends here, and stuff going on.'

'Another man?'

'No! Mum, God. I've only just broken up with Christopher.'

'Have you got any definite plans?'

I thought about this for a second. 'I'm writing a feature. But no, not really. I don't think it matters. I think maybe plans are overrated. I might knit some socks. I'm going to get back on with my novel, but I don't know how long that's going to take.'

'So you're all by yourself there, in this "cottage"?'

'B's here with me. She loves it. We've already been for a long walk down the beach this morning. We watched the sun come up. I had this amazing feeling when I got back, as if I had more empty space inside me than ever before. I made exactly the breakfast I wanted, and cleared away and washed up afterwards without anything being an issue. I haven't brought that much with me, but I put out a few books, and my guitar, and my favourite mug, and my jam-making pan and stuff, and I knew that no one was going to move them or wreck anything or come in and start an argument. I thought I'd be sad for ages and it would take months to make the transition properly, but I already feel like I would never go back. I just feel very . . . *serene* by myself. It's way less complicated. I bought so much cleaning stuff from the village shop you wouldn't believe it. I even got rubber gloves.' I didn't tell my mother that I wasn't planning to use any of it now I'd read Iris's book. I was going to use lemons, vinegar, baking soda, lavender oil and hot water instead. I'd been pleased to find there was an alternative to the other stuff, which all reminded me of advertisements containing people with perfect teeth, heroic expressions and offspring that looked like they were on their way to Hitler Youth rallies. Even the bottle of bleach I'd bought had a picture showing a woman's manicured hand opening the child-proof seal.

'Hmm,' my mother said. 'When I left your father I ate cakes. You probably remember; you liked eating them too. I had this feeling of just being able to do what I wanted without him disapproving of it all the time. He always disapproved of cakes. Not cheese, not wine, not meat, not salt: just cakes, probably because there's something feminine about them. He hated cakes because they're voluptuous and sticky and plump, and because they're what I liked, probably. He never had a sweet tooth, which is fine, but he looked down on everyone who did. I remember once I was next door having tea and pastries with Maddy Cooper. They were these delicate little things from a patisserie in London. We were celebrating something; I can't remember what. We had Earl Grey tea in bone china cups and these little pastries, and your father came in to lend Caleb a book, and he said — God, I remember this clearly — he said, "Are you two stuffing yourselves again?" What a bastard. And Rosa, dear little Rosa, who must have been all of about ten at the time, said seriously, "You're very mean, Mr Carpenter."'

My mother paused. I was about to point out that Rosa always had the knack of saying what other people were thinking, but had chosen, often for very good reasons, not to say. She was like a parrot, or a toddler, in that respect. But I didn't say anything because I could hear Mum starting to cry. 'Meg,' she said, 'there's no easy way to say this, but I've phoned to tell you that Rosa is dead. She killed herself yesterday. It's in all the papers.'

The village shop had fresh bread, and basil growing in pots, which I bought, as well as a small block of beeswax and some more lemons. I also bought a copy of every national newspaper they had. I was shaking as I picked up the papers and read all the headlines. Rosa, clearly inspired by *Anna Karenina*, had thrown herself under a train.

'Got a lot to read there,' said the woman at the till.

'Yeah,' I said. There were hyacinths in pots on the counter.

Some were already in flower: pink ones, purple ones and blue ones. I chose one that had tight green buds. It would be impossible to know what colour it would turn out to be. 'Can I take this as well?'

'They're two pounds fifty each,' she said.

'That's fine,' I said.

When I got back I put the hyacinth on the kitchen windowsill, built a fire and then spent the rest of the morning poring over the tabloids. B lay there in the warmth of the fire as if no one in the world had ever died. Rosa's suicide had taken place at a train station I'd never heard of and there had been no witnesses, or at least none had come forward yet. Rosa and Drew had been on their way back from a weekend in the countryside when it happened, but Drew was too devastated to say anything about it. In the end, there wasn't that much to find out from the papers, but I looked at every picture of Rosa, and read every obituary. I imagined a thousand journos all over Drew like funereal confetti.

After a lunch of pasta, olive oil, basil leaves and bread, I went online to look for furniture. I needed a kitchen table, chairs and a bed, at the very least. I looked again at the bed I'd decided I would buy on Saturday. It wasn't going to be available for a month. I couldn't sleep on the sofa for a month, could I? I'd never bought furniture in my life before. If I ordered it online, would men bring it in lorries? Would I have to assemble it myself? It seemed too complicated suddenly, and my eyes felt heavy, but I forced myself to at least order the basics before shutting down the laptop completely. The books for my feature were piled next to me, and I picked up *Mapping the Astral Plane* and yawned again. I settled down on the sofa, barely managing the first paragraph before my eyes started to close, and I pulled the blanket over me and slept.

'Oh, good,' Rosa said. 'I've been trying to phone you.'

This was a really bizarre dream, which I believed and

didn't believe all at the same time. In the dream I knew I'd fallen asleep on the sofa and had begun to imagine that I'd just finished reading the book about the astral plane. One of the things it told me to do was communicate with a dead person. In a dream-sense kind of way, I'd therefore decided to set up a séance with the only person I'd known who had died — thanks, Rosa! — and now we were in conversation.

'Me?' I said to her. We were standing in a vast, feature-less landscape of the kind I used to imagine when describ-ing the spaces between the cells in the cell-phone network in my Newtopia books. She was wearing a nurse's uniform, and I was wearing my usual jeans. The astral plane kept fading in and out and crackling at first, and then it settled into a dreamy hyacinth-blue.

'Yes. You're almost the only person I know who isn't fa-mous. No offence.'

I thought, not for the first time in a dream, that this dream would be something really good to write in a dream diary. I imagined someone like Josh's analyst or one of the authors of the New Age books in my sack telling me that this was very significant. I noted, also in the dream, that I was glad I was not in analysis.

'I'm not dead, you know,' she said. 'You should ring Drew and ask him.'

'I haven't spoken to Drew for seven years,' I said.

'I can see why you ditched him,' she said. 'My God, he's self-obsessed.'

'I left him for someone else,' I said. 'I thought he was very nice. I just wasn't desperately in love with him, and I thought I was desperately in love with his friend. What do you mean you're not dead?'

'I'm not dead. I'm in Hertfordshire.'

'If you're not dead, then how am I speaking to you?'

'That's the stupidest question I have ever heard. And that's saying something.'

'If you're not dead, well, then . . . I mean, all the tabloids think you're dead.'

'We had a big argument,' Rosa said. 'Me and Drew. About superobjectives. Then I pretended to kill myself.'

Rosa talked for ages about this argument and then her voice somehow faded out and I saw her getting out of a train and sitting on a bench at a deserted station, where she watched another woman pacing up and down until a train came and the other woman stepped in front of it.

'I made Drew say it was me,' she said. 'And now I'm with Caleb at last.'

I bumped into Andrew Glass when I was on my way to buy the papers the next morning. I'd had scrambled eggs on toast and a large cup of coffee for breakfast, but I didn't feel very awake. My strange dream the afternoon before had unsettled me, and I'd spent most of the night being afraid to go back to sleep, and playing Iris Glass's folk songs on my guitar instead. It was a little misty, but the bearded man was already setting up his tripod by the cliff-face. There was no sign of the woman and her daughter, or the couple I'd mistaken for Vi and Frank.

'How are you getting on in there?' Andrew said, nodding at the cottage.

'Oh, it's lovely. So peaceful.'

'No weird dreams, then?'

'Huh?'

'Funny dreams.' He laughed. 'No?'

'Why would you say that?'

'God — I could never sleep in there because of the dreams. It's because of all the witchcraft. It hangs around, you know, like cooking smells. Freaks you out.' He laughed again. 'Hey, I'm just kidding. That's not why I can't sleep in there. I mean, I can sleep in there. Obviously not now, but you know what I mean. Oh, dear. Sorry: I shouldn't mess around with you. Don't want to lose my tenant. I thought you were only using the place to work in. But Gill in the shop says you've been buying dog food and plants and all sorts.'

'Yeah. I broke up with my boyfriend.'

'Oh, shit, mate. I'm sorry to hear that. I'll definitely stop teasing you now.'

'No. It was the right thing to do. Totally my own choice, so tease me as much as you want. I'm much happier on my own, I've realised. But I have sort of moved in permanently. At least for the time being. I hope that's OK.'

'It's your place. You do what you want with it — I won't bother you. Gill's an old gossip. Wants to know who everyone is — even the holidaymakers.'

'Thanks. Well, I'm staying for a bit anyway. Unless the bad dreams drive me out, of course. We'll have to wait and see on that one.'

'Oh, dear. I hit a nerve there, I can tell.'

'Well, I did have a really weird dream last night. I wondered how you knew. But I always do when I'm stressed, and in a new place. I'm sure everyone does.'

'Well, don't be a stranger. Call in for dinner later if you fancy it. I won't give you raw pork or anything.'

'Thanks. I probably will. Especially if you don't give me raw pork.'

'That's what Mary Shelley ate, you know — to bring on *Frankenstein* in a dream. Actually . . .' He blushed a little. 'You told me that, didn't you?'

'I may have done. Sounds like something I'd say on a retreat.'

'You did. Yeah, that was it. You gave lots of good advice.'

'I'm not sure telling you to eat raw pork counts as good advice, but thanks.'

'Got a real problem now, though. Don't know if you dispense follow-up advice on the side . . . ?'

'What's the problem?'

'The ghosts. I don't know if I believe in them or not, you

know? If they're in me or outside. I don't want to have to make a decision on that in real life, let alone in the book.'

'I think it's fine if you don't. You can leave it open. Let the reader decide.'

The sea splashed gently behind us.

'Thanks. You know, you shocked me on that retreat,' Andrew said.

'Shocked you? How?'

'When you showed us that tape of all the TV programmes and adverts and explained how the seven basic plots are there in pretty much everything. It did my head in.'

I'd made the tape the previous year and used it for the first time on the retreat that Andrew, Lise and Tim had attended. There were the personal makeover shows that took a human being who didn't look like a character from a romantic comedy and changed her hair, make-up and clothes until she did, using a rags-to-riches structure complete with a crisis halfway through. There were home makeover shows that used the same rags-to-riches formula to turn the insides of people's houses into spaces resembling film sets, with any embarrassing old lino, faded photographs and comfortable old dog-beds removed. One of the clips I showed had an interior designer telling a young man to remove the soft monkey from his bed because it wasn't 'romantic' and no one would want to sleep with him if it was there. There were the talent shows where contestants had to cry before they could receive any good news, the dramas where selfish people learned to consider others, and the advertisements where women desired bright, clean kitchens in which their children could eat cereal and their husbands could read the newspaper and nothing would ever break or go rotten. Not one of these kitchens contained anyone rolling a joint, washing a muddy dog, having a huge row, making a messy stir-fry, picking their nose or anything that real people did in their kitchens. The kitchens on TV were made up, and so were the people inside them. It was as if the superobjective of everyone in the Western world was simply 'I wish to become a fictional character.' Of course, everybody knows all this. But at the same time most people don't really know that they know it.

'Yeah. God,' I said. 'I think it did my head in too, when I really thought about it.'

'It freaked me out because I don't have a TV and so it was all new to me. But then I started noticing it happening in my world as well. Blokes talking at the bar about a football match where the underdog has triumphed against the odds, or complaining because a woman is playing hard to get. I realised that when someone plays hard to get, they are making themselves into a character in a story, and they choose the story that leads to the outcome they want. If a woman puts a dragon between herself and the hero, it becomes an obstacle to be overcome. If she goes and knocks on his door and says "Fancy a bunk-up?" she becomes a slut: basically a conquest with no obstacles and therefore no value. It was like people wanted to put everything in a story because otherwise it wouldn't make any sense. The guys talking about the football wanted the "fairy tale" ending to the match they'd watched because they wanted it to be more satisfying, and they wanted to believe underdogs could win because they identified with them.'

I laughed. 'You can teach the next retreat if you like.'

'No, mate.' He laughed too. 'Thanks for the compliment, but I find it all a bit depressing.'

'Yeah. Well, I'm sure there's some other way. You can use conventional structure without letting it take over. You can still find ways of being original — not just in how you use formula, but *actually* original. You can put two new things together, or ask an important question. It's hard, but not impossible. In fact, Chekhov said that writing is all about formulating questions.'

Andrew raised his eyebrows. 'You didn't mention that on the retreat.'

'No, but that's because on the retreats I'm trying to show people how to write genre novels. But even then, the story-structure is just the container. The container might be strong and reliable and familiar, but you can put whatever you like inside it. It's the space that's important. There's no reason why you can't put something unfamiliar in a familiar container. Or lots of unfamiliar things. Or an interesting question. But you can't seal the container at the end . . .'

'Like a boat rather than a plane?'

I laughed again. 'I was thinking of a tea cup, but yes. Exactly.'

Andrew looked at his watch. 'Whoops. Late again. Better go and open the pub,' he said. 'But do drop in later. No raw pork, I promise.'

'Yeah. Thanks, Andrew. I probably will.'

When I got in I sat down with a cup of tea and the papers. Drew, much loved by the nation as the parochial sidekick of Inspector Bufo, aka 'The Toad', had been taken in for questioning, 'just as a routine part of the investigation.' The papers didn't seem to be making much of it. Someone had come forward as a witness, and explained how Rosa had paced up and down the train station, on her own, before walking in front of the train 'like she was crossing the road'. Columnists were already writing sharp pieces about the trappings of fame, and Rosa's obvious problems with her own success. Had all the dieting made her suicidal? Had she never recovered from the incident with the turquoise dress? While flicking through *The Guardian* looking for more about Rosa, I stopped on the national news page where stories appeared without headlines, but under headings like 'Science', 'Tourism' or 'Technology'. Under the weird heading 'Beast', which had caught my eye, I found a small story about the Beast of Dartmoor. There had been several more sightings of a large black wolf in gardens and on roadsides, but whenever anyone tried to take a picture it didn't work. New recruits of the Royal Auxiliary Air

Force were now trying to track the Beast as a 'fun' weekend exercise, and a way of learning how to use their observation equipment.

I couldn't quite remember what furniture I had chosen, so I looked again at the confirmation email. Yes, I had remembered to click on the table I wanted. And yes, I had ordered two sets of shelves rather than just one. I'd gone for a local place that said they'd deliver quickly. If I was lucky my furniture would arrive today or tomorrow. I wished I could have gone out and bought antiques and second-hand stuff, but I remembered what Conrad had said about Thomas Aquinas's paradox. Everything was an antique once; even the newest objects have really been around since the beginning of time. Did that make me feel better? I wasn't sure. A wagtail chirped outside.

I'd bought a little bag of coal from the shop, and added this to the fire. B got up, stretched, turned around and then lay back down again.

'We're going for a walk,' I said to her. 'When we get back the fire will be nice and warm. Come on.'

She looked at me with her big brown eyes and then rolled over on her other side.

'Come on,' I said again. 'We're going for a walk and then you can sleep while I get on with researching my stupid feature.'

She yawned, but didn't get up.

'Hurry up, or I'll feed you to the Beast,' I said. At this B looked startled and stood up immediately. I forgot that half the time she seemed to know what I was saying. 'I'm joking,' I added. 'But at least you're up now. Good girl. Off we go.'

I'd just slipped her lead on when my phone vibrated. It was a text message from Josh. *Christopher is here. His hand is totally healed by your Bach flower potion. Will you do me a remedy for my madness? And will you take Christopher back? He's driving us crazy. Actually, don't answer that. But are you com-*

ing to Newman still? With me? Shall I book a restaurant? It's
12 days from now. Laters, J x

'How am I going to write this feature?'

This seemed to be the safest question I could ask the Tarot cards that were shuffled and lying face down in front of me. I'd spent the rest of the morning and lunchtime examining the deck of cards and reading the book that came with them. It said you should ask the cards a question and then lay them out in a pattern. It gave several examples, but the simplest seemed to be a hexagram. I had a Post-it note stuck on the page that had a diagram of this pattern. I wasn't sure I'd read the instructions properly. As usual, I'd hurried through the book, noting some interesting moments, but failing to absorb the whole thing. I'd ended up quite fascinated with the cards themselves, though, each one of which seemed to tell a story that, according to the book, fitted into a bigger, more mysterious story in which the Fool was a clothed manifestation of the World, and the Hanged Man was someone in deep meditation, with his genitals pointing to his brain.

The book claimed that every story in the world, and therefore every human situation, could be represented with a pattern made from as few as six of the seventy-eight cards. I learned that the Major Arcana comprises twenty-two Trump cards, numbered from 0 to 21. The Minor Arcana has four suits of fourteen cards each: four Court cards, usually a King, Queen, Knight and Page — although sometimes a King, Queen, Prince and Princess — and then ten numbered cards. Although the Major Arcana cards have always contained what seem to be archetypal images based on one idea, the Minor Arcana cards were illustrated for the first time only in 1910, when the Rider-Waite deck, which I had in front of me, was produced.

I liked the Fool card best. Here was an androgynous, haphazard, dreamy figure wandering along looking a bit like Dick

Wittington, except with a dog instead of a cat. The Fool card, numbered 0, didn't represent what I'd first thought: a silly person about to step off a cliff because he's dreaming too much to even notice his dog jumping up and warning him of the dangers ahead. According to the book, the Fool card has always been fundamental: the Fool's number, 0, is a whole, a world, a circle; it is the non-existence that allows and precedes all other existence. The Fool card may therefore represent the basic nature of all of us: someone in an original state of being or enlightenment who is wandering around with few cares or possessions, uncorrupted by culture. This person seems foolish only to those who are unenlightened. The card also shows the innocent, natural wonder of stepping out into the unknown. We may assume that stepping over a cliff is dangerous, but perhaps the Fool knows he is simply stepping onto the next ledge down. We can't see what's beyond the card: it might be safety; it might be death. But he can see what we can't. The next card in the sequence of Trumps, and occupying position number 1, is the Magician: also a Trickster, but one who is firmly inside society. He is aware of his own power and importance and his ability to control nature. On the table in front of him he has a wand, a sword, a cup and a pentacle, representing the four suits of the Tarot. This is the socialised Fool, who has a long journey to go before reconnecting with the World, the twenty-second Trump card that some describe as the Fool as he or she really is: naked, and connected to everything.

The book suggested looking at each of the cards and writing down all the thoughts, images and associations that came with each one, in order that you could learn how to read them quickly. I didn't have time for that, but I had flicked through the deck and noted some interesting things. There was the Star card, where a naked woman had one foot in a pool of water, and one foot on land. She was pouring from two cups of water: from one the water fell on the land; from the other it replenished the pool. There were lots of other women in the deck: Strength, Justice, Temperance, Judgement and even the World cards were female, as well as the High Priestess and the Empress. There were some interesting male cards, like the Hierophant and the Hermit. There were cards of great destruction or fear, like the Tower, the Devil and Death. There was even a dog card which I'd pointed out to B: the Moon. I looked at the cards in front of me again and imagined Vi saying that the only true 'female' card was the Fool: the card of the void, of nothingness, of primal darkness and the beginnings of everything else.

Something popped in the fire, and B and I both jumped. Then there was a howling sound outside. It was the wind, blowing around the house and down the chimney. I went to the kitchen to get a tangerine. I ate it, then threw the peel in the fire. There was a little hiss and then all was quiet again.

The pattern I'd chosen for my Tarot reading was an imaginary hexagram with the cards at each of the six points. At first I thought I should read the cards clockwise, but in fact from the top going clockwise, the cards are numbered 1, 5, 2, 4, 3, 6. In this sequence, the first card represents the central issue, or the 'ordinary world' of the problem; the second represents the problem itself; the third represents the way to set out and resolve the issue; the fourth represents a previously unseen element in the central conflict that could make the problem seem insurmountable; the fifth represents a climax or turning point; and the sixth the resolution. I said all this to myself as I laid out the cards, and only when the pattern was formed did I realise that this exercise, whatever it revealed, would be ideal for an Orb Books retreat. This was a story-formula all over again. There is a problem, so you try to solve it. Although it goes well at first, there is something surprising about the problem that makes it more difficult to solve than you first thought. There is a moment when all seems to be lost, in the climax; but then the solution is found and the problem is overcome. If I could get ghostwriters to plot stories like this, with some Tarot cards, it would be good practice for them. But I felt a little sick as I thought of this.

In order from 1 to 6, my cards were as follows: Ace of Cups; Prince of Cups (reversed); the Star; Three of Wands (reversed); Three of Pentacles; and Justice (reversed). This, when I interpreted it, suggested that I wanted to set out for a great truth, something very worth while, as expressed by the Ace of Cups, but at the end I didn't want to come to a final judgement. I was somehow rejecting the Justice card, which is why it was reversed. In order to come to this non-conclusion, I needed balance, not dishonesty. I wanted to ask a question, but not answer it. Perhaps I wanted to create a storyless story. How that would work in my feature I wasn't sure. But I did suddenly realise that all the self-help books I'd rejected for being offensive or stupid were offensive or stupid precisely because they would take the Fool, about to step off his cliff, and they would stop him. They would put him and his dog in therapy and turn him back towards the 'real world', with its winding roads with signs pointing only to love, money and success. Then the doorbell rang and all my furniture arrived.

The delivery men took the flat-pack bed and mattress upstairs, but left the other boxes in the hallway. It took me half an hour to move them into the front room. Then I went back upstairs. The box of bed-parts was so heavy I couldn't move it. In the end I opened it haphazardly and about fifty pieces of pale wood fell on the floor, along with a bag containing a million billion screws and other metal objects, and a piece of paper with a picture of a bed on it. I couldn't even open the box properly; what chance was there that I would actually put all this stuff together? I tried sifting through the pieces and looking at the diagram, but it was no good; I didn't even know which way up anything went. I went downstairs and looked for Tim's number. I remembered that I needed to reply to Josh, not that I knew what to say. It was just like him to want to book a restaurant twelve days before an event.

Tim was in the *Yellow Pages,* under 'Handymen'. I rang the number. A woman — I assumed it was Heidi — answered.

'Hello,' I said. 'Is Tim there?'

'No, sorry,' she said. 'Who is this?'

'It's Meg Carpenter. I'm working with him on his book; he's probably mentioned me. Although really I wanted some help with a flat-pack. I guess he's on Dartmoor already?'

'What book?' said Heidi. 'Hello, by the way. I'm Heidi; Tim's wife.'

'Gosh,' I said. 'Sorry if I've . . .'

'He never said anything about a book. That's great.'

'It is,' I said. 'It's very . . .'

'God. How embarrassing.' She laughed. 'How stupid.'

'Huh?'

'How embarrassing and stupid to not know what your own husband is doing. Is it a good book?'

'Yeah. Well, it's a proposal at the moment. It will be good, I'm sure.'

'And you say he's on Dartmoor?'

'Honestly, I wouldn't know,' I said. 'It was a guess. I . . .'

Heidi laughed. 'I thought he was having an affair.'

'Um . . .'

'Sorry. I shouldn't tell you any of this. But I'm so glad he isn't having an affair. Isn't that pathetic? Unless, of course, you're his mistress and I'm making an even bigger fool of myself.' She sighed. 'What's he doing on Dartmoor?'

'He's researching a Beast,' I said.

'Not the one from the local paper? Oh, God.'

'I'm sure it'll be OK.'

'How can you say that? It's almost worse. I thought he was having an affair, and he's actually out there with some wild animal. Not that anyone feels safer inside, because apparently it finds ways into people's houses. Sorry — Meg, wasn't it? You've caught me at a strange moment, and I'm really rather embarrassed. I'm sorry.'

'Don't be, please,' I said. 'But look, I'm sure he had a good reason. What did you mean about —'

'You know, he accused me of having an affair once,' she said. 'Years ago, when we lived in London. I'd gone for dinner a couple of times with a colleague, and he thought that meant I must be sleeping with him. Now this. God.'

While Heidi was talking I'd walked to my front door, opened it as quietly as I could and rung the doorbell.

'Oh, sorry — *Hang on!* — Heidi, that's the door. I've got to go. Will you tell Tim I phoned? Sorry again. Got to go. Hope everything works out. Bye.'

I went to the village shop and got a Phillips screwdriver, a flat-head screwdriver, some more lemons, some bubble bath and the local paper. Gill didn't say anything at all, but shook her head a couple of times as she searched for the price on the flat-head screwdriver. I looked again at the books on the display behind the counter.

'It's Gill, isn't it?' I said to her.

'Yes,' she said. 'And you're Meg?'

I smiled. 'Yep. Sorry I keep buying such weird stuff.'

'Don't worry,' she said. 'We sell quite "weird stuff".' She smiled too.

'OK. Well, I need some more of those books. I'd like the one on embroidery, the one on building bat-houses, the one on watercolour painting and the one on birdwatching, please.'

When I got in I made some notes on my feature, but I still wasn't sure how to make it work. Then I went upstairs and put all the pieces of the bed into piles, and read the instructions twice. I realised I needed an electric screwdriver as well as the two I'd bought from the shop, so I went to borrow one from Andrew. I stayed for a quick fish stew and a pint of Beast. Then I went home to get on with my feature. I'd just settled down on the sofa with the sack of self-help books and the new books I'd bought from the village shop when my phone vibrated. There was a message from Libby: *I feel like a Stepford Wife. How are you? I've had sex three times today! Now I want to shoot myself.*

I added one more small log to the fire, and for a while it crackled in the fireplace, before settling into a kind of *Wishhh* noise, with the sea outside going *Shushhh* as the wind died down. I took out my Moleskine notebook and started writing, and the sound of my fountain pen on the thick pages was *Hushhh*. Wish, shush, hush. I wrote for two hours without stopping. Then I plugged in my laptop, made another cup of coffee and started typing, still surrounded by books with increasing numbers of Post-it notes stuck in them. When my feature was completely done and the fire had settled into a glow, I settled down to sleep with B on the sofa, thinking about what I'd written and hoping Oscar would publish it and Vi would read it, with the fire still *wish*ing, and projecting its own shadowy stories onto the walls.

I'd first met Vi on a drunken evening after a research seminar that Frank had given on Chekhov's letters and literary technique. One of my lecturers, Tony, was sitting next to an attractively weathered-looking woman I'd never seen before, who was wearing purple jeans, a Greenpeace T-shirt and big black DMs. She had the kind of tan you don't ever get in England, and several necklaces made from string and exotic-looking stones. After the seminar was over Frank invited everybody for a drink, but I was the only person who could make it apart from Tony and the mysterious woman, whom Frank then introduced as 'my other half: Violet Hayes, from anthropology'. Tony laughed at this, clapped Frank on the shoulder and said, 'Other half? Anthropology? How *sweet*.'

A drink turned into dinner in an Italian place down a side-street, and we all smoked and drank red wine as if we were immortal. The only person who didn't smoke was Vi, but she threw back her wine just as fast as the rest of us.

'Sometimes I yearn for a cigarette,' she said. 'Just one.'

Tony laughed. 'Chekhov gave up smoking eventually, didn't he?' he said to Frank. 'Didn't he say it had stopped him being gloomy and nervous?'

'Yeah,' Frank said. 'I hope that happens when I give up.'

'He went off Tolstoy as a direct result of giving up smoking, too, didn't he?' Vi said. 'I remembered that because I kind of went off certain things when I gave up. Like bad detective novels, for example.' She grinned. 'Hardly Tolstoy, but.'

Vi spoke English with the kind of accent that has evolved in a variety of different directions, like an adaptively radiated species. As I got to know her better I would begin to recognise or guess some of the origins of her different ways of constructing sentences. Using 'but' at the end of a sentence instead of 'though' was Antipodean — I knew this from watching soap operas, and from listening to Frank, who was Australian.

'Yeah,' said Frank. 'Sadly they didn't agree on the fundamental nature of existence. Tolstoy thought it was spiritual; Chekhov thought it was material. More or less.' He looked at me. 'Do you know Chekhov's letters, Meg?'

'No. I mean, I didn't before today. I'll get the book out of the library now, though. The letters sound great. So why exactly did he go off Tolstoy? How could anyone go off Tolstoy?' We'd reached Tolstoy on Frank's course, but not Chekhov.

'It was a class thing mainly,' Frank said. 'Chekhov was already making a distinction between his kind of writing and Tolstoy's in the letter I was talking about before, when he says Tolstoy and Turgenev are "fastidious" with their morals. Chekhov hated this. It wasn't just that he was a doctor. He came from a very poor background and most of his writing was done to make money to stop his family from starving. He supported them all throughout his life. His two older brothers were alcoholics, and didn't help much at all. He was very well acquainted with the lives of the lower classes: dirt, poverty — the "dung-heap" of life. He saw something too morally simplistic, or maybe naïve, in Tolstoy — or at least he said he did before he met him properly. Chekhov valued progress. He said something like "There is more love for mankind in electricity and steam than there is in chastity and abstaining from meat." I've been intrigued by that remark ever since I read it. Tolstoy, being rich, thinks that living like a peasant is virtuous in its simplicity. But Chekhov's been there and done that. He's eaten goose soup so thin that he says the only substance in it is like the scum you get in a bath after fat market women have been in it. He has slept in troughs. He was thrilled to leave his parochial home town, Taganrog, and loved spending time in St Petersburg, where there were proper intellectuals and good food. He doesn't have any romantic ideas about peasants and the countryside. It's interesting to compare his story "Peasants" with the sections in *Anna Karenina* where Levin thinks he will become enlightened if he works hard, like a peasant. But in Chekhov's story peasant life is simply dull, boring and painful. He became close to Tolstoy, of course, and they got on very well. Chekhov always looked up to him in some ways.'

'I don't want to be controversial here,' Tony said. 'But isn't it a bit misleading trying to reconstruct who these authors "really were" and what their great works "really meant"?'

'Of course,' Frank said, smiling. 'Chekhov said that himself. It's hardly a new idea. He would completely agree with what you just said. He was always being criticised for being too realistic. But he didn't want to be read as a liberal, or a conservative — just someone who told the truth and wasn't pretentious. He said it was up to the reader to judge, not the writer.'

'But do we need an author's permission to read their work how we like?'

'Well, no, but . . .'

'It's not as simple as reading "how we like", though, is it?' I said. 'There's the affective fallacy to think about as well.'

'So you do listen in lectures,' Tony said to me.

'Oh, I've heard that lecture,' Vi said to Tony. '"The Death of the Author", right? It's pretty good, except for the bit about infinity and monkeys.'

'How did you hear it?' he asked.

'Oh, I take tapes of other departments' lectures on planes with me when I travel. Ever since I gave up reading detective fiction I've needed to find something else to do on long trips. I read Zen stories too,' she said, 'but they're not very long. I mean, my reading pile is always taller than I am, but on plane journeys I just need something a bit dumb to help me switch off.'

'Thanks,' Tony said. 'Nice to know my "dumb" lectures help you switch off.'

'Don't be offended,' she said. 'Yours are pretty good. Maybe I don't exactly mean *dumb*. But you know those books that introduce a complicated subject for a general reader? There were more of them in the nineteenth century than there are now, which is a real shame. I'd like to be reading those books on a plane. Undergraduate lectures are the closest thing. I like the ones from the history of mathematics course as well. I'd like to listen to the actual maths ones, but they don't tape them because it's all done on a blackboard.'

'Vi's researching narrative theory,' Frank said. 'When she asked me whose lectures she should listen to from our department, I naturally suggested you.'

'How does anthropology fit in with narrative theory?' Tony said. 'And, er, *maths?*'

'Er, Claude Lévi-*Strauss?*' Vi said.

'Oh, of course.' Tony shook his head. 'And Vladimir Propp, I guess. All the folklorists and structuralists.' He looked at me. 'Did you come to my first-year lecture on structuralism?'

I shook my head. 'I don't remember it.'

'Lévi-Strauss thought that all stories could potentially be expressed as one single equation,' Vi said. 'The piece he writes about it is very moving. Having come up with a rough hypothetical "formula" for myths in general, he then says that because French anthropology is underfunded he can't complete his research, because he'd need a technical team and a bigger workshop. He was summarising myths and isolating their mythemes on big pieces of card and simply ran out of physical space to do it in. He had none of what he called "IBM equipment", although I can't imagine how a computer would help. Mine can't even hold a chapter of a book without wanting to die pathetically under the strain.'

'We'll come to Vladimir Propp on my course,' Frank said to me. 'He studied Russian folk tales and also came up with a "formula" for expressing them. He argued that they were all built from a finite number of story-elements, a bit like different recipes made from the same basic set of ingredients. For example, many folk tales begin with the hero being told not to do a certain thing, like look in a cupboard or pick an apple. In other words, an interdiction, which Propp gives the code Y^1.'

'And then the hero always does the thing he's been told not to do?' I said, although I knew the answer.

'They always do,' Frank said.

'So all fiction is the same?'

'No, no.' Vi shook her head. 'There are stories with no formula, but they are a bit harder to find. Mathematically they are expressed differently. You'd need imaginary numbers — the square roots of negatives — to express those stories in equations. I'm working on a paper about this at the moment.'

Our pizzas arrived, so Vi didn't say anything else about her paper.

'So what's wrong with my monkeys?' Tony asked Vi, once we'd started eating.

'Well, I liked what you said, up to a point, but I thought you misrepresented infinity. You said that if they were given an infinite amount of time, a million or more monkeys would eventually write Shakespeare, because of probability.'

He had, and then he'd asked us all to imagine we held a copy of *The Tempest* in our hands. In this thought-experiment, we did not know whether this was a text written by Shakespeare, or written randomly by monkeys. Did it make any difference which it was? Without intention behind them, would the words on the page still have meaning? I hadn't really been sure that anything not written by a human would be readable, and that anything non-human, even probability, could create *The Tempest*. But the argument had been logical enough, and we'd all concluded that it wouldn't matter — or at least it wouldn't make any difference to the meaning of the words on the page — whether the text had been written by Shakespeare, monkeys, a random word-generator or in any other way.

'In an infinite amount of time,' Frank said, 'things still "never" happen. The monkeys could create an infinite amount of gibberish before they wrote Shakespeare. That's assuming you could find monkeys that lived an infinitely long period of time as well, which seems unlikely.'

Vi laughed. 'In an infinite amount of time, at least one infinite monkey would evolve to *be* Shakespeare,' she said. 'Imagine that. Also,' she added, 'I wasn't a hundred per cent sure about your philosophical zombies.'

'Oh,' Tony said. 'I thought they were good.'

'Yes, I did too,' Vi said, laughing. 'I liked the idea that this being, the philosophical zombie, is purely hypothetical — that's a good paradox in itself. A being that cannot "be". I liked the way that this being could tell you it felt pain when it did not, and that you'd never be able to know either way. The idea that any one of us could be a philosophical zombie was quite chilling, and also very thought-provoking — well, assuming one is not a philosophical zombie. Because, of course, the point with philosophical zombies is that they have been programmed to respond as a human would, but they are not human. An outsider wouldn't be able to tell the difference, sure; but the zombie would not actually feel, or think, or know anything. So that's why I was wondering this: exactly how could a philosophical zombie write a novel?'

It was a good question. Tony had built a lot of his argument from this point that since you couldn't even tell whether another being — a novelist, for example — was a philosophical zombie or not, you certainly could not tell what they 'meant to say' in their fiction, even if you asked them and they told you.

'I guess', Tony said, 'a philosophical zombie *could* write a novel. I mean, if this is a being that's programmed to respond exactly as a human would, then if it strung a lot of these utterances about feelings and so on together, then maybe that would make a novel. Perhaps it could use one of Lévi-Strauss's equations, or Vladimir Propp's schema. But . . .'

'But what?'

'You're right. If you're implying that it wouldn't be much of a novel at all, then you're right. I hadn't exactly thought of that. So you're saying that there has to be a human essence at the heart of every work of art?'

'Yes,' Vi said. 'Although I'm not saying you can ever be sure about what it is. It's not something you can put your finger on exactly, but, scientifically speaking, it has to be there. Ha! Like consciousness, and dark matter, and "culture". The problem with you humanities people — if you don't mind me saying so — is that when you dabble in science, you always get it wrong. Or mostly. But that's OK. Scientists usually get science wrong too, but that's their job: to prove things wrong. That's all scientists ever do. Social scientists prove that society is wrong, probably. It's impossible to prove anything is a hundred per cent right. Can you pass the olives again?'

When I woke up in Torcross on Wednesday morning the fire was still glowing in the grate as if it had been enchanted, so I added another log and once the flames had taken hold of it I made some rosehip tea and ate a mashed banana on toast. When I opened my laptop, I had an email from Oscar. *Are you trying to give me a heart attack? Not only have you filed early, your copy is actually very good. In fact, this is a triumph. It's quite funny, and even topical if one believes all the economists saying that Western capitalism is in peril and we will soon need to make our own clothes because Chinese sweatshops won't exist any more (look at the News section on Sunday to see what I mean). Paul wants to lead with it in the Arts supplement this week. He's talking about giving you a column. You've really touched him with this 21st century hobby nonsense. He has a train set. Did you already know that?*

A column! That was the Holy Grail for any newspaper writer. But Oscar had done this before, I remembered. Whenever he really wanted me to do something I really didn't want to do he would invoke this idea that Paul was thinking about giving me a column. I'd met Paul at someone's launch party once. When I'd mentioned this column he'd looked at me as if I was mad. But this was different. I hadn't asked for more time, or tried to cancel the assignment. I looked at the email again in case I'd missed Oscar asking me to completely rewrite the piece by Thursday. But he wasn't asking me to do anything. Perhaps that email would follow this one and the column would be explained away.

Whenever someone praised something I'd written I read the piece back to myself as if I was that person. It was the only time I ever relaxed and enjoyed my own work, and it happened very rarely. I'd begun by making the fairly obvious point that the self-help industry functions by making people feel bad about themselves. I'd then described some of the ridiculous ways in which people were encouraged to 'fix' their own imperfections and become attractive as lovers, business contacts or whatever. You could learn, from a book, how to snare someone with an 'exclusive smile', how to set the agenda for any conversation you wanted to have, how to be the 'chooser' rather than the 'choosee', how to become 'magnetic' and attract the people and objects you want, how to harness the power of 'Screw you!', how to read other people's minds via their body language and also use your own body to communicate, and how to use ancient secrets of creativity to give your PowerPoint presentations more 'zing'.

If people couldn't get their life right in this world, then there was the Otherworld of fairies and guardian spirits, or past lives or afterlives. In these books there was always some way for the individual to become a hero. No one was encouraged to be a monster or a dragon or a helper along the way. No one was encouraged to be a fool or a hermit. Whether you got to transcend to a thousand years of perfection or simply spend the rest of your mortal life being 'perfect' and giving the best PowerPoint presentations in the world, this self-perfection was assumed to be everyone's goal. The whole of Western society seemed to be turning itself into a reality TV show in which everyone was supposed to want to be the most popular, the most talented, the biggest celebrity. I'd pastiched the self-help format in my feature, so that the feature itself offered tips for a life that looks outwards rather than inwards. I focused on the skills you might want to develop as an anti-hero, or, indeed, a fool, who does not desire riches and success and syrupy romance. I suggested that people who wanted to reject these ideas of perfection and individualistic heroism should get a pile of books that help them learn a new skill, or perhaps another language, not in order to become successful or fit in better, but just for the hell of it: to step over a cliff and see what happens. The anti-hero or fool could take up birdwatching or botany, fix something, translate something, embroider something or even knit a pair of socks. I said that unless we gave up on our addiction to the self-help industry — and the connected world of twenty-four-hour drama and entertainment — and reclaimed old skills and hobbies, we were in danger of turning ourselves into fictional characters with no use beyond entertaining people and being emotionally, aesthetically and psychologically neat and tidy. We would become cultural King Midases: unfeeling and untouchable. We would desire only what was immediately useful and relevant to our plot-lines: a pair of shoes, a new sofa, a home gym. And if those didn't work there were plenty of ways to buy our way out through box-sets, videogames and ready meals full of sugar and fat. We would become little more than character arcs, with nothing in our lives apart from getting to act two, and then act three and then dying. I wasn't completely sure about my feature as I read it back to myself. Was I just offering another kind of easy answer of my own? But maybe that didn't matter in a newspaper feature, and at least I'd got to mention some nice, little-known books. I started reading from the beginning again, this time not as someone who'd read it and liked it, but as my own harshest critic. I hadn't mentioned any of my absurd but well-meaning books in the end; I'd gone for the soft targets. Was I as much of a fraud as everyone else? But perhaps Vi would read it and see that I was at least trying to be genuine.

A few minutes later an email came in from Paul. *Bravo! Great feature. Reminded me of why I like my train set and walks in the countryside more than meetings with advertisers! Can you do regular weekly column? Each week another hobby + a book to go with it (or a CD or DVD or whatever you like—will be an Arts column, not in Books). Use 1st person style and OK if some hobbies fail. Just try things out. 600 wds/week and £1 a word. Let me know ASAP. P x*

I didn't want to make a big deal of my lunch with Rowan, but I hung up my only clean pair of jeans and T-shirt and my favourite cardigan on the back of the door while I had a long, hot bath and shaved my legs and plucked my eyebrows. While the steam unwrinkled my clothes I lay there thinking about my column, and what hobbies I might cover in the next few weeks. I wondered what Rowan would say when I told him. When the water went tepid I dried myself and got dressed. The bath was a state: it looked almost as bad as baths did after B had endured her annual shampoo: as well as all the froth from the foam I'd used, there were leg-hairs and bits of eyebrow stuck to the old enamel. In the bedroom, all the pieces of bed were on the floor exactly the way I'd left them. The pieces had made sense when I was sitting in amongst them the day before, with the instructions and the screwdrivers, but now the whole room was in a mess, as if all the bits of wood were from something breaking, not something waiting to be made.

When I got to Lucky's Rowan was already there, although I didn't notice him at first. We always used to try to sit at the nicest table: nestled in the bay window looking out at people walking past looking in at us. This table was free, but Rowan was right at the other end of the café with his back to me. I walked over.

It was one minute past one.

'Anyone sitting here?' I said, sitting down opposite him.

'Hi,' he said, smiling. 'How are you?'

'I'm OK,' I said. Then I realised how much had changed since I last saw him. 'Yeah, I'm OK,' I said again.

Rowan looked behind him and then back at me.

'It's all right,' I joked. 'I wasn't followed.'

'I wouldn't be so sure about that,' he said.

'Huh?'

'Don't worry.' He shook his head. 'I'm being silly.' He smiled.

Neither of us said anything for a few seconds. I didn't want to say any of the obvious things. I didn't want to tell him about Christopher, or ask him why he might think we were being followed, or ask about him and Lise. I thought about my column, but I didn't want to start by bragging about it.

'How's your yoga going?' I said, instead.

Rowan sighed. 'I haven't been for a couple of weeks. I'm missing it.'

'I've just started,' I said. 'It is quite calming.'

'Where are you doing it? Not Dartmouth?'

'No. From a book. How are you?' I asked. 'How are things?'

He picked up the menu. 'Let's order first. What do you want?' he said. 'I think I'm just going to have a smoked salmon sandwich and a coffee.'

'I'll have the same,' I said.

The waitress came over and I explained that I wanted the sandwich without the butter or cream cheese and my double espresso topped up with some water.

'It's good to be able to meet up outside Dartmouth,' Rowan said. 'Or is that just me? Sitting down to have a sandwich and a coffee, knowing we're not going to bump into anyone we know . . . It's nice.'

'I've kind of left Dartmouth,' I said. 'I've . . . Well, actually, I have some news. I've split up with Christopher. I've moved out. I'll give you my new address if you like, in case you want to send me a Christmas card or something. It's in Torcross.'

'What, on the beach?'

'Yeah. Right on the beach. It's this amazing cottage. I feel much better about everything. I've got so much time all of a sudden. Space to think. And everything's going quite well with work too, and . . .'

'God. You've actually split up with your partner. Not because . . .'

'No,' I said. 'Not "because". This has been on the cards for a long time.'

'How does it feel? If that's not an insensitive question. I mean, the idea of finally splitting up with Lise terrifies me, although it looks like it's on the cards too and I suppose it's what I've wanted for ages. Do you feel lonely?'

'No. Well, not until you mentioned it.' I laughed. 'Actually, it's wonderful. I feel like I can breathe for the first time in ages. It's probably the same for Christopher. We weren't doing each other any good.' I paused. 'It is kind of scary in a way too, I suppose. I don't know what it's going to be like in the winter when it's just me and the sea. I deleted the last bits of my novel before I went too. Clean slate.'

'Really?' He sounded alarmed.

'I'm always doing it. It's not a big deal.' I sighed. 'Oh, I suppose it is a bigger deal this time. This time I really am starting again from scratch. I'm going to try to write about real life for a change, not some pre-packaged idea of real life. You know that conversation we had at Libby and Bob's about omniscience? I think I'm going to try an omniscient narrator who sees everything and judges nothing. Maybe I'll set it on a ship. I'm going to take it quite slowly. And I got some good news from the paper this morning. They've given me a column. So I'll have enough money. It's all good.'

'That's fantastic.' He smiled. 'I'm jealous, I suppose, of you striking out on your own. I'd like to "ditch" everything and be able to breathe. And apart from anything else, you've actually left Dartmouth.'

'Do you really hate it?'

'Yes. It took me ages to realise, and I hate hating anything, if that makes sense, but I do. It's beautiful, of course, absolutely beautiful. When you first cross the river and see all the little houses there in all their pastel colours, it's gorgeous. It's as if real fishermen still lived in them alongside artists and intellectuals. You think that with all that water, and the old stone walls, and all the history, interesting people would want to be there. I mean, we decided to live there after all.'

'I actually moved there because there was no other option,' I said. 'Christopher knew someone who had a house to rent cheap.'

'I meant Lise and me. But it was Lise's choice, because of her family being in Kingswear. I wouldn't have chosen it. It has no cinema. I suppose the bookshop is quite good. But the whole atmosphere . . . Maybe when you first come, especially if you come across the river by ferry, you don't see the Naval College, and if you're lucky there aren't any warships in the harbour. Then it's very nice. We'd had holidays in Dartmouth in the past, but I never noticed how much I hated it until I lived there. That's why I spend most of my time in Torquay, especially now. It's more real.'

'Who knows what's real?' I said. 'Still at least in Torquay there's some sense of real drama and real problems. They seem to have to simulate that in Dartmouth by having military aircraft perform dangerous stunts over the river all the time as if there was no fossil-fuel crisis in the world.'

'When they're not doing that they like blacking-up and performing "old-fashioned minstrel" shows. I went to one once with Lise, and we had a massive row afterwards because I wanted to walk out, and she wanted to be polite because there were people there she knew from school, and some of Sacha's crowd.'

Our coffees arrived.

'Lise just couldn't see it,' Rowan said. 'I was so angry I didn't know what to say, so I just left. I ended up driving out of the place until I came to this country pub in Tuckenhay, where I got a little room for the night that looked directly onto Bow Creek, which is the best part of the River Dart, I think, because it has divorced itself from it. I woke up on my own and watched a white egret stirring up the mud to get his breakfast. It was the most peaceful morning I've had in years, because I wasn't with Lise and I wasn't in Dartmouth. My niece and nephew have become foodies, and that means they can just about cope in Dartmouth, although I think Bob's had enough and wants to go and live in London, but I can't imagine Conrad liking that much. Poor kid — he's got doting parents here, so he can't ever leave. And there's Libby with her — what did you call it? — her "tragic love affair".'

'I think that's over now, pretty much,' I said.

'Poor Libby. Or not?'

'Poor everyone,' I said.

'Oh.'

'Lots of affairs go on in Dartmouth,' I said. 'At least, among people who can't handle the place. It's something to do.' I remembered that one of the reasons we were here was Lise's affair. 'Sorry. That's not tactful, is it?'

Our sandwiches arrived, and we picked at them for a few moments. Rowan looked behind him, and then back at me.

'The night I went off to Tuckenhay,' he said, 'Lise went to stay in a hotel as well, in case I came back. She said she didn't want to be the drip who stayed at home, which I have to admit I respected. She said it was awful in lots of ways: a car park between the hotel and the river, so the "river view" was actually of cars, but she also said the food was really great. She persuaded me to go back there with her one night for dinner. I hated it instantly and we argued about that. God — I think we argue about everything. Maybe that's healthy. But she made me go in and said it would be a laugh. The conversations at the tables around us were quite hilarious. One woman was saying that she shouldn't have soup "this late" because she'd have to get up and pee in the night. It was only seven o'clock. We did end up having sort of a laugh, although even Lise had to admit the atmosphere was terrible, which more or less spoiled the food. It wasn't my kind of thing at all, especially since I'd rather cook my own fish on a beach somewhere. But that probably was the last time we had fun, I think. And sex.' He must have seen my face. 'Sorry.'

'There's no reason to apologise to me,' I said. 'Is there?'

'Well, no, but . . .'

'So what's happening with you and Lise? Have you been for counselling yet?'

'No. She's gone off that idea. In fact . . .' He looked over his shoulder again.

'What?'

He sighed. 'She's accused me of having an affair. Or wanting to.'

'What? Why? Who with?'

'With you. She's turned the whole thing around. Now she's saying that she only had an affair in the first place because she thought I was having one already. She said it was like having to go and stay in a hotel because I did. Again, she didn't want to be a drip. That's why I said no to lunch when we were on the ferry, and to be honest that's why I'm feeling really nervous about being seen with you now.'

'God. But that's . . .'

'Am I embarrassing you?' He sighed. 'This is all very hard to say. It's probably worse to listen to. I'm sorry.'

'I don't know if I'm embarrassed or not. Why me?'

'She knew about the lunches we had when we were both working in the library. I think I said you were interesting and good company. That was a big mistake. Apparently we exchanged "a look" at some dinner party.'

'Well, how does she know that? She wasn't even there.'

'Not Libby and Bob's. This was ages ago. After that she forbade me from ever seeing you again.'

'That's ridiculous.'

'I know.'

'And she really did have an affair?'

'Oh, yes. Like you said, everyone's at it in Dartmouth. Except us.'

'Seems a bit of a waste,' I said. Then I blushed. 'Sorry. Joke.'

'No. You're right. Of course, you're right in the sense that . . .'

'Anyway, I've left Dartmouth now.'

He nodded thoughtfully. 'That's probably a good thing.'

'What, for your relationship? Yeah, well, obviously that would have been my number-one priority when I left.'

'That's not really what I meant,' he said, looking at the table.

'No.'

'But I am asking a lot of you. I'm really sorry.'

'It's OK. I'm sorry I snapped. You're my friend. I shouldn't be . . .'

'I told Lise I didn't want to have an affair with you, but she didn't believe me.'

'Why?' I said.

'She said you were my type. She said she'd noticed you even before I did.'

'I didn't think I was anyone's type.'

'Meg . . .'

'And she was obviously wrong, wasn't she? I mean, you're obviously not attracted to me at all. Did you tell her that, when you were denying everything?'

Rowan looked at his fingers, clasped them together and then brought them up in front of his face. Then he rested his chin on his folded hands.

'No,' he said. 'No, I didn't tell her that.'

'Why not?'

'Because it's not true. You know that. You know how I feel about you. But I *can't* feel it, and I can't do anything about it. I thought that was the same for both of us. I thought that's why we never talked about it. Except now you've left Christopher, and . . .'

'I didn't leave him for you.'

'No, I wasn't implying . . .'

'I mean, well, we're not having an affair, are we? And I left him because I'd had enough of him. I should have done it years ago. I'm really enjoying being on my own.'

'I know.'

'And didn't you say I was too young for you?'

'That doesn't matter. Our ages don't matter. You said that.'

'It's not an issue anyway, if you're determined to stay with Lise.'

'I just don't see what else I can do. We'd have to leave Dartmouth. OK—I know—you've already left Dartmouth. But you've only gone a few miles down the coast. Everyone would disapprove of us. I'd lose contact with everyone I know in Devon, which I guess wouldn't be a great loss, but I don't know what else I have. I'd have to leave the Centre, I suppose.'

'Rowan?'

'What?'

'We're not going to run away together. There's no point thinking about it. You're going to stay with Lise and I'm going to . . . I don't know what I'm going to do. But there's no reason for you to think you owe me anything just because your wife accused you of having an affair with me.'

He took a deep breath, held it, and then slowly exhaled.

'She's not my wife.'

'She may as well be.'

We'd finished our sandwiches. At least, I'd picked at the middle of mine, and he'd eaten half of his and pushed the plate away. Now Rowan looked at his watch.

'I'm going to have to go in a bit,' he said. 'Lise has started calling the Centre every afternoon to check up on me.'

'Shouldn't you be the one doing that to her, since she's the one who had an affair?'

'You'd think so. Look. I'd like to finish this conversation properly. And also — didn't you have something to show me? A ship in a bottle?'

'You're welcome to drop in for a cup of tea at Torcross if you're passing.'

He breathed another deep, spring-tide breath, as if he was a river being filled and emptied more forcefully than usual.

'Yes. I'd love to. But . . .'

'We're not having an affair. There's nothing to feel guilty about. I'm not going to jump on you as soon as you walk in the door. I'll keep all my clothes on the whole time; I promise.'

'But if Lise found out . . .'

'God.' I sighed. 'This really is ridiculous. Well, it's up to you. I'll email you my address and my phone number.'

'Instead, can you . . . ?'

'What?'

'Can you put your number into my phone now? Don't email. I think Lise has my password. I'll text you if I'm in the area. Is that OK?'

He passed his phone to me. It was a bit bashed up around the edges and some of the markings on the keys had faded away completely. I opened his address book and saw about twenty numbers there, including Frank's mobile, and Vi's.

'What shall I put myself in as?' I said. 'The dry-cleaner?'

'No. I've never had anything dry-cleaned in my life. Just give yourself an alias of some sort.'

'I can't believe you're being serious. OK; I'll be Anna,' I said.

'Not a woman.'

'I'll be Anton, then.'

'I'm so sorry about this. You can stop speaking to me if you like, and have nothing more to do with me. I'd understand.'

'Do you want me to stop speaking to you?'

'Of course not. I need a friend, like I said.'

'A secret friend.'

'Yes.'

I sighed again. 'This is very weird.'

'I'm sorry. It's the best I can do.' He looked at his watch again. 'I've got to go. See you soon?'

'Yeah, whatever.' I felt like crying, suddenly.

He reached across the table and touched my hand. 'Meg?'

'It's OK,' I said. 'Go.'

'I'll see you soon. I mean, I want to see you soon, if you want to see me.'

'OK.'

'Don't get in touch with me. I'll contact you.'

When Rowan left I just sat there with all the sandwich crusts. After a few minutes I took out my phone and replied to Josh. *Sorry for one day delay. Yes, I'll come to Newman with you, and for pizza. Tell me what time to meet you at Rumour.*

• • •

A week later I still hadn't heard from Rowan. I hadn't heard from Christopher either, although Josh had confirmed that he'd booked Rumour for the evening of 20th March. My feature had been published in the paper, and various people had written me congratulatory emails, but not Vi. I'd been back to the house in Dartmouth and removed the last of my stuff except the rest of my books, which I'd arranged to have picked up by a Man with a Van that Andrew knew. I'd finished constructing my bed and had made it up with the plain white organic cotton bedding I'd bought from Greenfibres. I'd been working my way through Iris's book in the evenings, and, using her instructions, had appliquéd an image of a wagtail onto the bottom right-hand corner of the duvet cover, using scraps from an old pillow-case. I cut up the rest of the pillow-case into fairly neat squares and added them to my newly constructed bag of patchwork materials. I was going to make a patchwork quilt for the winter, I'd decided, and write a column about it.

I'd got into a good rhythm of living by myself. Some evenings or lunchtimes I'd pop into the Foghorn for something to eat and a pint of Beast. Other times I cooked pasta or omelettes for myself. I learned how to pick the leaves from my basil plant in such a way that new ones grew in their place. And my hyacinth bloomed: it was blue, like the sea. I spoke to my mother a couple of times, and Libby. Claudia rang to let me know the arrangements for next week's editorial board meeting. I wanted to ask her about Vi, but the words didn't come out. In the evenings, when the phone stopped ringing, and after a couple of pints of Beast, I'd get out my guitar and play one of Iris's folk songs, or a version of some blues song I already knew. I couldn't help myself playing all the songs I'd ever talked about with Rowan. I'd decided to write my first weekly column about playing guitar, which I already knew how to do. Between songs I checked my phone for messages that I wouldn't have heard over the music, but each time I saw that no one had texted me, not even Libby. At some point I went on the Internet and worked out how to text myself, to see if it was still working. It was. My message, when it came through, said *You're an idiot.*

As well as all this, I finished knitting my slippers and found it was quite easy to rinse the pieces and lay them out on the kitchen table to dry and take shape. But Libby had been right about sewing them up. It was both boring and stressful in a way very few things are: as if someone has given you a priceless antique and told you to stand there holding it for five hours. The last time I'd been in Totnes I'd bought organic unbleached wool and a set of four double-pointed bamboo needles, along with a sweet little zip-up bag in which to carry my sock-knitting. The needles were odd-looking things, like giants' cocktail sticks. I was going to have a go at Iris Glass's pattern and write about it in my second column, and had decided that I should start trying now, as Libby had said it was so hard.

To knit a sock you have to cast on some stitches to one of your double-pointed needles and then distribute the stitches around two of the other needles, so you have something wigwam-ish and triangular, with none of your stitches 'twisted'. I didn't know what that meant exactly, but Iris's other instructions had all made sense in the end, although usually only as the activity was being performed. So one evening, after the sun had gone down and while the fire was crackling in the grate, I got a couple of bottles of Beast from Andrew and sat down to work it all out. I'd already done a swatch, which I'd cast off and was now using as a beer mat. My wool gave me six stitches per inch, so I used Iris's table to work out that for an 'adult medium' sock in this yarn I should cast on fifty-two stitches and then divide them on the needles so the first and last needle held seventeen stitches, and the middle one eighteen. This took a few attempts. I had no idea which the 'first' and 'last' needles would be until I tried it out, got it wrong, read that the tail of the wool dangles between them like a rat's tail and tried again.

To knit a tube, which is basically what a sock is until you get to the heel and 'turn' it to get to the foot, you simply knit the stitches off whichever needle carries the live yarn onto a 'free' needle. It's similar to juggling, which I'd also learned from a book, years before. With juggling, you only have to remember to throw the ball from the hand that is about to receive a ball. Knitting socks turned out to be oddly similar. By midnight I'd got a rhythm going, and I'd knitted seven rows in a K2 P2 rib. After that, I moved on to a simple knit-stitch to carry on making a stocking-stitch tube. My sock looked like the beginning of a sock! I couldn't believe it. That night I went to bed without putting my phone on the pillow beside me. In fact, in the morning I couldn't remember where I'd left it. Rowan could have been texting me all night and I'd never have known.

When I found it, it was textless. I rang Libby.

'You'll never, ever guess what I'm doing,' I said to her.

'Shagging Bob's uncle?'

'Libby!'

'Sorry.'

'You can't keep saying that.'

'Yeah, yeah.'

'Anyway, guess again.'

'You're making rhubarb jam for the shop? I bet you're not. But everyone's asking, now that the forced rhubarb's in.' She sighed. 'That bloody shop. All people care about is food. There must be more to life than eating nice food and getting fat in front of the telly.'

'Are you OK?' I asked her.

'I'm totally, totally in the shit again. I was going to ring you today anyway. Are you busy at lunchtime?'

'No, why?'

'I'll come to you. Meet you in the Foghorn? You can show me your new place.'

'Sure.'

Libby hadn't been more specific than 'lunchtime', so I went into the Foghorn at quarter past twelve with my knitting and settled by the fire to wait for her. Andrew brought me over a half of Beast and a pink straw.

He laughed as he waved the straw in front of me. 'We all know you're multi-talented. But even you can't drink and knit at the same time. Thus the straw. Aunt Iris used to drink through a straw when she was knitting. Used to get totally pissed, drop stitches all over the place and sing sea-shanties, sometimes until the sun came up. Even had a couple of knitting songs too, I think, although I'm sure she invented those.'

'I've been reading her book,' I said. 'It's how I learned how to do this.'

I held up the sock, which, to an objective observer, probably wasn't much of a sock yet. Still, I'd done thirty-six rows, and I thought it was really beginning to look like something. I'd expected Andrew to glance at it vaguely and pretend to be impressed, but he leaned down, took off his glasses and touched the fabric gently with his big fingers.

'That's pretty good,' he said. 'Don't worry about the knobbly bits and the dust. That'll all come out the first time you wash them. Nice wool. You taking orders?'

'Orders?' I laughed. 'I haven't even got to the heel yet. My first-ever sock might be my last-ever sock if that doesn't go right. It could still turn into a legwarmer.'

'Nothing like hand-knitted socks,' he said. 'She used to make them for me.'

'Iris?'

'Yeah. Made them for half the village. You can't buy socks after you've had home-made ones. It's not the same.'

'I'll tell you what,' I said. 'If I can get one pair done — which

I warn you might be in about a million years — I'll make you a pair next. Say thanks for the cottage and stuff. I'm really enjoying living there, I can't tell you how much.'

'Oh, there's no need,' he said, putting his glasses back on. 'I'm only kidding with you.'

I shrugged. 'Oh, well. I'm going to write about Iris's book in the newspaper, though. You might want to tell the publisher.'

Andrew smiled. 'Thanks, mate. And actually, what am I saying? I must be mad. Give me a pair of hand-knitted socks and you can have all the logs you want for free. And a few pints — lots of pints — of Beast on the house.'

'You're on.'

Andrew drifted away to wash up glasses. I carried on knitting until Libby came in about half an hour later, carrying a box of rhubarb.

'Ha, ha!' she said.

'Ha, ha,' I said back. 'Yes, I'll make the jam.'

She put the rhubarb down on the end of the table, sat next to me and took off her sunglasses.

'Holy shit, you're knitting a sock.'

'I am.'

'Where in God's name did you learn to do that? Have you got a new best friend?'

'Well, sort of, but she's dead.' I told Libby all about Iris Glass. 'The coolest thing is that I've been given a column at the paper and each week I have to "try out" a different hobby. I'm going to do sock-knitting for the next one.'

Andrew came over and addressed Libby. 'She's in that cottage all the time knitting and sewing and making things. You want to take her clubbing or something before she becomes a complete hermit.' He laughed. 'What can I get you to drink?'

'Same as Meg,' Libby said. 'I think we're too old for clubbing.'

'I'm only teasing,' Andrew said. 'I'm a hermit myself. Nothing wrong with it. Do you know what you want to eat? We've got oysters in, and some nice pollock.'

We ordered both and Libby looked properly at my sock, squealing with astonishment as she saw that it really was progressing as a sock should.

'No one learns to knit socks from a book,' she said. 'It's too hard.'

'Lots of people learn things from books. Usually the wrong things. But my column's all about how to learn good things — like knitting socks — from books.'

'God. It'll be like being back at school and having projects where you have to go to the library and learn how to build a campfire or put up a shelf or sew your own apron.'

'It doesn't have to be like that.'

'I think you know how to knit socks because you cosmically ordered it.'

'God, I did, didn't I?' I laughed.

'It's the most rational explanation.'

I looked more closely at Libby. She seemed to have aged a couple of years since I last saw her. 'You OK? You look very tired and a bit ethereal, if you don't mind me saying so.'

'Oh, that's because I forgot to put mascara on.' She sighed. 'I'm back with Mark. Or, at least, we're sleeping together again.'

'Shit. Why? How?'

'Maybe he's my destiny.'

'You don't believe in destiny.'

'Bob does. He said I'm his destiny.'

'OK. Tell me from the beginning.'

Libby sighed. As we ate our way through first oysters, and then pollock with roast beetroot and mashed potatoes, she explained what had happened.

'It was like I had this dead feeling in my head all the time. Something between concrete and cotton wool. When I tried to think, nothing happened. I didn't know what to talk to Bob about, all of a sudden. When I was with Mark I was always so busy rushing here and there, and trying to catch up with stuff all the time. Life felt exciting, you know? And real. Being with Bob felt more dishonest than being with Bob-and-Mark. Before, I had to pretend to love Bob — well, you know, to love him "like that" — while really loving Mark. Once Mark was out of the equation I was just left with "pretending to love Bob" as my whole entire life. I've thought about this a lot. Maybe I'm just trying to justify myself. But I was getting seriously stressed and a bit depressed. I never understood when you told me about your depression: that feeling of nothing really meaning anything, or having any point. But that's what I started to feel. I literally have to plan conversations to have with Bob. I make notes beforehand. But it doesn't really help. You know when you're a kid and you've got double biology with the most boring teacher in the world, and anticipating it just makes you want to go to sleep? That's how I started to feel every time I thought about talking to Bob. I used to get through it by imagining being with Mark, you know, thinking about the last time I'd been with him, or the next time I was going to see him and what I might wear. I used to book hair appointments and do my nails because of Mark. I just didn't have any motivation to bother to do it for Bob. Does all this sound awful?'

'No, of course not. I know the depressed feeling you're talking about. When I had it really badly I could hardly speak to anyone. I had absolutely nothing to say. If my mum phoned up and asked what I'd been doing, I wouldn't be able to remember.'

'Yeah, that's exactly it. And it's spilling over into the rest of my life as well. I stand in the shop all day with nothing to look forward to, and I can't even be bothered to make new displays when we're quiet. I just go out the back and cry, because at least that feels real, and dramatic: like something's actually happening — must be happening — in my life. I've found my-self putting on mascara in the mornings and wondering why I bother. I wondered why I bother with anything at all. Didn't Darwin say that more or less everything is about sex? And sex is for reproduction. What use is my life if it's all about sex with no reproduction? Does it mean everything I do is pointless?'

'I think you can help the species without making babies yourself,' I said.

'But not by wearing mascara, presumably? I mean, does it matter whether I wear mascara or not?' Libby sighed. 'Does it matter if I'm attractive? Poor Bob. It's not as if he's objectively boring or anything like that; it's just that I don't desire him and I'm not interested in him. I have baths all the time just to get away from him. He came into the bathroom the other day when I was in the bath, just to have a piss, and then he wanted to stay and chat. I ended up crying and telling him to go away, for no reason — just because I couldn't bear to be in a room with him, even for ten minutes, and I couldn't believe he'd actually started to invade my last bit of private space. And I didn't want to have to pretend to be interested in the graphic novel he's just read, or the song he's learning. Did I tell you that his latest plan is that we form a band? He wants us to go on tour in a year or so — because we've been talking about go-ing away, and he thinks that would be a really good excuse. I can't sing for nuts, but he thinks I can. He says I have an "inter-esting" voice. We've had a couple of practices, and both times I just longed for someone else to be there, because singing to him, or with him, felt worse even than singing by myself.'

'Sounds pretty miserable,' I said.

'Yeah. And on top of all that I've had to keep going out every Friday night, because I couldn't suddenly say, "Oh, yeah, by the way, I dumped my book group." I'd just drive out to Paignton and look at the sea. That was where Mark and I first kissed. The second time I went there, Mark turned up too. We didn't talk. We just went back to his place and made love. I cried. I said it was goodbye sex, it had to be. He said he didn't care any more; he'd take whatever I had to offer. He didn't want me to leave Bob, even. I thought, "Why me?" I mean, surely Mark could find someone better than me, who's single. So the whole thing has started again, and I'm not depressed any more, but I don't know what to do.'

'You have to leave Bob,' I said, surprising myself.

'Seriously?'

'Yeah. Well, I don't know. It has to be your decision. I shouldn't have said that.'

'You're right, though. I have to leave him. But I'm still not sure I can. Everything's set up with Bob: the house, the business. You and Christopher didn't really have anything like that together. It must have been easier for you . . . Oh, shit. What am I saying? It's never easy, is it?'

'Honestly, Lib, for about six years I thought about leaving and I told myself I couldn't do it. I told myself I didn't have enough money; I couldn't leave Christopher to pay for the house on his own; things would work out. We gave up a lot to be together, as you know. I couldn't leave him with nothing after all that. I couldn't admit to myself that at the beginning with him it actually wasn't about us having things in common or wanting to share our lives. I just wanted to fuck him, and I was prepared to seriously disrupt people's lives in order to do it. If I admitted that was the real story, then what sort of character would that make me? There are always a million good reasons not to split up with someone. And so many of them are complicated reasons about how you define yourself, and under what circumstances you can even live with yourself.'

'Maybe I'm just a coward.'

'I don't think it's as simple as that. No one just "is" a coward.'

'But if everyone split up with their partner every time they felt like it there'd be no relationships in the world.'

'Yeah, but when you've been feeling like it for years . . . ?'

'I thought you weren't ever going to tell me what to do.'

'Yeah. I know. But from everything you've just said, it's kind of obvious. I'm just telling you back what you're telling me. Apart from everything else, it's not fair on Mark. It's definitely not fair on Bob.'

'I'm a terrible person.'

'No, silly. You're a lovely person. That's why you've got all these men wanting you. You're a bit confused, though, and you're trying to do the right thing. I thought it made sense to stay with Christopher, even though I knew we were wrong for each other, because I thought passion could be worked at, or learned. But you can't just decide to be happy, or learn passion, I don't think. And like we said before, who knows what the "right thing" is?'

'Yeah, but how important is my happiness in the scheme of things? Loads of people in the world are miserable, and they just get on with their lives. My problems are just trivial and pathetic. If Bob was my disabled parent, for example, I wouldn't be able to leave him; I'd just have to get on with it. I kept telling myself to pretend he was my disabled parent. But it didn't work.'

I laughed. 'No wonder the sex didn't go well.'

'Yes; ha, ha.'

'Anyway, disabled parents don't prevent you from falling in love.'

'The ones on TV do.'

'Yeah, but no one would hold it against you on TV — falling in love, I mean. Isn't that the point of the disabled parents on TV shows? They just function as an obstacle in the way of the hero or heroine. Just another version of the parents who want to tie you down or arrange your marriage or make you take over the family business. With an obstacle like that it's your moral *duty* to fall in love, so that your disabled parents can lead a fulfilled life of their own without having to rely on you.'

'Yeah, that's true.'

'And your relationship with Bob is completely different. You do have to have sex with him, and you can't love anyone else.'

Libby covered her mouth with her hands, and then uncovered it again.

'Oh, my God. You're right.'

'Sorry to be so blunt.'

'God. No, it's all become clear now. I'm really going to do it. I'm going to split up with him.'

'It does make sense. Just like you said.'

'Oh, fuck.'

'Yeah.'

'So my downfall continues.'

'It doesn't have to be a downfall. You can't predict what's going to happen. I thought I was doing a really bad thing when I left Drew for Christopher, but after we split up Drew's career took off and he ended up with Rosa Cooper. He'd always had a thing for her, so it all ended up OK for him, at least for a while . . . And I ended up like something caught in a gum trap, stuck in Dartmouth with Christopher.'

One of Vi's favourite folk tales was about a rabbit that becomes stuck in a farmer's gum trap. A coyote comes along and asks the rabbit what he's doing and why he's stuck there. The rabbit tells him that the farmer was annoyed with him because he refused to eat melons with him, and now he's trapped him and is going to force him to eat chicken with him instead. The coyote frees the rabbit and sticks himself to the gum trap, because he wants to be the one to eat chicken with the farmer. But of course when the farmer comes he shoots the coyote. This wasn't exactly a storyless story. In fact, it was a conventional story with all kinds of reversals (the coyote goes from free to trapped; the rabbit moves from tricked to Trickster and so on) that seem satisfying only because the rabbit, being weak and cunning, is positioned as morally superior to the coyote, who is strong but stupid. But in real life strength and stupidity normally win, and rabbits can't speak.

Libby had blushed, and was looking down at the table.

'Oh, shit,' she said. 'I never thought to say anything about Rosa. God, Meg, I'm really sorry. I know you sort of hated her, but she was your oldest friend, wasn't she? I'm a selfish, self-obsessed cow. I completely forgot.'

'It's OK,' I said. 'You're right. I did sort of hate her.'

'But you're not glad she's dead?'

'No. Of course not.'

We finished our drinks in silence, and when Andrew came over I insisted on paying. Libby picked up the box of rhubarb.

'You don't have to make jam, really,' she said. 'It was a joke.'

'No; I'll make it. I want to.'

'I'm so embarrassed about everything. Can I look at your house now?'

After Libby had gone the day darkened and it started to rain. I curled up on the sofa in front of the fire and knitted some more of my sock, while listening to the spit and hiss of the logs and the lazy rolling of the sea. Now that I was into a rhythm with the sock I could just about think of other things while knitting it, and so my thoughts drizzled along with the rain. At one point I imagined myself with Rowan, and colours formed in my mind like an unexpected rainbow. I imagined walking down the beach with him and getting him to promise me — to swear on his life — that the moment he stopped loving me he would leave me. Not a year later, or seven years later, or thirty years later: the very moment it happened. But I couldn't even imagine walking down the beach with Rowan, not really. I could barely imagine sharing a cup of tea together in this cottage. I couldn't imagine us ever going on a train together, or taking it in turns with the review section of

317

the newspaper, or him walking B because I had a headache. I couldn't imagine ever looking in my purse for 50p for something and then him automatically looking in his pocket or wallet when I couldn't find it. He'd have to start loving me before he could stop. There'd have to be a beginning and an end to the rainbow, both of which were impossible to contemplate.

The gloom never lifted, and at about four I took B for a walk down the beach. Startlingly red seaweed lay across the tide-line like picked scabs. B found a beat-up piece of driftwood and brought it to me. Then she crouched down with her back half in the air, her tail wagging wildly. This was code for 'throw the stick'. I thought about all the ways we subtly understood each other. I knew all her codes for 'I'm hungry'; 'I'm thirsty'; 'I want to play'; 'I don't want to play' and so on. She knew to connect shopping bags with treats, and so put her head in every shopping bag she ever came across. She knew to connect having a bath with her annual trip to the French vet, who always gave her lots of biscuits, and then examined her fur, saying, 'Now let's see if there's anybody living on you,' before doing her vaccinations. She knew that big cardboard boxes meant moving house. She knew that the sound of a little bell anywhere meant that there could be a pussycat attached to it, and that the sound of quick footsteps and rustling envelopes meant that the postman was coming. She was almost eight. So in a few years' time, in my early forties, I would finally be alone: a miserable old spinster with a thousand hobbies. I'd have hundreds of pairs of socks by then, all made for myself. What was wrong with me? There had to be more to life than that. I tried to imagine lots of good novels, interesting CDs and lovely dinners, with B living on and on. But it was too late. My breath started to come out in short, thin bursts and then before I knew it I was crying. What was wrong with me? I had my column, and some friends, and even an emerging plan for my new novel. I had money, and my cottage.

When I got in I just wanted to get into bed and sleep off this feeling, but my phone started ringing as soon as I got to the top of the stairs. It was Tim.

'Hello?' he said. 'Meg?'

I could hear wind and rain in the background.

'How are you?' I said.

'Heidi said you rang me. Was it about the book?'

'Oh — no. Sorry. The board meeting's not until Friday. I'll ring as soon as I know anything. It was just, well, nothing really. I wondered if you'd already left to go looking for the Beast. Wondered how you were getting on.'

'It's exhilarating out here,' he said. 'Magical.'

'Any sightings?'

There was a huge gust of wind at his end as I said this.

'Sorry?' Tim said.

I repeated the question, and from his broken-up reply managed to work out that he'd been moving camp every couple of days according to where sightings were, and on the basis of the tracks he'd picked up. But he was always one day behind the Beast. He'd get to a new location and set up his camp. Then he'd find a local pub or B&B and they'd tell him that the night before they'd heard awful howling and then found a bag of potatoes missing — or something like that. But the next night there'd be nothing but some tracks and a huge pile of shit. He thought the Beast was following the line of the River Dart, but he wasn't yet sure.

'There's stuff that no one's really saying as well,' he said.

'Like what?'

'I met this woman in Dartmeet called Margaret, who made me swear never to tell anyone what she'd seen.'

'What had she seen?'

Tim paused. 'The Beast. In her bedroom on the stroke of midnight.'

'Seriously?'

'It was panting softly. Just standing there panting and watching her sleep. All her doors were locked, and there were no windows open. I wrote it all down.'

There was another big gust of wind at Tim's end and the signal dropped out for a second.

'What will you do if you see it?' I asked when the line came back.

'I've got a gun,' he said. 'My mate's a farmer. He lent it to me, but don't tell anyone. I don't want to shoot it, really. I just want to see what it is. But better safe than sorry.'

'I can't remember exactly how this is going to help with the book,' I said.

'What do you mean?'

'Well, surely in the book the Beast turns out not to be real.'

'Why?'

'Well, that's the Zeb Ross formula. We talked about this. It's in your proposal.'

'Yeah, but if it does turn out to be real that would only make the book better, surely? If I can prove it.'

'Not in fiction. Especially not if it's by Zeb Ross. Remember, the books have to be realistic, in the sense that anything mysterious is explained as something rational that just seemed to be something irrational.'

'But what if that isn't actually realistic?'

'Then you write a philosophy book about it or something. Zeb Ross novels are not the place to start questioning the true nature of reality. They're supposed to make sense of the world for teenagers. They have to tell a good story.'

'I'm not sure I know what a good story is.'

'Well, ditto. I do understand, believe me. But there's a real difference between what you can do in fiction and non-fiction. For example, if you had a character in a novel who finds aliens, the character would have to turn out to be mistaken or deluded — otherwise you'd have to make the novel take place in a different kind of world from this one: maybe in the future, or in a parallel universe. It wouldn't chime with what we understand to be reality now. But if you were a scientist you could write a book speculating about aliens and no one would think that was odd. Well, I guess some people would, but . . . Look, do you still want me to put this proposal through on Friday?'

Tim went silent.

'Tim?' I said. 'Are you still there?'

'You're going to reject my proposal because I'm looking for the Beast?'

'No! I'm just saying that if you wanted to turn this into a different kind of book altogether, you could withdraw the proposal from Orb Books. They're not the only publisher in the world.'

'But they're quite close to accepting it. I've never had a chance like this before.'

'Yes, exactly, so . . .'

'So I should give up and go home? I can't do that now. The *Totnes Times* is phoning to interview me tomorrow. And this American writer's coming next week. He wants to record my heroic journey for an anthology. He was really interested in the way I'm doing it: camping, living on velvet shanks and morels when I can find them . . .'

'What's his name?'

'I can't remember, but he's quite famous.'

'Is it Kelsey Newman?'

'That sounds familiar. He's coming to Totnes next week to give a talk.'

'Yeah; I'm supposed to be going to that. It must be him. He could be a useful contact for you. Ask him what you should do about the Beast.'

'Yeah. I might do. Anyway, I can't give up now.'

'I'm not saying you should give up. But if you don't find the Beast it might be helpful for the book. Just don't pin all your hopes on seeing it, that's all. And if you do, just be really careful with that gun.' I realised I was straying outside my role as the possible commissioning editor of this book. 'Just be careful,' I said again.

'You sound like my wife,' he said.

'Yeah. Sorry. Look, I'll let you know what happens on Friday.'

The next day was bright and still. It wasn't cold enough for the fire, although B thought it was. It was hard to sit on the sofa and knit my sock, because at regular intervals she would fix me with a stare and then go and stand by the fire and look at it meaningfully. At one point she swiped the matchbox with her paw so it turned over and clattered. It was like the electric fan heater all over again.

In the end I gave up trying to knit and replied to a few emails at the new kitchen table before taking B for a long walk in the weakening sunlight. I could see dark clouds coming from beyond Start Point, and just as we'd got in it started to rain. B settled down with her rawhide chew, and I made rhubarb jam while the rain turned to hail and then back again. I'd just finished putting the jam into jars when my phone vibrated. It was a text message from Rowan. *Can I come and look at your ship at 5 P.M.? I hope you're OK.* 5 P.M.? I looked at the kitchen clock. It was already coming up for three. How would I ever get ready in time? Then again, what did I need to get ready for, exactly? We were just two people, two of what Tolstoy called randomly united and fermenting 'lumps of something', and we were going to be in a room together. That was all.

B got out of her basket, stretched, came over and wagged her tail, before circling me twice and going to get a leftover biscuit from her bowl. She headed for the sitting room. 'B,' I said, following her, 'please don't cover the rug in bits of biscuit today. We've got a visitor coming.' The more I told her not to make a mess, the more excited she became, until there were biscuits all over the rug, and in B's fur, and I was on the rug

too, rolling around and tickling her. 'I've got to brush you,' I
said. 'And I've got to change the bedding, just in case. I've got
to clean the bathroom, and the kitchen. I've got to have a bath
and wash my hair. I'll never have time, and it's all your fault.
I don't know how, but it is, you silly dog.' B seemed to love
this, and by the time I went upstairs to have a bath she was
brushed and happily asleep on the sofa and I was the one covered in biscuits.

'Tarot cards?' said Rowan, as he walked into the sitting room.
    There they still were, on the desk by the window.
    'Long story,' I said, my voice surprising me. It sounded
as if I was reading lines on the radio, and my laugh sounded
canned. 'Can I get you a glass of wine, or a cup of tea or something?'
    'I'd love a glass of wine.'
    When I came back he was sitting on the sofa, looking at
the Tarot cards.
    'I didn't have you down as a Tarot reader,' he said.
    I gave him a glass of the Syrah I'd bought from Andrew ear-
lier and sat cross-legged at the other end of the sofa.
    'Oh, don't worry, I'm not. They were research. For my
newspaper feature.'
    'The one from Sunday? I meant to say — I liked that.'
    'Thanks.'
    'But there weren't any Tarot cards in it, were there?'
    'No. Not really.'
    'There was something about the Fool, though?'
    'Yeah.'
    'So . . .'
    I sighed. 'I was commissioned to write a feature exposing
New Age books, which to be honest isn't that hard when you
see what's out there. My editor sent me a big sack of books
on everything from cosmic ordering to meeting your own
spirit guide. In amongst them were some books that, well . . .

I don't quite know how to describe them. They weren't things I'd choose to read on my own, but they weren't awful either. At first I thought I'd do my feature on them, just because they seemed the least painful to read. But they didn't make such good copy. I was supposed to be putting myself in the story, which I didn't really do in the end. The idea was that I'd do a Tarot reading on myself and go out and do something ridiculous on the basis of it and write about how hilariously stupid the advice was. But in fact I found the advice quite useful. Why am I telling you this? You'll think I'm a freak.'

He shook his head. 'No. I don't think you're a freak. This is a nice deck. I'm glad they've re-issued it. You know who designed these?'

I shook my head. 'Not really. I read the information card but forgot what it said. Some spiritualist guy?'

'Arthur Edward Waite? Well, yes, he commissioned them. But all the work was done by a woman called Pamela Colman Smith, who must have been born at the end of the nineteenth century in England, but grew up in Jamaica. She did illustrations for Yeats, and drawings of Anansi the Spider for books of Jamaican folklore. All the innovations in this deck were hers. The idea of illustrating every card, not just the Trumps, came from her. She died penniless and unknown, with no family except for a woman companion.' He laughed. 'God, sorry. I feel like an encyclopaedia sometimes. Lise complains about it.'

'Sounds as if you know more about Tarot than I do.'

'Yeah.' He looked at his glass of wine as if it was a crystal ball and he didn't like what it was telling him. 'Yeah. I know a bit.'

'You're the Tarot reader!'

'Well, sort of,' he said. 'Just for one summer. Probably before you were born.'

I rolled my eyes. 'I was born in 1969.'

'This was in . . .' He frowned. 'Must have been 1970, I think. So it was just after you were born. I was about twenty-two and

I'd gone hitchhiking around Europe with my first girlfriend. The idea was we'd spend the summer doing that before both going back to Cambridge to do our PhDs. Oh, how our lives were mapped out. It was all so over-determined and planned. She must have thought so too, because she dumped me somewhere in France and I ended up going on to Spain and then Italy by myself. In Italy I got a ride in a hippy bus and ended up hanging out on a beach with a bunch of Cornish musicians. That was when I learned to play guitar. This woman, Maisie, taught me. She taught me guitar, and then late one night we sat on the beach and she taught me Tarot. She looked . . . I hate to say it, but she looked a lot like you. A late-sixties version. A twenty-two-year-old version. Long hair, blue eyes, thick eyebrows. She was my first true love. I hope you don't mind me talking about this . . .'

'Why would I?' I smiled. 'I don't mind you saying my eyebrows are thick.'

He laughed. 'Your eyebrows are lovely.' He looked down at the cards, and then put them all in his left hand while he drank some wine. He swallowed, then took another sip and swallowed that. He looked at the cards again. 'She almost died. God, how weird to be thinking about this. I haven't really thought about Maisie for years. Or Tarot cards. I never thought I'd touch them ever again. But it's actually soothing looking at yours. I'm having a million memories. I hope you don't mind.'

I wondered why Rowan kept asking if I minded, and realised that Lise probably minded almost everything he did, just as Christopher had minded everything I did. It seemed to be a feature of most long-term relationships that you realised you'd ended up with someone who constantly minded everything you did.

'How did Maisie almost die?' I asked.

He bit his lip. 'The Tarot cards — or one Tarot card — got her. Pretty wild, huh? She was in a coma for a week.'

'Oh, my God. How is that . . . ? What happened?'

'When I met Maisie she had just started to give Tarot readings to tourists for money. I'd run out of cash back in Spain, and since I wasn't good enough on the guitar yet to join in with the musicians, I learned how to make friendship bracelets out of embroidery thread, and so I'd sell those out of a newspaper on the ground while Maisie did her readings next to me. Maisie was a bit of a loner at heart, and she'd had enough of travelling in a big group. So had I. We set off down the coast together with our knapsacks and her travelling card table. We stopped in villages on the way and she did readings. At first I felt a bit useless. I spoke no Italian, and I had no way of contributing to the venture myself except with my bracelets, but they took a long time to make and didn't sell for very much. While I was sitting there, I watched Maisie, and that was how I learned about the cards. I found I picked it up very easily. You've noticed that I remember historical details, especially about people. I used this — and everything I'd learned on my degree — to start doing readings of my own. If the Chariot came up for a woman, I'd imagine Boadicea. For a man, I'd imagine Caesar. I was able to pick out the archetypal elements of each card by thinking about all the historical situations I could connect with it. I saw so much in each card, in the end, and it was all new to me and so exciting. It was probably more exciting because I was in love, and charged with energy. I didn't feel that way again for years and years.' He sighed. 'Soon I did readings of my own, and for a few weeks it was all Maisie and I talked about. We really connected through these cards. If we wanted to talk about clarity and focus, we'd discuss the Ace of Swords. If we wanted to talk about decision-making, we'd use Justice. I got better and better at reading, and also at playing the old guitar I'd picked up in Genoa. We travelled and travelled, searching for English-speaking communities for whom we could do deeper readings than just "You have problem with husband." We took a boat to Sicily, and then another boat to Malta. Maisie and I were planning to keep travelling, and eventually get to Africa and maybe go around the world together. I had decided not to go back to Cambridge. It was a magical time. We washed in the sea and slept on beaches. At some point we took a boat from Malta up to the island of Gozo, where there was a commune we'd heard about, with revolutionaries from all over the world waiting to help stage revolution and help the Maltese and Gozitan people get independence from Britain. That was probably the happiest time of my life. We drank Gozitan wine, got stoned, talked about politics and, of course, did Tarot readings. Lots of the communists said Tarot was decadent and bourgeois, of course.'

'So what happened to Maisie?'

Rowan sighed again, and took a big sip of wine. 'Her sister was coming out to meet us and spend some time at the commune. We'd written to her to ask for some supplies. This was stuff like needles and thread, writing paper, pens and pencils, Bob Dylan tapes — and a new pack of Tarot cards. It was hard to buy Tarot cards then, although I'd picked up my own deck in Italy. But Maisie's were virtually worn out. We would never have thought to ask for antiseptic or anything grown-up like that. We were young and we would never die. Especially not of something as stupid as septicaemia.'

'Is that what happened? She got blood poisoning?'

He nodded. 'Yeah. Liz, Maisie's sister, had brought some bad news from home. Maisie was upset, and asked me to do a reading for her. We hardly ever read for each other, because it felt weird, but she was desperate. We used her new cards. She was the querent — the one asking for the reading — so she had to shuffle them. They were new, of course, and she was used to shuffling old cards. While she was doing it she got a papercut on the back of her little finger, just above the first joint. We didn't make a big deal of it. As the cards turned over we both realised we were seeing a pretty terrible spread.' He frowned. 'At that stage we were so immersed in the meanings of the cards that we knew every little nuance of them — or thought we did. In Tarot, Death doesn't mean death. It can mean a new beginning, for example. But however much you know that, it's still awful when Death comes up in a significant position. I think in this case it came up second, as the "Cross" card that covers the first card. There was Death, and at some point there was the Three of Swords and the Nine of Swords. I can't remember the others, but I think the Six of Swords was in the "Outcome" position. It was just terrible. Maisie became convinced that she was cursed — even though she knew the cards didn't work that way, and, unlike a lot of people, didn't believe you could tell anything about the future from them, only the present — and fell into a depression. When her finger got infected she didn't do anything about it. I hardly noticed until it was too late and she had blood poisoning. She lost consciousness on the boat back to Malta, on her way to hospital. At one point it looked as if she was going to die.'

Rowan had been shuffling the cards, face up, as he spoke. Now he pulled out the Six of Swords and passed it to me.

'You know,' he said, 'every deck of Tarot cards is different. But the main idea on each card remains the same.' He moved along the sofa and pointed at the Six of Swords that I was holding. Our arms lightly touched as he pointed out the details. 'This card always has a boat, with someone — usually a woman — on it, and the sense is of a difficult or sad journey on water. One thing Tarot never does is depict anything literal. But this is pretty close to what happened to Maisie.' He sighed. 'I'm so sorry,' he said, after a few seconds. 'I'm all right, really. It's fine. It's just the memories, and maybe remembering being young and free and then it all stopping.' But his eyes were filling with tears.

'It's OK,' I said.

The wave function of everything that I could possibly have said — that Maisie would certainly have taken a trip on water from a small island, that the nocebo effect could have led to her coma, that my grandmother, Margaret, after whom I was named, was also known as Maisie, that I was jealous of Rowan's first love, that I wanted to know how Lise acted when Rowan was emotional, that it was still possible for him to be free, if not young — collapsed and I found myself holding onto him, wrapping my arms around him and stroking his soft, thinning hair and saying, 'It's OK. I understand.'

'We can't . . .' he said, pulling away only a little.

'We're not,' I said. 'Don't worry; I'm not so insensitive that I'd . . .'

And then he clutched me harder. 'I know,' he said.

We didn't speak for a few minutes, until Rowan said he wanted to go for a pee and I pointed him towards the bathroom upstairs. While he was gone I started building a fire. B, clearly realising what I was doing, came out from wherever she had been and plonked herself down on the hearth, virtually in the fire, getting ash in her fur.

'Come on, silly,' I said to her. 'Out of the fire.'

Rowan came back. 'What did you say?'

'Oh,' I smiled at him. 'How are you?' He shrugged and smiled. 'I was just suggesting to Bess that she might like to get out of the fire. She's pretty keen for me to get it going.' B jumped onto the sofa. I struck a match underneath my wigwam of logs and newspaper, and the firelighters caught immediately.

Rowan sat down on the sofa too and poured more wine for both of us.

'That's impressive,' he said, gesturing at the fire.

'Oh — that's just the firelighters.' I put the guard in front of the fire. 'Just cross your fingers that the heat is enough to make the logs catch. They don't always. But this should be OK. It sparks a lot at the beginning, when it does catch — thus the fire guard — and then . . . Why am I telling you this? Presumably you know about open fires.'

'Yeah. Although we never had firelighters when I used

to make them, usually on beaches. I've never had a fire in a house. We didn't have them when I was growing up, and Lise never wanted one because of the mess and the fuss. You've made it look easy.'

'Well, it's nowhere near properly lit yet. I guess it's the same with campfires. They take ages and ages to get going, and you have to poke them and fuss over them and move the logs around so that there's enough oxygen for the fire to breathe, but not so much that the whole thing falls in on itself and suffocates. But once it's going it seems as if it will never go out. Sorry. I'm waffling about nothing. I've got quite into my fires since I've been living here. I'm sure the novelty will wear off. How are you feeling?'

'I like hearing you talk. And I'm fine.'

I sat back on the sofa. Instead of being at either end of it, we were now side by side in the middle, with B at one end like a single bookend. Since we'd been touching before, it now didn't seem so odd when Rowan took my hand and held it.

'Is this OK?' he asked.

'Yes. Of course.'

We sat there like that for a minute or two.

'I came round to see your ship in a bottle, didn't I?'

'Yeah.' I took my hand away. 'I'll go and get it.'

It was on the mantelpiece in the bedroom. I brought it down and gave it to Rowan.

'Here,' I said. 'I don't expect you to make anything of this, but I'd be reassured if you told me that there's some completely rational reason for it washing up at my feet — especially as I'd just asked the universe for a sign. It was all Vi's idea.'

He didn't seem to be listening. He was poring over the ship in a bottle as if it was the denouement in a murder-mystery.

'I'm very glad you asked me to come and look at this,' he said, without taking his eyes off it.

'Why?'

'It's very interesting.'

'Why do you say that?'

He looked up. 'You tell me your bit first. Where did you find it? Why were you asking the universe for a sign?'

'Oh. I thought you missed that bit. Well, it's all a bit improbable,' I said. 'Or I think it is.'

'I can take it,' he said, and poured more wine. 'I'd better not have any more after this. I've got to drive back.'

'You're welcome to sleep on the sofa by the fire if it comes to it,' I said.

'Thanks, but . . . Anyway, tell me about how you came to have this.'

I'd always meant to simply tell him that I was walking along the beach and there it was. But instead I ended up telling him about Robert in the forest and his ship in a bottle, and Vi, and my argument with her, and how depressed I'd felt on New Year's Day, when there didn't seem to be anything worth living for.

'So you asked the universe for help and it gave you this?'

'Yeah. I think I was actually asking the sea for help, but it amounts to the same thing. Funny kind of help, wherever it came from. I mean, obviously the rational explanation is that whatever I saw after I asked for help would have been meaningful in some way. But this?'

Rowan turned the ship over in his hands.

'Yeah. This is really something.'

'Really?'

'Oh, yes. It's a bit fucked-up, though. You thought that Robert's ship was the original and this was some sort of copy, sent by the universe to freak you out. It's the other way around. This should be in a museum. It's quite famous.' He smiled. 'You might like this. It was famous anyway, but the reason it's really famous is because there was a book in the early seventies called *Make Your Own* . . . You could make your own Mona Lisa, your own Roman coin and so on. You could also make your own ship in a bottle, based on this one. There was a time when lots of households had a home-made copy of this on the mantelpiece underneath the flying ducks on the wall. You don't see them so much any more.'

'So you're not saying that someone simply knocked it up one weekend from instructions in a book and then threw it in the sea?'

'No. This is the original. Look at the age of the cork, and the precision of the sails. The glass is thick too. I'm fairly sure it used to be part of the William H. Dawe collection, but I can't imagine how it ended up in the sea. I don't know why the universe gave it to you — probably so you could give it to me and I could put it back with the rest of the collection in the Maritime Centre.'

'How efficient of the universe.'

'Good old universe,' Rowan said. 'Very kind of it to give you the original rather than the copy. So much less probable, of course, considering that there's one of these in the world, and a good few thousand copies.'

I shrugged. 'You could say that everything that happens is random, so why not this? Why is it that when something has meaning for us we assume the meaning is made by a higher force or even a tricksy human? Why can't things just happen?'

'Nothing "just happens".'

'What do you mean?'

'There's always some motivation somewhere. There's always something you can't see behind everything you can see. Not ghosts and monsters, but people, usually, doing things for good reasons.'

'Yeah. I guess that's right.'

'Hey, tell me — why do you want a rational, scientific explanation for this? Or, to re-phrase that a bit: why do people — including me — want scientific explanations for things? Isn't it more romantic and interesting if the universe has magically given you the ship for some reason?'

'No.'

'Why?'

'I don't know.' I frowned and remembered the scratching at the door in Dartmouth. 'Maybe because it's frightening and creepy that way.'

'But why?'

'I don't know, exactly. But if the universe is somehow conscious, then everything about living in it is different. It takes free choice away from you somehow. I don't want to live in a universe with a fixed meaning, and the end of mystery. The universe should be unfathomable. You shouldn't be able to fix the meaning of the universe, just as you shouldn't be able to reduce *Hamlet* or *Anna Karenina* to a sentence or say what they "really mean". I want a tragic universe, not a nice rounded-off universe with a moral at the end. And I don't think looking for a final meaning for the universe is rewarding either. Tolstoy tried, and his results are far less interesting than his fiction.'

'What were his results?'

'A religion called Tolstoyanism. I guess it is interesting in a way. He advocates vegetarianism and pacifism. But he also claims to have all the answers, which I don't want particularly.'

'What led to all this?'

'He had a breakdown when he was in his fifties. By then he was famous and successful and had a big house and a family, but he couldn't see the meaning of life. So he set out on a spiritual odyssey and went madder and madder, squeezing the universe for its last drops of meaning, desperately trying to get some sense out of it and find out exactly why he existed. When he eventually tried to explain his idea of the afterlife to Chekhov — a place that Chekhov describes as being like "jelly", where you dissolve and lose your individuality, but live on for ever — Chekhov just didn't understand it. It seemed pointless to him. He wasn't bothered about the meaning of life in general, but life as it is lived. He was more interested in what people around him said and did. He was obsessed with the detail of life. Tolstoy always saw his own writing as "teach-

333

ing" and had his breakdown partly because he was so anxious that he didn't have anything to teach. But Chekhov only ever saw his own writing as the formulation of questions, and so didn't need to have a crisis about it. While Tolstoy was founding Tolstoyanism, Chekhov was gardening, and trying to cope with his TB. In the last letter he wrote before he died, he complained of German women's dress-sense. Interesting, though, that Tolstoy managed to write these vast novels—before he had his breakdown, that is—and Chekhov never did, even though he wanted to. Mind you, Tolstoy was rich and Chekhov was poor. I think I identify more with Chekhov.'

While we had been talking, we had somehow started to hold hands again.

'So if you saw a fairy . . .' Rowan said. 'What would you do?'

'You were going to tell me something about fairies, weren't you? The Cottingley Fairies.'

'Yes. But first I'm interested. What would you do?'

'What would I do? I don't know. Probably tell myself I hadn't seen it.'

'But because you want the universe to make less sense, not more? I mean, you wouldn't go out and look for evidence of more fairies, for example? You'd rather look the other way?'

'Yeah, I think so. I'd want to be uncertain about what I'd seen.'

'Me too. I thought I was weird.'

'You are weird. I think most people do want to know things for definite.'

'Oh. That's probably true.'

'But you didn't see fairies?'

He laughed. 'No. Neither did the girls from Cottingley who claimed they had. At least, they almost certainly didn't. My grandparents lived just down the road from where it all happened, and they believed in the Cottingley Fairies, which made it all a bit of a shock for me later when I found out they didn't exist—the fairies, that is, not my grandparents. The

basic story is that in 1917 two girls, Frances Griffiths and Elsie Wright, took photographs of fairies. Frances kept getting into trouble for playing in Cottingley Beck — a kind of
stream — and ended up telling her mother she went there to
see the fairies. No one believed she'd seen fairies, so she borrowed her father's camera and set off to lure them out so that
Elsie could take a picture of them. When he developed the
photo her father thought it was a fake. But Frances's mother
was involved with the Theosophists, and eventually news
of this extraordinary photograph got back to Arthur Conan
Doyle. He ended up writing a book about it. Perhaps like Tolstoy, Conan Doyle discovered spirituality later in life. His book
The Coming of the Fairies is quite bizarre. He absolutely believed in the story of the fairies, and the photographs, and saw
them as evidence for a complex spirit world. It took years for
Frances and Elsie to own up to the fact that they had faked the
photographs. In fact, it wasn't quite as simple as that. They
kept hinting at it in the sixties — on chat-shows and in magazine interviews. At one point they admitted that the cut-out
images had been stuck to trees with hat-pins. In the end they
admitted that they'd faked "all but one" of them, and said that
they really had seen fairies but couldn't get them to keep still
for real photographs.'

'That's amazing,' I said. 'What did they look like, these
fairies?'

'They looked like cut-out illustrations from fairy stories.'

'Seriously?'

'Yeah. You'd think so, if you saw them now. But Conan
Doyle saw something else. Or he wanted to see something
else. It wasn't just him — all sorts of "experts" looked at the
pictures. One woman said that this was the discovery of a new
world, even while commenting that the fairies were artificial-
looking and flat, and that one of the gnomes had hands like
fins. This was, of course, because Frances and Elsie hadn't
done a very good job of cutting him out. What fascinated me

wasn't whether or not the fairies "really existed", but why and how those girls faked them, and why people like Conan Doyle believed it would be impossible for these girls — one merely the daughter of a mechanic — to have the depth of character to forge anything. He was much more prepared to believe in fairies than to believe in these girls, in fact. But Elsie had been working in a darkroom at a greeting card factory, faking pictures of dead soldiers and their families looking happy together. She had good technical experience making composite photographs. And Frances was an interesting character. She had grown up in South Africa and must have been pretty freaked out to end up in Cottingley. I certainly was when I lived there for a while before university. One of the really strange things is going from a hot country to a cold country. The cold doesn't hit you for a few days; it's as if you've got out of a warm bath at first, and you carry some of the heat with you. But when it does hit you, it's awful. You need more clothes, and you feel like you're starting to rot inside them. And everybody stays indoors all the time, in the cold and the dark. I could easily imagine Frances going out on the first warm day of spring and seeing magic and mystery and fairies. I also like the story of how the photograph ended up in the hands of Conan Doyle. By chance, Elsie's mother's Theosophical Society meeting that night was all about fairies. So she happened to say that her daughter had this picture, and so on. The girls didn't set out to be notorious, but they were, for their whole lives.'

'I guess they couldn't let Conan Doyle down, once he believed in their fairies?'

'Exactly.'

'So the "reasons" for the fairies are very complex, in the end — almost as complex as fairies themselves. Hmm.' I sipped my wine. 'I reckon everything is more complicated than people think, not simpler. And there's so much that people feel they can't say, or can't ever explain to anyone.'

Rowan sighed. 'That's certainly true.'

'Are you OK?'

'Yes, of course.' He looked at his watch. 'I'd better go. Lise is getting the last train back from London. I need to go and pick her up from the station.'

'Oh.'

He took his hand away from mine. 'I'm sorry.'

'I don't know why you're apologising to me. You're right. You should go.'

'Meg . . .'

'Look, Rowan, I'm not cross. I've got no claim on you, and who knows what would happen between us if we were single. It might be awful. Maybe I only want you because you're attached. But you said that you wanted to feel passionate and free again. So why don't you just do it? Leave Lise. Not to come and move in with me — you could go travelling, or anything you wanted. You find out what things feel like by acting them out in your professional life. I can't understand why you don't do it in your real life.'

'You do want me?' he said.

'Of course. I thought you knew that. You do know that, or you wouldn't keep apologising to me all the time and making me feel as if I'm making demands that you can't satisfy — which, by the way, I'm not.'

'But you do want me.'

'Yes.'

'It's so complicated,' he said. 'But can I kiss you, just once more?'

'I don't know,' I said, but I leaned towards him, and we kissed.

'I shouldn't be doing any of this.'

'Neither should I. I'm not going to be your mistress. You know that.'

'Of course. I wouldn't ask you to be. But I can't leave Lise. You know that too.'

'Why not?'

He sighed. 'It's not simple. It's not as if we have young children — or even any children. It's not as if Lise has a terminal disease. But she does need me. I do a lot for her mother, for example. And Lise herself has terrible anxiety attacks, and I'm the only one who can talk her down from them. There are other things. We own a house. We have a holiday booked for later in the year. We've got a joint bank account. Our lives are completely bound together.'

'I'm not being cruel,' I said, 'but it sounds like a normal relationship to me. It's never easy to leave. I didn't even know I was going to leave Christopher until the last minute. I'm not saying you should go out and pursue your own selfish adventures, having dumped someone who was holding you back. That's not exactly going to make you feel good about yourself. But can't you just talk to Lise and tell her how you feel?'

'That would be dynamite. She'd say I was abandoning her for you, and then if we — me and you — did try something together, she'd be convinced she was right. She'd try to ruin my life. I know what she's like. If I split up with her, the one thing I couldn't do would be to get involved with you.'

'God.'

He looked at his watch again. 'We'll talk soon?'

'Maybe. I guess so.'

He got up, slipped on his jacket and walked to the door.

'I want you too,' he said. 'Very much. I wish I could do something about it.'

'So do I,' I said.

And then he left.

I sat on the sofa for a long time, watching the fire burn and listening to the sea outside sucking gently on the sand, lapping at it and licking it and kissing it. I imagined it nibbling and nuzzling the shingle, breaking it down, breaking it down, saying 'Shhh' and 'Please'. It sounded as gentle as a whisper, as a promise. But as the night went on, the sea began to throw itself on the sand harder and harder, and the sand breathed 'Yes' and they drowned in one another, all night long.

'I've got the answer,' Josh said.

It was half past five on the evening of Kelsey Newman's talk, and Totnes was bathed in twilight. Rumour was half empty or half full, depending on how you looked at it. Almost all the wooden tables had little signs on them saying they were reserved at 7, or 8, or 9 P.M., and most people were just having after-work drinks. There was a family sitting looking at menus at a big table by the window. Two women with crew-cuts and feminist earrings sat together at the other window. Well-thumbed newspapers were strewn around on the bar. An old Barrington Levy track was playing. I knew it from my Brighton days when I used to sometimes go with Christopher to score dope from an old Rasta DJ who kept trying to sell us vinyl as well.

'Hello,' I said to Josh, and sat down. 'What was the question?'

'The question was, "Why can only some people do magic in Kelsey Newman's universe?" But let's order first, and get some wine and stuff. I can drink now that I'm not on such strong medication. I'm going to dazzle you with my improved theory of the universe. Then I'm going to dazzle Kelsey New-man with a super-improved version, once you've picked up all the flaws.'

'What time's he on? I've forgotten.'

'Seven P.M. in Birdwood House.'

'OK.'

'I think we've got enough time for dinner and pudding. In case you're worried, Christopher isn't going to burst in on us. He's gone to live with Becca.'

'God. What about Milly?'

'She's gone too. Having Christopher in the house didn't really make it easier for her and Dad to get back together, as you can imagine. What do you want to drink?'

'Sauvignon? But whatever. I've got to drive back later. And of course I want to be able to concentrate on what Newman's got to say. That's such a shame about Milly.'

'Well, shall we get a bottle? That way you can have two glasses, and I can have about three. I think that will be OK.'

'Yeah. OK.'

'I'll order some food when I get the wine. What do you want?'

'Oh, a pizza with extra chillies and no cheese, thanks. Here's some money.' I gave him a £20 note. 'I've got some news for you when you get back. And then you can tell me your theory of everything.'

'It's going to blow you away,' he said. 'It's a theory of the anti-hero. The last part of it fell into place when I read that piece in the paper at the weekend by Vi Hayes. The second-last part happened when I read your feature. I think Vi Hayes might have read your feature too; she sort of replies to it. I brought her piece along with me in case you didn't see it. Here.' He took a print-out of the online version of the article out of his leather briefcase and gave it to me. I hadn't seen it. I'd been too busy finishing my first sock and getting over my trip to London for my last-ever editorial board meeting.

As he got up to go to the bar, I realised he was wearing aftershave: it smelled like Ceylon tea and cinnamon. I looked at my phone. I hadn't heard anything from Rowan since I saw him at my place, and there was still nothing. Then I looked at Vi's piece. It was what she'd been talking about for such a long time: her theory of the 'storyless story'. She argued that, although she had named and analysed it, the storyless story was not new. However, it had almost been forgotten in the West in recent years. The whole point of a storyless story, she said, is the subtle rejection of story within its own structure. In this sense, the storyless story is almost what we would recognise as metafiction, but more delicate. Rather than being similar to a snake swallowing its own tail (or tale) the storyless story is closer to a snake letting go of itself. Vi had written a manifesto for the storyless story that suggested that the author of the storyless story would usually be a Trickster, as would his or her characters. The storyless story has no moral centre. It is not something from which a reader should strive to learn something, but rather a puzzle or a paradox with no 'answer' or 'solution', except for false ones. The reader is not encouraged to 'get into' the storyless story but to stay outside. One of the items on the manifesto was this: *A story about a hermit making jam could be as interesting as a story about a hero overcoming a dragon, except that it would be likely that the writer would make the hermit overcome the jam in the same way the hero overcomes the dragon. The storyless story shows the hermit making the jam while the hero overcomes the dragon, and then the hermit giving remedies and aid — and jam — to both the hero and the dragon before going to bed with a book.*

Why jam? The only person Vi knew who made jam was me. As I read on I realised that Josh was right and she had read my feature from the week before. I smiled. Characters in storyless stories, she said, didn't worry about what they wore or said or did. They were Fools stepping over the edge of the cliff on all our behalves, so that we can also step out of the restrictive frame of contemporary Western narrative. Surely, she argued, we should have stories not to tell us how to live and turn our lives into copies of stories, but to *prevent* us from having to fictionalise ourselves. Maui is a Trickster who shows us the non-sense of the world. Perhaps Tricksters, the characters you're not supposed to identify with, are in the end much more interesting role models than the princes and princesses of fairy tales, and the characters in American sitcoms that only exist in order to make us feel that we should be perfect, like them. Towards the end of the piece she recounted a

Chinese fairy story about a tiger who catches a fox. The fox tells the tiger that he can't eat him, because he, the fox, is revered as the most important animal in the world. 'Walk behind me for a while,' the fox says, 'and you'll see the way the other animals respect me.' The tiger agrees, and they set off. The other animals, seeing the fierce tiger walking behind the fox, decide that he must indeed be the most important animal in the world and flee. The tiger, impressed, then lets the fox go on his way.

At the end of the article Vi said she was putting the finishing touches on a book that covered not just the storyless story, which was her theory of folklore and fairy tales, but also the historyless history, the fictionless fiction, the romanceless romance, the unproven proof and the uncertain certainty. The idea of the whole book was the rejection of what she called 'totalitarian' structures in science and the humanities, and the acceptance of paradox in all disciplines. Fictionless fiction, I realised, was what all realist writers, including me, wanted to create: something super-authentic and with so much emotional truth that none of it seems like a story at all. I remembered Chekhov saying that a writer should practise 'total objectivity'. At the time I hadn't understood how that could be possible. But fictionless fiction would be totally objective; it would have to be.

'What's the news?' Josh said when he came back.

I put the print-out down on the table.

'It's good news, I think. You are now officially Zeb Ross.'

'Wow! That's amazing. Thank you. Have I got a disability?'

'Yes. You've got a disability. I hope this doesn't freak you out too much, but your "disability", not that I should probably call it that, is OCD. This was a complete coincidence. They'd already decided that this was something "romantic" and "cool" that might nevertheless stop Zeb appearing in public. I have to say it helped when I said that you really had it. I hope you don't mind.'

'I don't think I do. Will you be my boss?'

'No. No, in fact I've left Orb Books, as of Friday. You're on your own. Do feel free to turn them down if you want to. But it's a pretty good job, and the pay's OK.'

'Why did you leave?'

'I want to spend some proper time on my novel. My' — I glanced down at the print-out of Vi's article — '"fictionless fiction". I've also got some more work at the paper, which means I can leave genre writing behind completely for a while. I think it'll be good for me. Unlike Kelsey Newman I don't think we're immortal beings and I want to try to do something worthwhile while I'm still alive. Not to get to some other dimension, but because this is probably my only chance. I'm not doing down Zeb Ross, and I think you'll have fun being him, but I think I've had enough for a while.'

'No more narrative arcs in Torquay for you, then?'

'I guess not.'

'Are you abandoning the three-act structure as well?'

'I don't know. Maybe.' I sighed and then sipped my wine. 'You know, I really don't understand why Vi blurbed Kelsey Newman's book, when she's obviously so against it. It's a puzzle.'

'One that may well be solved later. Or now, if you like.'

'Huh?'

'Vi Hayes is coming to Kelsey Newman's talk. She's going to confront him about it.'

'Confront him about what? And how do you know this?'

'I Googled her. I've been reading and re-reading *Second World* since you gave it to me. Her quote has been staring at me the whole time. So when I saw her piece in the paper, and it said the opposite of what Kelsey Newman had said, I emailed her to ask why she'd given such a good quote to his book when she'd mentioned it in her piece as an example of bad narrative theory. I said I knew you; I hope you don't mind. She emailed back and told me that her quote had been taken out of context.' Josh pulled another piece of paper from his briefcase. 'What she'd actually written to the publishers was this: "No doubt many people will think this provides a blueprint for living based on what we have learned from the most well-loved fiction. But we don't need blueprints for living, and all we learn from the most well-loved fiction is that the moral high ground protects you from almost anything, and the way you get on in this world is to go out and kill anything monstrous, other or different because you don't like it, and that if you do this you end up with treasure and a princess — money and sex. I have studied forms of fiction for the last thirty-five years, on Pacific islands, in Russia, in South America and even in the kitchen of a nursing home in Brighton, and I have discovered that the Hero's Journey is not as universal as Joseph Campbell and now Kelsey Newman have suggested. The Hero's Journey is actually the colonial journey. It's the journey of the American Dream. There are many different types of story-pattern all over the world that don't show a hero going to good fortune from bad fortune through overcoming. Of course, at the moment, the loudest voices do tell these hero-myths, and claim that this has been so since the beginning of time. In fact, the abundance of this story-type at this point in history is a cultural, not an essential, fact. It's an interesting word, *Overcoming*. Newman uses it all the time in his book and each time it occurs I read it as a verb applied to a man who ejaculates too much, also in every sense. He comes onto everything. There are enough moralising neo-liberal forces in the world without Kelsey Newman adding a cosmic version, and therefore making the logic of globalisation universal."'

I was giggling by the end. 'Go, Vi,' I said.

'She's pretty cool. I wonder what she'll think of my theory of everything.'

I smiled. 'Go on, then. Tell me how your universe works.'

'Well, it might cheer you up to realise we are immortal after all.'

'It might not.'

'We'll see. So I know you're into the Periodic Table of Elements, but you're not so into Jung and archetypes. So maybe I'll leave those bits out.'

'I can take it,' I said. 'I know even more about archetypes now, because of you.'

'Why because of me?'

'Because of you I reviewed the wrong book. Because of that I got a new commission that meant I got sent not one, not two, but seven Tarot sets. They're full of archetypes, and all come with books that are in some way about Jung. It's more complicated than that, of course, but it's still your fault.' I'd actually been sent six Tarot sets, but I thought this might disturb him.

'Ah. Well, my theory may also explain why everything is my fault.'

'I should hope so if it's a theory of everything.'

'All right. Here goes. OK. Well, last time we talked about it you were right. It is a creepy idea that we have to keep being re-born into the Second World to have adventures until we get one of them right, and then we get sucked into the Omega Point to live on for all eternity in this, this . . .'

'Hell? Vacuum of morals?'

'Yes. Well, sort of, except it's not enough of a vacuum. There are some logical flaws in Newman's argument right from the start, the main one being that if the Omega Point is an infinite moment of pure love and total omniscience, then why would it put us through all this shit? OK, I accept that this is the usual question people ask about God, and in a sense it's proof either of the non-existence of God, or of God's knowledge that we are going to go to heaven after we die and everything will be OK. So I started thinking again about other ideas of the afterlife and reincarnation, and most of them take you into a void, a nothingness: some deeply cosmic and mysterious non-place. But Newman and Tipler's Omega Point keeps

345

you trapped for ever at the entrance to this void: the end of time and the beginning of nothingness. This, I thought, can't be right, like you said.'

'Did I say that?'

'I'm sure you did. Or something like it. Another thing that struck me was that Newman said that people were constantly becoming heroic enough to be enlightened and then being transported off to the Road to Perfection. Remember that only pizza-guzzlers would remain? I wondered how this squared with an increasing population, if indeed this is supposed to be the Second World. After all, this is a system where people are leaving or coming back, but not actually being generated. All "possible" humans have already been generated by the Omega Point at the end of time, so after that there are not any more humans left that you could possibly generate. And then it came to me. Remember I was, when I set out, also trying to solve this problem of why some people can do magic and others can't, and also why some people are wise and other people are stupid, which has always bugged me. So I'm just going to tell you this from the beginning of time, and you can see what you think. I don't think there are many logical flaws left.'

Our pizzas came. 'From the beginning of time?' I said. 'Wow.'

'Don't mock. You'll see. So you'll know, presumably, that the first element in the universe was hydrogen, which is why it is the first thing on the Periodic Table and has atomic number 1. Everything is made from the void, as the Taoists tell us, but everything is also made from hydrogen. It is the one atom on which all others are based.'

'Could you not say that everything is based on quarks?'

'Well, yes. It doesn't matter, because this is a sort of metaphor. It doesn't matter exactly how the chemical world was formed. Well, obviously it does, but all we need to know is that it was formed, from one essential piece, from which all the other essential pieces, or elements, were also formed. These elements in combination form basically everything in the universe. There can seem to be more or fewer "things", but there's always the same amount of matter in the universe. And matter changes its form all the time. The cheese on my pizza was once partly grass, in a sense. What I'm proposing is that this also happened with spirit, and this is how people's souls were formed. There was one great spirit, which was split up into many spirits — but all still essential. These are the archetypes. It's really interesting that so many disciplines recognise archetypes, or elemental spirits. In homoeopathy archetypes are often connected with elements. So the Mother, for example, is linked with Natrum Muriaticum, or sea salt, and her essence is the sea. She is the vast ocean from which we all emerge. The Wise Old Man is sulphur. The Trickster is mercury. And so on. But it's hard to find people who are pure archetypes. Most people have bits of this and bits of that in them. In Hindu philosophy, the universe is seen to be a cosmic dance where everything gets worse and worse until Shiva simultaneously destroys and re-creates it for the dance to begin again. The idea is that people also get worse and worse. How could this be? Well, think back to our example of original human spirits as pure elements. What if they start to combine and form molecules, and these molecules combine and form compounds and so forth? Fundamental spirit, while there in essence, as a memory or a component of being, becomes reduced further and further and you can't then isolate the original spirit very easily. It would end up spread all over the place. The pizza-guzzlers that Newman talks about are these highly diluted spirits: people with only long-lost memories of the pure form they once were. The most fucked-up people are the most diluted spirits.'

'We are guzzling pizza,' I said.

'Speak for yourself. I do not guzzle. Anyway, this is why the amount of spirits stays the same, but the population increases. The fundamental Mother archetype, or spirit, is now divided over, say, a million people. How does she come back together? I want to propose that the purpose of living is to get back to your essential spiritual nature, and there are various ways of doing this, although no one does it quite consciously. It's the spiritual version of evolution, or genetics — but it's not quite either.' Josh pulled another document out of his bag. 'If you don't mind, I'm going to read to you from this for a bit in case I leave anything out. It's quite complicated, I think. So every Higher Spirit, or Elemental Soul, exists in its pure state on something like a cosmic Periodic Table. You naturally have things in common with the elements nearest you, as arsenicum does with phosphorus, or palladium with platinum. Indeed, your ultimate cosmic soul mate is always right there next to you on this "table". But the dance of the universe is first about these spirits splitting and breaking and becoming mortal, and then splitting further, and then coming back together. When the table is complete, the final step is for all the spirits to merge in one monumental orgasm of spirit before collapsing into the void once more. The Periodic Table of Elemental Spirits is very different from the real Periodic Table of physical elements, but the latter serves as a useful analogy for the former, as I said. We have to use lots of analogies, because we are seeking to describe here something that cannot be described.'

'I like the "monumental orgasm of spirit",' I said.

'So do I. This is why I'm reading this. It sounds better.' He looked down at his sheet of paper again. There was a howling sound in the distance, like the wind. Then there was a bang, like a gunshot or a firework, but Josh didn't even look up. The howling continued for a few seconds and then stopped. 'So each imperfect being that we see around us contains the spiritual debris from various fundamental spirits. We are attracted to people who may help us shed some of this debris, or add new pieces that then purify what we already have. Think of interactions with people as being spiritual reactions or explosions, just like chemical reactions. Tragic interactions are interesting because they lead to the smashing up of these compounds, and the release of energy, just as Nietzsche said. And so it goes, on through time, as some higher spirits are distilled by life, and some made even more complex. Happily-ever-after leads to more bonding, or more bondage, if you see what I mean.'

Josh flicked through his pieces of paper. 'I'm going to skip the next bit because it's quite long. But I'll email you the full version. OK. The universe has two "operating systems" or "natures". One is the physical world as charted by scientists. So there are gravity and quarks and evolution and so on. But, as I have always said, there is also magic, and an unseen world of energy: Qi, the Force, whatever you want to call it. This is, if you like, another manifestation of the physical universe. In the same way that light is sometimes waves and sometimes particles, and mass can be seen as energy, the universe is sometimes physical, or "being"; and sometimes energetic, or "non-being". It is made, as we have seen, of both matter and spirit. Magic is simply when someone uses an unseen, non-physical energy to work on another energy or vibration. It is very subtle. It can have physical effects, but it is not physical in itself. For example, falling in love may have physical effects, like making someone lose weight, produce more hormones, have erections or whatever. But this is not the result of something solid and physical acting on something else that is solid and physical: it is the result of energy, or the non-physical, acting on the spirit, which is also non-physical, which leads to changes in the body, which *is* physical. In this way, there is no simple deterministic link between energy and matter. Most of the time energy works on other energy, and then it has a subtle effect on the matter around it. This is why there are no such things as spoon-bending and conjuring: they are tricks. But it is also why homoeopathy, flower remedies and Reiki work.

'The closer to being fully *spiritualised* you are — do you like that term? I'm not sure about it — the wiser you are, and the more easily you can use things like energy and magic. But also, in a sense, the less likely to use them, because you don't really desire anything that magic could give you. You pointed that out; more or less. I was thinking of making a website where you put in your basic opinions, attributes and so on, and then it calculates whether you're a 10,000th-level Hermit, or a 783rd-level Trickster. But I thought that might take something away from the theory, which is quite serious. What do you think?'

'God,' I said. 'You've really thought this through.'

'One thing that's quite neat about it is that it probably negates Newman's theory altogether,' Josh said. 'If "true" heroes are being sent off on the Road to Perfection all the time, and the freaks, fools and tragic heroes get obliterated and come back to hang out, in purer form, with the pizza-guzzlers, then eventually what you'll have left in the Second World is the whole Periodic Table of Spirits, all the ultimate superbeings who refuse to act like pathetic heroes, and they can form the one basic spirit and then overthrow the Omega Point. But it seems unlikely that the fundamental spirits, who when they re-form become guardians of the universe, would let the Omega Point be created in the first place. So there you have it. An afterlife that I hope you'll agree is better than Newman's.'

'It is better than Newman's,' I said. 'Why are you so down on the hero all of a sudden?'

'Well, I've realised that I'm never going to be one.' Josh looked at the wall and then back at me. 'I think that's a good thing, though. I like all that stuff Vi says about globalisation and power and the stories told by Western governments that means that they are the heroes fighting terrorism or whatever. She's also right that the very concept of "hero" is a paradox, especially in Christian democracies. The hero is the person who has the right to kill to get what they want. Who gives that right? It has to be God, otherwise anyone could give themselves that right — and they do, of course, but other people disagree. It can't be a cultural right because culture isn't permanent. But what sort of God would decide that people can be divided into those who can kill, and those who must be killed? Surely a God would love us all equally. So the hero can't exist. But what do you think of the whole theory? Are you convinced?'

'Honestly?'

'Yes.'

'I think you should fictionalise it. Spend some time at Orb Books, and then suggest it as a series to Claudia. I think it would be excellent.' I saw his face falling. 'Look, Josh, I'm a novelist. I think fiction is a great place for these ideas. I'm not doing them down by saying that they'd work well as fiction. And I'm not even doing them down by saying that Orb Books should be the publisher. I'm guessing you want a big audience for all the work you've done. One of the paradoxes of writing is that when you write non-fiction everyone tries to prove that it's wrong, and when you publish fiction, everyone tries to see the truth in it.' I bit my lip. 'Of all the theories of the universe I've come across, it's probably the best one. Honestly. But I can't accept theories of the universe. I think it's too big to theorise.'

'But isn't the point of being alive to try to answer the big questions?'

I shook my head. 'For me it's about trying to work out what the questions are.'

We finished our pizzas. Josh wanted to have ice-cream, and there was still wine left to drink. 'Hey,' I said. 'You could run something weird that happened to me through your theory if you like, and see what you come up with.'

'But you don't believe it.'

'Ignore me. I don't believe anything. But you might like this.'

'Go on.'

'OK, well, you know that Rosa Cooper — the famous actress who died, the one who was going out with Drew — was a childhood friend of mine?'

'No. Was she? That's weird that she ended up with Drew.'

'Yeah. After she died, I had this vivid dream. It was very realistic. Well, sort of. The content seemed realistic at the time. We were on a kind of astral plane, and she basically told me that she wasn't dead. She showed me how she'd faked her suicide.' I filled in the rest of the details for Josh, including Rosa's revelation about her relationship with Caleb.

'Uh-huh.' Josh looked interested now.

'So while I was in London I saw that one of the newspapers had the following headline: *Rosa Cooper Still Alive?* I couldn't believe it. There'd been a sighting in Hertfordshire of someone who looked just like Rosa. Hertfordshire was where she told me she'd gone. By the time the *Evening Standard* came out, dental records had shown that it was definitely Rosa who had died. But there was a moment when I thought my dream had been real. Everyone half-believes in telepathy and stuff. Even me. I'm not sure about a grand theory to explain it, but . . .'

'Keep reading the papers,' Josh said. 'I bet you anything she'll turn up alive, just as you dreamed it. I've already worked out that you're a 40th-level High Priestess. Or possibly a 38th-level Hermit. I'm not entirely sure. But you should certainly have some telepathic powers, healing skills and access to some pretty powerful magic.'

'Gosh. The numbers go . . . ?'

'Down to one, which is the archetype.'

'What are you?'

'I'm not sure. I know I'm a Trickster of some sort. I don't have any real powers of my own, but I can discern powers around me. I don't know what that means. I think I'm between levels fifty to a hundred. Probably an even number. It's pretty good. But you're better. You're psychic, and, like I said, I bet you anything that what you dreamed will turn out to be true.'

'But I don't really want it to be true,' I said. 'I mean, it's not that I want her to be dead. I just don't want to be in any way psychic. I half-want to vaguely believe that some of this stuff is possible, but I don't want "special powers".'

'Most people do.'

'Most people want to be millionaires, and then when they are they're miserable because they haven't got anything left to do except go shopping.'

'Jung said that everyone secretly believes in magic and the supernatural. He says that in public people say they don't believe, but privately, everyone does.'

'Maybe that's right.' I shrugged as if I didn't have an opinion.

By the time we paid the bill it was gone five to seven. We hurried out of Rumour and up to Birdwood House. I wondered what I could say to Vi. Would just 'Sorry' be enough? Perhaps we'd already said sorry to one another in our newspaper articles. There were about fifty chairs set out in the long, thin room, and about a third of them were filled. But I couldn't see Vi anywhere.

'I thought you said Vi was coming?' I said to Josh.

'She said she was. She and Frank are staying in the organic vegetarian B&B at the top of Cistern Street specifically so they could come to this tonight and hang out in Totnes a bit. They arrived yesterday. You know, of course, that she's officially in Devon to open that Labyrinth tomorrow? They're planning to go to Dartmouth on a River Link ferry. I think me and Dad are going to go on one too, maybe a bit later. Vi said she wanted to go earlier to "try out" the Labyrinth.'

'Yes, I knew about the Labyrinth. I wonder where they are, then.'

'No Kelsey Newman either.'

'Well, it's only . . .' I got my phone out of my bag to check the time. 'Oh, it's one minute past seven. God, what's this? I've got eleven missed calls. Who . . . ?' I mumbled away to myself as I found the command that phoned my voicemail service. Then the phone started to vibrate again just as I heard Tim's voice begin speaking on voicemail. He must have heard about his book. Since Newman had yet to show, I gestured to Josh that I would just be a minute, and pressed the button to abort the voicemail and answer the call.

'Hello?' I said.

'Oh God, Meg. Thank God you're there. Do you have a car and a torch?'

'Tim? Hello? What's wrong? Your voice . . .'

'It's the Beast. It's eaten Kelsey Newman.'

'What? Tim? What did you say?'

'The Beast has eaten Kelsey Newman. I tried to shoot it, but it didn't work. There are people here who say they know you. Can you come? Do you have a car and a torch?'

'Where?'

'Longmarsh. It's on the river . . .'

'I know Longmarsh. Where's the Beast now?'

'He swam away.'

'Are you sure?'

'I don't know.'

'Why are you phoning me? I don't understand . . .'

'These people. They . . .'

There was the sound of rustling, and the phone being passed to someone else.

'Meg? This is Vi.'

'Vi. What's happened?'

'I've got no idea.'

'Did the Beast . . . ?'

'I don't know. I'm not sure there is a Beast. But Kelsey has disappeared and I'm worried about him. It's too dark to see anything here now. Have you got your car with you? And a torch?'

'Yes.'

'Can you come? I don't think there's any danger. But if you think there is we can just leave.'

'What about Tim?'

'He's in a bad way. I think we need to get him out of here too.'

'OK.'

'I'll explain more when you get here.'

I hung up. Josh had come out to look for me.

'What's up?' he said.

'I don't know. Something really weird has happened.'

'Is it Dad? Or . . .' He started to twitch, and I wondered what he was counting.

'No,' I said quickly. 'It's Kelsey Newman. I don't want to tell you what's happened, because I think you won't like it and I'm not sure it has really happened. But I've got to go. Vi and Frank are there, and an Orb Books author. I think you should go home. There isn't going to be an event.'

'I think I want to come with you.'

'There won't be space in the car. I've got to bring at least three people back into town.'

'OK,' he said. 'Well, thanks for having dinner with me.'

'Thanks for asking me.' I turned to go.

'Use your magic,' he said. 'I mean, use it to solve whatever crisis there is. Use it to protect yourself if you have to.'

I remembered Robert in the forest saying that magic always had consequences.

'There is no magic,' I said. 'But don't worry; I'm sure I'll be fine.'

The almost-full moon was coming up behind the hills. It was big, white and haunting, like the entrance to a tunnel out of the universe. I drove past Baltic Wharf to the Longmarsh car park. Totnes was where the River Dart properly became a working waterway, and although the river traffic was now mainly ferries and tourist boats, commercial ships had travelled between Totnes and Dartmouth for hundreds of years. I imagined getting into a boat and sailing home. I would go past Longmarsh on the left-hand side of the river and St Peter's Quay on the other, as St Mary's Church marked Totnes disappearing behind me. I'd pass the lightning-struck tree full of cormorants' nests, and the skeletal wreck of a condemned medical boat from the First World War. I'd glide through stretches of river as wide as lakes and held in place by damp green hills with ruins on their tops. I'd pass the oldest yew tree in Britain and the boathouse in which Agatha Christie and Max Mallowan lived while Greenway was full of American troops in the Second World War. I'd pass smugglers' cottages and clapped-out boathouses. I'd drift past Long Wood, the steam railway, the Naval College and the Higher Ferry, and then beyond Dartmouth Castle and Kingswear Folly to the sea. I would navigate around the coast until I reached Torcross, where I could build a fire and curl up with B until the morning. But I wasn't doing that. I was getting out of the car on my own in the dark.

I used to walk B at Longmarsh when I lived in Totnes, but she never liked going there after dark, and neither did I. I didn't believe in ghosts, but the place still felt haunted, as if there were wrecked spirits in the air to go with the wrecked boats at the bottom of the river. Moonlight didn't help. It made everything silvery and ethereal and the shadows it cast looked wrong, as if they were from an alternative reality. There were dim lights on the path for a hundred yards or so, and then darkness. From the car I couldn't see anything very much. There was no sign of Vi, Frank, Kelsey Newman, Tim or the Beast. I had to get out of the car. I made myself remember a book I'd had as a child where a tiger turns up at a suburban family house. The mother feeds the tiger with all the food in the house and then the family has to go out for dinner. After this, the mother makes sure she has a tin of Tiger Food in the cupboard. The tin in the book was very impressive, much bigger than the little tins from which the Cooper cats were fed. I begged my mother to get some Tiger Food for our cupboards, just in case, but she said it didn't really exist. Suburbia stopped things from existing in all sorts of ways, and so I decided I would pretend that I was taking a walk there: a place where tigers could be made to sit at dinner tables and Beasts probably wore bowler hats.

I got out of the car with the torch. I coughed, and it echoed.

'Hello?' I called. 'Vi?'

Nothing. I went through the gate and started walking down the path, with the black river sloshing on my right. *This is fine,* I said in a loud whisper, to cover the hollow, echoing sound of my footsteps. *Look, there's the meadow where I played football with Josh however many summers ago. How peculiar it looks in the dark.* I made a point of stomping along while I spoke into the darkness. *Hello? Vi?* Nothing. *OK. So let's pretend I'm a 38th-level Hermit. I have magical powers. Brilliant. OK. Remember every film I've ever seen and every book I've ever read about magic.* I clicked my fingers. *I am protected. Ha, ha. Yeah, whatever. Frank? Tim?* After I'd walked about fifty yards, and nothing bad had happened to me, I stopped talking out loud and instead told myself cheerful things in my head as the path darkened and I had to rely on my torch to see where I was going. I told myself that the dark felt womblike, and that it was better not being able to see very much because in dark like this the meadow could be full of dancing headless ghouls and I would never know. I remembered an Orb Books retreat where we'd brainstormed effective ways of conveying fear that weren't as bland as 'Her heart was hammering in her chest,' or 'His skull felt like it might explode.' No one came up with anything to describe what my body was doing now. I ended up walking along muttering again: *Fuck, fuck, fuck, fuck, fuck.* There wasn't anything to be scared of, I knew that. But I kept remembering Tim's slightly crazed voice. *The Beast has eaten Kelsey Newman.* People had seen the Beast; it had been on the news. But any rational person wouldn't believe in it.

After a minute or so a large shadow came towards me, and I jumped.

'Meg?'

'Oh, my God. Frank? I can hardly see you. You're just a shape.'

'Sorry. I was on my way to meet you at the car park.'

'Where's Vi?'

'She's down there on a bench with Tim. He's a mess. We need to get him back to Totnes. Are you all right?'

'I think so. It's a bit creepy out here.'

'It is a bit.'

'There's no Beast, is there?'

'I don't think so. Not now anyway.'

'What happened to Kelsey Newman?'

'We don't know. Come on.'

We walked down the path until it ended. There was a patch of grass with a picnic table that in the day would offer a good view downriver. Now there were two shadows sitting at it. The shadows must have been watching us approach. One of them got up. It was Vi. She came and hugged me. The water lapped darkly at the river bank beyond the bench. In order to walk any further on this side of the river you would have to wade through water for a while. On the other side of the river you could walk a path all the way to Cornworthy.

'Great. A torch,' said Vi. 'OK, Tim. Now you have to tell us: what really happened to Kelsey Newman?'

In the torchlight I could see that Tim was wrapped in a blanket and shaking. His big rucksack was a dark shape by his side. A pan-shape and a kettle-shape hung off it. He didn't say anything.

'Tim?' I said. 'What happened?'

'You'll think I'm crazy,' he said. 'Maybe I think I'm crazy. Maybe it's the mushrooms. Maybe Kelsey Newman wasn't even here.'

'He was here,' Vi said. 'We had afternoon tea with him and then he said he was coming here. We saw him leave.'

'How did you end up here?' I asked Vi.

'We just came because of Alice Oswald's poem,' Frank said. 'We wanted to see as much of the River Dart as possible, and Vi thought she might find something to use in her speech.'

'Kelsey said he was coming here too, but it was clear he wanted to come on his own,' said Vi. 'He had a big bag and a camera. He said he had arranged to interview Tim, so we left him to it. We had more cake and went shopping and then we walked down here. We haven't seen him since he left the café.'

'Tim?' I said.

'I told you that the Beast ate him. I told all of you that. But if you don't want to believe me it's up to you. I feel sick. I know whatever I say is going to sound completely mad, so I think I might just shut up now.'

'I heard a gunshot before,' I said. 'Was that you?'

Tim nodded.

'You didn't shoot Kelsey Newman?' I said.

'Why would I do that? He was going to put me in his anthology. We'd already done most of the interview. Anyway, I'd never shoot anyone.'

'Should we look for Kelsey?' I asked Vi.

She glanced at Frank. 'Yeah, I think so.'

'I can't even describe properly what happened,' Tim said, as I started flashing the torch around behind him, into bushes and beyond them. 'But it grew. The Beast grew from twice the size of an Alsatian into something bigger than a house.

I hadn't even seen him before today, but I was right: he had been following the river. As soon as I arrived I knew the Beast had been here too, but I thought he'd gone further down the Dart already. Anyway, I was telling Kelsey Newman about my adventure so far. He wanted to know what the Beast represented for me. What was I trying to overcome? I said the Beast was actually a Beast and I wasn't trying to overcome anything. I told him about my book. Then, suddenly, there was this flashing light coming from behind Kelsey Newman's head. The light turned streaky and dark: a kind of grey light or black light. I can't really describe it. Then I realised that the Beast was standing behind Kelsey Newman, panting. His edges were blurred, but he was black with pricked ears and a long pink tongue. He looked very calm. Kelsey asked me what I was looking at, and I whispered, "The Beast is behind you." Kelsey said, "What is it? What does it look like to you?" I said he could look for himself. Kelsey turned around. He was obviously terrified when he saw the Beast, and he told me to shoot. First I couldn't do it. Then I tried to shoot into the air to scare him, but it made no difference. At that moment the Beast began to grow. The dark light ribboned around everything and I couldn't see properly. The world started fading in and out, and I thought I saw black balloons in the sky. Kelsey Newman was running down the path, but by then the Beast had grown even bigger. He just put his head down and ripped into Kelsey with his teeth. He threw him up in the air, and after he'd fallen on the ground and stopped struggling, the Beast ate him.'

'That's horrible,' I said. 'I couldn't make that up.'

'And you don't believe it either,' Tim said. 'I can tell. It's just like a Zeb Ross story to you. You want everything to have a nice, normal outcome. You think Kelsey's hiding in the bushes or something.'

'No,' I said. 'It's not like a Zeb Ross story at all, because it's real. I think Kelsey Newman is injured, or just gone. If he thought he saw something frightening, he probably did run away. Maybe he twisted his ankle and went to casualty. There are so many logical explanations for this.'

Tim shrugged. 'You don't think he was injured by the Beast?'

'No. I don't think so. If the Beast is so violent, why didn't it eat that woman in Dartmeet? Why did it eat all those dog biscuits and potatoes? I think the Beast is probably just a poor, lost dog having to take part in everyone's monster fantasies. Where is the gun now?'

'I threw it in the river.'

'We saw him,' said Frank. 'That bit is true.'

'I didn't even want to have a gun,' Tim said. 'I could never shoot anything or anyone.'

Vi put her hand on Tim's shoulder and patted it.

'I'm not a violent person,' Tim said. 'Maybe I'm lost too. I really didn't do anything bad. I just sat here not believing my own eyes.'

No one said anything for a minute.

'What happened to the Beast?' I said. 'After it "ate" Kelsey Newman?'

'He shrunk. He went back to normal. All the flashing stopped. He looked at me as if he was sorry or ashamed and then he slipped into the river and swam away. Again, you don't have to believe any of that. Believe what you like. I'm really sorry you had to come out here, and I'm sorry about the book and . . .' Tim started to cry. 'I don't know what's wrong with me. Everything seems strange. I probably did imagine everything, but where did Kelsey Newman go?'

'You're tired,' Vi said to Tim. 'You've been out on the moors for a long time. I think we should take you to Totnes and get you in a warm bed for the night.'

'Where did he go?' Tim said.

'Well, he didn't make it to his talk at Birdwood House,' I said. I was in the car with Vi and Frank. We'd taken Tim to their B&B and arranged for him to take over their room. We hadn't told the landlady very much, just that Tim felt a bit ill and might need to see a doctor in the morning. We paid the bill and then I drove back down the Lanes towards the sea. Vi and Frank were going to stay with me in Seashell Cottage. It seemed like the most sensible plan.

In the car Vi told me in more detail about what had happened that afternoon. She and Frank had gone for afternoon tea with Kelsey Newman in a café by the river. Vi had been intending to really have it out with him about the quote and tell him everything that was wrong with his theories. But as soon as she'd told him about the quote, and how out of context it was, he got out his BlackBerry and rang his publisher to tell them to change it. He was on the phone to them for ages and then apologised and insisted on paying for tea.

'He was an OK guy,' Vi had said, as we drove down the Lanes. 'He kept apologising about the quote. I think he seemed embarrassed.'

'Do you think he's OK?' I said. 'Should we ring around the hospitals?'

'I'm not sure,' Vi said. 'We don't even know him. But I'm pretty convinced that he wasn't at Longmarsh when we got there. I don't know why Tim had such a vivid hallucination. Poor bloke. Hey,' she said to me, 'why were you so angry with him?'

'I don't know,' I said. 'I shouldn't have been, really. I was just a bit freaked out in the dark, I guess, and his story of the Beast eating Kelsey Newman was just so unnecessary.'

'Did you believe it?' Frank asked.

'No, of course not,' I said.

'Then why were you scared?'

'I found it unsettling too,' Vi said. 'But you have to feel a bit sorry for him. He obviously hadn't been eating properly for a good while. I probably wouldn't have spoken to him at all if I hadn't seen his scissors.'

'What scissors?'

'The Orb Books scissors. Claudia has them too. Don't you have a pair? He was cutting up pieces of paper and throwing them in the Dart. He said it was some sort of proposal. At first I thought he meant it was a marriage proposal, and I wondered why he'd written it down. Then he explained that it was a book proposal, and all the connections fell into place.'

'Oh, I see. He must have heard it had been turned down.'

'He was saying that the proposal had led to everything going wrong in his life. He seemed to think that getting rid of what he'd written about the Beast would get rid of the actual Beast. Anyway, by the time he told us what he thought had happened it was getting dark and it was obvious we needed to check Kelsey wasn't injured in the bushes somewhere and get Tim back to Totnes. I hope you didn't mind that we suggested he call you . . . We didn't have our phones.'

'No. It's really good to see you both again. Anyway, I'm sorry. I'm the one who encouraged Tim to get into all this stuff. And maybe he was right. Maybe his version of the Beast didn't exist until he started writing about it. Maybe he needed to get it out of his system in some way.' I put the car into second gear to go round a sharp uphill bend. The moon had shrunk as it had risen and now looked completely normal. 'Do you think the Beast is real?' I asked.

'I think there's something,' Frank said. 'But I don't think it ate Kelsey Newman.'

'I saw it,' Vi said. 'Or what must have been it. It was a dog — very big and black, like a huge version of Bess. But it was just a dog.'

'Really?'

'Yeah.'

'Where did you see it?'

'On the path.'

'Frank?'

'Oh, I was answering a call of nature. I didn't see him.'

'Actually,' Vi said, 'I think the Beast was a "her" not a "him".'

'What did you do?' I said.

'I did what I always do when I see a dog with no owner around. I told her to go home,' Vi said. 'And she did. She trotted off down the path and disappeared.'

Back at the cottage I lit a fire and B curled up in front of it. Vi, Frank and I got through a bottle of red wine in about fifteen minutes and all I had left was a crate of Beast, so then we started drinking that. I was driving myself—and probably them—mad by trying to work out what had gone on, and where Kelsey Newman was. Frank had picked up my guitar and was gently playing a folk song I half-remembered.

'He didn't make it to his talk,' I said again. 'That's the bit that bothers me.'

'You want to go back and look for him again?' Frank said, while still playing the guitar.

'No. But I want to know he's all right.'

I went and sat at the table in the window, opened my laptop and Googled Kelsey Newman. There were a few interviews, and an out-of-date website. There was a phone number for a New York agent, but it was too late to ring New York even if I had known what to say.

'There aren't any pictures of him,' I said. 'What was he like?'

Vi and Frank looked at one another.

'Dark hair . . .' Frank said. Then he laughed. 'I can't actually remember. Maybe the Alzheimer's is kicking in at last. Can you remember, my love?'

Vi shook her head. 'I have no picture of him in my mind at all.'

'You only met him this afternoon,' I said.

'It wasn't for long,' Frank said. 'He was on the phone most of the time.'

'I'm not that good on appearances,' Vi said. 'I always had to make notes when I did my fieldwork, and nowadays if I don't make notes I don't retain anything. If I closed my eyes at this moment, I couldn't tell you what I was wearing.'

'And I think I've just had too many students,' said Frank. 'He did look a bit like a student. Maybe jeans, maybe trainers. It's odd that I can't remember anything.'

'God. It's almost as if he never existed at all,' I said.

'There's a picture on his book, isn't there?' Vi said. 'Get that. You'll see what he looks like. It'll probably jog our memories.'

But I searched the house and I couldn't find the book.

'Maybe we all imagined him,' Frank said. 'Maybe he was a mass hallucination.'

I kept fiddling around on the Internet until I found a number for the University of California Press that published his books. It wasn't too late to ring Berkeley. I got the phone, but I didn't dial the number.

'Why do you want to know that he's all right?' Frank said. 'Do you really care?'

'Don't you?'

'Well, sort of, but I suppose I just think that whatever has happened now just "is" and there's not a lot we can do about it. I don't think he was swallowed into the belly of the Beast. I don't think he's still at Longmarsh, because we looked. He must have just left. We did our best.'

I sighed. 'Maybe I want to know for sure that the Beast doesn't exist. I want to know that Kelsey Newman is fine and out there somewhere thinking up some new terrible book. I want to believe that Tim has gone a bit mad but will get over it. I don't know why. Isn't it normal to want to know that everything's OK?'

'Most of the time everything actually isn't OK,' Vi said. 'In so many complicated ways. We just tell ourselves that it is. We have to find a way to tell ourselves that it is. Out of the six billion people in the world, how many of them are happy and have lives that make perfect sense? I bet not even one.'

'I suppose so.' As I said this I remembered my conversation with Rowan and all my struggles against plots and outcomes and formulae, and my argument with Vi in Scotland. 'I wish I didn't have to try to rationalise this,' I said. 'I mean, on a deep level I don't want to make sense of anything. Everything you said in Scotland was right. I just can't help doing it.'

'Just stop,' Vi said. 'Let it go. Why not?'

'We didn't just let things go with Tim. We helped him.'

'We could help him. He was there.'

'What about Kelsey Newman? Even though he wasn't there . . .'

'Maybe we all imagined him,' Frank said again, with a strange smile.

I considered this, even though it was ridiculous. If you took Kelsey Newman out of the world, what would happen? My recent life would unravel, for a start.

'All right, let's say he *did* exist,' I said. 'But maybe he was immortal and just visiting us in the Second World—or whatever this world is. Maybe the Beast ate him because he didn't belong here.' I closed the lid of my laptop and went and put another log on the fire. 'Here's another non-rational explanation. According to my friend I am something close to an "elemental spirit", like something in a picture on a Tarot card, and because of this I have magical powers. A long time ago I met someone else with magical powers—another of these, well, let's call them "superbeings". Let's say that you are both superbeings too: I mean, if I am, you must be. Anyway, this first superbeing I met told me that if I used magic in the wrong way then I would unleash a monster. The other week I ended up accidentally cosmically ordering all kinds of things. So I obviously created the Beast by doing this, and you, Vi, made it go away again because you're an even higher spirit than I am.

There. That explains everything, almost. And who cares about Kelsey Newman if we're superbeings? He's probably one too. Anyway, we're all immortal — kind of like Kelsey Newman said — and so being eaten by Beasts doesn't really matter.'

I laughed, but Frank carried on playing the guitar and Vi patted my arm.

'These superpowers sound pretty cool,' Vi said. 'But you'd need to be careful with them. I've probably told you before that most of the shamans and healers I've come across had lots of knowledge but no magical powers. But every so often you'd meet one who did have something more. They were the ones with the most practical skills and the biggest pharmacopoeias, because they knew how easily magic could go wrong.'

I laughed again. 'It's OK. I was just messing around. I don't believe any of that stuff. I'm just trying not to be rational.'

'It sounds as if your friend's idea was actually highly rational,' Vi said. 'Too rational. But it would be because it was worked out in the language of this world, with the concepts of this world.'

Vi took another bottle of Beast from the crate, and I did too. Then I realised we were all pretty drunk. B was probably the only being left in the room with any sensible thoughts at all. She snored and turned over.

'Did I ever tell you about the goldfish that went missing from my mother's pond years ago?' Frank said. 'Precisely half the fish went. Then a week later they came back. I won't go into the details now, but we knew for certain they'd gone, and how many. We couldn't fathom it, however hard we tried. The whole family made up theories about aliens and pond-poltergeists. It was quite entertaining. My sister had the wildest theories of all.'

'So what happened?'

'It turned out my sister had done it. We'd been looking for a natural or a supernatural answer, because we couldn't work out the objective of someone who would do that. But it was quite simple in the end. She wanted to freak us out because we'd been mean to her about one of her boyfriends.'

My phone vibrated. It was a text message from Josh. *KN is OK after dog bite. I guess you didn't find him. Come for dinner with me again tomorrow? I have something to add to my theory.*

I breathed out. 'OK. Listen to this.' I read the text message. 'For some stupid reason I can relax now. Who wants a cup of tea?'

'Who's Josh?' Vi said.

'My friend with the wild theory of everything. I think he emailed you as well.'

'Oh, yes. Are you going to go and hear more of his theory?'

'No. I don't think so. I think I'm going to stay in tomorrow night and knit my sock. Cup of tea?'

The sea splashed outside and Vi picked up my knitting.

'Yes, please,' she said. 'And then you can tell me all about this and we can talk about more interesting things than Kelsey Newman.'

After I'd made the tea I explained how I'd come to start knitting socks, and at some point we all hugged and apologised properly for what had happened in Scotland. Then Frank and Vi filled me in on Sebastian, and the dogs, and Frank's retirement plans, and Vi's ideas for her next two books. The first one would be a collection of storyless stories from around the world, and the second would be a collection of historyless histories: re-enactments that she and others had performed over the years, in which history had been relocated in the present. I told them how I'd come to read the Kelsey Newman books, and how I'd left Christopher and moved into this cottage.

'To be a hermit and write about your hobbies in a column,' Vi said. 'I like that.'

'Yeah. Well, I'm a heartbroken hermit at the moment. I've never been good at relationships, have I?'

'This one is worth sticking with,' Vi said. 'He loves you.'

I looked at Vi as if she'd just correctly told me what I'd eaten for breakfast for the last seven days, and what I had in each of my pockets. Maybe she was in fact a superbeing.

'You don't even know who it is.'

'Yes, we do. He phoned us to talk it over.'

'When?'

'Last week. It's not going to be easy for him. Just be patient.'

'Really? He told you about it? I thought if I told anyone about this they'd say he was messing me around and not to have anything to do with him, especially as he's too old for me. I feel sorry for him, because if he left Lise for me he'd be labelled a philanderer, or someone who's traded a perfectly good partner in for a younger model — you know all the things people say about men who leave long-term relationships for a younger partner. But I didn't make their relationship rocky: it already was. If he has anything to do with me in the meantime then it would seem as if he's messing both of us around because he's not being honest with her, and he's not properly committing to me. But if he does nothing then he's, well, he's sort of giving up on life, surely. And even doing that, the least wrong of all the options, wouldn't be fair on Lise, who presumably wants her partner to love her and not be staying with her out of a sense of duty.'

'He knows all that,' Frank said. 'He's working through it.'

'Sometimes I wish life could be more storyless,' I said.

'I know,' Vi said. 'Well, in some ways it is. You just have to let go of the plot when it gets too much. Do something else.'

'I wish he'd just phone me or something.'

'He will when he's got something to say.'

'Why can't he write me a love letter?'

'Because it would be dishonest. Not because he doesn't love you, but because he knows he's not doing anything concrete about it. Rowan has never told a lie in all the years we've known him.'

'He must lie to Lise all the time.'

Frank shrugged. 'Maybe. Or maybe he doesn't say anything.'

'Be patient,' Vi said. 'Things will work out.'

'I've got a friend who's in a similar situation,' I said. 'She can't work out whether to leave her husband for this other guy. I suppose it's not the same situation, really.' I thought about it some more. 'No. They're complicated in different ways. But she can't act either.'

I hadn't heard from Libby since I'd seen her the week before, which I thought meant she probably hadn't left Bob.

'Just wait,' Frank said.

'I guess I'll have to. I guess I'll just knit another sock and wait for the spring.'

The Labyrinth was beautiful. It was a simple pattern laid out in pale stone, with benches made from the same stone and set out so that you could sit on any of them and look at the Labyrinth and the river at the same time. The sycamore tree was there between two of the benches. It didn't have its helicopters any more; instead, it had the beginnings of buds. Vi, Frank and I had got up at six and come to walk the Labyrinth to see what it was like so that Vi could compose her speech for later. B had come too, and sat there looking puzzled while we took it in turns to follow the single path from the edge to the centre as the sun came up over Kingswear. Vi went first, then Frank, then me. Afterwards we sat huddled together on one of the benches and said nothing. At about seven Vi looked at her watch, and then a few minutes later Rowan came, walking down the dawn-lit embankment in his duffel coat. He walked the Labyrinth too, more slowly than the rest of us had, and then we all went for breakfast.

Josh and Peter came to the opening, along with everyone else you would expect: Old Mary, Reg, Libby and Bob, everyone

I'd ever seen in the Three Ships and around town. Even Andrew came over from Torcross. Josh had his briefcase with him, and I promised to introduce him to Vi properly over a drink later on. At twelve o'clock the ceremony opened, and Vi walked the Labyrinth again, silently, slowly, while everyone watched. The town council had originally wanted her to cut a ribbon, but couldn't work out where you'd put a ribbon on a labyrinth. In the end they'd improvised and done what Vi suggested: they'd left just a small piece of red ribbon in the pale circle at the centre. Having walked the Labyrinth myself, I had some idea of what Vi might be thinking, although of course I would never know. I had been surprised myself—we all had, we found, when we talked about it over breakfast—that just walking one short path could make you feel hopeful, frustrated, bored, excited or even nothing at all, and that this could change from one step to the next. You are aware that you want to reach the centre, and also aware that the Labyrinth keeps taking you away from it. Just as you seem to be getting close, you turn and end up walking almost around its outer limits. As you do this, you realise that there is a ring that forms the outer limit that you will never reach if you keep walking the path. This is a path all of its own, connected to nothing and going nowhere. When you get to the centre, you feel an odd sense of achievement, even though you've simply walked on a path that's been laid down for you. You love the Labyrinth and you hate it at different moments, but you never feel like you've conquered it, because that would be ridiculous.

'What's perhaps most exciting about this process,' Vi said in her speech, 'is that at any time you can choose to leave the path and just walk straight to the centre. Why does no one do that?' I remembered that this was precisely what B had done earlier, as if to demonstrate to us where we were going wrong. Perhaps Vi remembered this too, because she looked at B and smiled. B was looking resplendent, I thought, in some of the discarded red ribbon. Vi continued, 'Or almost no one. This is a path that is determined for you in advance, but no one can tell you what to think while you're walking it. It's not like a maze: you can't get lost. No one's playing any tricks on you. There aren't any monsters lurking around any corners. You can see the end and yet you walk calmly towards it, following perhaps the least logical route — in mathematical terms, at least. Perhaps the Labyrinth tells us why we don't simply read the last pages of books, why we don't hurry through life looking for outcomes all the time, however many times we're told that we should, and that we should be overtaking people, and overcoming things as we go. The Labyrinth doesn't tell us how to live; it shows us how we do live. There is no drama in the centre of the Labyrinth, just a place where you have come to rest for a while before you walk the path out again. Perhaps walking the Labyrinth is the path of the storyless story, or perhaps that's just my labyrinth. You will all find your own way, I'm sure, even though to an external observer who hasn't walked the path it will seem to be the same objective experience for everyone.'

Vi picked up the piece of red ribbon from the centre of the Labyrinth and walked with it back to the beginning, holding it in her left hand the whole way. Every so often I glanced beyond her, to the river. There were so many things in the Dart, unseen: pieces of old shipwrecked ferries and designs for follies; love tokens and manuscripts; Libby's car; Tim's gun; even the Beast, perhaps, swimming for its life. I waited for something to wash up, but nothing did. As Vi returned to the beginning of the Labyrinth, I looked at the river again, and I was almost sure that something black swam past. I imagined it dog-shaped and wolfish: prick-eared, black-nosed, pink-tongued; and in my mind it was swimming away from this world and into another one.

ACKNOWLEDGEMENTS

Lots of people (and one dog) helped directly or indirectly with this novel: Rod Edmond, Francesca Ashurst, Couze Venn, Sam Ashurst, Hari Ashurst-Venn, Dreamer Thomas, Simon Trewin, Francis Bickmore, Sarah Moss, Dan Mandel, Jenna Johnson, Jamie Byng, Jenny Todd, Jennie Batchelor, Karen Donaghay, Alice Furse, Vybarr Cregan-Reid, Ariane Mildenberg, David Stirrup, Abdulrazak Gurnah, Jan Montefiore, Rosanna Cox, Suzi Feay, Jon Gray, Caroline Rooney, David Herd, Donna Landry, Will Norman, Graham English, Steven Hall, Tom Boncza-Tomaszewski, Mudassar Iqbal, Laurence Goldstein, Jason Kennedy, Kirsty Crawford, Leo Hollis, Zahid Warley, Sheila Browne, Murray Edmond, Andrew Crumey, Emilie Clarke, Allen Clarke, Philip Pullman, Ian Stewart, Doug Coupland, Norah Perkins, Janine Cook and Anne Makepeace. Thanks also to Tony Mann, Don Knuth and everyone else at the 2009 Mathematics and Fiction conference. I am grateful to all my colleagues in the School of English at the University of Kent, particularly those in the Centre for Creative Writing. I have learned something from (almost) all the students I have ever taught, so if you've ever sat through my Plato lecture or a class on compassion in writing then thanks to you too. I am hugely grateful to everyone at Canongate.

Parts of this novel were written in the following locations in Devon, UK: the Maltsters Arms, Tuckenhay; the Barrel House café, Totnes; Number 12 B&B, Totnes; and the Sea Breeze Hotel, Torcross.

I have tried to acknowledge some of the many books I have used for research within the text of the novel. Most of the books I mention are real, except for those by Kelsey Newman and Zeb Ross, *Household Tips* by Iris Glass, *Teach Yourself Tantric Sex* and all the books in the sack sent by Oscar. The following real books are not mentioned in the text, but were very useful: *Zen Flesh, Zen Bones,* compiled by Paul Reps; *Meaning, Medicine and the Placebo Effect* by Daniel Moerman; *A Life in Letters* by Anton Chekhov, translated by Rosamund Bartlett and Anthony Phillips; the *Tao Te Ching,* translated by Stephen Mitchell; *Russian Fairy Tales,* translated by Norbert Guterman (for the story called 'The Goat Comes Back' on pages 56–57); *Chinese Fairy Tales & Fantasies,* translated and edited by Moss Roberts; *Trickster Makes This World* by Lewis Hyde; *A River to Cross* by David Stranack; *The Book* by Alan Watts (for the cat image); *Knitting Socks* by Ann Budd; *The Case of the Cottingley Fairies* by Joe Cooper; *The Forgotten Dead* by Ken Small; *A Witch Alone* by Marian Green; *Hedge Witch* by Rae Beth; *Bach Flower Therapy* by Mechthild Scheffer; and *Seventy-Eight Degrees of Wisdom* by Rachel Pollack. I could not, of course, have written my novel without Frank Tipler's book *The Physics of Immortality.*